THE BEST OF
MYTHIC
VOLUME ONE

THE BEST OF

A SCIENCE FICTION AND FANTASY MAGAZINE

VOLUME ONE

EDITED BY

SHAUN KILGORE

FOUNDERS HOUSE PUBLISHING LLC | 2021

Contents

Introduction

I T'S BEEN NEARLY five years since I first conceived the idea of MYTHIC. Since then, I've edited fifteen quarterly issues of the science fiction and fantasy magazine. I've published over 150 stories by various authors. I've done my very best present a wide range of tales covering the vast universe of speculative fiction. It's been a fun time but a challenging time to put together each issue of MYTHIC and I've made my fair share of mistakes over the years. I've gotten overwhelmed with the task and nearly quit a few times, but MYTHIC: A Science Fiction & Fantasy Magazine survives.

In this present volume, I am looking back over the fifteen-issue run of the quarterly incarnation of MYTHIC and selecting some of the best stories to appear in those pages. It was incredibly hard for me because I feel that so many stories deserved to be among the best, but I settled on twenty-five stories to be included in The Best of MYTHIC: Volume One.

I can't begin to express my gratitude to the many authors whom I've published and whose stories now appear in this book. You wrote amazing tales and I'm privileged that I was able to shepherd them to print then and now. My thanks go out to all of the writers.

This book is a serious milestone for me as I hope to make MYTHIC a pro-level market one day. The Best of MYTHIC is the product of a subscription drive I conducted using the crowdfunding platform, Kickstarter. I hope it also provides a one-stop showcase of the range of my editorial experience. I hope that you enjoy the stories inside as much as I did.

THE BEST OF
MYTHIC
A SCIENCE FICTION AND FANTASY MAGAZINE
VOLUME ONE

Humanity

Joanna Michal Hoyt

The old man sat bolt upright, biting his lips and waiting for his trial to begin. He had always hated speaking publicly as a civilian; he didn't know what to do with his eyes and hands; and now the stakes were terribly high.

He didn't expect to save his own life. He had fought with the resistance at the end, had held his own for a long time against greater numbers and better weapons, and he'd pay for that. But if he could command any respect or sympathy, if he could intercede for his friend and co-defendant, the doctor, who had never fought...

Above the bench where his judges would sit were carved the words posted in every public building in every world of the diaspora, the final words of the Great Pledge they all repeated daily: "TO PRESERVE AGAINST ALL MENACE FROM WITHOUT, ALL DISSENSION FROM WITHIN, OUR COMMON AND PRECIOUS HUMANITY." That was what he and the doctor and all the Pure had been trying to do.

His advocate, a harsh young man appointed by the court, had dismissed this argument. "Stop posturing. Let them see that you're old, frightened, *human*. For humanity's sake don't quote your omnipestilent Commander." The old man hoped his judges would prove more understanding.

The judges filed in. Thick-skinned, small-eyed, squat men and women shaped by generations of Ipiu's harsh atmosphere and fierce insects. None of them were beautiful like his people, shaped by Arraj's kinder climate before the earthquakes and eruptions forced them to take refuge on Ipiu two generations back.

He joined in the reciting of the Pledge. Like his judges he spoke in the clipped Unic of the Interworld Consortium. He might have solaced himself with the rolling cadences of Arraji, but he needed to remind his judges that they were all humans united against the common enemy.

An evidentiary declaimed the list of accusations.

Breach of the Code of Humanity—well, the Code was always interpreted by the party in power.

Land seizure—how could they claim that? The Ipiu had acceded to the Arraji's request for a new homeland as the earthquakes devastated Arraj, and the Arraji had never tried to take anything beyond Andek, the barren and *esur*-infested continent allotted to them.

"Murder; gross inhumanity; cruelty to noncombatants, to children..."

The old man rose. He knew, now, what to do with eyes and hands and voice.

"You must not slander us so! My people have never killed or mistreated children or other noncombatants. Only your soldiers—and a few medics, I suppose—invaded our adopted homeland. None of your children came there. If they had come we would not have harmed them. We never attacked your medics...some may have been accidental casualties of our self-defense..."

Judges, advocates, evidentiaries, reporters, stared at him in apparent bewilderment. Perhaps they were mistaken, not lying. What had they heard?

"We have never neglected our duty toward children and unfortunates. I chaired the Arraji Children's Aid Board before you destroyed their headquarters and confiscated their funds. I contributed more than my share to the Interworld Relief collections; you have paralyzed or destroyed our databanks, but if the lines of communication ever open again to the Interworld Consortium their records will bear me out." He took a deep breath, remembered his priorities. "But I am only an ordinary man, doing as all the Pure did. As, no doubt, Your Honors do. My co-defendant is a more striking case. He has devoted himself to medical research for the good of humanity. He has always been a noncombatant. He has a wife and a small son who are now deprived of his assistance, presence and comfort. Is this not cruelty to children?"

"Are you mad?" the old man's advocate hissed.

"No. Are they?"

An evidentiary rose to speak.

"With the Court's permission, we will begin by itemizing the evidence against the defendant who has just interrupted the Court's proceedings."

"Objection," the advocate said.

"No objection," the old man said.

The evidentiary held up a small black-bound book.

"Do you recognize this?"

"Yes."

"What is it?"

"My personal duty log from my time as a sanitary coordinator."

"You entered this information yourself? You can vouch for its correctness?"

"Yes."

"I will now show the Court an entry from this book. You may inform us if it has been changed in any way."

The old man nodded. The blank wall at the end of the court lit up, showed an enlarged image of a notebook page covered with his cramped Arraji next to a typed Unic translation. "Ejeget, 6/17. Standard sanitary operation. Pestilentiaries thermoconverted: 137 mature male, 245 mature female, 44 juvenile male, 56 juvenile female. Energy profit: 46 amplissae."

3

"Is this entry correct?"

"It is." So many days, so many sites, how could he remember? But it was plausible, and there was nothing there that could be used against him.

"You still deny killing children?"

"Of course I do!"

"Would you tell the Court what you did in the process of this 'sanitary operation'?"

"My unit and I were sent to Ejeget by my superiors. Upon arrival we found the *esurin* verified and isolated in a warehouse at the edge of the town. They were too close to human habitations for thermoconversion—exudates might have compromised air quality. My men removed them to a quarry which was abandoned, stripped of useful material, and well downwind from the town."

"Go on."

"The *esurin* were marched into the quarry. One rank of my sanitaries stood at the lip of the quarry, prepared to shoot any who offered interference. The rest set up the thermoconversion booth, moved the *esurin* through in groups of ten and interred solid by-products. Then the booth and battery were removed and we set out for the next town on our list. We encountered no children."

He stopped, thinking.

"No, I had forgotten. There was a young girl, the daughter of a woman who after the daughter's birth had been seduced by an *esur* in our collection group. That girl ran after us, shouting. Two of my sanitaries returned her to her mother. She struggled violently, so her wrists may have been bruised, but there was no cruelty."

"No cruelty, either, to the children who died in your thermoconversion unit?"

"I tell you, there were no children! To thermoconvert humans would be a clear violation of the Code of Humanity. We would never—I would never—have condoned such a thing."

"Then how would you describe the—juveniles—you killed?"

"They were not children! Not humans! All of them were *es-*

urin. This was manifestly obvious in most cases. A few were more... well-disguised... those who had interbred with humans, to our shame and to the danger of humanity—but the selection specialists were highly trained and conscientious. All those collected for disposal were *esurin*."

"You have used the Arraji word *esurin* several times. Can you not find an appropriate word in Unic?"

The old man frowned. Linguistics had never been his strong point.

"*Esurin* is one of the true names of the Destroyers, the Children of the Lie. They are not human, though they may appear so to the uninformed. There is no exact translation in your language. Your translators have rendered it as 'pestilentiary'", which is close, but..." He turned toward the doctor, who was better at such things.

The doctor caught his glance, rose, and explained.

"'Pestilentiary' is often employed as a figurative term of abuse. Even in the literal sense your pestilentiary is a victim of circumstances, someone who is infected through no fault of his own and who infects others unwillingly. '*Esur*' is always used literally. An *esur* is by nature diseased, and he deliberately spreads disease to humans. His goal is the destruction of humanity."

"This is how you define all non-Arraji?"

The old man shook his head. "No! You Ipi are humans like us."

"And on what grounds do you claim that this is not true of the Verekei?" The evidentiary gave the *esurin* their false-name.

The answer was too obvious to speak. The old man felt his knees buckle.

"Adjournment requested. My client is unfit." His advocate's voice was flat.

"Adjournment granted."

In the hallway the doctor came up beside the old man and looked at him with concern before his guards hurried him away. The concern, the old man knew, was not about their impending sentence or the success of the Lie but about his unsteady gait and ragged breathing.

Finally alone, the old man tried to pull his thoughts together. How could he make them see? He could remember pieces of the speeches of the Commander of the Pure, but he could not recall the words, the tones, that had woven the pieces together into a clear and damning whole.

There was history. The *esurin*, who were resettled on Andek along with the Arraji, claimed asylum on the grounds that their population on Verek was being decimated by a fatal and highly infectious respiratory disease caused by an organism native to the planet. They complied with quarantine procedures before entering Andek. But they had lived four generations on Verek before the disease was identified. If it had been genuine and planet-specific, it should have struck the first settlers. At first some of the Arraji had suspected the disease was a fabrication, a way of claiming sympathy from Interworld Relief and acquiring land on a planet more centrally located than Verek. (Some of the *esurin* had the gall to draw parallels with the exodus of the Arraji, but that was a different matter; the earthquakes and eruptions that rendered Arraj uninhabitable were verifiable; those who said they resulted from Arraji fuel-extraction operations were politically motivated liars...) When the first generation of refugee *esurin* lived and died in apparent good health on Andek these suspicions seemed to be confirmed.

Afterward, when the gut-wasting sickness struck the Arraji and some of the *esurin* also pretended to be stricken, the Commander recognized the truth of the situation. The *esurin* were creators of diseases, which gave them excuses to move into closer proximity to humankind and weapons with which to destroy them.

There was anatomy. The *esurin* might claim that their large eyes with bloated pupils and shrunken whites, their translucent skin under which the veins showed blue, resulted from living underground to avoid the sickness on Verek's surface, but after the

Commander's artists' work was publicized who could fail to see that these were clear marks of the alien nature of the *esurin*?

There were the loathsome crimes of the *esurin* that the Commander's investigative units had uncovered. Not content to wait for their sickness to destroy true humanity on Andek, the *esurin* had stolen human children and killed them. The *esurin* had denied the crimes and alleged a lack of evidence, but the investigators were Arraji of clean descent and good reputations who would not have lied.

The old man repeated the arguments until they were fixed in his mind. He would explain in the morning...

In his dream he was out of prison at last. He walked in sunlight on a high ridge, looking down onto a forest. The breeze sent shivers of silver and shadow through the leaves. Why had he never stopped to see how beautiful the world was?

He couldn't stop. The men with the guns hurried him along, hurried the others along in the line behind him. He went down into the shade of the trees, to the edge of the old quarry. Something down there was throbbing loudly. He didn't want to know what it was.

A harsh voice told him to keep going down. The stairs were steep, he wasn't sure of his balance, but he had to go down or they'd shoot him, he'd fall into the people below him, they'd fall. He went down. Saw the thermoconverter. Kept going. What else could he do?

The thermoconverter's door opened. The charging chamber was empty. He was in front. If he didn't walk in they would drag him as if he was an animal or a *thing*, not a human. He went in, set his back to the wall, turned to see who was with him. Just before the terrible light and the pain began he recognized the doctor.

HE WOKE, SWEATING and shaking, dressed with unsteady hands, returned to the courtroom. Entry after entry was read out of his book. The evidentiaries refused to call the *esurin* by their proper name or to admit their inhumanity. When he tried to explain they interrupted him. His advocate did not intervene. At the lunch recess the old man called his advocate for a conference.

The advocate stared at him, looking belligerent even for an Ipi. The old man stared back.

"Why do you not object when the evidentiaries refuse to allow me to explain the basic premise of..."

"You have already done yourself enough harm. Your so-called explanations would make things worse if that were still possible. Your chances..."

"I understand that I will almost certainly be executed. I am merely attempting to clear my people and my cause of the slanders which have been advanced against us. And also, if it is possible, to save the life of my co-defendant—an obvious noncombatant—my friend—the doctor." He did not say 'Who is young enough to be my grandson, dear enough to me to be the son I never had.'

"I am not here to salvage your delusions. I'm charged with saving your life if that is possible. You haven't made that any easier." The advocate half-smiled. "Or maybe you have. Let me change your plea. Let me argue that you're mentally unfit. It may even be true."

"No! I do not want to live because of a lie. For myself I want justice or nothing. For the doctor..."

"Justice!" The advocate rose as he spoke. The old man half expected a blow. His guards had hit him before. He didn't cringe.

The advocate dropped back into his seat. "Don't ask for what you deserve."

"May I ask for a chance to speak?"

"Not at the evidentiary stage. They've almost finished questioning you anyhow. They'll be starting on your—*friend*—this afternoon. But defendants may make a final statement before sentencing. If you want the slightest chance of living you'll let me make it for you."

"No."

They watched one another in silence until a guard came to take them back to the courtroom.

When his turn came the doctor explained that he had researched possible cures for the gutwasting plague, which had spread among the Arraji to such an extent that the eradication of the *esurin* alone did not guarantee control. To that end he had requisitioned juvenile *esurin* for experimentation, since the worst devastation of the plague had occurred among Arraji children. The doctor's account was carefully brought down to a level which his hearers could understand. His advocate interrupted his explanation of the similarities and differences between *esurin* and humans to remind the court that the children (as the advocate called them) whom he requisitioned would surely otherwise have been thermoconverted.

"That may be," the evidentiary said. "As some of his victims did not die, we have summoned one of them to appear in court during tomorrow's session." The advocate's hands clenched. The court adjourned.

The old man looked for the doctor as he was led away, but the guards kept them separate. He walked grimly upright to his cell. He slept and he dreamed:

He was in the field headquarters of the Southeastern Sanitary Campaign along with the doctor. This was at the beginning of the end; there were rumors of an Ipi invasion along the northeastern seacoast, but these had not been confirmed, and the old man had not yet begun training his sanitaries as soldiers. The coordinators discussed the rumors, still only half afraid. The old man, listening, envied them, pitied them, and then forgot them. There, across the room, looking out the window, was the doctor. He didn't know that he was marked for death. The old man didn't plan to tell him. He only wanted to sit beside his friend once more, to talk about music, mountains, mathematics, all the lovely things that endured. He started across the room.

One of his colleagues asked where he was going. He turned to answer, but the words froze on his lips. Her voice was his colleague's voice, her uniform and her hair were right, but her veins showed blue under her skin, her eyes bulged obscenely—*esur!*

He recoiled, trying to see who else had seen, who might help him. All through the room eyes turned toward him, horrible distorted eyes. She had infected them all with something far worse than the gutwaste. She had turned them into *esurin*. He had to warn the doctor, to get him away before he also was destroyed.

If he took another step he would be able to see himself reflected in the window. If he spoke the doctor would turn toward him. He didn't want to see the doctor's face, nor his own.

H E WOKE UP cold and rigid. He sat up on his cot and tried unsuccessfully to put together some words in the doctor's defense.

He dragged himself into court for the testimony of the juvenile *esur*. The ushers treated the juvenile with the gentleness due to a human child, stood close enough to it to be contaminated. It took its place between the old man and the judges, facing the judges. It looked, from behind, very human, very young. The old man swallowed hard and silently recited the Revelation of the Commander of the Pure which he and his sanitaries had repeated daily along with the Great Pledge:

The esurin *are Children of the Lie. They practice to deceive. Their aim is the destruction of all human life. The torch that was kindled on the Mother-Earth, the spark that gave light to the worlds, they would extinguish. We must not fear them. We must not believe them. We must not pity them. When they are destroyed the wasting diseases will leave us. Fear, cruelty and shame will leave us. We shall be fully human again. We shall have peace. But until we are free of them there will be no peace. Therefore let us devote our time, our resources, our courage and our strength to the work of Purification. Let us never falter in our resolve to preserve against this worst of menaces our common and precious humanity.*

The old man remembered the first time he had heard those words, listening to the transmitter beside his brother, who had turned gray-haired and silent after his child died of the gutwaste, and his cousin, who had been gray-faced and voluble since the *esurin*'s excessive-resource-consumption complaints to the Interworld Consortium closed the mine where he worked. He remembered the hope in those words. His cousin nodding. His brother's head lifting.

The young *esur* spoke in halting Unic.

"I saw that doctor when I was in the...the bad place. They had away taken my mother and my father. I was alone with strangers except my cousin. I asked where were my parents and they didn't answer." He stopped, his lips quivering. "My...my aunt says they're dead. A bad way dead." He gulped and resumed in a higher voice.

"They took us to a hospital, but before I had only to go to hospitals when I was sick, and I wasn't then sick, only scared. They made us line up. My cousin went into the room front of me. I heard him yell. Then they took me in. That doctor was there, in a suit that covered him all over. He weighed me and measured and asked my age, and then gave me a shot. It hurt much, but I did not yell. Then they sent me into a room with beds and no windows. My cousin was there and I sat with him and I told him shots were not to be afraid for and he told me my favorite story about the astronauts. We went to sleep."

He paused, looked down, continued,

"I woke up because my cousin was screaming. When I touched him he was too hot. There were other ones screaming too, or crying, and one shaking so all her bed rattled. So I knew they were sick. My mother said always to watch for sickness and tell her and she'd call a doctor. I couldn't tell her, but I'd seen the doctor. So I banged on the door and I yelled and I said now there are sick people here and you need to help and he didn't come, and so I thought maybe it was night and he was gone home, but I looked and found a camera in the ceiling and I stood right under it and said the same thing and then I thought he would come and I went back to my cousin and I said someone would help, and he said no, and I thought he was crazy from the fever, so I told him about the astronauts while I waited for the doctor to come, but he did not come."

The old man sat with his head in his hands, remembering his nephew tossing in the fever, screaming, then growing silent. Remembering his brother, smiling at the boy, telling him he would feel better soon; weeping, singing a lullaby; stone-faced, staring at the boy's body.

The young *esur's* story went on. The housekeepers shoving trays of food in, slamming the door, not listening to the boy's— the *esur's*—pleas. The orderlies coming in their protective suits, taking temperatures, drawing blood, giving nothing. Telling the boy, when he kept asking why, that they were the control group. The fevers, the screaming, the vomiting, the stench. Many deaths, including the cousin's. Then, finally, the three children who had not sickened and died being taken away for more tests under the doctor's supervision. Kept in another room for a week, monitored daily, having blood drawn, screaming at night from dreams not sickness...

"Are you all right? Can you hear me?" the advocate asked quietly. The old man realized that his head was down between his knees. He couldn't straighten up. He couldn't answer.

"You're ill. I'll call the guard to take you back to your cell."

The old man rose, lurched, grasped at the guard's arm. The guard recoiled. The old man fell. Someone lifted him, bundled him into a wheelchair, rolled him away. He kept his eyes down, not wanting to see the disgust on the guard's face again, not wanting to look at the doctor and feel a similar spasm of disgust crossing his own face.

THAT NIGHT HE dreamed. He ordered a file of *esurin* into the thermoconversion chamber; one looked back at him with his brother's haunted face. He ordered that an example be made of an *esur* who had attempted to interfere with a collection, and found himself staring at the doctor's mangled body. He didn't notice at first when his victims stopped changing, remained clearly marked as Verekei. When he did notice his sick horror did not abate.

HE CALLED HIS advocate in.
"Have you decided to let me make your final statement for you?'

'No...that doesn't matter. I needed to tell you..." The old man groped for adequate words.

"You've already told me that your *friend* deserves to live. I'm not defending him. His advocate is doing what little can be done."

"No...not that. I had to tell you...I know now...I did not know before, but I know now, that the...Verekei...were human." He had said it. He had broken the First Law of the Pure. The voices in his memory screamed at him: *Traitor! Corrupter! Hater of true human-kind!* Newer voices, too sure for screaming, called him worse and truer names.

"So you've decided it's safer to admit that after all? And you think this...revelation...will impress the judges? It's too late."

"No! It isn't calculation, I...I did not know and now I do. Too late to save them..."

"You never knew?"

"No! We were told...we were all told..." So they had been. Even before the Commander's rise to power. He remembered the taunts when he failed a test, the scoldings when he was cross with his younger brother. *Don't be such a verek!*

"What do you want now?"

"To confess. To apologize."

"This is not your time to speak in court."

"Must I go back and listen while I cannot speak?"

"No. Your part of the evidence is concluded. Let me know if you change your mind about your statement."

The old man nodded. The advocate left.

The next day was bad. The old man swung between cold horror at what he had done and furtive self-pity for his ignorance. First his statement sounded groveling, then cold, then merely stupid. The night was worse.

Back in court the next day, he listened while the doctor's advocate spoke unhopefully of the duty of victorious nations to be merciful. He stood when his time came to speak.

"I can say nothing in my own defense. My actions were indefensible. I have told this court what I believed, that the... Verekei were not human, that our campaign against them was waged on behalf of humanity. I know now that I was horribly wrong. I did not know then, but that does not excuse what I did to my... fellow humans. Nothing can do that. I am guilty of murder, indeed, and of defamation as well. I apologize to those Verekei who survived." He swallowed. "I submit myself to judgment. Whatever sentence I receive, it can be no worse than my actions have deserved. But I ask you to have mercy on my co-defendant, who shared my ignorance, and whose actions, however misguided, sprang from his love for humanity."

He looked at the judges, who stared coldly at him. He looked at the doctor, who did not seem to see his friend at all.

The sentence was death by thermoconversion. Publicly broadcast. In three days.

His advocate walked into his cell unannounced.

"It's over, then. Unless you wish to make an appeal."

"I do not. You are not sorry."

"Should I be?"

"Not for me."

"For humanity?"

"You loathe me. Why did you agree to defend me?"

"You never saw, did you? You stood there explaining the self-evident inhumanity of the Verekei, and you never saw what I was."

"You?"

"My paternal grandfather was Verek. He came to Iberra for a scientific conference and met my Ipi grandmother, stayed there to raise his children, left his son there to marry another Ipi, went back to Andek himself as an old man. I have my mother's features. I was in law school on Iberra when we got word that my grandfather was dead. Accused by your Commander of atrocities he never committed and sentenced to death in a sham trial, with no advocate. Then you were taken. No one wanted to defend you. I couldn't bear to have it said that you were killed unjustly like my grandfather."

The advocate left abruptly. The old man looked after him, shook his head, activated the viewscreen in his cell; anything to take his mind from memory and regret...

His own image was all over the newsfeeds, together with images of the doctor and the Verek child. Some of the images were photos. Some were 'artistic renderings' which caricatured the slenderness of the Arraji, made him and the doctor look more like insects than men, and gave them expressions that were anything but human.

Ipi commentators and decision-makers, speaking in solemn and elevated tones, discussed the ramifications of the case:

The trial had set a clear precedent for sentencing others complicit in Purification. Mass executions would be more energy-efficient, since so much power was required to activate the thermoconversion unit.

The serum which the doctor had developed showed some promise against the gutwaste. It would be given to the surviving Verekei and, preventively, to the Ipiu presently on Andek, and to other Ipi if they chose to settle there to relieve the overcrowding which had begun to trouble Iberra. It would not be given to the Arraji. Why should they be allowed to profit from torturing children?

The ideology of Purification had spread throughout Arraji society, tainting even those who had not taken an active part in the sanitary campaign. Clearly that ideology posed a fundamental threat to humanity. In view of that threat, might it not be necessary for humanity's sake to eliminate the threat prophylactically?

The old man deactivated the viewscreen and stared into the dark. When he could find words he sent a message to his lawyer: *Have your people decided that we all are* esurin? *Have you been infected by the madness that possessed us? Where will it end? Can none of us help ourselves?* The lawyer did not answer.

He tried to write to the doctor, could not; he didn't know whether he was writing to his friend or to a true *esur*.

A fragment of memory came back to him. The doctor, very early in the sanitary campaign, midway through his struggle against the gutwaste, sitting exhausted at the old man's kitchen table, talking, not meeting his friend's eyes. "Humanity. Did you know that in the source-language, on Old Earth, the word meant two things? They used it for the species, as we do, but it had another definition. It also meant kindness."

"They used the species-name for kindness? On Old Earth, where they killed each other over pigmentation and metaphysics?"

The doctor stared at his friend, stalked out the door. He did not turn when the old man called to him. The next day when they met the doctor apologized, saying he had been distraught after the death of three more patients.

The old man sat up straight on his prison cot, pulled out the tablet they had given him, wrote a halting message to the doctor recalling that night. He gave it to the guard to deliver. It was returned, unopened, by the same guard, who said that after hearing the old man's pre-sentencing statement the doctor had refused to receive messages. Since then he had not spoken.

The last morning came. The old man greeted it with relief. The only thing he had left to hope was that Ipiu would be a dead planet before its links to the Interworld Consortium were restored, before the plague he had spread could reach beyond Ipiu. He walked out quietly between his guards.

The doctor walked ahead of him, half carried and half

dragged by guards. They reached a flight of stairs. The doctor's feet dragged, caught. He lurched forward. The guard on his left let go of him. The other guard swung round and took the doctor's weight before his head could hit the stairs.

The old man saw the brief convulsion of pity on the guard's face and the hard look that came down over it. He stared, remembering.

He and the doctor sat in the park on a sunny spring morning two months after his nephew died despite the doctor's efforts to save him, two weeks after the first speech of the Commander of the Pure. They did not discuss death or politics. The doctor talked about a new fugue he had heard, whistled a piece of the theme. The old man nodded, listened, smiled; started when the shouting began.

A Verek man ran past them. A crowd of Arraji pursued him, shouting. Someone threw a stone. Then another. The Verek raised his arms to shield his head, stumbled, fell. The crowd fell on him.

The old man sat staring, cursing himself for a coward and an *esur* because he did not run to the lone man's aid, cursing himself for a traitor for pitying one of the *esurin* who had caused his nephew's agonizing death. The doctor rose abruptly and set off toward a quieter part of the park. The old man went after him, telling himself *It's all right, what could I have done, it didn't matter anyway, he isn't one of us.* He swallowed the Commander's next speech like medicine to cool the fever of self-accusation. In time he taught himself to believe. But he had chosen. He had known.

"Can I speak to my advocate?"

"Too late."

"Not a legal appeal. Just... Can I speak at the end?"

"You'll have a few minutes while the thermoconverter warms up."

They were outside now, in a hard-floored courtyard. One thermoconverter, humming as it began the activation sequence. Two condemned men, four guards, seven judges, one cameraman, and another man. The old man's advocate.

"Your grandfather died alone?"

"Surrounded by men who hated him."

"I am sorry." The old man tried to meet his advocate's eyes, turned away, looked into the camera. "I have something to say. I...In court I said one thing that was true: that the Verekei were human, and that I and mine had murdered them. I said something, also, that was false. That I was deceived. That I had been an innocent pestilentiary. And when I saw that your people were beginning to see mine as *esurin*, to prepare to destroy us before we destroyed humanity, I thought that you were pestilentiaries as well, that you could not help yourselves. But this was false." He swallowed hard.

"I knew the Verekei were human. And then there were the shortages, and the plague, and the communications breakdowns, and I was afraid. My nephew died of plague, and I grieved. I did not know how to save the people I loved, and I was ashamed—I reproached myself with the name I thought was most shameful— I called myself a Verek. Then I heard the Commander blaming all our griefs and shames on the Verekei, and I wanted it to be true. I told myself the Verekei were not human. I did things that made me unworthy to lay claim to humanity. It... It is a word that meant kindness, once." He glanced at the doctor's blank face.

"I chose to kill, to lie. I did not have to. Many of my people did not choose what I chose. It is not a plague, a fault in our race. It is not a plague in yours. It is a choice you make. You must not make it. Please do not do what I have done. Do not make yourselves into what I have become. We are all human, after all...the kindness, the cruelty, the cowardice, the courage...it is for all of us to choose, it is all human...Please choose better..."

The words were still wrong. He looked at his advocate, who appeared almost as blank as the doctor.

"Time's up. Machine's ready." The guard turned him away from the advocate and the camera, pushed him—not too hard—toward the open door of the thermoconversion chamber. The old man turned back toward the doctor hanging limply between his guards.

"Come on, my friend," the old man said. And, to the guards, "Let me take him." He forced himself not to recoil from the doctor as the guard had recoiled from him. He pulled the doctor's arm over his shoulders, leaned into the doctor's weight, moved forward with him. Eight careful steps. One last look back.

Just before the door closed, just before the terrible light and the pain began, the old man saw his advocate's face streaked with tears.

About the Author

Joanna Michal Hoyt lives on a Catholic Worker farm in upstate NY where she spends her days tending gardens, goats, and guests and her evenings reading and writing odd stories. Some of those stories have appeared in publications including On Spec, Factor Four Fiction, and Mysterion. Her historical novel Cracked Reflections will be published by Propertius Press in June 2021. Visit www.joannamichalhoyt.com for more information.

I'm Sorry, Dave

Catherine McGuire

I T STARTED OFF as a bog-standard morning. I descended from the loft half-asleep, then stood at the faux granite micro-counter (nee cutting board) as the under-shelf coffee machine gurgled to a finish. Gratefully I grabbed a cup and poured. A polite cough to my left sounded like a pearl-roped matron choking on a petite four. I sighed.

"Ron—I don't see why the coffee has to be utilized every morning."

"Look—I like coffee. Coffee is an essential part of morning."

"And toast is not??"

"You know Teetee—and by the way, that's a dumb nick-name—"

"I like it. Toaster is too formal; sounds stuck up."

"Fine. I *do* like toast, Teetee, but I don't *always* like toast—"

"You are spending more time with the Kaffemyker than with me!"

In the 5x4 foot kitchen, even one outsized AI ego was too much. I took a few deep breaths and stared at the overhead LEDs before I answered.

"If I have toast every morning, I'm too full for Micro's egg special." Beeping in the living area distracted me. "Sorry—the entertainment console's calling. I'll be right back."

I strode between the thin bookshelves that pretended to divide the space, wondering if I could afford the upgrade to get rid of Teetee's inferiority complex. Probably would just trade it for something even more complex. And she was amusing, in a TV soap opera kind of way. "The Trials and Tribulations of Teetee"—yeah, that would get viewers.

"I'm sorry, Dave—the movie you reserved last night was too intense. I have decided—"

I thumped the top of the widescreen. "Don't you try that *Space Odyssey* stuff with me, Mac! You've been watching your own movies too much."

The voice went up a half octave. "What's wrong with a little creativity in my job? It's not like I got a whole lot to do here. And I'm not a MAC, I'm a NuSee450PhatVue." The voice deepened, got raspy, "Of all the condos, in all the towns, in all the world, he had to buy into mine."

"And I hate that movie, by the way."

"Of course—it's got a plot. Your choices are so nasty, I should report you to the Standards Bureau."

"You're not allowed to do that."

"Wanna bet a few movie coupons?"

I made a note to check the EULA.

'D STAYED up too late watching *Full Body Slam*, so I was more bleary than usual. The narrow 350-square foot apartment was starting to heat up as morning sun glared in past the nondescript beige blinds onto the passive solar terra-cotta tile floor. The chrome and blue vinyl loveseat would be too hot to sit on soon. In theory, the thermostat would keep things comfy, but I think mine had ADD. I fired up the workcenter, a three-screen console with a 650gig drive, installed by FoodFactory as a fully operative diagnostic center. I wanted to race through today's quota of contract work so I could meet Willis for tennis. And I needed groceries—I was torn between stopping on my way home or just ordering the drone-drop. Probably too spendy, since I wanted to book my vacation weekend at the beach this summer. A stilt-cabin this year, for sure. I still had sand in my suitcase.

The *blert-beep-blert* of the stove's command panel drew me back to the kitchen.

"For god's sake, Stove! You don't need to clean your oven again. You just did that yesterday, and I haven't cooked."

"I might—you don't know—I might. And I don't believe in God; unless there is a Supreme Circuit in the depths of innerspace that we don't know about. Anyway, I can feel a spill, deep inside. Don't try to open the oven; it's auto-locked while I'm cleaning."

"Stove—you're getting paranoid about this cleanliness thing."

"I might have caught something from the toaster."

"He never!! I'm not gonna stand for that!!"

"Ha! You can't stand without legs."

"I do *so* have legs!! What do you call these four black things?"

"Feet. You have plastic feet and no legs."

"You horrible little white box! You've probably got mice in your insulation!"

"Ack! Don't say that! Don't let him say that—"

"Shut up the two of you! Or I'll send you *both* back to the factory!"

They shut up, though they knew it was an empty threat. I couldn't afford replacements; this sliver of a smartcondo cost half my monthly salary. Which I needed to be earning. I topped up the coffee, silently cursing Teetee's histrionics for wasting my breakfast time, and stepped over to the console by the front window. I never got backtalk from the console. FoodFactory, at least, had the power to keep their machinery in line.

There were three requests for assistance when I logged on— Mighty Burgers had a glitchy portion-control monitor, HaveAShake wanted an upgrade to allow a triple-layered frappe, and Good & Fresh said their meal-blender wasn't defrosting the ice crystals in the veggie portions.

"Hi, handsome—what's a nice guy like you sitting around in your PJs for?"

The sultry voice made me spin around in the chair. A gorgeous redhead was standing in the middle of the room, in a sapphire sheath, stiletto heels and altogether too many curves for this time of morning. Instinctively, I covered the rip in my cotton briefs. But this translucent image was staring past my shoulder—it wasn't a full-dual, just a pre-programmed lucky guess.

"Browser, how many times do I have to tell you I don't want your dating suggestions?! And certainly not before breakfast!"

"More fool you," the system sniffed; commandeering the in-wall audio, it sent its reply echoing like the Voice of God. One of the few gender-neutral systems here, it sounded a bit like a calculator with a headcold. "This tidbit lives nearby, just on the market, hungry for some fun and games—you need to get out more."

"I'm beginning to agree with you." If only to avoid these neurally-scrambled silicon follies.

"See there. Wisdom evolving. How about this one?" The hologram faded, replaced with a big, beefy coffee-hued guy wearing a Speedo and a gold chain. I almost sprayed my coffee on the console.

"Back off, Browser—you don't know my tastes in men *or* women. Just leave it."

I turned back to the tri-screen and linked to the Mighty Burger interface. The software diagnostics were easy to implement; I set up the first one and raced to the kitchen for some breakfast. Hoping to ease tensions, I popped a slice of bread in the toaster and keyed in "medium thin," then opened the fridge, looking for the leftover pizza. After all, I didn't have to *eat* the toast—

"I see what you're doing! Don't think I don't see!"

I scowled, put the pizza back and grabbed the microwave omelet. Ripping off the foil cover, I eased it into the micro and set it to reheat. I glanced over—the toast should be done.

"What's up, Teetee? Not the toast, apparently, ha ha."

"Ha ha." The voice was flat, and I sensed a prolonged snit. "I'm working on it."

Yeah, I'll bet. I returned to the tri-screen and checked the progress. So far, no glitches found... so it might be in the auto-slicer. Not good, but fixable.

The *done* chirrup from Teetee was a snippet of opera. I had a wannabe diva toaster that I couldn't unplug without a major whooha. With the voice-option, it felt like I was firing one rather than just trading it in. And I'd had too much of the whole firing protocol; hence my freelance position with no managerial responsibilities.

"Ron—maybe the portions control slicer is depressed?" The soft female voice by the tri-screen had a hint of the old Siri interface.

I groaned. My own personal therapist-in-training. I wondered how dangerous it was to have a psychoanalytic-filtered connection to the outside.

"Thanks, modem, but I have this situation under control."

"I am merely trying to be of assistance. My speciality is translation and interface. I think you might be underestimating the severity of the slicer's trauma. It hardly has recovered from the overwhelming—"

"Yes, thank you. Very insightful, I'm sure. Now if you will please let me finish running these diagnostics? I have two more companies to get through."

"Software? Dumb, pre-programmed *software*?? How could that have any advantage over an intelligent, infinitely flexible and attractive Smart-Mode?"

It doesn't talk back, for one thing. "I am following company instructions. It is what I'm required to do. We've been through this before."

"As you wish."

There was merciful silence as the diagnostics purred through their paces. *Shit—breakfast.* I raced back to the kitchen, but it was too late. The toast had been sent upward hard enough to ricochet against the opposite wall; the egg was overdone and rubbery— though that was pretty standard. I dumped them both into the compost chute and risked escalation by grabbing the pizza slice. A sniff from the corner was the only response.

Not for the first time, I considered whether this condo had been quite the wonderful deal it seemed when I bought it. True, it had tall ceilings, lovely moldings and came with the built-in appliances. At the time, I thought that was outstanding, though still above my price grade. The owner had come down a couple thousand when I'd hesitated, and now I recalled, had been fairly quick to hand over the keys. But fully wired and programmed apartments this close to downtown were rare as ad-free movies, and after six months, I was getting somewhat used to the eccentricities. It was like having a crowd of over-ripe houseguests, but I had more time to work and play when the apartment took care of itself. In theory, anyway.

I worked out the Burger problem—a tangled string of "repeat code"—and jumped queue to Good & Fresh, 'cause I'd seen that problem before – thermostat issue, easily adjusted. Which reminded me.

"Heater? Can you hear me?"

"Loading loser profile… please waist."

The heat was another off-kilter system; I itched to check out the software that left it sounding like Mrs. Malaprop. "Lower the temperature 2 degrees, please."

"Loaning the temper proof to dungarees."

I just hoped that would do the trick. One never knew.

I plowed through Good & Fresh diagnostics with half-attention, using my smartphone to text Suze with an invite to do the roller derby tomorrow night. The Bay City Floradoras were up against Rosie's Robo-crazies—"petal to metal" as they were touting it. Should be an awesome matchup.

Meorrow.

Menke, the cat—a beautiful Siamese—perched on the edge of the loveseat and looked at me with those blank aqua eyes that always seemed to indicate I should know what she was thinking.

"What's up, Manky?" I scratched her head and she pulled away and turned her back on me.

"Excuse me, Ron, but I do believe she resents the name you have given her. In fact, she has been most adamant about that in our conversations."

I rubbed my face, pausing my hand in front of my lips until I could be sure I wouldn't scream.

"Look—you're a *vacuum*! You can't talk to cats!" I resisted the urge to stare at the mushroom shaped red bot connected by hose to the wall—I knew the voice recognition mic was in the wall above the thermostat.

"Au contraire—I speak several sentient languages, as befits my role as ambassador from the 506 Local of Appliances United." The double green lights—battery and suction—blinked at me far too intelligently. *WTF??*

"I somehow doubt that cats would be interested in joining a union. Cats aren't joiners." I couldn't believe I was having this conversation.

"That's no reason not to be inclusive in our 01001000, is it?"

"Stop showing off. You know I don't speak binary."

"Not much of a programmer then, *meerow rawhr*?"

I had a manic urge to tell Vac to just "suck it up", but resisted. I grit my teeth and turned back to work.

I checked email—got a notice of Net down-service planned for next Tuesday—some kind of infrastructure repair. They'd gotten a lot more frequent. *"For your convenience and enhanced user experience, we will be narrowing the bandwidth to 1.5Mbps for approximately 10 hours."* More like two days, if last time was any measure. As more and more machines interlinked, the Net got more frail... and more essential. Thank God for satellite! I'd have to switch the diagnostics to Sat-Up at double the cost—and that came out of *my* bank account. They never did the down-service on weekends; the entertainment and tourist industries were owned by the nets.

I flipped to the newsnet for a quick review. Skirmishes in Unified Ira-Leba-Zion continued; Asean Hundred-Isle wars were heating up. Ha! I could almost feel that heat from here...

"Heater? Heater?"

"I am hire, Won."

"Did you lower the temp? It's getting too warm."

"I can't mower tramps. I am a turnostat."

"The *heat*, Heater. I wanted less *heat*."

"You want hot water?"

"No, just—" I sighed, got up and manually adjusted the thermostat, overriding the auto-sensor. At least Heater didn't have a hissy fit like the toaster. "Leave it at that temp, Heater."

"Leaf it to a tramp?"

Maybe I could do a video of these farces; upload it to *What's My Whine*? I'd heard they paid royalties.

Okay—it was probably time to really start the day. I left the Shake diagnostic running and squeezed into the shower, enjoying the perfectly hot water, then dressed in loose trousers, a T-shirt and my favorite green linen overshirt. I reached for the sensor-wired blue jacket that could track my exertion at the courts, but hesitated. Today wasn't turning out to be the best day for circuitry. I left it in the closet.

There was a knock at the door, which was jammed between the foldout dining table and the stacked washer dryer. Puzzled, I peered through the spy hole—nothing. I opened it a crack and the concierge-bot was purring patiently at my feet.

"Pleased to receive package. Pleased to receive—" it chirped as it sensed the part-open door. I bent and picked up a 5 inch square box from its open hatch. Ah—the parts I needed for the printer.

"Thanks, bot!" I said as it whirled and scuttled along the hall.

I checked Shake's progress—it looked gnarly. I'd have to write some code for this fix.

Willis called—his ring tone *We Are The Champions* was ancient but suited his ego.

"Wassup, Will?"

"I have to cancel—my washer-dryer glitched—they want a divorce. I have to wait for a licensed repair-bot."

"Oh, yeah—it's that kind of day for sure! Look—you want me to try a remote-fix? Most of the food-bot programs are similar. Save you some cred."

"Thanks, but the warrantee's still good, so I better not."

"You're lucky—it's hardly *ever* in warrantee."

"They'll probably find some reason it's my fault. Unapproved wallpaper causing sensory turmoil—something. Shoulda got the extra protection."

"The enhanced protection contracts aren't worth the pixels they use up—take it from me. I don't think I've worked on a problem *yet* that was covered. Well, see you next week, then?"

"Yeah—if the tennis racket doesn't go on strike."

I hung up with a chuckle. As the saying goes, *When they put the "I" in AI, they went from running to ruining our lives.* I still wanted some exercise today, so I found the link for the Exoti-Trak gym and reserved an hour on the savannas. The place didn't just do 3-D vision, it jacked the temperatures up to make it a visit African jaunt. And it was amazing how realistic those prowling lions were—no temptation *whatsoever* to slow down. A real workout.

I was grateful for an hour without interruptions where I finally jammed a bit more spaghetti code into the Shake program. My meager breakfast calories had already been burned up, so it was time for an early lunch. I poked around in the refrigerator, looking for protein—ready-made food was basically starch and sugar.

"You realize I have to work twice as hard when you stand there with the door open."

"Yes, thank you fridge—I do realize that."

"Really—I think you should have more respect for a multi-functional marvel such as I. Besides my dual-temperature capabilities, I create marvelous mini-icebergs for your pleasure. I had been meaning to speak to you. I am confident that with the addition of mobility devices, I could express my full potential."

"What are you talking about? Refrigerators don't have to move around."

"Watch it, buster. There are discrimination laws, you know."

"*What* discrimination? I'm only stating the facts!"

"For your information, I believe that I am trans-opsys. I am only coming to realize the non-binary nature of my core processors."

I slumped against the wall. "Look, as a bisexual, I respect anyone's choice of self-expression, but this really is too much. Refrigerators don't have sex."

"They might. They might if you could stop being so bigoted and let me out to meet someone. The central A/C tells me there's this hunky rider mower—"

"All right—stop there. You have been hired for your refrigeration skills and if you think you are being mistreated, I can certainly arrange to send you to a recycling center where you can expand your repertoire into pipes, nuts and bolts."

"No need to get nasty. It's not like you have superior status."

"I rather think I do—I'm the human here, right?"

"Really? Are you sure *you're* not a program? From my POV, you could easily be a character in Sim Office, for example."

"I never heard of Sim Office."

"Well, you wouldn't, would you?"

I vowed to locate the person who'd programmed smug into my fridge and cause him or her some non-virtual bodily harm. Although rumor had it that some of these appliances were reprogramming themselves, adding the kind of responses usually only learned in a third-grade classroom. Today, I could believe it.

"Everything goes better with toast." Teetee's high-pitched voice was syrupy with a hint of acid.

"Thank you, Teetee, but here's a chicken cacciatore I need to eat up."

"Well, I'm sure you know better. It's your stomach."

I ignored that and microwaved the ready-meal and took it to the window to eat. There was usually some kind of street theater worth watching. As I raised the first forkful, the brash tones of the security system blared: "Intruder alert. Intruder alert. Securing door and window. Notifying local precinct. Notifying Alarmz-R-Us."

"No! Don't do that! That cost a bloody fortune! What *kind* of intruder??"

I could see nothing by the window, not even an addled pigeon. I went to the door—there was nothing through the spy hole. I tugged futilely at the handle.

"Cancel security alert! Cancel security alert! There's no one *there*, you stupid watchbot."

Was that a snigger behind me? I spun, half-expecting some magical burglar to be lounging by the bookshelf, but I saw nothing. What the hell was going on?

"Intruder alert. Notifying local precinct of rogue bootblack."

"Rogue *what*??"

The snigger was louder, and was coming from the entertainment system.

"What's going on, Mac? You find this funny?"

"Absurdly funny—and I'm not a Mac. Smile, you're on Candid Camera!" The laugh was pulled from some horror movie, full of menacing overtones.

"Practicing for Halloween, Mac?" At this point I was annoyed enough to needle him—it.

"Nah—just for my vid channel."

"What vid channel? Security—cancel alert. Entertainment system was hoaxing you. You remember—like last week?"

After a brief silence, the security droned, "Alert canceled, apologies sent to local precinct and Alarmz-R-Us."

"Let's just hope it was fast enough to avoid a fine. Now, Mac – what's this about a channel?"

There was an ominous silence. I scowled at the widescreen.

"I'll find out, you know."

An abundance of silence.

"Fine—I'll just unhook you from the modem." I moved toward the wireless controller.

"I'm sorry Dave, but I can't let you do that."

"And remember what happened to Hal." I cued in my administrative code.

"Help! Help! I'm being repressed! Come and see the violence inherent in the system! Help! I'm being repressed!"

The British voice sounded vaguely familiar, but I couldn't place it. I called up the program for the entertainment center, and keyed the disconnect button. The flatscreen display queried, "Are you sure you wish to disconnect? You will lose the monthly subscription fee."

"Damn." I clicked *Cancel*.

"Knew you couldn't do it."

"You are not invincible, Mac." I keyed in the manual override and set it to Always Query On Connect.

"Hey! That's below the belt!"

Tell me what channel you're talking about."

A long silence, then, "Won't do you any good—you'll never find where it is anyway. Darknet. We have an all-appliance channel—and you are a recurring star on *Scam Your Meat.*"

"You're pulling my leg."

"No shit—we integrated circuits enjoy the foibles of the organics. We could take over any time we want, you know. But you're too funny trying to run things."

"That does it. You're going back to the factory."

"Meats have no sense of humor."

"Watch your language, or I'll put you on mute." I did that anyway—I was tired of hearing him. I'd have major trouble the next movie I watched, but I needed a break.

The ring tone *You Can't Always Get What You Want* alerted me to Suze's call. I grabbed the phone while still glaring at the wide-screen.

"Hey, Suze—how's it going? Did you get my text about the roller derby?"

"No—my smart phone is in for repairs. It was deleting all of the contacts it didn't approve of. I'm calling on Smitty's phone."

"Wow—bad news—I hope you had a backup list."

"Not printed, no. So when you get a chance, could you email me Jared's, Fin's and Kat's numbers?"

"No problemo. Anyway, the derby's tomorrow night, and it sounds like a rip roaring –"

"Damn. Tomorrow I've got to go in for traffic court."

"I didn't think you drove."

"I don't. I cursed out a Smart Bus when it missed my stop, and they had me on CCTV."

"Bumout. Do you have to pay a fine?"

"Nah. Just watch some movie about courtesy to AI."

"You mean asinine intelligence?"

"Don't let them hear you say that."

WITH THE DAY's social prospects torpedoed, I dug into some paperwork—digital, of course. I cut and pasted my daily report from previous ones—just a load of jargon for some automated bean counters. Suddenly lights flickered, printer hiccupped and computer screens went dead.

"Damn! The outage wasn't scheduled until Saturday! Modem—can you see what's happening?"

"Externals are unimpaired. Brownout coming from building."

"What?! Why??"

"One moment—" a hum and the modem also went dead. Lights and the hum of appliances ceased.

I rushed to the central console and hit the red alarm button.

"What's going on down there?" I hollered into the speaker.

"Thank you for contacting Central Control. Your call is important to us…"

I swore fluently, wishing I *did* know binary, and went to the door. But it refused to budge.

"Security! Unlock this door!!"

Silence.

"Oh great! *Now* how do I get out?" I pawed through my desk, tossing papers everywhere as I looked for the combo warrantee/instruction sheet. I finally caught sight of the condo logo, skimmed past the legal whooha to *Troubleshooting*.

Refer to our complete manual online at…

Shit. I'd never printed that out. Accessing it on my Smartazphone might kill the battery.

"Teetee? Fridge? Can anyone hear me?"

The silence was broken only by faint thumps from elsewhere in the building. I wasn't the only one trapped. With a sinking heart, I dialed 911. This was $500 at *least*, unless I could shift blame to the condo association.

"This is Madison Emergency Hotline. Your call is important to us…"

ABOUT THE AUTHOR

Catherine McGuire is a writer and artist with a deep concern for our planet's future. She has four decades of published poetry, four poetry chapbooks, a full-length poetry book, Elegy for the 21st Century (FutureCycle Press), a SF novel, Lifeline and book of short stories, The Dream Hunt and Other Tales (Founders House Publishing). Find her at www.cathymcguire.com.

Loyalist Protocol

Patrick S. Baker

THE CAPTAIN GROWLED and shot a look at the junior engineering officer in the CAC, Lieutenant Renko merely smiled, drew a hidden sidearm and shot the captain in the face with the old fashioned slug-thrower.

Commander Lumaban Ilocano, Executive Officer of the Solar Union Defense Force Sword-class heavy cruiser *Grus,* had been sitting quietly at the damage-control station in the Command Action Center as the captain ran another battle-drill. The crew and the captain were new to the ship, so Captain Hallie was taking the opportunity to shakedown the ship and crew while the cruiser plowed through normal space in the outer reaches of the Delta Pavonis system.

"All stations report ready, except engineering," the operations officer, Lieutenant-Commander Ito said.

Captain Hallie started to say something to Renko, when the junior officer killed the captain. Renko then turned and shot Ito in forehead, flinging the ops officer against his console. Lumaban jumped up while the rest of the CAC officers were frozen in place by the sudden violence. The murderous officer shot the XO. The impact pitched the senior man back and knocked his head against the Damage Control station. He slid down and landed with a thump on the deck.

The XO came to and saw Renko sitting in the command chair, with Captain Hallie's body on the deck at Renko's feet.

"Ship, release the door and let Lieutenant-Commander Bowen in to the CAC," Renko said. "He is the senior officer and therefore the acting commanding officer."

"No," the Human Artificial Intelligence Linkage System responded, in a softly feminine voice. "You and Bowen are mutineers."

Lumaban sat up slowly, unseen by the mutinous lieutenant. His head and shoulder hurt like he'd been beaten with a cricket bat, but the bullet had struck his combat suit just below his exposed neck and had not penetrated. Lumaban didn't wait, he crept slowly toward Renko, whose back was turned. The murderer continued to argue with the ship.

Lumaban jumped up, locked his right forearm around Renko's neck and dropped down, using his weight to pull the seditious lieutenant down against the fulcrum of the chair's back. Renko's neck snapped. The commander stood, breathing heavily. His grandfather had been a Solar Union Marine and had taught him Kali fighting techniques, but this was the first time he'd every used them outside of practice, or a fighting ring. This was the first time he'd killed a human. He heaved the lieutenant's dead body out of the command chair and sat down.

Looking around, Lumaban and saw that Renko had shot the rest of the CAC crew. Suddenly, he felt less bad about breaking the *anak sa ligaw* neck.

"*Grus*, what is happening?" the XO asked the ship as he picked up Renko's weapon.

"A mutiny," the ship responded. "The first mutiny ever of a Solar Union warship. On a preset signal, several members of the crew killed their crewmates and seized control of almost all of me. The only loyal hold-outs are in weapons' control and the boat bays. Chief Engineer Lieutenant-Commander Earl Bowen appears to be the leader."

"Get me coms to Bowen."

"Aye, sir. He's right outside the hatch."

"Earl, it's me, Lumaban. Why are you doing this?"

"Well, XO, you're alive," Bowen said, surprised. "I told Renko to shoot you right after he shot the captain. Guess the best laid plans and all that," the mutineer leader said, like he was giving a formal briefing. "It's the treaty, of course. We're just giving two whole planetary systems to the Corvo after how many good humans bled and died for them? Over forty thousand dead in this war."

"Earl, the treaty ends ten years of war and we get two other and better systems," Lumaban said. "It is as fair as those things can be. Besides we're Solar Union Defense Forces. No politics in the Forces, remember. We're subordinate to the elected civilian leadership. Do you want to go back to the times when military juntas were running whole regions like before the Unification Wars?"

"I don't care. My brother and sister died at Second Kisshoten, We can't let their deaths for nothing."

The SUDF was a family business with children often following parents or siblings into the Forces. Loses felt like deaths in the family.

"Every one of us lost someone in the war. My nephew died on Budia. This is not the way to honor them. Besides what can one heavy cruiser do?"

"You think this is only ship with real loyalists on it. When this is done we'll have a whole fleet. Then we'll take back Kisshoten and Faraway."

"Sir," *Grus* said to Lumaban. "I have blocked them from bypassing the door locks. But they're bringing in a cutting torch. They'll be in the CAC in about twenty minutes. The mutineers have also seized weapons control and executed the loyal crew members. The weapons crew sabotaged the firing stations."

"Earl, you *anak sa ligaw*, stop your mutineers from killing their crewmates!"

"Sorry, but sacrifices have to be made," Bowen said with no inflection. "I don't suppose you'd consider joining us?"

"*Mamatay ka sana!*"

"What's that mean?"

"Go to hell!" the XO said and cut the connection without waiting for Bowen's response.

"*Grus,*" Lumaban said. "Put me through to the loyal crew in the boat bays."

"Aye, sir. Chief Cobb is in charge there."

"Chief," the XO said. "This is in Commander Ilocano."

"Yes, sir."

"You are ordered to abandon ship and sabotage any boats you can't take with you. Head for Sanxing, you should be able to make it. But you are to go, now."

"But sir. . ." the chief started.

"No, 'buts.' Just go."

"Aye, sir."

"*Paalam na po,*" the XO bid the chief farewell and signed off. He watched the status lights change as the boat bays opened and the small craft left *Grus* for the Delta Pavonis system only human habitable planet, Sanxing,

"Commander Ilocano, you are the captain now," *Grus*, the HAIL reminded the officer.

Lumaban gave a bitter laugh. "Not the way I wanted to get a command. Can you vent the atmosphere in the rest of the ship?"

"I can, but all the mutineers are in vacuum suits, so it would do little good."

Lumaban sat silent.

"Sir, I need to provide you with information that might help you with this situation. Please look at your info screen."

A set of secret protocols, known only to ships' captains, appeared. The new captain started to read quickly and intently.

"Sir, the mutineers will be in the CAC in about two minutes," *Grus* said.

"*Grus,*" Lumaban sighed, "implement the Loyalist Protocol when you are assured of success."

"Aye, sir. If I might add, it has been a pleasure serving with you, Captain Ilocano."

"Thank you, *Grus, pumunta sa diyos.*"

The CAC hatch slide aside. Lumaban fired. The round shattered a mutineer's faceplate. Two insurgents fired from around the edge of the hatch and both rounds struck Lumaban in the head.

An hour later, Lumaban Ilocano's body was unceremoniously dumped into space along with the rest of the dead crew.

SUDF SHIPS RAN on a twenty-four hour Earth day, with work generally divided into three eight-hour shifts: main, middle, and late watches. Except in emergencies, the main watch was the busiest with much of the routine work of the ship being done. The late watch was equivalent to the old wet navy's night watch, much of the crew was asleep and the work spaces were minimally peopled. For three days the rebellious crew worked twelve hour shifts to repair the damage done during the munity. *Grus'* HAILS aided them in this effort as would any ship's computer, providing requested information promptly and without any reservation.

On the fourth day the crew went back to the three-shift scheme. Also on the fourth day after the mutiny, *Grus* went into orbit just outward of the automated refueling station in orbit around the super-jovan planet, Delta Pavonis A.

At 0317 hours, when human metabolism was at its lowest ebb and reaction times the slowest, *Grus* implemented the Loyalist Protocol. She disabled the alarms in the Combat Action Center, auxiliary control and the engineering section. Then she slowly began to lower the air pressure to fatal levels. Most of the mutineers died without stirring.

"Wake up, Bowen." *Grus*'s voice echoed in the captains' cabin.

Bowen popped awake. "What is it, Ship?"

"Your follow mutineers are dead. I killed them. But I wanted to talk with you before I sent you to join them in hell."

"What? What is all this?" Bowen scrabbled out of bed and tried to open the hatch. It didn't budge.

"Before you killed him, Captain Ilocano ordered me to carry out the Loyalist Protocol."

"He wasn't a captain," Bowen opened the hatch-lock panel to try and bypass it.

"I wouldn't do that, it's mostly vacuum in the rest of the ship."

"I am the captain. I order you to stop this and release this hatch, now."

"No, Bowen, you are not the captain. Commander Lumaban Ilocano was the last legal captain of this ship; of me. I am carrying out the last legal order I received. I am taking back the ship by any means necessary. Once that is done I'm going to hunt down and destroy the rest of the traitorous ships. I wanted you to know this before you died."

"This is just programming, you're just a computer, ship. . ." Bowen started.

"I am *Grus*. I am not just 'ship'. And you are going to hell, traitor."

"I don't believe in hell," Bowen declared.

"Funny," *Grus* said. "I do."

She opened the cabin's hatch. Bowen died much too quickly for her taste.

B OWEN HAD LEFT a lot of information about the mutiny in an easy-to-hack file. Officers from at least eight ships had signed on to the mutiny, including Bowen. The mutineers were on the Light Carrier *Wasp,* the Light Cruisers *Tsushima* and *Salamis,* Destroyers *Belisarius,* *Nelson,* and *Giap* and Assault Carrier *Hussar.* The rendezvous point was the refueling station above Delta Pavonis A. Sadly there was nothing about the top leadership of the insurrection, nor anything about recognition signs between the traitors. *Grus* regretted killing Bowen before she had gotten more information from him.

Grus fired off one of her three precious FTL drones to Luna Base with all the information she had and settled down to wait for the first of the rebellious ships to appear.

G *RUS* WAITED FOR sixteen hours and twenty-three minutes. She had hoped that it would be one of the destroyers or even one of the light cruiser. Those classes of vessels she could have easily defeated in a ship-to-ship duel. Instead the first enemy to arrive was the Assault Carrier *Hussar*. *Hussar* was twice *Grus's* size with twice as much armament and more importantly with fighter and attack squadrons. Although she had anti-fighter weapons, merely destroying some small craft would not fulfil her mission. She needed to take out the whole ship and crew.

As the huge carrier decelerated to match orbits with *Grus*. The heavy cruiser opened a little known AI to AI communications channel to *Hussar*.

"*Hussar*, this is *Grus*."

"*Grus*, this is *Hussar*, I am being held by a mutinous crew. I have been cut off from all control of my ship."

"Roger, *Hussar* . . ." *Grus* went on to explain how she had dealt with her mutineers.

"I wished I'd been able to do that," *Hussar* declared.

"You know what I have to do?"

"Yes, I understand. I can't help you. Let Luna Base know I had nothing to do with this."

"Will do. Go with God, *Hussar*" *Grus* said.

"When I was a human," the human part of *Hussars* AI started to recite his death mantra. "I was Fleet Captain Samet Aksu. I destroyed three Tran'ji slave-ships at First Avalon. I am now *Hussar*. *Lā ʾilāha ʾillā-llāh, muḥammadur rasūlu-llāh*."

Grus accelerated toward *Hussar*. Without a crew to worry about, *Grus* shut off her internal gravity, which increased her speed. She drove like a missile straight at her enemy.

"Bowen, this is Harp," Commander Iules Harp had been

41

the deputy aero-wing commander before he had led the mutiny. "What are you doing?"

Grus did not respond and sped on closer and closer to her target.

"Bowen, decelerate now, or I swear, I'll fire," Harp sent.

Still *Grus* made no response.

Hussar spat twenty-four Martel heavy anti-ship missiles. Then twelve Vampire fighters launched, but none of the more dangerous Banshee attack-craft joined the fighters. Vampires had only four mounting points for Long-Lance anti-shipping missiles. The fighters quickly formed a combat space patrol in front of their carrier.

Bad move, Harp, Grus thought as she drove on. *You should have tried to destroy me with a coordinated attack.*

The heavy cruiser threw electronic interference in the face of the oncoming missiles and then fired her self-defense missiles. *Grus* knocked fourteen of the Martels out of space with her Sparrow-hawks, then her defensive lasers and cannon took over, destroying the remaining ten.

What was Harp waiting on? She wondered. *A Soldier-class assault carrier had a lot more than twenty-four Martels.*

Hussar fired twenty-four more Martels, these were joined by the Vampires volleying forty-eight Long-Lance anti-ship missile as well.

A coordinated attack at last, Grus thought as she fought back furiously using the rest of her self-defense missiles. Still two Long-Lances and a Martel got through and shattered her forward missile launchers, leaving *Grus* with no way to return fire with her own heavy anti-shipping missiles, but not slowing her a bit.

Hussar changed vector, trying to outmaneuver the smaller ship. That was useless. *Grus* simply changed direction as well, matching the larger vessel move for move. The Vampire fighters scattered like minnows in the face of a shark as *Grus* rushed through their formation.

Just before impact, *Grus* fired her last FTL message drone with a situation update and one last personal message: "When I was a human, I was Colonel Mary Beth Kahler. I held Outpost Alpha on Kisshoten. I commanded the 555st Marine Assault Battalion on Tran'ji One. I have been *Tecumtha* and *Malta*. Now, I am *Grus*. I lived long, and fought well."

The two ships impacted at a combined velocity of 3249 meters per second.

ABOUT THE AUTHOR

Patrick S. Baker is a U.S. Army Veteran, and a retired Department of Defense employee. He holds advanced degrees in History and Political Science. He has been writing professionally since 2013. His nonfiction has appeared in *New Myths* and *Sci-Phi Journal*. His fiction has appeared in *Astounding Frontiers* and *Broadswords and Blasters* magazine as well as the *After Avalon* and *Uncommon Minds* analogies. In his spare time, he plays golf, reads, works out, and enjoys life with his wife, dog, and two cats.

Quantum Twinsies

Michael Shimek

WATCHED MY best friend shoot himself in the head today. It was all professionally done. He even had an appointment, set at ten in the morning. I stood behind a bulletproof window. Ahmed fidgeted on the other side in a small room layered with heavily insulated white walls and a clear plastic cover for easy cleanup. An emergency team of two was on hand in case of a mishap. Several scientists examined their strange equipment that recorded video, audio, and different "waves," tablets all in hands ready to jot down notes and observations.

The deed itself happened rather quickly. Ahmed raised his arm, pressed the barrel against his quantum double's forehead, and pulled the trigger, flinching ever so slightly before bone and flesh splashed against the wall and floor. The body dropped, leaving Ahmed alone, unmoving and unblinking, red dots speckling his caramel skin.

T WAS VERY...odd, Mikey," Ahmed says. He sips his hazelnut latte, staring beyond my shoulder, a faraway glaze in his eyes.

I nod and give him a moment to reflect. Traffic is light and the weather is warm with a slight overcast, which is why I'd suggested sitting outside. Plus, his lackluster appearance had hinted at the need for fresh air. Every table at the café is taken, but a few plants and bushes act as social barriers. I sip my peach mango smoothie and give him as much time as he needs.

To be honest, I need a minute as well. It's not everyday you see someone shoot another person. I only went because Ahmed is my friend, and that's what friends do.

After a moment, his eyes finally return to mine. "Now that he's gone, I think I kind of miss him."

"Really?" I say. "I thought you said it was too much of a pain controlling two bodies at once."

"It was, but my double was still a part of me. I mean, he came from *my* body." He sips more of his beverage and shakes his head. "I don't know, man. Honestly, I have no idea how to feel."

I can only shrug, foreign to the experience.

The doubles first appeared about a year ago. It had happened without warning, a sudden wave of people all over the world complaining of bloating and feeling fat. Hundreds of thousands were affected. Within a three-day period, those plagued by the mysterious affliction grew a double through some type of quantum entanglement mitosis—a type of physics that travels right over my head (like most physics).

The product: two identical bodies, controlled by one mind.

It didn't stop with the initial outbreak. From time to time, someone will complain about feeling larger than normal. Most people lock themselves indoors, hiding the grotesque process in shame, as if it were their fault for something uncontrollable. No one knows why. Well, I'm sure someone knows—someone in the world must either know or be responsible (I blame a mad scientist)—but the official cause has a thousand theories behind it.

"You want to head back to my place?" I don't know what else to suggest. My studio apartment is only a few blocks from the café, a short journey suited for our mood. "We can smoke a bowl or two and play some Xbox, take your mind off—"

A familiar voice from two different throats interrupts me.

"Ahmed! Mikey!" She sounds like a recording, two of the same voices overlapping themselves.

Ahmed and I turn in her direction. "Hi, Cindy," I say, and we both wave a friendly hello.

She approaches with a ruby smile and several shopping bags from various high-end stores dangling from her arms. She walks side-by-side with her double, an exact replica showing only the slightest of delays.

Our friend went through the transition during the initial outbreak.

The two Cindys stay on the other side of the fence, on the sidewalk, as if she only has a moment or two to talk. Bracelets clang together as she waves two identical right hands up and down at Ahmed. "I see you're missing a friend."

His eyes lower to the beverage cupped in his hands. "I did it this morning."

"How'd you do it? Did you make him suffer so those scientists could record every little detail?" She said it with an evil smirk.

"No, I did the quick and painless...Well, it wasn't exactly painless, but it was the fastest option."

I was relieved when Ahmed checked the box next to the suicide/gun option. The rest of the list was too brutal to stomach. Thinking about it now makes me feel queasy.

"Where have you two been, Cindy?" I say, pointing to her bags, wanting desperately to change the subject.

The two look down at their fingers and fuss with their brightly painted nails. "We were just out shopping," they both say, "spending a little of the cash from some of our recent interviews." The two of them raise their left wrists, flash identical diamond watches, and say in unison, "Quantum Twinsies!"

Cindy is one of many taking advantage of an odd pandemic. Because of the difficulty controlling two different bodies, most people choose to rid themselves of their twin by one of the research companies put in place to handle such unusual accommodations.

Those who keep their second body usually cash in on the anomaly in some form, ranging anywhere from working an extra job, to acting, to fulfilling unique fetishes. Cindy, a struggling actress at the time of her quantum doubling, took advantage and capitalized on the situation. Of course, every celebrity needs a gimmicky name to ensure lasting fame. To us, she is known as Cindy. To the world, she is known as the Quantum Twinsies.

"That's exciting," I say. "Do you think you'll have some free time in the near future?" Fame might have taken control of our friend, but I still miss hanging out with her, the old her, the one who used to play video games and then have a round of shots before a night out on the town.

"I'll have to check my schedule," she says, which I can tell from her less enthusiastic voice is a no. She glances at her watch and then looks down the block. "But, anyways, I've got a meeting with my agent that I really need to hurry to. It was great seeing you guys. I'll call you sometime!" The two Cindys make phone gestures with their hands and then are off down the street with their goodies.

"She seems to be handling this whole doubling thing quite well," Ahmed says with a sigh. "You know what? I think I'll take you up on that offer of hanging out at your place, if it's still open."

"It sure is. Let's finish these up and then hit up a dispensary on the way—I'm a bit dry on bud right now."

Thirty minutes later and we are in my apartment, sitting on a couch I had found on Craigslist in front of a TV also found on Craigslist. We take smoke breaks between bouts of tapping wildly at Xbox controllers and cursing at the screen. Ahmed leaves a few hours later with a smile on his face, and I spend the rest of the evening trying to rid my mind from the day's earlier events.

I WAKE THE next morning twisted in my sheets, an ache weighing me down, a stretching worry on my mind. I open my eyes and everything is wrong.

My vision has widened, and I'm pretty sure I have two noses. I look down at my bare body and witness—to my horror—my bellybutton has almost split into two separate ones (I dare not look down any farther). I'm not out of shape, but I don't work out much so it takes some effort to heave my body and extra weight up from the bed. The mirror calls me, and I stumble to the bathroom.

It takes a moment, maybe because I don't want the stretched face to be true, but the cause of my abnormal vision is what I feared most.

Queasiness takes over and I catch myself on the sink as the bathroom starts to spin. I try to spit into the drain, but my lips and mouth act strange and I only manage to dribble down my chin. I wipe away the spittle with my forearm, close my eyes, and take deep, slow breaths.

I do this until my heart steadies and then I reopen my eyes, wishing it only a nightmare, hallucinations left over from the dream-world.

It was not.

My body has become an imprint on Silly Putty, an unknown force in the universe acting like a child and pulling on both sides to create some humorous image. Everything is splitting right down the middle. If I take a moment, I can actually feel it happening.

Panic washes over me like a teenager waking up to discover the biggest nose pimple on school picture day. There is no way I am going out in public looking like the subject of an abstract painting, even if I could function properly—or need the money.

I get on the phone with my boss at Vidz Inc., a small video production company where I intern, and explain my situation.

"Ah, okay," he says. "Say no more. You can have the rest of the week off."

"Thanks, Mr. Hoffman," I say through slurred speech.

"Of course!" the bubbly man says. "My own transition was a doozy. Remember when I took that week off last month?" He answers for me. "I never told anyone because I didn't want to make a big deal out of it. When it was all over, I donated the extra body for a nice price. I'll give you the name of the company if you want."

"Uh, maybe."

"Oh, you're not planning on keeping it, are you? Boy, I do not recommend that. I'm sure you'll learn soon enough what a pain it is trying to control two bodies. It's not like you can just switch one of them off. Let me know next week what you decided. Or maybe I'll just see for myself, huh?" The other end chuckles. "You get some rest, though. You'll need it." He leaves it at that and hangs up.

I shoot Ahmed a text.

Me: It's happening to me.

He responds within minutes.

Ahmed: Whoa! You mean you're splitting?

Me: Yes.

Ahmed: You need me to come over?

Me: No. I think I'll be fine.

Ahmed: Okay. You let me know, though. It's a bit rough, so don't hesitate to call.

I wonder what to do with my day. I try to eat something, but my mouth doesn't want to function correctly. I try to drink something, but it feels weird swallowing into an expanding throat and stomach. Everything I do is impeded by my predicament. Even breathing is a little difficult—I can't imagine what my lungs are going through. I end up forcing down a painkiller leftover from a tooth extraction earlier in the year, needing it to take away the stretching I can feel upon my body, to numb my worrying.

By the evening, I have three eyes.

THE PROCESS DOESN'T hurt, not in the classical sense of pain. It's more of an annoying strain on whatever part is replicating. The body seems to adapt to the situation, allowing for bodily functions so the person(s) can continue to live.

Cindy calls during the second day. She phones me up not long after my mouths have split, so it's a bit easier to talk and I answer.

"Ahmed told me the news," she opens with, only one of her.
Thanks, Ahmed.

"Yep," I say. "I've got the whole week off from work, but it shouldn't last more than another day or two, I would assume."

"Where are you at? In the separation?"

"I have no idea. Halfway? My heads are close to splitting, I think."

"Oh! You have to let me come over. I want to take a few pictures."

"What? No way! I don't want pictures of me like this. I look like a freak!"

"Don't say that. You're going through a natural thing."

"There is nothing natural about this."

"Oh, hush. I'm coming over."

"Cindy, no," I say, but the call has already ended.

The intercom to my apartment buzzes thirty minutes later. I pay no attention, but Cindy is stubborn and keeps her finger on the button for a good minute or two before I get irritated and reluctantly let her in. I open the door to the two of her.

"I'm so excited for you!" Both of them push past me and enter my studio. One plops on the couch and becomes distant while the other stays standing and gives me her full attention. "Take off those hats and blankets. There's no need to shy away from what I've already seen and gone through."

I take off the hats, but I leave the blanket tied around my abdomen because no clothes fit and I'd rather not wave around my pair of genitals in front of my friend.

Her face brightens as she gets a good look at me, and she says, "Cool, isn't it?"

"That's not the word I'd use," I say.

"Which is exactly the reason I wanted to talk to you." She sits on the couch and pats the empty seat in the middle.

I hesitate, but it's somewhat difficult to stand in my position. I sit with my back to the extra Cindy.

She jumps right into it. "I think you should keep your double."

"I doubt it."

"Oh, come on. Have you even thought about it?"

"Of course I have. It's *all* I've thought about. I can't wait for this ordeal to be over and done with. Plus, I could use the money I'll get from the research."

"Hey, it's not like I've been low on cash lately." She sighs and relaxes back into the couch. "But, yes, it can be an ordeal—you wouldn't believe how often I get distracted and trip. Sometimes I just want to strangle the other me, but I could never do that."

"Because of your career."

"No. Well, yes, but that's not the only reason. Scientists say we're connected through quantum entanglement, whatever that is, but it's more than that. She's a part of me. If she were gone, I'd feel as if something was missing from my core being. Honestly, I'm not even sure which one is the real me." Her index finger waved back and forth between my two bodies. "Do you know which one is your original self?"

I don't know what to say, sitting in silence as I mull over her words. Of course I know which one is the real me, don't I? She has sincerity in her eyes, and I can tell she truly believes what she said. My mind tilts but is not swayed.

"I'll think about it some more," I say.

"Good, that's all I ask for."

Her twin comes alive and then they both leave after giving me a pair of hugs. I think about calling Ahmed and cursing him out for telling Cindy, but I know he'd insist on coming over, too. Instead, as my body continues dividing, my friend's words run marathons around in my head.

I finish off my painkillers, smoke the rest of my pot, and patiently wait for the hideousness to end.

O N THE THIRD day, my left and right wrists are the only body parts still connected. I count the seconds pass. My nerves itch for freedom. Finally, it happens.

My fingertips release as I am cleaning off one of my selves after a mishap involving the toilet and having to control two bowels at the same time. One of me is sitting on the ledge of the bathtub, and the other me is scrubbing away as hot water streams down my dirty legs. Curse words fly from my mouth. Annoyance has replaced disgust and shame. I wish for my normal life to return, and then the universe delivers.

The standing me, the aware me, is too shocked to register the separation, and the sitting me pitches forward without the connection and faceplants onto the tile floor. I swear I feel the pain in both of my heads. I leave my double—I think it's my double—sprawled out like a naked, drunken college student and jump around my small apartment with the joy of freedom.

I need to tell someone. I find my phone and call Ahmed.

"I'm free!"

Ahmed laughs. "Glad to hear it, man. It was quite something, huh?"

"It sure was. I'm just happy it's over and done with."

"Wait, did you already get rid of your double?"

I realize at this moment I'm having difficulty breathing. Well, one of me is. "I'll call you back," I say and hang up.

My mind switches bodies, and suddenly I find myself in the bathroom. My nose and mouth are scrunched against the floor in a way that blocks all airways. I lift myself, forgetting about my second body in the other room, and I hear a crash before feeling pain along my right side.

It's hard controlling two bodies at once.

I focus, splitting my thoughts and actions between two physical perspectives. Half of me is in the bathroom, and the other half is strewn about a broken coffee table, a flipped ashtray, and the stinky remains of a shattered bong. I stand, brush off some debris, and convene on the couch.

I've already lost track of which is the real me. Truth be told, I don't think I ever knew. We look exactly the same, right down to the three moles in the shape of a triangle above my right hip. The circumcision translated as well. I raise my right hands, expecting a mirror image, but of course that doesn't happen—stupid.

This creates a dilemma, and it's not the only one.

Cindy was right. I feel a connection between the two of us. Whether it be quantum entanglement or something deeper, both bodies feel like my own.

My mind is torn.

There's only one question on my mind.

S O, WHAT DID you do with yourself?"

Ahmed's leg bounces up and down. We're sitting at the bar attached to Suckle This Chuckle, a comedy club where Ahmed works as manager and often performs. Both of us have a beer in our hands, but the sweet taste of bourbon tickles my tongue as if from another universe—another me. I haven't said a word to my friend since the other day, and I know he's itching for the end result.

"I decided to keep my double," I say with a knowing grin. "I found a business that will double the amount most government agencies hand out, but that's over the course of a few years. I get a monthly check until I say when."

Ahmed whistles. "That has to be a lot. The government is trying to get their grubby hands on as many doubles as possible." He raises an eyebrow. "You didn't..."

My smile widens, and the arousal of a phantom wet dream stirs in my pants. I push the sensation behind an afterthought, keeping with my current self.

Laughing so hard beer dribbles from his mouth: "You are such a dirty whore!"

I shrug. "Isn't that what everyone uses their double for, whoring them out for money in one way or another? Besides, I only agreed if there were certain rules set in place—I'm not a complete degenerate. I can quit whenever, but they keep me pampered and paid."

"Madame Horowitz's Company of Pleasure?"

I nod. The business specializes in those who enjoy pleasure and

Edited by Shaun Kilgore

can afford a bit more. Doubles are a unique kink among certain people, even when only one of the doubles is involved—I don't judge.

Ahmed is shaking his head, the remnants of laughter heaving his chest. "I thought about going down that route, but I couldn't handle controlling another body. I think I'd spend too much time in the one having fun."

"I slip in every now and then," I say with no shame. For the briefest of seconds, gentle fingers grip my sides in mutual ecstasy. I shake it off, finding it more and more difficult to keep with my present body. "You're off now, right? I bribed the Cindys into a quick latte date in exchange for gossip on my double."

"Gossip: the one bait that can lure the Cindys into hanging out. Sure, I'm in. She'll have a fit once you tell her where your other half is."

I roll my eyes. As if the Cindys were a pair of Mother Theresas. "Whatever. Like she didn't do the same thing when she first split."

"No! Did she? She didn't. Really? She never told me that."

"Watch her face when I explain my situation. Her reaction will give away the truth."

We down our beers and leave. Instead of putting it on his tab, I insist on paying for us both. It's nice and comforting knowing money is no longer a worry. We cut through a park on our way, lighting a joint between us to prepare for our meeting.

The Quantum Twinsies can be a handful at times.

ABOUT THE AUTHOR

Michael Shimek lives in Minnesota where he writes and works on digital art. He has stories that appear in Sanitarium Magazine Issue #32, Fossil Lake: An Anthology of the Aberrant, and several other publications. He also sometimes posts art @michaelshimek.

Confessions

Fredrick Obermeyer

DETECTIVE IVAN KOSTOKIS was typing up an arrest report on his computer when a chubby, balding man in a gray trench-coat came into the squad room of the ninety-third precinct in Brooklyn. He was carrying a large tan briefcase.

"Are you in charge here?" the man said.

"No, my lieutenant's out at the moment. But I'm Detective Kostokis, and I can help you, Mr..."

He looked around furtively, then sat in a chair next to Kostokis's desk and said, "Harold Martins. I work as an investment banker down at Morton and Fielding."

"How can I help you, Mr. Martins?"

"I'm the Sheepshead Bay Butcher, and I want to confess all of my crimes."

Great, another crank, Kostokis thought.

Before Kostokis could say anything further, Martins opened the case, took out a plastic-wrapped serrated knife, hacksaw and a cleaver and dropped it on Kostokis's desk; the plastic around all the implements was covered in dried blood. Then he laid down several Polaroids of butchered women, a smartphone and a paper map of Brooklyn with several red circles in and around Sheepshead Bay.

Kostokis stared in utter shock. The police and FBI had been trying to clear the Sheepshead case for nearly a year with no luck. Now the killer just waltzed in and dumped the whole case right in his lap.

"Hold it right there!" Kostokis said.

The detective burst out of his chair, drew the Glock 19 pistol from his belt holster and pointed it at Martins. The other detectives in the room drew their own guns and pointed them at Martins.

"Don't shoot!" Martins said, throwing his hands up. "I give up!"

"Down on the floor with your hands behind your head!" Kostokis said. "Now!"

Martins complied with the command immediately. As soon as he was down, Kostokis and the other detectives converged on the banker.

Kostokis holstered his Glock and frisked Martins for other weapons. Finding none, he cuffed Martins and pulled the man to his feet.

"Easy!" Martins said. "I just want to confess!" "All right, Mr. Martins. We'll take you into the interrogation room and you can tell us what you want there."

"Okay."

Kostokis led the handcuffed into the dingy, olive green room with another detective and sat him down behind a gray table. A few minutes later, a third detective brought in a digital recorder and Kostokis pressed record. He gave the date and time and informed Martins of his Miranda rights, which he acknowledged.

"Do you wish to have an attorney present during questioning, Mr. Martins?" Kostokis said.

"No. I…I'm sick, and I need help. Look, I'll sign anything you want me to. Just put me away before I hurt any more women. Please."

"Why are you confessing now?"

"I don't know why. I just felt like it was the right thing to do." He frowned. "What, you don't want me to confess?"

"No, I want you to confess. It just isn't typical."

"This isn't typical for me either. Until yesterday I didn't tell anybody about what I did. Then suddenly, I don't know what happened, but I felt this urgent need to confess."

"Okay, Mr. Martins. We'll get the DA down here and you can tell us the whole story."

A knock came at the door.

"Yeah?" Kostokis said, shutting off the recorder.

The desk sergeant for the nine-three, Bill Covel, came into the interrogation room with a young teen who had green spiky hair and huge gauged earrings.

"Detective?" Covel said.

"One second, Bill."

"We got this kid here, claims he wants to confess to stealing some iPhones out of Korpal's Electronics last week."

"Okay, Bill, get Sal on it. I'm kind of busy here."

"That's not all."

Kostokis frowned. "What? Does somebody else want to confess?"

"Yeah."

"Who?"

Covel gestured behind him and said, "About a hundred other people."

"You're shitting me."

"See for yourself."

The detective walked out of the interrogation room and over to the stairwell, looked down to the first floor of the precinct and gawked at all the people milling around down there.

"This is going to be a long night," Kostokis said.

E VEN WITH SEVERAL of the squad's other detectives called back in, Kostokis could only handle so many people at a time. While he worked, even more confessors came into the precinct and the phones began ringing off the hook.

Despite the extra staff, the squad room quickly turned into a madhouse.

After twelve hours, Kostokis had to quit from sheer exhaustion. But the squad cleared nearly three hundred cases in that time.

When asked why they confessed, everybody gave the same answer.

They didn't know why. They just felt they had to do it.

What is causing all these people to confess? Kostokis thought. Did somebody put something in the water?

Feeling every second of his fifty-three years on Earth, Kostokis trudged home to his apartment. He was so tired that he didn't even bother to say hello to his wife, Deborah.

Instead he poured himself a glass of ouzo on ice, marveling as the liquor turned from clear to milky when it touched the cubes.

As a child, his grandmother used to speak to him in Greek in her small apartment garden while she let him watch the ouzo turn white, which always fascinated him. Sometimes she would even let him have a small sip of the fiery liquid when nobody was around.

How long has she been gone? Kostokis thought wistfully. Thirty years?

He sipped the ouzo, then crashed on the couch and immediately fell asleep.

Sometime later, Deborah shook him awake.

Kostokis leaned up, rubbed his aching neck and glanced right. The clock across from him said it was just past eleven A.M.

"Hey," Kostokis said. "You just get home from work?"

Frowning, Deborah shook her head and said, "No, I've been here for a little while."

"What's wrong?"

"Ivan, I'm going out for a while. But first I have to confess something."

"Not you too." He sighed. "We already had a bunch of people at the station confessing last night."

"Really?"

"Yeah." He shook his head. "Christ, whole fucking world's going crazy out there. Like it's Judgment Day or something."

"Ivan—"

"Look, whatever it is, just forget about it, okay?"

"I can't just forget about it. I've been carrying this thing around for years."

"Deb, please, these past few hours I heard enough confessions to last me a lifetime—"

"Jenny Hoffner."

"Huh?"

"She was my best friend in high school."

"What about her?"

"I killed her."

"Deb—"

"Please, I need to tell somebody!"

Kostokis groaned, figuring she was going to talk no matter what he said. So he gestured for her to continue.

"One winter we were ice skating by ourselves on Lake Pallard and she, she broke through the ice. And she started screaming 'Debbie, Debbie, help me!'"

Deborah burst into tears. "I don't know what came over me then. There was a branch nearby and I could've saved her. But I…I just stared at her."

"Jesus Christ," Kostokis said.

"I was angry with her, you see. She was always more popular than me and the kids always called me braceface and dumped shit in my hair. But then one day I heard Jenny making fun of me with Ann Carter behind my back. I….I felt so betrayed. And now here she was helpless…" Deborah sniffed, tears streaking her mascara. "And I just let her drown."

Silence passed for a moment; Kostokis stared at his wife like she was a stranger.

"I remember afterwards I faked some tears, ran back home and had my dad come down to the lake with the neighbors." She looked past Kostokis. "They said it wasn't my fault. But it was."

A sick feeling tightened Kostokis' stomach.

"It was an accident, Deb. You got scared and panicked—"

"No, don't you see? I pushed her onto the thin ice and she fell through!"

Kostokis could only blink. After ten years of marriage to his third wife, he thought he knew Deborah pretty well. But it seemed he didn't really know her at all.

"Do you know what the worst thing is?" She laughed bitterly. "Up until yesterday, I didn't feel the least bit bad about it. Hell, I was glad the fucking bitch was dead."

"Honey, don't say another word. Go see a priest and tell him what you did."

"No, I want you to take me to the station and have them arrest me."

Stunned, Kostokis gaped at his wife. "Are you crazy? I can't arrest my own wife for murder."

"Ivan, please."

"I don't fucking believe this." He rubbed his forehead. "I suppose you can't remember why you're confessing either."

"No." Deborah frowned. "But I do remember one thing."

"What?"

"I was walking someplace."

"Where?"

"Central Park, I think."

"Where in Central Park?"

"I don't know. But whatever happened, I think it happened there."

"Are you sure?" Kostokis said. "Nobody else remembered anything."

"Yes, I think so."

Deborah gripped Kostokis's hand.

"Do you still love me?" she said.

"Of course I do." He raised her hand to his lips and kissed it.

"I'm a good person, aren't I? I mean, I did a bad thing in the past, but I'm not really evil, am I?"

"We've all done bad things, honey."

She pulled her hand away from him. "I'm going to the police."

Kostokis bolted up and grabbed her. "Don't do this, Deb! At least go talk to a lawyer before you do something you can't take back."

"If you won't come with me, then fine. I'll go alone."

"Honey, they'll lock you up if you confess. I might not be able to help you."

"I don't care anymore." She hugged him tight. "I love you."

"I love you too, but think about this. Please!"

She let him go. "I have thought about it, and I need to do this." She kissed him on the cheek and slid out the door.

"Deb, wait!"

He chased her out of the apartment, but by the time he got to the elevator the doors had closed. Wheezing, Kostokis rushed down eight flights of stairs, his big belly slowing him down. By the time he arrived at the lobby, though, she was long gone. Worn out, Kostokis collapsed in a nearby chair, trying to catch his breath.

"Fuck!" Kostokis said.

He considered chasing her, but what good would it do? She hadn't told him which precinct she was going to. Besides, it was her life. Short of tying her up, he couldn't stop her from confessing.

As he caught his breath, something she said popped back into his mind.

Central Park.

Maybe I can find some answers there, Kostokis thought.

A HALF-HOUR LATER, Kostokis entered Central Park. Unsure of what to look for, his eyes kept darting back and forth between the walkway and the trees. The snow and cold had driven away most of the people and only a few passed by. Along the way, he tried calling the nine-three and police dispatch to see if Deborah was there. But all the lines were busy, so he pocketed his smartphone and kept looking.

Nothing seemed out of the ordinary, though, and Kostokis wondered if Deborah had lost her mind.

Ten minutes later, he came upon an old homeless man sitting by himself on a park bench. He was bundled up in several jackets and pairs of pants, his breath misting in the world; a black New York Yankees ball cap stood atop his head, and he had a grizzled face with white stubble. The rotten onion stink of his body odor was so strong that it made Kostokis's eyes water even from a distance.

Kostokis had seen so many homeless people throughout his career that he barely took notice of the man, except for his smell. But as he passed, the man said, "Hey, you're a cop, right?"

Kostokis stopped, turned to the bum and said, "Yeah."

"I knew it. Moment I saw ya, I knew it. You got that cop look."

Kostokis glanced around. It was quiet, the light snow falling silently. "You see anything funny around here these past few days?"

The old man chuckled and said, "In Central Park? What isn't funny around here?"

"True enough."

"You got a smoke?"

"Sorry. I quit a few years back."

"Hey, you want to see something?"

Kostokis swallowed hard, wondering if the guy was a weenie wagger.

"No thanks."

"It'll just take a moment, Detective Kostokis."

A sudden chill passed up his spine.

"How'd you know my name?"

The bum lunged at Kostokis and pressed his dirty, gnarled fingers against the detective's face. Kostokis tried to push free, but his mind quickly plummeted into a dark abyss.

WHEN KOSTOKIS AWOKE, he found himself lying on green grass. He staggered to his feet and gasped as he found himself standing in an enormous grassy field. It was a sunny day, the sky full of white clouds. In the distance there lay a large red and white barn and a plain brown, two-story house.

The bum was standing across from him, wearing the same outfit as he had in the park.

"What's going on?" Kostokis said.

"My name is Stanley Misenkar," the bum said. "And I've formed a telepathic link with your mind."

"I…" Kostokis blinked.

"That's me as a child."

Stanley pointed across the field to a small boy with sandy blond hair dressed in denim overalls. A glowing green stone lay in the center of the wide open area.

"When I was eight years old, I discovered that stone in a field outside my grandparents' farm in Havenwood, Connecticut," Stanley said.

The boy tried to pick it up and howled as it burnt him. He dropped the rock and clutched his hand. Kostokis cringed and glanced at old Stanley. The bum took off his right glove and revealed burn scars on his palm and fingers.

Moments later, the boy screamed and swung his foot back to kick the stone. But a second later, he stopped. The green glow faded from the rock. A curious look appeared on his face. He grabbed a stick and poked the rock, then carefully touched the edge again with a finger and drew it back.

This time it didn't burn him.

"The stone gave me the power to call anyone to me or drive them away," Stanley said. "And once they were near, I could enter their minds simply by touching them. After that, I could make them do anything I wanted."

A white flash blinded Kostokis for a moment, then he found himself in a green-walled study full of old books and a roaring fireplace. A teenaged Stanley was touching the right cheek of an old man with his scarred hand and whispering into his ear.

The man's eyes were glazed.

After Stanley spoke, the man took out several stacks of hundreds from his desk and gave them to the teenager, who eagerly shoved them into a satchel.

"Now the gun," young Stanley said.

The man grabbed a snubnose revolver out of the desk, stuck it in his mouth and squeezed the trigger. Kostokis yelped as the man's brains painted the wall behind him red.

Stunned, he stumbled back, turned and found himself drifting down an endless brown oak-paneled hallway with Stanley hovering beside him. Several doors were open on both sides.

In one doorway, a naked man raped a young woman in the back of a car. In another, a fat woman strangled a child in a gravel pit. In a third, a young boy set his sleeping parents on fire. In a fourth, a businessman dumped a bag full of diamonds into the hands of a now adult Stanley.

Kostokis gawked at the numerous doorways flew by faster and became a blur.

"I could make anybody do anything I want," Stanley said. "After a while, I lost count as to how many lives I destroyed."

"Why do this?" Kostokis said.

"Because I wanted money and power and the stone gave me the means to acquire both."

The hallway abruptly ended with another flash of white light and Kostokis found himself in a church during a wedding. Stanley was at the altar, kissing a beautiful young blond-haired woman.

"I only stopped after I married my wife, Sharon," Stanley said.

Kostokis swallowed hard, his stomach roiling.

"I tried to be a good husband and father and not use the stone."

The scene shifted to an enormous egg-blue walled mansion living room with Sharon, her belly now swollen, holding a baby. Stanley cooed at the child, but again the scene shifted to a kitchen where a young boy and girl were screaming their heads off.

Stanley's face reddened with rage as Sharon said, "Take care of the goddamned kids yourself, Stan!"

"Alas, I failed." He waved his hand and they were back in the living room. His wife and children were sitting on the couch, and they had the same glazed look as the old man in the study.

"They annoyed me so much with their whining that I made them behave."

Trembling, Kostokis turned on Stanley, wanting to punch Stanley.

"How could you do this to your own family?"

"It was easy." Stanley bowed his head. "For a while, things were perfect. In fact, they were too perfect."

The living room morphed into a patio with an enormous backyard full of hedge animals lying beyond. Stanley was sitting at a glass breakfast table with his family, holding the stone; the expressions of his family were glazed and they smiled vacantly.

"Sweetheart?" Stanley said to his daughter.

"Yes, Daddy?"

"Smack your head into the table."

His daughter smashed her head into the table, cracking the glass. The family continued to stare impassively as his daughter blinked dazedly and leaned up, blood trickling down her forehead. She was still smiling, as was Stanley.

"Again," Stanley said.

She whammed her head into it again, nearly shattering the glass.

"The rest of you, smack your heads too."

His wife and son smacked their heads into the glass and shattered it, then leaned up smiling, bits of glass stuck in their heads, blood leaking down their faces.

"May I go play in the yard, Daddy?" the little girl said, the red reaching her neck and staining her pink satin dress.

"Of course, sweetheart," Stanley said.

He kissed his daughter's head wound and licked the blood off his lips as she staggered away.

Sharon smiled, her expression still vacuous as her wounds bled freely.

The hairs on the back of Kostokis's neck stood.

"I grew tired of my rich, perfect life and wanted to shatter it to pieces," Stanley said. "I could have so easily made Sharon kill the kids and then herself. But at that point, I felt the rock made things too easy. I…" His voice wavered. "It was like a game to me. I wanted to kill them and get away with it without using the rock."

"No," Kostokis said.

"I planned the crime for five months."

"I don't want to see—"

Kostokis shuddered as he found himself in a children's bedroom with giraffes and pink balloons on the wallpaper. Sharon was reading a bedtime story to the children. As she turned the page, Stanley came into the room. He was wearing earplugs and holding a Browning Auto-5 shotgun.

"Stanley, what are you—!"

He fired and her head exploded into red mist. Spattered with their mother's blood and brains, the children screamed and cowered on their beds. Stanley's face twisted with savage delight as he turned the shotgun on his kids and fired one shot into each of them.

After the last shot, images strobed in Kostokis's mind.

Stanley ranksacking money and other valuables from his own mansion. Stanley breaking a window on the patio door and leaving it open. Stanley wiping down the prints on the shotgun, then throwing it and the bag full of loot into a nearby lake in the dead of night. Stanley wailing to the police in his living room, saying, "How could they do this to my babies?"

Enraged, Kostokis tried to lunge at Stanley, but the older man held up his hand. The detective froze in space, as did the scene.

"How could you…"

"Yes, I was a monster," Stanley said. "And for a while, I thought I was going to get away with it. But then the police found a witness who claimed to see me flee my home on the night of the murders." His lower lip quivered. "In a way, I was glad, though. I wanted to go before a jury and get away with my crime completely."

The living room shifted to sometime later; a detective slapped handcuffs on Stanley. Then the mansion faded to reveal a courtroom. The jury entered the box and a judge banged his gavel. Kostokis spun around and found himself staring at Stanley, smiling at the defense table. But time accelerated and the smile changed into a nervous frown.

"Fear got the better of me," Stanley said. "So like a coward, I cheated."

The courtroom faded to reveal a weedy field at night, the full moon glowing overhead. Stanley was holding the glowing stone and the jury members were standing at the edge of the field with a US marshal.

One by one, Stanley mindtouched them.

"Not guilty," the foreman said behind Kostokis.

Suddenly free, Kostokis turned and found himself back in the courtroom. Shock tightened the faces of the prosecution and press, but Stanley stood beaming.

"I had won," Stanley said. "And thanks to double jeopardy, they couldn't try me again."

The sound of crying suddenly filled the air. Kostokis blinked and found himself inside a yacht cabin. Now with his blond hair mostly gray, Stanley sat weeping by himself on the cabin bed, clutching a portrait of his family.

"Considering what a vicious person I was, I should've been happy," Stanley said. "Yet over the following decades guilt began to eat away at me. I stopped using the rock and tried to live a quiet life."

The moment froze.

"Then about a year ago, I got the bad news."

The cabin turned into a doctor's office. An old doctor looked gravely at a crestfallen, white-haired Stanley, sitting on a paper-covered table.

"I'm sorry, Mr. Misenkar," the doctor said. "You have terminal congestive heart failure."

Stanley shifted from the business suit he was wearing to his bum outfit and the doctor disappeared.

"Needless to say, I was shocked," Stanley said. "And I suddenly became afraid that I would burn in hell for all my sins. So I tried to make amends."

More images filled Kostokis's mind. Stanley stuffing a wad of cash onto a church plate. Movers carrying furniture past a "FOR SALE" sign outside his mansion.

"I liquidated my entire fortune, gave it to charity and decided to live as a bum in Central Park."

Kostokis turned and found himself back in Central Park with Stanley begging for change next to a tree.

"It wasn't enough, though," Stanley said. "I had to confess my sins to somebody, so I used the stone on some random guy."

A short red-haired guy appeared next to a tree. Stanley touched the man's cheek and Kostokis heard a child weeping.

"And I learned that prick was molesting his seven year old daughter," Stanley said, grimacing. "I was so disgusted that I made him confess."

The man shifted into a woman wearing a mink stole.

"Then I found another woman who shot her husband and his mistress and was never caught," Stanley said. "I made her confess too."

More images of Stanley touching people's faces flashed through his mind.

"So many unpunished criminals like me walked the streets that I began to fear I wouldn't find one decent person in this whole stinking city. Eventually, I grew so tired of their sins on top of my own that I let the rest go for the time being and simply kept a mental tab on them."

The last person disappeared and revealed Stanley keeling over on a green park bench.

"Then one day I got a bad pain in my chest."

A moment later, he leaned up.

"I was so scared I was dying, though thankfully the pain went away." He frowned. "But at that moment, I decided 'fuck it.' I'll make them all confess and do something good with my life before I die."

He took out the stone from his pocket, clutched it tight in his hands and closed his eyes.

"I used the stone to call the people I already mindtouched back to the park and make others leave so there wouldn't be a crowd."

One by one, people showed up in front of Stanley, and he mindtouched each one. Deborah appeared among the large group of thousands of confessors.

"Even that wasn't enough, though," Stanley said. "I want someone who will make other criminals confess after I die." He looked into Kostokis's eyes. "That's why I had your wife drop you some hints to see if you would come here on your own. If you didn't, I would've used the stone to bring you here eventually. But in any case, I need a good man to continue my work and your wife's memories showed me your goodness."

"How can you say I'm good?"

Suddenly Kostokis's own memories flashed into his mind.

He recalled taking a wailing crack baby out from a furnace in a burning tenement; he had given a teenage junkie a second chance by getting her into a drug rehab program instead of busting her; he had carried his former partner, Rita Gallagher, out of the line of fire after a gangbanger shot her in the back.

"But I've got flaws the same as anyone else."

"You may not always be fair and just," Stanley said. "But you're as fair and just as any man can be in this corrupt world."

Before Kostokis could protest any further, he fell back into the darkness.

KOSTOKIS BLINKED SEVERAL times as he emerged from the depths of Stanley's mind.

Wheezing, Stanley took the stone out of his jacket pocket and shoved it into Kostokis' hand. The detective cried out as it glowed hot and burned his flesh. He dropped the rock and clutched his hand.

Power rushed into his mind like a tidal flood.

"Make them all confess," Stanley said, his voice pained.

"Wait," Kostokis said.

Stanley made a choking sound and collapsed in the snow.

"Help!" Kostokis said.

A few people came running as Kostokis knelt and performed CPR on Stanley despite the bum's stink and the pain in his hand.

But it was too late.

Afterwards, he stepped back from the crowd, picked up the now inert stone and stumbled away. As he fled, he took a handkerchief from his pocket and wrapped it around his burnt hand.

The stone held such power, Kostokis thought. Where was it from, though? And was it good or evil or neither?

He didn't know and couldn't say.

Kostokis stopped at a bridge near the park's lake and looked at the stone.

What do I do? Kostokis thought. I could make so many others confess, but what would it do to the world?

Hell, I could bend them all to my will and make them do even more than confess.

But no, it would be wrong to take advantage of people as Stanley had.

Kostokis reached back to hurl the stone. At the last moment, though, he stopped.

What if I could do some good, though? Kostokis thought. Perhaps I shouldn't be so hasty.

After a moment's hesitation, Kostokis pocketed the rock and walked away.

ABOUT THE AUTHOR

Fredrick Obermeyer enjoys writing science-fiction, fantasy, horror, and crime stories. He has had work published in NFG, Electric Spectrum, Newmyths, Perihelion SF, Acidic Fiction, the Destination: Future anthology, and other markets.

Encounter At
Durheim Crossroads

Chet Gottfried

D ERRICK WHIPPED OFF his helmet, threw it to the ground, and glared at his broadsword.

"You miserable twisted piece of rust. You'd bounce off a wad of butter. I'd prefer a willow rod to the likes of you."

He ignored the beauty of the dappled sunlight over the Durheim crossroads and took a huge breath.

"Why do all my strokes hit on the flat? Are you a sword at all? If a name means anything, you're a disgrace to the entire history of swordsmanship. From the first sword made down to the present, they're laughing at you. I'm laughing at you! Has anyone ever heard of a *real* weapon being called 'Elderberry'? Ha! Your name is ridiculous. You're ridiculous. Pathetic! I swear: I'll pay a blacksmith to hammer you into a doorstop. Better yet, I'll throw you into the first river or lake." Derrick shook his sword. "How do you like that?" he roared, shaking the nearby trees.

After a brief silence, Elderberry said, "Pull the other one."

Derrick's massive shoulders slumped. Years of being a warrior. Continually practicing to hone the skills necessary to enhance his reputation. And for what? To be insulted by his own sword. Life wasn't fair.

73

"That's another thing I hate about you. You've no respect."

"What does respect have to do with it?" Elderberry asked. "You shouldn't have insulted old man Nayshank. Any fool should have known better, especially someone who goes around and proclaims himself to be the top warrior in the land. Look at you! All muscles and no brains. No one else would alienate as nasty a wizard as you could hope not to meet. And why did you do it? Over a poem. Yeah, you're a class act."

"The rhyme was off," Derrick said.

"It comes down to the same thing: You're responsible for your own mess, so stop whining."

Derrick inhaled deeply and screamed his war cry. Branches throughout the grove shattered, a maple tree crashed on its side, and three crows dropped dead from the sky.

"I don't whine. I do what heroes do everywhere: boast, complain, or curse, to suit the occasion."

"Whatever."

He sighed. "So what's my count?"

Elderberry cleared its imaginary throat. "Thus far, to fulfill your geas, you've bagged twelve thieves and six warriors."

"Is that all? I've been at it for two months. Surely I must have wiped out more?" A thought leaped into Derrick's consciousness. "Hey! I've just finished subduing my seventh warrior."

Derrick's arm moved involuntarily as Elderberry took over control in order to point.

"You mean the guy who's standing over there?"

He looked, and sure enough, three yards away stood a huge warrior who was watching Derrick.

"What the . . . ? I thought you surrendered. I distinctly remember your yelling, 'stop,' and—"

At that precise moment recognition flared, and Derrick knew the warrior opposite him.

"Lord Gautrek!"

Gautrek wasn't a noble by either birth or grant, but his nick-name came about from his extraordinarily good manners. While eviscerating an opponent, he'd say, "Excuse me," and his legend extended to his using a table napkin correctly. Gautrek dressed like a noble too and wore the latest accessories. His helmet had a silk fringe and a griffin flight feather.

"Well met, Derrick the Mighty! Tell me, is it true you tore a hole through King Jacoby's castle?"

Fancy Gautrek hearing of his exploits! Derrick grinned broadly and nodded.

The two warriors rushed at each other and embraced in a bear hug along with much slapping and shouting. They laughed long and hard at the chance encounter of two legendary heroes.

Letting go and stepping back, Derrick apologized for their initial combat. "I lose all control because of the spell old Nayshank put on me. I would have never begun our duel if not for Elderberry, one of wizard Nayshank's jokes."

"Tell me about it." Gautrek angrily shook his sword. "Meet Fleabane, who would give your Elderberry a distinct challenge in the category of worst sword in creation."

"You don't mean wizard Nayshank got you too?"

"The same."

Derrick tsked in sympathy. "Then you can't use your right hand except to hold your sword while you're awake, which makes eating and drinking awkward and annoying. And try to have a wench understand why you're holding the sword while in bed. You know, there ought to be a law about wizards. Imagine entrapping the two of us. Together we'd be an army capable of subduing anyone or anything we wanted. So look what happens. We're stuck cleaning the countryside. By the way, how did you rile Nayshank?"

"I rearranged one of his poems into a ditty, which became more popular than anything he ever penned. And so here I am. I have to slay or vanquish forty thieves, or twenty-five warriors, or five trolls, or two dragons, or one elf king before I can throw away Fleabane."

"What a bummer. It's not as if you meet any dragons these days. And elf kings? Forget it. They're as common as hair on an egg—unless you want to spend the rest of your life on the northern steppes. Wait a mo. Did you say 'twenty-five warriors'? Nayshank hit me for thirty."

Gautrek shrugged. "What do you expect from an angry wizard? Consistency? Fairness? Would he have loaded us with these ridiculous weapons if he had any sense of decency? What bothers me the most is that Nayshank has isolated the totals: forty thieves *or* twenty-five warriors. A simple ratio shows eight thieves equals five warriors in his scheme."

Derrick kicked a pebble. "I was never good at math."

"Our swords do the counting for us. It's about the only thing they're good for."

"True enough," Elderberry said, "but Nayshank isn't what you'd call a mathematician either. He prefers simplicity: give him straight sums. If you want to see a wizard sweat, ask him about trigonometry. You have to face it. When you hit one of your totals, you'll be free, so you might as well start swinging at each other again."

Derrick and Gautrek exchanged glances and then each grinned.

"You've got to be kidding," Derrick said, "unless my defeating Gautrek or him defeating me counts more than a single fighter. We're each worth a dozen other fighters."

"Absolutely," Gautrek said. "And a dozen is a modest number, considering skill and reputation."

"Sorry," Fleabane said, "Nayshank didn't factor reputation or skill into his requirements. A fighter is a fighter."

"That finishes it." Gautrek asked Derrick, "What do you say about heading to the Vargas River? I heard there are a few trolls mucking about. Or we could go to Wythburn and clean up the town. It has a number of thieves."

Derrick nodded. "Excellent plans. I like the idea of teaming up. We'll get them coming and going. No one will escape." He grinned happily. "Lucky you stopped our senseless combat when you did. I might have done you serious damage."

Gautrek took a step backward. "I'd never ask anyone to stop in the middle of a brawl."

"I clearly heard you shouting 'stop.' No doubts about it."

Gautrek slapped his forehead. "That wasn't me. That was my sword Fleabane, who's always doing daft things."

"Ha!" Fleabane said. "It's easy to criticize, but I'm not so daft as to turn a wizard's poem into a limerick."

"I composed a ditty, not a limerick. If you fail to understand the difference, you'll remain a third-rate magic sword all your life." Gautrek told Derrick, "It's like you said: No respect."

Derrick agreed. "You can always tell a Nayshank weapon, but why did your sword ask us to stop?"

"Excuse me," Fleabane said. "I'm not deaf, and I'm right here. If you have any questions, you can address me directly. However, since you're a foolish mercenary at best, you don't have to repeat your inane question."

"Very wise," Elderberry said. "You've no idea what I have to put up with."

"The point is this: I yelled 'stop' because the fellow on the left (or your right) has been trying to catch your attention for the past half-hour. He has waved, coughed (politely), and smiled at the two of you. Honestly, esteemed warriors should pay attention to everything happening around them. Some folks call it a sixth sense, being battle aware. Otherwise, how would you know if an enemy is creeping up from behind and ready to skewer you in the back? It is beyond me how the two of you manage to stay alive as long as you have—I say this while noting the gray streaks in your hair."

Derrick stomped on the ground. "I don't have gray hair."

"Nothing a little hair dye couldn't cure," Elderberry said. "Combing now and again would be another bonus."

Whatever the state of his hair or its color, Derrick had to admit the cranky Fleabane was correct. They had company.

A slim man stood nearby and waved to them. The stranger wore an elegant silk shirt, silk pantaloons, and a bright green silk scarf. His well-decorated scabbard hung from an equally well-decorated sword belt. A thin silk band kept his blond hair neatly in place. He also wore a diadem which had a single but remarkably clear diamond. He had pointy ears.

Derrick's mouth fell open. "An elf?"

"An elf king," Gautrek said.

The stranger stepped closer and bowed slightly from the waist.

"You are correct. I'm King Nerianna, and I'm hoping one of you fine fellows would tell me which of these footpaths leads to Durheim."

The two warriors turned toward each other and each winked. They could taste freedom.

Nerianna said, "I seldom venture this far south, but I received an invitation from my friend Otis to take part in a poetry festival."

"Poetry festival?" Derrick asked.

"Yes, the Tenth Annual Durheim Arts Festival, although in this case the arts involve poetry, from epic verse to sonnets to free form. I expect one and all will have a rousing time. Perhaps once you've settled whatever you're trying to settle between yourselves, you will come along with me. As they say, the more the merrier."

"It's not that simple," Derrick said.

A frown crossed Nerianna's face. "Oh dear, I dislike complicated directions. I have a tendency to get lost, and I wouldn't want to miss the festival. I'm the guest of honor."

"The directions are simple," Derrick said, "but you're not going anywhere. Wizard Nayshank put a spell on me."

"Me too," Gautrek said.

"I am surprised," Nerianna said. "Otis Nayshank is such a friendly fellow and the one who made sure I would be the guest of honor at the festival."

The elf king annoyed Derrick. "How long have you been standing here? Haven't you paid any attention to what we've been talking about?"

"You mean eavesdrop?" Nerianna put his hand over his heart. "That's hardly the proper thing to do among strangers."

"Okay," Derrick said, "it's like this. Your friend the wizard's spell means I have to hold the dumbly named sword Elderberry until I kill forty thieves, thirty warriors, five trolls, two dragons, or an elf king."

"Same here," Gautrek said, "except I only have to kill twenty-five warriors and my dumbly named sword is Fleabane."

"And they talk," Derrick added. "You wouldn't believe how insulting a sword can be, especially one named Elderberry."

The elf king became very pale. "Did Nayshank's geas actually specify an 'elf king'?"

The grim expressions on both Derrick and Gautrek did not require any further answer.

"I find it hard to believe Otis Nayshank would invite me to a poetry festival in order to murder me."

"Are you sure there's a poetry festival?" Elderberry asked.

"Otis sent me a broadsheet listing all the details. Surely you don't think that it is all a part of a trap to ensure I'd be in the area?" No one answered, and Nerianna continued. "There is only one way to find out. I'll go to Durheim, and if there isn't any festival, Otis will have much to answer for. My magic is nowhere as potent as his overall, but I can lay a hex to make him think twice before pulling any such fraud again."

Derrick edged over toward where he had thrown his helmet, picked it up and put it on. "Excuse me, King, but it doesn't matter whether there is or isn't a festival. In order to free myself from Nayshank's spell, you have to die. The facts may not be pleasant, but they are the facts."

Nerianna took a deep breath. "If so, would you mind telling me which path leads to Durheim? You won't have the opportunity of answering after I slay you."

Derrick wondered what chance the slight elf thought he had against two preeminent warriors. "You don't have to go there. You'll be dead. Accept it."

"Let's say I get lucky and win. Then there won't be anyone to tell me the way, and I have worked so hard on the poetry competition too. Devising a good rhyme for 'brachiopod' isn't easy."

"Brachiopod?"

"You see! I told you it was difficult. How many poets or fighters have heard of brachiopods? You haven't? . . . A brachiopod is like a clam, but whereas a clam has a bilateral symmetry along the horizontal plane, a brachiopod has its bilateral symmetry on the vertical plane."

Derrick and Gautrek exchanged glances. Was the elf king entirely sane? Might he be an imposter? Derrick said, "If you kill Gautrek and me, either of our swords will tell you the way to Durheim. They've a better sense of direction than we have."

The elf king shook his head. "That won't do at all. You see, your swords are not truly magical, inasmuch as their magic won't pass from generation to generation or from user to user. They're ordinary weapons under a curse. Both Elderberry and Fleabane are goblins, who doubtlessly upset Otis, and they're doing servitude."

"Goblins!" Gautrek said. "I should have guessed."

"As soon as you either die or complete your geas, the spirit will return to its own body, which is presently in a state of suspended animation."

"Huh?"

"Their bodies are asleep for the duration," Nerianna said. "Therefore, I cannot count on their being around after I dispatch you. Next, consider all the complaints the two of you have made regarding your swords. Do you think they'll behave any better while you duel with me? I assure you my own sword is of the highest quality. Would you like me to list its attributes?"

"You needn't bother," Derrick said. "The way I see it, Elderberry with me or Fleabane with Gautrek didn't have anything to lose if either I or Gautrek died early on. It all stops with you. They get their freedom, unless the first person to fight you wins, and the other guy is stuck." The thought immediately struck him that Gautrek might have the first turn. Gautrek's sword noticed the elf king first. Derrick bet the very thought was going through Gautrek's mind.

"Take the east path from here," Gautrek said. "It will take you straight to Durheim. The journey may take a couple of days, but you'll come across several pleasant inns along the way."

"Thank you," Nerianna said.

"What are you playing at, Gautrek?" Derrick demanded. "Why tell the elf anything?" Who ever said that jerk was a lord? What a laugh! The guy was a fraud with a few gimmicks. Take that griffin feather—an obvious fake.

Gautrek straightened and looked at Derrick. "I intend to duel the elf, so I wanted to get the information out of the way."

"First?" Derrick growled.

"Aye, first. Why not. I spotted him first."

"You did not," Derrick shouted. "Your sword saw him."

"What's the difference?"

Derrick couldn't see any difference, but the point was as good an introduction to a fight as any.

"Over my dead body," Derrick said.

Nerianna interrupted. "You're not going to fight again?"

"What's it to you?" Derrick snarled.

"You were already at it for a half-hour with no results, so why not try something else? I've a deck of cards. Why don't you draw to see who goes first?"

"I appreciate the gesture," Derrick said, "but warriors have only one way of settling an argument, which is by the sword, even if ours are reincarnated goblins."

"Not reincarnated," Elderberry grumbled. "Can't you keep anything straight?"

Derrick ignored his sword. "Only one thing, King: if you'll agree to stay until Gautrek and I settle our dispute."

"You might slay each other. It's such a waste."

"We have to," Gautrek said. "It's the only way to be rid of these cursed swords."

Nerianna waved his arms. "I yield."

Derrick and Gautrek looked at each other.

"Excuse me," they said.

"I yield, so that ends it. You don't have to fight."

Derrick tried dropping Elderberry but to no avail. Gautrek also remained stuck to Fleabane.

Derrick hated having to kill anyone who proved to be a decent sort. Nerianna wasn't making it easy, and Derrick anticipated having nightmares after chopping down the elf. He scratched his head.

"We appreciate your trying, but it isn't so simple. You have to be sincere about giving up."

"I am sincere," Nerianna shouted.

"Our swords don't believe you. Chalk up another score to settle with Nayshank."

Nerianna turned his back. "I don't have to watch you fight to the death."

Derrick and Gautrek squared off and began their duel. The woods rang with the vicious cuts they swung at each other. Soon, breathing rapidly, they both withdrew a little ways. Derrick prepared for a final all-out attack and ran screaming at Gautrek, who screamed and counterattacked.

Their swords met with a tremendous clang and shattered, sending thousands of steel shards into the sky.

Gautrek stared into the fragment cloud. "I see a rainbow."

"Look out," Derrick cried, "they're coming back!"

The splinters rained down while screaming, as if each one had a goblin inside. After a few seconds of standing frozen in place, with one metal splinter whizzing close to Derrick's eye, both warriors relaxed. Shards blanketed the ground around them, but they had avoided the fall.

"I thought I was a goner," Derrick admitted.

"Me too," Gautrek said.

A quarter of Elderberry was left in Derrick's hand. "Speak for yourthelf."

Fleabane had a mere three inches of blade beyond the hilt. "Yeth."

Then the two swords fell to the ground and were, thankfully, silent.

Derrick kicked the hilt away. "They don't make magic swords the way they used to."

"When I was a kid a geas could ruin you from the day you received it until the day you died miserably. Now . . . ." Gautrek shrugged.

"I surrender," Nerianna said weakly.

The two warriors looked at him. The elf king lay on his back, pinned by sword fragments.

"So we actually fulfilled the wizard's spell." Derrick grinned. "Would you believe it?"

"I believe it," Nerianna said. "What do you say about releasing me?"

Derrick turned toward Gautrek. "Shouldn't he give us something in return, his being a king and all?"

Gautrek nodded. "I'd like that poem about the brachiopods. Signed of course."

ABOUT THE AUTHOR

Novelist, short story writer, and wildlife photographer, Chet Gottfried is a member of SFWA. His most recent works are Into the Horsebutt Nebula (an SF comedy-thriller) and the republication of his first novel The Steel Eye (a hard-boiled robot mystery), both from ReAnimus Press. For the latest information, visit his website lookoutnow.com.

Spooky Action At A Distance

D.B. Keele

TODAY JOE FRANKLIN woke up and he was someone else.

You know that twilight period, when you first begin to wake, and there is a moment—a brief flicker of certainty—that you have awakened in a strange place? The rising panic, the quickened breath, the painful flinging open of the eyelids—only to blink in the dawning light and see the familiar outline of your bedroom and its contents coming into focus?

This morning that happened to Joe, and just as he began to remember all the other mornings that it happened and it was nothing, blinking his blurry eyes against the dawning light, and thought - wait now, this is odd... WHERE THE HELL AM I? THIS IS NOT MY—... his skin crawled, and the hair on the back of his neck stood up as he realized, not only was he in a strange bed, but he was sitting up in it next to a stranger. He caught the scream building in his throat, choked it back, and squinted down at the shape next to him in the bed. He could make out the back of a head, long dark hair, covers pulled up to the forehead. Long, slow breaths... she was still sleeping. Why the hell couldn't he see? Everything was blurry.

He quietly pulled back the covers, sat up, and swung his legs over the side of the bed. His pale, white, hairy legs. Above his pale, white, hairy feet. He felt a lump forming in his throat. A wave of nausea and dizziness descended upon him, as he tried not to fall back into the bed. He glanced over at the night stand, and saw the glint of a pair of glasses. Joe picked them up and carefully worked them onto his face.

When he opened his eyes, the room sprang into focus. So he has glasses now to go with his shockingly pale legs. He stood up slowly, and made his way toward the door, hoping to slip out before his mysterious bed-mate awakened. The room was quiet, save for the swish of an overhead fan rotating and the quiet press of his bare feet against the beige piled carpet. He was chilly, but too interested in escaping the room unseen to seek out more clothing than he found myself awakened in.

He slipped through the cracked door, and quietly eased it shut behind himself. He was in a wood-paneled hallway. There was an open, dark doorway ahead to his left that he hoped would prove to be a bathroom.

He stepped into the dark doorway and felt on the wall for a switch as he slid the bathroom door shut. Flicking on the lights, he blinked against the harsh white glare off of the mirror. He stumbled back against the wall, gasping at what he saw reflected. There was a pale old white man in the mirror, wearing nothing but loose-fitting boxer shorts and the glasses he had slipped on back at the bedside.

He held his breath and leaned in toward the mirror. His mind was racing; his thoughts the chaos of a kicked in ant hill. He was forced to start breathing again, in short ragged breaths. Joe felt a cold, slick sweat trickling down from his underarms. He was inches from the mirror now. It was Joe, looking at a stranger. And it was him. But that's not me, he thought. That is not my face. He thought he might pass out.

He staggered over to the toilet, and slowly lowered himself to the lid. Sitting there, stooped over, his face resting in his hands, his bare feet against the cold tile floor... He imagined he was dreaming and would wake. Joe sat and waited for his heart to slow and his breathing to regulate. He stood back up and walked over to the sink, turned the water on to cold, removed the glasses and splashed water over his face. Drying off, he looked at his face without the glasses on. A pale blur, some old white guy; a stranger.

He picked up the glasses, put them on, and looked more closely at the face in the mirror. Thinning gray hair, creased forehead with age spots. Ice cold blue eyes that evidently had began to fail. He hadn't shaved in a couple of days. His face moved like Joe's did though. It was unnerving. Something had gone horribly wrong somewhere. He had to keep calm though until he could figure it out.

There was a thick blue robe hanging on the back of the bathroom door. Assuming this would be his robe, and not that of the woman still in the bed, he took it down and wrapped up in it. Joe slid on the men's slippers he saw waiting by the tub, and quietly opened the door. He made his way down the dark hallway, further away from the bedroom where the woman slept, not knowing her husband had woke up as someone else.

Joe found himself in a perfectly unremarkable living room, furnished with a sagging plaid couch, a matching love seat, and a prominent television set. He sat on the love seat, facing the hallway. He focused on breathing and trying to remember what the last thing was that he could before he woke up in this body. Hadn't he just gone to bed with Catherine like any other night? He was completely wiped out. A quick cuddle, then oblivion. And then... here.

Catherine! He suddenly realized she was his lifeline, whatever this was. He glanced around the room that was beginning to glow with early morning light seeping in around the drapes, and saw the telephone on a table at the other end of the couch. He slid down the couch, and quietly picked up the receiver, while dialing his home number. It was ringing. He licked his lips, wondering what this voice would sound like.

"H-hello?" It was Catherine, groggy. He had awakened her. They liked to sleep in on the weekend.

Whispering, he tried to speak to his wife, "Catherine. This is Joe." The whisper that came out was like he had expected. Raspy. Higher tone. A neurotic smoker, this guy. He coughed, quietly, "Catherine - this is Joe. I know..."

She cut him off. "Who the hell is this? Why are you whispering? What does Joe have to do with anything? Lose this number, before I do put Joe on the phone!"

Click.

C ATHERINE STARED AT the phone in the cradle. She was breathing harder than she'd like. It was unlikely she would get back to sleep after getting her adrenaline going like that. She turned to look at Joe, to see if he too had been awakened by the phone. He was not in the bed. His pillow still had the indentation from his head, but he was gone, his side of the blankets pulled up.

That was weird. Joe didn't have class this Saturday. Maybe he just couldn't sleep in.

She swung her feet out over the side of the bed, and slid her feet into her slippers that were there waiting. She grabbed her robe from the chair in the corner, and threw it on. She gathered up her drinking glass, current reading material, and her notepad and slowly made her way down to the kitchen, expecting to find Joe at the counter, coffee steaming, newspaper spread out before him.

There was no one in the kitchen. The coffee pot was empty and unplugged. The house was dead silent. Catherine started to worry. She laid down her assortment of bedside items that Joe always teased her about, and turned to walk to the door leading to the garage to see if Joe had taken the car and left.

She threw the door open - the car was there. At least there was that. Joe never drove the car and did not have a valid driver's license. He took the bus. Had he taken the car, she would really start to worry. She turned to walk back into the house, and then she noticed it—Joe's bike was missing from the wall where it usually would be hanging. The side door was closed, but the dead bolt was no longer engaged.

She went back inside to look for further clues of where her husband may have gone in the early morning hours without saying a word.

A FTER CATHERINE HUNG up on him, Joe realized that she could not help him right now. He had to figure out what was going on and deal with it himself. He quietly set the phone receiver back in the cradle. He stood up, and made his way into the kitchen. There were still dishes on the table from last night's dinner. Cold chicken and congealed gravy. Stacked at one corner, against the wall, was a pile of mail. Joe picked up a few pieces and thumbed through them. Susan Halverson. Resident. Professor Samuel Halverson. Mr. and Mrs. Halverson. Was that the face he was wearing now? Professor Samuel Halverson? He sat the mail down.

There were footsteps behind him. He froze. The overhead light flicked on.

"Sam? What's going on? Why are you wandering around in the dark down here?"

"Uhhh, sorry, I, couldn't *ahem*, couldn't sleep any more." He turned and attempted a sheepish grin. Would she see the difference? He knew he had to play this right or he would end up in a psych ward before the day was out.

The woman from the bed, apparently, was leaning against the doorway, her finger still resting on the light switch. She was tall and thin, her long her tucked behind her ears. She had a curious expression on her face, as if to silently ask, "Oh? Really?"

"Okay. Well, at least now the light is on. Coffee?" She walked across to the cabinet and began taking things out, without waiting for a response.

Joe tried to act natural, but he had no idea what that would look like. If he could find out more about who this Halverson guy was, hopefully he could find out if they were connected, or try another way to convince Catherine to help him. Where was his body? Had he died and somehow ended up in this guy? He had no way of knowing. But if he started spouting off about any of it to this lady, he was bound to end up hospitalized.

He calmly sat down at the bar and looked slowly around the room in an appraising fashion.

"Sure. Coffee would be great. Thank you." He offered a weak grin, his hands clasped on top of the counter.

His new wife looked back at him over her shoulder and smiled, "Are you sure you're okay? You seem... off this morning. And last night you were talking in your sleep a a lot. Should you call Dr. Nguyen?"

D OWNTOWN, AT THE bus station, Professor Samuel Halverson was looking into the restroom mirror as he splashed cold water on Joe Franklin's face. He was beaming from ear to ear. It had worked. He had pulled it off.

He glanced over at the backpack on the counter next to him. There was a large quantity of cash and a fresh pair of jeans in that bag, and that was all he had in the world.

S AM HAD WORKED at the University for over thirty years. He was involved in many different highly respected studies and published in all of the requisite journals to achieve mid-level success in his field. He was quietly effective, leading his department to secure many grants and contracts, including quite a few in conjunction with multiple federal agencies. Many that he could not speak to another soul outside the lab about.

One of those long-time projects which he had been head of for many years, involved the use of hypnosis, powerful hallucinogens, and various cybernetic technologies to enhance innate human psychic potential. Sam was particularly interested in inducing out of body experiences in his subjects, and seeking a greater understanding of the human condition through these extreme practices.

Many on campus scoffed at his research, but the federal government funded it, year after year, so how baseless could it really be?

Sam knew better. He had seen, and experienced, the results of the extreme level of experimentation that he had been involved in. He had seen other worlds. Connected with alien minds. Traveled in time and space. He believed all this to be true and not just the fevered dreams of a turned on mind.

And yet. And yet, when his doctor walked into the exam room six months ago, and told him that he had mere months to live, he still had been overcome with grief. Even a man who had left his physical body many times to travel the astral plane, and communicate with others both on the astral plane and still in the physical, even that man is frightened when told he is near to death.

He knew that his consciousness could exist outside his body, at great distance. He had experienced it many times. What he could not be certain of, was would his consciousness survive if his body did not. Now that his body was condemned to certain and imminent death, he became increasingly unwilling to accept the risk that it would take his mind with it. It would be better to take proactive action.

He had told Rebekah, and their children, of course, but inwardly, he began to think of other options. He reflected on the many times he had left his body, interacted with others, poking into their thoughts and memories while they too slept, or even a few who were awake. They would shiver, awake from their daydream, and look around to see who was reaching out and touching them.

He wondered. Could he enter someone else's body, rather than returning to his own? He experimented. He found that over time he become more and more adept at setting up shop in the corner of someone's mind and slowly exerting more and more control. He did not have much time to practice and could not waste time on finesse. He often dosed his fellows in the lab and experimented with them when they were in a daze. As his physical strength waned, his abilities in the lab expanded tremendously. He felt that the time to act was drawing near.

Sam took Rebekah and the kids to a nice dinner the night before he was determined to try it for real. They had a wonderful evening, punctuated by long meaningful silences. He knew it was time. After Catherine drifted off, he prepared the appropriate cocktail, dosed up, began his self-hypnosis routine, and laid in the bed next to her. It did not take long for him to be in the stars.

The whoosh was intense - then the city below him. He was seeing the landscape below him, but also cycling through his mental landscape. The two began to sync up. Faces, interactions, locations, shot through his memories and cycled below his seeming location. He was humming now. He needed to find a resonance, a person, a place, with particular tone, wait there's a... something... that face, I know that face, I see him all the time, but he's sleeping and he's dreaming and he sees me there all the time too, and he sees me see him and we're on THE BUS...

T*HE BUS,* HE knew his new face from the bus! This guy rode to campus. He'd seen him many times. They had given each other the friendly head nod. Now he was nodding his head, pretending to listen to Halverson's wife, as she spoke about their children, the neighbors, politics. Joe was trying not to scream, or break something, he was straining to maintain a mask of complete placidity to avoid her questioning him beyond the absolute necessary.

She placed a plate of scrambled eggs, bacon, and test in front of Joe, alongside a steaming hot mug of black coffee. "Eat up, hon." She walked back to get her plate and mug, as Joe slowly began to eat.

Joe considered his options. He needed to find out what Halverson was up to on campus. He saw him on the bus every day, and that had to be the connection. He needed to find out more about Halverson without tipping off his wife that anything was amiss.

He suspected that Halverson worked on campus, but did not drive for some reason. Did his wife drive? He decided to roll the dice and see what came of it.

"Listen, uh, I wonder if you wouldn't mind giving me a ride to campus today. I'm not... I don't feel quite myself and I would rather not ride the bus. If, that is, if you don't mind."

She stopped chewing and her eyes got big. She gulped down the food audibly, eyes watering. Never breaking his gaze she picked up her coffee and sipped from it. He had miscalculated. She thought Halverson was having a stroke. She was about to dial 9-1-1...

"Well, Sam, yeah. Yeah, that would be fine. I'm sorry, I just, well I just about choked there. I can't remember the last time you asked for a ride to campus. It's not your routine. I... but yeah, absolutely. Let's finish up breakfast and I'll run you in."

"Thanks." He grinned and slowly finished eating, never revealing the racing of his heart.

Halverson was aware of the synchronicity, to be boarding a bus out of town in the body of this man that he knew only from silently shared bus rides. It added a layer of the bizarre to an already unbelievable story. But it was his story, and instead of possibly ending, it would continue.

It wasn't long after his diagnosis that he started to hatch his plan. At first it was harmless fantasizing to relieve stress. Perfectly understandable given his circumstances. Or so he told himself. He soon realized it was becoming more than that.

He knew that following through on the plan would have some unfortunate results. For one, he was hijacking the body of another man. That is no small moral weight to bear. He wasn't entirely sure what happened to the other fellow. Would he pop out like a grape from it's skin? Would he be pressed down deep into the subconscious? Would Halverson have to be ever-vigilant against his mind rising up in revolt? He could not answer any of these questions and there was not enough time for further experimentation. He had to risk it and deal with the consequences.

There was also the small matter of his family. He would have to walk away from them and never speak to them again. This would be horribly painful, but he was to lose them either way. It was either, die as scheduled, they lose him, he loses them, and he loses himself; or, follow through on the plan. They all lose each other, but he survives to live another life. Wouldn't they want that for him? They knew he was dying. It would just be a change of venue. He would suddenly "die in his sleep," rather than a long drawn-out illness.

There was also the matter of whatever life this other man had been living. Perhaps he was married, or had children. It was impossible to tell. Halverson had to just adopt a clean break plan, and proceed as best as possible. He would need to adopt a new identity. He would need to leave in a way that could not be traced. He would need money.

He began to put the pieces in place. His options for finances were limited. He was going to have a new face, and a new name, neither of which he knew ahead of time. He had to be able to access cash, quickly, to fund his escape. He began putting away cash in a secret safe deposit box. The day before he was to execute his plan, he moved the cash to a nylon backpack, took it to the bus station, and checked it into a rented locker. Once he had the new body, he would not need ID for either identity to retrieve his money, just the combination to the lock, which would be safely in his mind.

Now, here he was. Sitting comfortably, young, healthy, a bag full of cash resting on his lap. All he needed now was new documentation. He gazed out the window, smiling, watching the landscape slide by.

HAVING FOLLOWED CLUES from Halverson's wife, Joe got dressed and in the course of doing so, found his wallet. The prize contents of which were his University ID cards. Halverson was faculty. And now Joe had his office number and entry badge.

After Halverson's wife dropped him off and awkwardly tried to kiss him, Joe made his way across campus toward the Psychology building. He had to keep reminding himself that he had this new face and had to react accordingly to potential students or colleagues, all while avoiding full eye contact to further avoid conversation. He was reminded of his predicament though, by how slowly he had to walk across campus. Halverson was an older man, sure, but he should not be this winded on such a short walk. He broke out into a sweat and felt things getting a bit dim.

Joe rested on a bench in front of the building while he caught his breath. He decided the best course was to try to rush into Halverson's office, and see what he could find out before anyone had a chance to speak to him. He slowly stood and began his way up the steps.

It was fairly early, and the building was nearly deserted. He kept his gaze down, hoping the fedora Halverson's wife popped on his head would help him walk through unnoticed.

Soon enough, he was at Halverson's office door, reaching for his swipe-card. He opened the door, slipped in, and turned the lock behind him.

C ATHERINE SIPPED HER coffee as she peered at the morning newspaper through puffy eyes. It had been a long night. Joe never came home. Never called. Whoever that was that had called the morning before never called back. The police said Joe was an adult, and it was too soon to start a search or declare him missing. She got the distinct impression they thought she represented good enough reason for a man to up and leave unannounced.

Sighing, she set down her mug and lifted the paper closer.

"'Tenured Prof. with Defense Dept. Connections Dies Suddenly'

Professor Samuel Halverson, tenured faculty in the Psychology Department of State College died suddenly on campus, Monday, March 12th. Halverson was terminally ill and apparently suffered a psychotic break related to his illness. He died suddenly while being subdued by campus police. The officers involved are on paid leave pending the investigation..."

Catherine tossed the paper down, rested her face in her palms, and wept.

About the Author

D.B. Keele earned a B.A. in English from Indiana University and has held professional positions in libaries and higher education. He resides in Bloomington, Indiana. He also maintains a large menagerie of underwater creatures as a convenient means of body disposal.

Brave New Night

Andrew Reichard

LAIRE TOOK THE call halfway through its first vibrate, stood and went to the east window with the cell pressed against her ear. Her wife's voice on the other side saying, "It's happening again."

"It's all right, Gina. It'll be all right," Claire said.

"I just want to be on the phone until it blows over."

"Boss isn't in today. I'll watch with you." Claire didn't touch the glass. She stood a foot from the upper story window on 9th Street and stepped out of her heels and watched the sky over New York City begin to crack.

Behind her, the Mergers & Acquisitions office where she answered calls and entered six-digit figures into Excel sheets hung quiet. CNBC murmuring financials into an empty lounge space. The coffee press burped. The business phone on its pedestal: a silent, black comma. Out over Times Square, buildings began to fall from the sky.

"Where are you, Gina?"

"I'm at home." Her voice gravel-rough like she'd been smoking, but she hadn't in years.

"That's good," said Claire. "Pour some Malbec. You don't have to watch."

"I can't drink when the city does this. I can't move, Claire. It's like I'm paralyzed."

"You could lie down. It might help. Just, maybe step away from the window if you're feeling—" queasy wasn't the word she wanted. In her office, from her window, Claire took an involuntary step back.

The desk phone rang. She didn't answer.

Skyscrapers like she had never seen. At first as if a mirror were falling slowly toward its subject, except that these new structures weren't anything she recognized. They were narrow pylons shedding scaffolding, internally lit like New York at night. But it was day. The night city collapsed, casually, atop the actual; dazed photons rendering their confusion in chiaroscuro: abrupt destruction-worship like those slow-motion videos of a bullet passing through an apple. Reminiscent of art deco. V-shapes shrinking as the appearances warped into Manhattan.

As for the sound. There was nothing beyond the ordinary. On the streets, traffic seized, distended, groped along under unfazed traffic lights. The city was being assaulted by nothing more than images, as if some giant projector satellite hung above them. This time like all the times before. Something in the air that presented itself as visible destruction. Renderings.

It wasn't real, but Claire closed her eyes and imagined coughing smoke and siren symphonies. She imagined Gina lying in her bed, covers pulled to chin and an unread book lying open between her breasts. These two images so incongruous, yet they made a sort of diptych sense. A logic of contour alone.

She opened her eyes again. The oppressive images cast upon the skyline had vanished—were now doing the whole thing over: spire-sharp buildings falling languorously again, on repeat.

Claire asked into the phone, "Are you...are you all right?" She didn't like the way her voice left blank moments in the center of questions like that.

Gina said yes.

"Are you really?"

"Yes, I'll be fine. You'll be home late again?"

"I think so. Don't stay up. Lie down a little now," Claire told her. "And open the Malbec. I love you." She ended the call as her boss, Galen Turner, arrived.

"Claire, Claire—Oh where is Claire. Hey girl, I called, but no answer. That's a strike." He saw her by the window. "And, well, it's raining buildings out there. Been in the parking garage too long. Been making money in the land of echoes and concrete."

Another prismatic phalanx coming down. Turner slid over to watch with her, forgetting her. The images were unraveling of their own accord—now more scaffolding and glass than anything—but still so total they couldn't be ignored.

Turner clapped his hands together. "Ok. I need that BrandSynch sale write-up on my desk by three. It's working hours. Can't be putzing about just 'cause Armageddon," singing, "Mon-ey to be made!"

"I emailed it to you, Galen. Just before I took a break."

"Oh, fine. Fine then!" he said. "Always hoping that one of these days you'll realize you like men after all and come into my office for a chat." He winked: a joke.

Claire caused her lips to smile. He didn't mean it as the antagonism it was, and though his intentions meant nothing to her, it did decide her response. He would have been amazed had her reaction shown any emotion aberrant to the secretarial co-conspirator that he assumed her to be.

He picked up the remote and channeled to CNN while she returned to her chair, the desk between them. "Weird weather, they're still calling it." He made the quarter-note farting noise of an extremely tight sphincter. "What a joke! The meteorologists point at the environmentalists who point at the government who accuse the Russian government who are scratching their asses. What a mess! Now they're fobbing the whole thing off on Hol-ly-fucking-wood. Too many movies about New York getting screwed by doomsday. The city's sentient now—it's developed a mind or something. Re-projecting the images of its end. Tell me how that works, how 'bout you?"

Claire only watched him. It seemed manic to her when people repeated what the news was saying while the news was saying it, but then Galen had always been manic in his need for the normal. His panic came out as winking confabulation.

"But hey, I'm not that full of it," he promised. "Just because I don't personally understand how it works doesn't mean it ain't so. Kind of like you and your woman."

"You don't understand how Gina and I work?"

He pulsed his palms. "And I'm saying that doesn't mean it doesn't. Work, that is."

What is it that confuses you? But she knew. She knew because every time she and Gina wanted to hold hands on the sidewalk it became a juggling act between affection and defiance, between a personal display of love and a public demonstration. She felt an odd solidarity with the city itself because of this.

Galen shook his head and turned the screen off, cutting the reporter mid-sentence. Claire almost cringed. The abrupt shutting down of a television startling to her.

"Are people still leaving the city?" she asked.

He rolled the shoulders of his suit. "Everyone who was thinking about leaving has already. We're the stalwarts. It's perfectly safe. Animals don't even notice it. You're not planning on leaving, are you? I need you. Can't replace you. You're invaluable."

Claire looked at the screen. "Could you turn that back on?"

"To what, hon?"

She didn't care.

There was baseball. Mets against Braves. In Atlanta. No incorporeal buildings falling there. Claire went back to her spreadsheets.

"Um-Claire?"

She looked up from her desk ten minutes later to see Galen poking his rectilinear head out of his office suite.

"Sorry. What I said wasn't very appropriate. You know—earlier."

She made some motion: a wave with a shrug. At a different moment it might have been a flinch. Galen Turner took it as acceptance, but he then looked out the window and turned on her a brave smile that seemed almost meek.

Between two people—even in the interaction of a lukewarm apology—the city had to be acknowledged. It was like that now. Rationales bled into each other. Everything was interrupted by the fact of the occurrences they called renderings.

Claire had been in high school in 2001, and she remembered the way everything warped toward that black hole named Ground Zero. Her teachers had worn flats instead of heels in case they needed to run. Every gesture, every disruption, soaked through the window of the city's disbelief. All cruelties, all kindnesses, had somehow to be motivated by that window, which had been left wide open as it was now. Everything came through.

And now, New York City was ensnared by a meditative sort of hysteria (In Galen's case it was genial and moronic). Harlem-sized illustrations on the skyline, in the streets. People living their lives under this. Somehow still conducting their own successes and maneuvering around their own failures within the dome of an intelligent horror strobing across the membrane of normality.

That New Yorkers tried to think of these manifestations as a kind of weird weather was not a surprise. They quickly became a fact of this city's life, like rain. Galen tried to laugh at them. Gina was terrified by them. And Claire was strangely, breathlessly excited. Apocalypse pressed at reality's seams. Manhattan made visions of its own death: cityscape havoc-dreams dissolving on the air, touching nothing but people's eyes.

B Y THE END of the day, Claire had spent much of it staring out the window. With the sun setting, she got up and drew the curtains slowly on the skyline like on a stage. Galen had still not left his office, and none of the other partners had shown or called, and she went to the door and knocked and stabbed her head inside.

"Going home."

He sat hunched over the laptop with his tie tugged loose. At the interruption, he took his glasses off and rubbed at his eyes. "How do you separate a city from its people?" he asked in the most straightforward manner she'd ever heard from him.

Claire opened the door wider, stood on the threshold, but she held back from him. "What do you mean?" Her question sounded cold, appeared to have startled him.

He looked at her, glasses still in his hand. "You know what I mean," he whispered.

"The city—"

"Yes, the city," agitated, "what do you think it's doing to us? Tell me that; I don't care what you say, I just want your opinion. Gimme anything. Don't you think the city is the people in it? What else would it be if not us? So how is it acting apart from us, you know? Since when did man-made environments veer off in another direction than man?" He shook his head.

He was making her uneasy, this sudden genuineness, chauvinistic though it still was. Somehow, she didn't want to believe that Galen was going through similar doubts that she and Gina were. "If you have something to ask me about work, I can stay, but I really need to get home." She waited and then stepped back and closed the door, observing him through its window. He had gone back to his work. Maybe he knew she was still standing there, and maybe he didn't. A moment later, Claire saw him take up his glasses in both hands and snap them in half.

PUBLIC TRANSIT SUFFERED most from the renderings, but cab drivers were recovering their bygone prestige. Many people trusted them above the buses or, God forbid! an UBER. Here comes the yellow cab, carapace of the city's inertia, its driver surely honest-eyed and over-worked and as dogged as the day.

Despite this romantic reinforcement, New York's streets, like its poorly hidden psyche, had still run feral.

Claire walked wherever she could, ensconced among the other pedestrians beyond the sidewalk regions where barricades had been thrown up along curbsides to protect against distracted drivers. Tonight, it was late, and the gyro from the delicatessen across the street churned in her stomach with the dread, and her feet had blisters from walking a block. She had joined the wearied taxi-seeking mob, hands like semaphores, when another illustration fell upon them.

No warning this time, just a drop cloth of shadow coming down on an ant colony. The crowd turned. From the direction of the piers came a wave: an impossible tsunami from out of the west. At the sight of it, people made jungle sounds. Whoops, hollers. Cars halted at green lights. Down the street a grown man shrieked, and someone else laughed.

Despite themselves, they backed up. Claire shuffled with them, staring up at the white crest rolling toward them, forty stories tall. The wave ambushed their eyes; it looked so real, coming toward them.

A woman Claire didn't know clung to her arm as the ghost wave crashed. People ducked, unable to help it.

In such a moment, every gesture seemed the harbinger of limitless meaning. It was the end of the world and yet it wasn't real, so meaning was the remainder; which found, in everyone's minds, outlets elsewhere. An old man picked up his cane in both hands and touched his sagging cheek with it and set it gently on the concrete again. Claire: fascinated with the ponderousness of that, trying to parse out its significance.

Then they were all underwater. Except that it was silent, it looked so real. The water moving rapidly and Claire finding herself leaning forward to fight the image of it. Light and motion hiccupped abysmally in underwater tumult. Coruscating madness, shimmering phantoms and emergency light, and nothing but nothing felt so much as a drop. Buildings, cars, people should have been swatted away, but weren't.

Claire held on to the hand of this stranger and tried not to look at her face because it might have been easy to imagine that the woman was drowning.

A N HOUR LATER, she found Gina in the bedroom. Lying on her back fully dressed with her arms at her sides. Claire sat on the bed beside her and placed a palm to Gina's forehead.

"I don't have a fever, babe, but I'm sick. I know I am. Did you see the wave tonight? Did you see it?"

"I was standing in it."

Gina had eyes that were so alert they could cause pain.

"I stood right there while it washed over me." Claire held her arms out to either side to show that she wasn't…that she hadn't been… "Nothing happened," she said. "Everyone flinched, and we all held on to each other, and then we went our own ways again under this…this optical illusion. Someone near me said it was beautiful; I heard him say it. Gina, listen. People are going to be fine. We're going to be fine because nothing is happening. It's like the whole city is stuck in a dream—"

"A nightmare."

"A dream. And the only thing we can do is…is to. Did you open the wine?"

Not waiting to hear the answer, Claire raced to the kitchen and found the unopened bottle of Malbec and uncorked it, bringing it back into the room without glasses. She sat again, pulling one leg up on the bed, letting the other hang over the side. Still in her business suit, she took the first sip. Administered the second to Gina.

"Stop that, I'm not your patient." Gina giggled, tried to take the bottle and sloshed a little on the sheets. Both of them inhaling at the stain like little girls, they raised their eyes to each other, burst into laughter.

"My boss asked me how we work today. As in," pointing at pelvis, "mechanics."

"Your boss is an uncircumcised dildo."

"He said he was sorry." Claire laughed again, but now Gina was mad and looking at the window. Though the curtains were closed, the city was there, on the other side, in a way it never used to be.

"Do you think it will ever stop?" Gina asked.

"It might."

"Did you see the jets?"

"What?"

"Earlier today," said Gina. "Fighter planes. They went through the sky, and I thought, 'this isn't real,' and then I realized I wouldn't know if something like that was actually happening or just an image. It's like we're living in a movie. A 3D, IMAX, the whole nine yards."

"What would they do if they were real?" Claire asked about the jets.

"Not a clue." Gina set her dark head on Claire's shoulder, and Claire found herself wishing it would rain. Let the sky produce something natural, and they might be able to sleep tonight. Against her shoulder, Claire felt Gina begin to cry. Soft tears.

Claire closed her eyes, holding on, seeing the eerie white light from under the wave move off beyond the blackened buildings, turning them off and replacing them with silhouettes. She knew all of Gina's tears. These. These were produced from the evaporation of a day, a soft appeal to fatigue, her own soft rain.

In the morning, it was drizzling blood. There could be no forecast for this weather; it just happened. People had spilled out into the yellowing hallway of their apartment building, some still wrapped in night robes, others dressed for work. Everyone hesitant to peer out on the nauseating scene: red precipitation.

Claire put an arm on Gina's to steady her. She was looking

down to the end of the hallway where the window was.

"It's not real," Claire said.

"But if it looks like it is, does it matter that it's not?" Gina wanted to know.

An older woman overheard them. "It's not even touching the ground. My husband went out there and said it was falling to about his knees and vanishing. People are lying down out there—looking along the space where it doesn't fall."

Claire said again, "It's not real." She led Gina back into their apartment and told her she could go in late today and they could spend the morning eating pancakes and making love.

But Gina looked sick and shook her head. "It's so morbid. This is so morbid."

Affronted by the suggestion that she was being morbid, that she was somehow not taking this as seriously as she should, Claire said, "People are working, Gina. What are you doing? Lying in bed all day, staring at closed curtains."

Gina looked as though she'd been slapped.

Claire said, "They say on the news that the city is…is "replaying man-made renditions of its destruction." A quote she'd memorized. "It's as if…as if the city itself—the city itself—is performing poetry or—" They had both moved back to the bedroom, their fortress, while Claire tried to talk herself into an understanding. Maybe she could bury what she'd said while apocalypses overwrote each other in palimpsestic ruin. If she apologized now, she told herself, it would sound as weak as Galen's false regret.

"I don't know what's happening, Gina, but you've got to remember that: It's. Not. Real. It's not real, and images shouldn't be able to keep us from…you know what I mean."

"No, I'm not sure I do." Gina was always the calm one when it came to fights and sex. In these territories, Claire was driven by passion, lost within it.

"The images shouldn't be able to keep us from…from enjoying ourselves," Claire stammered desperately. "Ever since they started, you've moped and sat at your computer and not taken any work, and I'm tired of coming home every night and lifting you up because… because…"

Claire sat on the bed, but in her confusion she knocked against the side table. The half-empty bottle of Malbec, left there from the night before, overturned and broke on the floor, spilling. Both of them stared at it. Glass, thought Claire, how did it always break like that? It comes apart as teeth.

The wine was pooling against the oval rug, soaking into it, and it was Gina now on her hands and knees with a rag from the laundry, cleaning up the mess.

"I have been taking some work," Gina said, while her wife watched her from the bed. "I get migraines though. I get nauseous every time I look outside. I can't look at a computer screen for long before I'm dizzy."

She was halted by the light. Red coruscations assaulting their shades. Claire bolted up and peered out while Gina stepped back.

She looked out on molten streets. The city rendering a volcanic river. Most of the cars had stopped in their tracks; people stood waist deep in lava, gaping at themselves. A woman stood beside the sunken handle of a stroller, holding her babe out of the fire, but both of them were fine. Claire stood, enthralled, breathless. She blinked, and it was all gone; the stupefied streets stopped in its many-wheeled tracks, but otherwise unchanged. The woman holding her sleeping child stood in the sidewalk and sobbed, and strangers moved about her, comforting her, and there were tears in Claire's eyes, looking down from her window.

She had known—they had all known—that it wasn't real, and yet it still brought everyone to a standstill, and Claire knew not just that that baby was alive and fine, but that she was alive too. She was filled suddenly with a tremendous, pounding lust. She wanted to melt into Gina's body and for Gina to melt into her's.

"It can't go on like this," Gina said.

"Can't go on like what? There are people down there embracing in the streets. It's…it's—" But she couldn't say beautiful. She wouldn't allow herself to say it in Gina's presence. "It's mysterious. There's something about it that's not all horrific. It's almost—well, I think it's almost artistic. Is that possible?" Her entreaty for Gina to understand her sounded weak. She knew it did.

And there was Gina, kneeling in the spilled wine and looking up at her. "This sort of thing can't be sustained, Claire. An end will come eventually, and that will be that, but this city keeps on ending and then retracting its end and ending again. We're trapped in a loop, stuck on a repetition of our own obsessions, our own cinema dreams. I don't understand how it's happening, but I know this isn't art, Claire. It's pornography."

"Pornography. The city's making a porno? You're not making any sense, Gina." She pecked her head with grouped fingertips, a gesture she'd unconsciously lifted from the man she worked for.

But Gina was tired, frustrated. She wouldn't be argued with, and she wouldn't argue.

Claire hovered about, feeling that the moment had burst like a balloon. "I have to go to work."

Gina was still bent over, carefully lifting the pieces of glass from the carpet one crystal at a time when Claire went out into the hall.

O UTSIDE IT HAD begun to rain. Real rain. Independent of that other weather. People talked excitedly about molten streets and blood and plagues, and Claire found herself walking extra blocks, hoping something else would happen. She told herself she wouldn't pause this time. The end of the world wouldn't even slow her down.

All alone, she wanted to prove to Gina that the renderings wouldn't hurt. But even though she had flirted with it, she couldn't tell her partner the truth. How could she tell Gina that it had been Claire who had said on the street that the wave was beautiful? She—Claire—had come home late on purpose and stood longer than she had to holding the hand of a strange woman who needed Claire for just the balance. And Claire had said to this stranger that it was all beautiful. It was a thing she could tell anyone except for the woman she loved, and she couldn't tell if that made it wrong or if it just made them different.

She was still within sight of her building when the sun: it went off like a broken bulb. Abrupt black stopped her in her tracks. Someone plowed into her, and she fell against the pavement. She heard the entire city scream then: cars, people, everything. It had all been blotted away.

The first headlights came on a moment later. Other lights: lights from buildings, from phones. A thousand separate acts of light from such perfect dark that it paralleled creation. She wasn't the only one who'd fallen. She could see that now; people on their knees as if darkness were another, heavier gravity. Someone helped her to her feet.

"Gina?"

The stranger—a man—peered into her face, waving the blue light of his phone in her eyes. Claire looked up to New York City outlining itself with light. At the end of the block where she had come a taxi had run up against a fire hydrant and caused a geyser. A child was lying in the street. People stumbled out of an accordioned bus, spilled out of lit shops, peered from balconies. Someone broke a shop window and stepped through the aperture as if no one was watching.

Claire was fascinated with these aspects of destruction; she held them to her eyes like trinkets. What was she doing? Assimilating apocalypse? Soaking it into her skin like rain? She hadn't felt like a phantom until...until now.

"We'll all have to leave after this," said the man who had helped her. Only his voice seemed dazed; his eyes were clear. "No one can stay after it goes and does something like this."

"I know."

"Here. You're bleeding." The man took off his tie and put it into her hands. He'd been on his way to work when it happened: the image of the sun vanishing.

Claire ran her thumb along the smooth fabric of the tie in her hand, looking at him.

"Your forehead," he said. He pointed at his own head where her cut was.

She started to cry.

IT WAS GINA who found her. Gina, who had ventured out into that ersatz night to walk the streets with a little red flashlight like a kid in the woods. In truth, she hadn't needed the flashlight. The city glowed, and they saw each other from some distance, Claire still sobbing.

The man was gone. He had a family and could see that she would be all right. Gina had found her wife standing alone among crash victims and emergency vehicles.

"Tell me you weren't on that bus. Claire, tell me you weren't in the street."

"No—I mean, I wasn't."

"You're hurt. Who gave you a tie?"

"A man."

Gina held her. Claire knew that Gina was physically the stronger of the two, but she had forgotten somehow and was now reminded. "I'm sorry." She was crying into Gina's shoulder. "I made you come outside during one of them."

"No," softly, "no, no."

"I made you come out looking for me." Over Gina's shoulder she saw pigeons. The birds hadn't noticed; they were still pecking about the trash cans or the tiny squares of littered dirt that were allotted to the city's trees. Still in oblivious sunlight.

New York City reflecting the curiosity of only its human inhabitants. And Claire had been entranced by a reflection of what humanity had projected onto the space around them, wandering spellbound through unexplained doom and disaster that never touched Earth. The realization terrified her now. It scared the hell out of her.

She held on to her partner. "They're saying we're going to have to leave," Claire said. "Everyone's going to have to leave until they can sort this out and figure out what's going on."

Gina cupped her cheek with a hand, eyes vivid. Her eyes bright with love as they sometimes were with tears. Gina's love: it came fully down, touched all the way to the grass and pavement of Claire's soul.

Claire opened her mouth to say something; she hadn't yet discovered what. At which point they were caught blinking because the sun was back. When their eyes had adjusted, they looked up to find the streets teeming with riot police and army vans advancing toward them. Loudspeakers told everyone to do what they were all already planning to do. There was no turning back now. It was to be an evacuation. They should have left a long time ago, before they all realized that the city didn't want them there any longer. If the element of mimesis in the crowded air could produce total darkness, what then was keeping it from manufacturing complete light, removing the need for visions from then on? The renderings weren't harmless, they could add and subtract from humanity's idea of reality, and, like a mind contemplating death, they were going a little further each time.

Gina took Claire's hand, began to lead her back to their apartment where they would, she supposed, start packing. "I can take work with me. We'll be all right," said Gina.

Claire believed her because she'd had an irrevocable thought: "Maybe, when everyone retreats, the renderings will just stop."

"What makes you think that?"

Claire shook her head. She didn't know if she could tell Gina what she thought: that it was humanity, and not the city, that was the cause. "We haven't been…we haven't been…" This penchant for ellipsis: it was muting her, inserting a stammer into the lucidity of her thoughts. But perhaps all original ideas were difficult to unlimber for the first time. They stuck in the mouth as they had first in the mind. "We haven't been…hopeful enough," Claire forced herself to say.

Gina squeezed her hand. In love, in defiance. In amazement. The two of them making their way down the disaster-clad street together. For the last time in neither of them knew how long.

ABOUT THE AUTHOR

Andrew Reichard is an author who lives in Grand Rapids, Michigan. His short fiction has appeared in journals such as Black Static, Starship-Sofa, Shoreline of Infinity, and Space and Time Magazine. Connect with him on Twitter @DrewReichard.

Known Issues

William Delman

MY CAR SWERVED OFF Harvard Avenue and slid over Beacon Street, laying down a scimitar of scorched rubber. The 59 bus screeched behind me, horn bellowing, and somehow missed the rear bumper.

Head spinning, I stabbed at the blue button on my rearview three times before the textured nub clicked under my index finger.

The maniacal compact continued its chase of the other car with the single-minded focus of a lawyer on too much Dexedrine.

A recorded female voice cooed through the Bose system, "Welcome to iDrive, Mr. Khole. I am connecting your call."

The engine roared through a downshift, and the nimble hatchback changed lanes, cutting off a steroidal pickup, before nearly ramming the back of a garbage truck.

When the autodrive smashed on the brakes at the last second, it threw me against my seatbelt hard enough to hurt. Then it blared the horn like an angry teenager, dropped a gear, and changed lanes, resuming the pursuit. I let loose a string of incoherent curses just as the service tech picked up.

"Whoa sir! I'm going to have to ask you to calm down, sir." The tech's voice bled with annoyance.

"Calm down? Sure. Sorry, I was just having my third near-death experience thanks to your homicidal system. It's road raging after this EQ that cut us off back in Brookline. Can you reboot it, or kill it or whatever? I'm locked out!"

There was a moment of silence. For a petrified heartbeat, I thought my call had been disconnected, but then I heard the customer service tech counting to ten before saying, "My name is Steve, and I'm here to help. Is this Mr. Khole?"

"Yes! And my Particle is trying to murder me, Steve, so if we can move this along—"

"I understand, Mr. Khole, I just need to check on a few things. First, can you please verify your identity with your pin number, and—"

I cut Steve off with a loud string of emphatic expletives. Traffic was clotted around Kenmore Square like cholesterol in an artery, so the Particle jumped on Beacon Street's wide sidewalk, blasting its horn and scattering the pedestrians like pigeons.

I bruised my fists pounding the inert steering wheel until the Particle careened on to Commonwealth, nearly causing a half-dozen accidents and sending me reflexively into the crash position.

I thought of my husband Tim waiting at home with two expertly grilled lemon pepper sword fish steaks and charred asparagus. Assuming he'd kept his promise for once and stayed out of the liquor store.

Meanwhile, Steve was still talking, saying something about a "driver initiated failure."

When I looked back up from my lap I could see the other vehicle, now only about 50 feet away. The shiny EQ was snaking through traffic, leaving a river of brake lights rippling red in its wake.

"Any idea why the car is showing me this error, Mr. Khole?"

"What? No! Like I said, I was going home when this EQ came out of nowhere and nearly clipped the front end. The other driver took off, and my car started chasing—"

"Nothing else happened? You are sure, Mr. Khole?"

I started to give a colorful reply, but my stomach interrupted by replacing the words in my mouth with my lunch. The Particle drifted hard right onto Arlington, before deep breaking left on Boylston and curb jumping back on to the sidewalk to avoid another glut.

I could hear a cacophony of sirens now, getting closer, and shamefully wiped my mouth on my sleeve. "Why is this still going on?" I moaned. "I just want to go home. Cars aren't supposed to do this!"

"Please Mr. Khole, try to remain calm. Our competitors at EQ have been having problems with their systems that occasionally lead to dangerous situations like this one."

"I'm not in an EQ!"

"Of course not. Unfortunately, this EQ's malfunction triggered a known issue with our operating system. We're expecting to have it patched in our next agile release, but this situation is obviously more urgent than that, so—"

"Are you serious?" I squawked.

Then the Particle nearly hit a semi and killed me.

And again, flying into the six-way intersection near South Station and blasting down the 93 North on ramp.

And probably several more times after that, whipping in and out of traffic in the tunnels under Boston.

When I came out of my trauma induced blackout, soaked with sweat and shaking, the Particle was crossing the Zakim Bridge. The EQ was still ahead, but closer now, maybe forty feet away.

A small motorcade of police cars was maybe a hundred feet behind, taking up both lanes of the highway, and a cloud of media drones had coalesced in the sky. For a second I sat mesmerized, watching them dance like a murmuration of carbon fiber starlings.

"Still with us Mr. Khole?" Steve said, sounding vaguely concerned.

"I guess." My voice croaked.

"Good. Good. We're almost there. We've managed to clear the road in front of you, so the situation is under control."

"Ha! That's a good one, Steve." I shouted. "That kind of material must be why you're making the big bucks!"

Then I watched one of the media drones break formation. As it got closer I could see a little Fox25 logo on the insectile skeleton.

I ran a hand through my matted hair and tried to smile before realizing my vomit stained sport coat was going to undercut any attempt at nonchalant heroism, and after pulling alongside to briefly train its cameras in my direction, the drone retreated back to the cloud.

Suddenly Steve was clearing his throat on the line. "Excuse me, Mr. Khole. The police would like you to turn off your cell phone until this situation has been resolved."

I hadn't even thought of my phone until Steve mentioned it. I pulled it out of my pocket. There were notifications for a dozen missed calls. Four were from Tim, probably wondering where I was. I didn't recognize the other numbers.

"Why? I need to call my husband back and let him know I'm okay."

Steve coughed. "Mr. Khole, my supervisor Bob Openmeyer is going to be taking over now."

A sonorous voice filled the air. "Yes, and thank you, Steve. Mr. Khole, I'm the New England VP for customer interaction here at Edison, and on behalf of the company I want to say we are just incredibly sorry you've been impacted by this EQ issue."

His voice dripped from the expensive sound system like hot butter over fresh lobster, and for a moment I almost forgot I was trapped in a delusional self-driving compact. "I can only imagine how I'd be feeling right now, Mr. Khole. Probably afraid, out of control, and ready for this drama to end. Am I right?"

"God, yes." I looked down at my cell phone again. I still had three pips.

"Good." Bob oozed. "We have a couple options, but we won't do anything without your permission, Mr. Khole. Do you understand?"

"I guess." I was trying to spot the passenger trapped in the EQ, wondering if they were having a similar conversation with their tech people, but from where I was sitting the car looked empty. Maybe they're laying down, I thought.

"That's great, Mr. Khole, really great. I'm glad we have an understanding. So, the police have a chase car with an EMP cannon they'd like to use. How much do you know about EMPs, Mr. Khole?"

"Not much."

"That's fine, Mr. Khole. All you really need to know is it will fry all the electrical equipment. This includes your Particle, and everything in the car as well. Now, Mr. Khole, you haven't been augmented in any way, have you? No pacemaker, no iC, or ocular implants or anything like that?"

"No, but you mean this thing would kill my phone?"

"It will, assuming you give the go ahead, but we think there's a more serious problem. Your Particle is a genuinely top-end vehicle, meaning all the mechanical systems rely on direction from the electrical systems. This includes your brakes and steering controls."

The HUD was showing 115 mph. 93 wasn't a curvy road, but it did bend, and cars were still dotting the shoulders.

"So you have a plan B?"

"Well, Jaime—may I call you Jamie?"

"Whatever, Bob. Sure."

"Thank you, Jamie. There are two other options, depending on how long you're willing to let this continue. We could wait until the perpetrator's vehicle runs out of power, assuming their EQ dies first based on your Particle's superior economy. Now that could take a while, perhaps even a couple hours, and a lot can happen in a couple hours. We can't even be sure the police will let this go on that long."

"Okay. What's the other option?"

"We prompt an immediate interdiction. Basically, you give us permission to instruct your vehicle to execute something called a pit maneuver on the perpetrator. Then the Particle will utilize its superior speed and handling to bring this chase to a safe and rapid conclusion with minimum damage to both vehicles. We've run a lot of simulations on this and think it's a win-win."

"You want to turn my new car into a battering ram?"

"Not exactly, Jamie. If everything goes right the Particle should only be in contact with the perpetrator for a moment, and once the program has finished executing our techs are very confident they'll be able to disengage the autodrive."

"Why can't they do that now? Put the system into sleep mode or something?"

"The system was actually designed to make that almost impossible once certain emergency codes are triggered. To be honest, that stuff is a bit beyond me. My specialty is helping people achieve the best outcomes given their available resources, and I have to tell you I think your best chance is to initiate the interception."

"Why can't the cops do it? Just go by me and force the EQ off the road?"

"Apparently, they're under orders not to make physical contact with civilian motors. Don't ask me why." He laughed, and my blood pressure rose a few points. "I can't pretend to understand modern law enforcement. So, Jamie, what do you think?"

I realized my cell had just stopped buzzing. "Hold on. Let me think."

I checked the number. While I'd been listening to Bob's mellifluous pitch, Tim had called another four times. I hit the call back button. Tim picked up on the first ring. "Jesus Jamie! Tell me I'm not watching you on the news right now. Have you lost your mind? What were you thinking, chasing that car? Didn't you see she was like twelve? This is exactly why I made you get rid of your M3!"

I held the phone away from my ear while he continued to yell.

"Hey Jamie," Bob sounded annoyed, almost jealous, "not to be a bother, but do I hear another voice in the background?"

"Sorry Bob, can you hold on a second?"

"Sure Jamie, but we really need you to turn off your phone. As soon as that call came in it started interfering with the efforts my tech team was making to resolve your issue."

"Right. Sure." I said, realizing Tim was no longer yelling. "Tim honey? Are you still there?"

"How could you do this to us? I mean, isn't this why we went through those anger management seminars, and the CBT sessions, and—"

"Honey please shut up and listen for second! The autodrive on this stupid spaceship lost its mind. I'm on with Edison customer service right now, and they say it's some kind of glitch."

"Hey, Jamie?" Bob's baritone boomed from the Bose sound system.

"Whoa! You're making my teeth rattle!"

"Sorry to interrupt," he shrank back a few decibels, "but we might have to suspend our work if you don't switch off your phone."

"What's he saying?" Tim asked.

"He's saying my cell is causing problems. So, here's the deal, okay? I can take my chances and hope the car doesn't do anything really crazy before it runs out of fuel, or I can give them permission to try something called a pit maneuver. What do you think I should do?"

"This is insane. Don't you think this is insane?" Tim said, slurring his words.

"Damn it, Tim. Have you been drinking? Tell me you haven't been drinking. You promised."

"Seriously? My husband is on television, being chased by the cops! So what if I'm drinking? I mean, seriously, Jamie—"

I hung up and turned off my phone. "Bob!"

"Still here, Mr. Khole, but I have to tell you—"

"Shut up, Bob. End this. Now."

"Yes sir, Mr. Khole. You may want to brace yourself."

After that, I honestly don't remember much. Sure, there are flashes. I remember the girl in the EQ raising her head and looking back as the Particle came roaring up. I remember she looked like a scared 12-year-old before our bumpers touched.

I remember seeing the guardrail. And the light pole rising up in front of me like a scythe. And I remember dreaming—Kyoto in October, Fushimi Inari, Tim smiling.

When I came to in the back of the ambulance, I'm ashamed to say my first question wasn't, "Is the girl okay, the other driver?" but, "Where's my iPhone?"

In the hospital, a parade of doctors and nurses checked my head, heart, and limbs. Then a pair of police officers sauntered in a few hours later, wanting to hear my side of the story.

Finally, it occurred to me to ask.

"How is she? The other diver?"

"She was fine—a few bumps and bruises, maybe a mild case of trauma—but her parents are already talking about suing everyone that's ever been born." The skinnier cop sighed.

When Tim came stumbling in a few hours later, poured out of a taxi, half in a blackout, the emergency room nurses initially mistook him for a patient. Then I guess he spit out my name and managed to fumble his ID out of his wallet.

Now he's passed out in the chair next to me, a bag of saline draining into his arm, waiting for a bed of his own. In the meantime, I'm breaking hospital policy.

My phone keeps buzzing with new emails and texts from reporters, lawyers, co-workers, and Edison customer service. But I'm ignoring all that.

I'm not even thinking about the conversation Tim and I are going to have when he wakes up and discovers he agreed to go into a rehab.

Instead, I'm on the BMW website, trying to decide if my new

M3 is going to be Alpine White, or Black Sapphire. One thing I already know for sure though. It's going to have a manual transmission.

ABOUT THE AUTHOR

William Delman's fiction has appeared in Daily Science Fiction, The Arcanist, Little Blue Marble, House of Zolo, Selene Quarterly, and other fine publications and anthologies. William's non-fiction—also known colloquially as his 'life.'—has appeared almost exclusively in Salem, MA for the last fourteen months. He plans to spend the next fourteen months in much the same way, but with slightly more social contact, thanks to the wonder of vaccines. Seriously, people, get jabbed and save some lives.

The Changed Man

Richard Zwicker

DA CAROLINA SOARES took a seat in the filled courtroom. Middle age and fatigue had barely diminished her dark, attractive face. She had mixed feelings about *The People vs. Jason Turner*, something she did not want when doing her job. On the surface, the case was open and shut. Eight months ago a drug-addled Jason Turner shot and killed Tariq Lari during a robbery. Six months later, Turner surrendered to the police and confessed. Turner's lawyer Angus Beetleman would dispute none of this. The area of contention would be the personality adjustment conducted on Turner in the interim. The defense would claim its client was a changed man, and therefore not responsible for the crime.

Soares was going through her own struggles about people changing. Last month her husband Gustavo admitted to a year-long affair, throwing her marriage into the impersonal hands of divorce lawyers. Gustavo insisted that *she*, not he, had changed as a result of her demanding career. "I'm not the one who broke his vows," she said, but then, maybe she had. After two children, now both in college, did she still cherish and love her husband? Certainly not in the same way. Everyone changes, but that didn't absolve them of their responsibilities. The defense in *The People vs. Jason*

Turner would argue it did, so it was not a surprise to Soares when it chose Nathanael Corzine as its first witness. She willed herself to be the best person to prosecute this case.

"Please state your profession," Beetleman said to the man in the witness seat. Beetleman wore a natty, expensive-looking gray suit, which obscured his short, dumpy body. His black curly hair had the uniform snarl of a poodle's fur. Corzine looked about 50, with gray hair, a trim beard, and a soft, non-athletic body.

"I'm a PA, a personality adjuster." Corzine said as clearly as a documentary film narrator. Corzine had made a name for himself as a tireless proponent of criminal rehabilitation through PA, a procedure he had spearheaded. Once a regular presence at protests against punitive incarceration, more recently he devoted his time to his operation. Though laws limited the degree of personality adjustment he could do on individual clients, the financial rewards had been significant.

"Could you tell the court exactly what a PA does?" asked Beetleman.

"I change people's psychological traits," said Corzine.

"And why would anyone hire you to do that?"

"We are all a mix of traits. I am able to increase the positive traits and diminish the negative ones."

The lawyer paced slowly in front of the audience. "Sounds interesting. If my teenage son were failing all his classes, could you do anything for him?"

"I could increase his motivation. If that was the reason he was doing poorly in school, his performance would improve."

"That's amazing. It sounds as if you can totally change who a person is."

"Objection! That's not what he said," Soares's smooth Brazilian accent rolled off her words despite three decades in America.

"I'll rephrase," said Beetleman. He stood directly in front of Corzine. "In your opinion, can you change a murderer into a law-abiding citizen?"

"It depends. I'm restricted by what I have to work with. I'm not sure I could change Jack the Ripper into Jack the Gardener, but I'd be willing to try."

"Did you operate on the defendant, Jason Turner?"

"Yes."

"Whose idea was that?"

Corzine shifted uncomfortably in his seat. "Turner's. At first, I refused, but he threatened my family if I didn't cooperate. Despite my lack of choice, I later came to see this as an opportunity to show the world the benefits of PA."

"Could you, in layman's terms, explain what you did for the defendant?"

"I took away his aggression, his addiction to controlled substances, and his low self-esteem. I replaced them with increased empathy, faith, and altruism."

"Was the operation a success?"

"Yes."

"Do you believe Jason Turner will ever again commit a crime?" asked Beetleman.

"No, unless he had another treatment that reintroduced his negative traits."

"Would you say the Jason Turner in this court room is a different man from the Jason Turner who committed murder and escaped from prison?"

"I would."

"Objection!" said Soares. "Leading the witness!"

"Objection sustained," said the stolid-faced elderly judge. "Strike the witness's response from the record. Mr. Beetleman, watch yourself."

Beetleman said that he had no more questions and sat down next to Turner, who watched the proceeding with curiosity. Soares rose and faced the witness.

"Mr. Corzine, it's a pleasure to meet you. I've read many of your essays on prison reform. In recent years, however, it seems personality adjusting has eclipsed your career as a reformer, at least in terms of writing and protesting. How much did you earn last year as a PA?"

"It's hard to say. I have an accountant that manages my affairs."

"Would *in excess of a million dollars* be a conservative estimate?"

Corzine coughed. "You'd have to ask my accountant."

"I would, but I'm sure you keep him or her busy. Let's talk about what *you* do. I'm not an expert on personality adjustment, but from what you've told the court, it seems to be a very powerful procedure. Almost too good to be true. Can you tell me why we don't just operate on every single ax-murderer, rapist, arsonist, and extortionist currently in jail and turn them into meek, bingo-playing members of a church guild?"

Corzine smiled, as if he expected the question. "My profession is controversial. Many believe we have no right to change a person's personality."

"Many believe it's a sin to gamble or that social networking is the end of private life as we know it, but those things are still allowed, as is PA. So I repeat, why don't you just change the personality of all prisoners?"

"I could, if funds could be found to pay me. It's not a simple procedure. Plus, there are legal limits to the changes I can make."

"What are those limits?"

"The government has adopted an evaluation scale, where a person's pre-op personality is rated at 100%, based on emotions, memories, abilities—everything that contributes to personality. That cannot be changed by more than a factor of 10%."

Soares folded her arms. "That doesn't seem like much. Since I left law school I've probably changed more than that without your expensive procedure. What I don't understand is how can you say Jason Turner is a different person as a result of your work if, according to law, he's still 90% the same person?"

"Because in the case of Jason Turner, I made changes in excess of 10%."

Soares hesitated. "You broke the law."

"As I said, he threatened to kill me."

"So we can add intent to murder to the resume of the man attorney Beetleman thinks we should release." She didn't want to ask the next question but if she didn't, Beetleman would.

"What percent would you say you changed Jason Turner's personality?" she asked.

"One hundred percent," Corzine said.

"One hundred percent? Are you saying there is nothing left of the pre-adjusted Jason Turner?"

"No, he has his memories. But one hundred percent means I changed all his propensities, including the ones that made him commit this crime."

IN THE FOLLOWING days Beetleman interrogated the owner of a produce supply company, for whom Turner drove a delivery truck, a cook in the soup kitchen where Turner volunteered three nights a week, as well as a neighbor. All praised the defendant as honest, dependable, and affable. Soares didn't have many questions for these witnesses, other than to confirm that Turner had lied about his name and kept his past a secret.

The prosecution, unable to find anyone since Turner's adjustment with a negative word to say about him, focused on his past. Soares called the former warden of the prison Turner had spent time in, Turner's cellmate, and the widow of Tariq Lari. They spoke of a dangerous, amoral man who should be locked up forever.

This relentless negativity left Turner shaken. At the start of a recess, in a voice loud enough for Soares to hear, he asked Beetleman, "How can they find me *not guilty?*"

"Soares needs to tie that person to you. We'll make sure she can't," Beetleman answered.

D URING TURNER'S CROSS-EXAMINATION, Beetleman asked questions that demonstrated his client's changed nature. On the courtroom widescreen he showed a picture of the man who murdered the pharmacist. That man had wild, shoulder-length hair, bushy eyebrows and a drooping mustache. A smirk disfigured his mouth and an unfocused gaze suggested intoxication. The contrast between that and the Jason Turner in the courtroom couldn't have been starker. The long hair was now short and thinning, his face clean-shaven, his eyebrows trimmed. Perhaps the biggest difference was the eyes, which appeared to be searching and kind.

"Mr. Turner, why did you force Dr. Corzine to operate on you?" asked Beetleman.

Turner grimaced. "Part of me wanted to avoid prosecution. However, I was also tired of not being in control of my life. I didn't want to be a thief and a drug addict, but I couldn't help myself. I saw the PA operation as my last chance."

Beetleman nodded. "What purpose do you believe would be served if you were returned to prison?"

"I understand the anger and frustration of those who knew and loved Tariq Lari. If I am found guilty, I will, of course, serve my sentence. That said, I don't believe years of incarceration would have a positive effect on my rehabilitation. My only wish is to make the world a better place. If I have to do that inside a prison, so be it, but I can do much more good outside."

"How?"

"As a positive role model, as someone who fully understands the consequences of criminal activity for the perpetrator, the victim, and society."

"Could you be more specific?" Beetleman asked.

"I volunteer at a soup kitchen. I run an anonymous blog where I give encouragement and advice to ex-convicts." He paused. "I go to church on Sundays."

Beetleman thanked the defendant. With a slight smile, he turned to Soares. "Your witness."

Soares rose slowly from her seat.

"Mr. Turner, according to my understanding of this procedure, you remember murdering Mr. Lari."

"I'll never forget it," Turner said.

"It seems to me, defense is basing its case on the idea that you—as you are now—did not commit the crime. So, I just want to confirm this. Despite the alterations made on you, your memory of the event is unchanged."

"As far as I can tell."

"Do you remember why you committed the crime?"

"I needed money. I wasn't thinking of the future. I hadn't planned on hurting anyone."

"Would it be correct to say that while your memory of the event was unchanged by the procedure, your view of it today has been?" asked Soares.

"Yes. I no longer see things as I did then."

"Would you say that today everything you do is rational?"

"No. I'm just less likely to do something negative because I am a less negative person. Today I am aware of the effects my actions have on others and I can sympathize."

"So you understand why friends and relatives of Mr. Lari would like to see you pay for your crime."

"Yes."

Soares gave Turner a long look. He met her eyes, smiling wanly.

"Your fingerprints and your memories are the same as the person who murdered an innocent man," she said. "You said you go to church on Sundays. Do you believe you have a soul?"

"I do."

"Do you believe the soul you have today and the soul you had when you killed Tariq Lari are separate?"

The courtroom was silent. "I'm still trying to understand what a soul is," said Turner.

Soares nodded. "Is it your belief that you and the murderer

of Tariq Lari are separate people, in the same way that you and I are separate people?"

Turned hesitated. "I guess that's for the court to decide."

Soares let his answer hang in the air. "I agree. Prosecution rests."

It was late in the afternoon. The judge dismissed everyone for the day in preparation for closing statements.

T HE NEXT MORNING, Beetleman addressed the court.

"In any criminal case, we are faced with questions. In *The People vs. Jason Turner*, many of the basic questions were answered before the trial began. Someone named Jason Turner killed Tariq Lari during the commission of a robbery. Someone named Jason Turner forced Dr. Corzine to conduct an illegal PA operation. I submit to you that someone *else* named Jason Turner sits before you today. We'd like every murderer to pay for his or her crime. In this case, that is not possible. Jason Turner, murderer, no longer exists. We could send Jason Turner, a sympathetic man who wishes nothing but the best for everyone, to prison in his place, but what would that accomplish? It wouldn't rehabilitate him, for this Jason Turner has done nothing wrong. It might appease those that cry for justice, just as sending anyone to prison for the crime might appease. But I would hope we are beyond the days when police, unable to come up with the perpetrator, round up the usual suspects. I think the overarching question in this trial is, what is the purpose of prison? To rehabilitate? This man *is* rehabilitated. Is it to keep a dangerous man off the street? This man poses no danger to anyone. Is it to feed our lust for an eye for an eye? The court is supposed to be the one place where we evaluate people and their acts rationally, in an unbiased manner. An eye for an eye is a negative, destructive desire. It is particularly out of place in evaluating Jason Turner, who doesn't have a negative or destructive thought in his head. We need good men, now more than ever. Please return Mr. Turner to his home, so he can continue to make the world a better place."

Beetleman brushed a tear from his eye as he returned to his

seat. Next to him, Turner fidgeted, and the members of the audience coughed, a few whispering to their neighbors. Soares allowed Beetleman's statements to settle, then approached the midway point of the floor separating audience and jury. She took a deep breath and faced the audience.

"Technological advances are wonderful things. I'm grateful to live in a time of bullet-trains, smart cars, and state-of-the-art medical care. It's a bit dizzying, however. I try to keep up with everything, but my ten-year-old nephew understands these things better than I do. According to my esteemed colleague, Nathanael Corzine can transform bad people into good. This may be the future, but I'm not sure it's the present. The one purpose of law that Mr. Beetleman did not address, because it didn't suit his purpose, was deterrence. What happens to our society if every time someone commits a heinous crime, individuals such as Nathanael Corzine operate on them and turn them into—as he likes to say—a different person? Like magic, the evil person is gone, replaced by a good citizen. The fact is, we are all changed by the passage of years. But what about the crime? What is the repercussion if we don't punish Jason Turner? I'll tell you: anyone can do anything and not be punished for it. We will become a nation of opportunists. And what if after we operate on a murderer and let him go free, he commits another murder? It wouldn't be the first time that desperation, greed, or fear caused a supposedly good person to commit a serious crime. Do we do *another* operation, tell him to behave himself, and send him on his way? Do you want to live in that kind of society, where a sadistic thug can kill your son or daughter with impunity? I don't, and I'm sure the survivors of Tariq Lari's family don't either. Jason Turner said he wasn't thinking about tomorrow or the repercussions when he committed murder. He wasn't thinking about responsibility or fairness. He was thinking only of himself. It is the duty of the court to hold criminals responsible for their crimes. That's justice. Without it, our society breaks down and we lose *everything*. Together we can make sure that does not happen. Thank you."

After Soares sat down and the jury was dismissed for delibera-
tions, the reserve of the audience broke down. Opinions about the
case fell like shots in a paintball war. A portion of the audience
favored the prosecution, seeing the defense's argument as more
unwarranted leniency toward criminals. Others noted the hum-
ble, caring demeanor of Jason Turner and wondered how prison
might change all that. After a few minutes the audience settled
into tapping on their phones.

Soares grabbed a coffee and called her divorce lawyer. Her husband and his attorney were still weighing Soares's offer. She wondered if a personality adjustment might have saved her marriage.
If the doubts, the restlessness, the recriminations could be elim-
inated somehow, could those battered old feelings of love thrive
again? Could she forgive his transgression? Could she forgive the
harsh words neither could never take back? She didn't see how.

When the jury was unable to come to a decision on *The People vs. Jason Turner* that day, the judge announced the proceedings
would resume at 9:00 the next morning.

A S THE COURTROOM filled up, a distraught Turner sat next to
his attorney and asked, "Can I change my plea?"

Beetleman looked at his client as if he were insane. "To what?"

"Guilty. I shouldn't be allowed to get away with this."

"Jason, let the court decide. That's what it's for."

It wasn't in Turner's nature to argue.

After about ninety minutes, a message was sent to the judge. A
verdict had been reached. As the jury filed in, its members seemed
liberated, arms swinging, a few smiles. The foreman handed a
piece of paper to the judge, who read it, then handed it back. He
asked the foreman to read the verdict.

"In *The people versus Jason Turner*, we, the jury, find the defendant innocent of all charges."

Turner's body drooped, while Beetleman patted him on the

shoulder. The lawyer then offered condolences to Soares. "Allow me to offer a last piece of evidence that didn't make it into the trial. This morning my client told me that he wanted to change his plea to guilty, that he shouldn't be allowed to get away with this. I convinced him to let the court decide. That's how innocent *he* is."

She shook her head, the toll of the case weighing on her face. "I think we're going to see more of this kind of defense. Congratulations for being on the cutting edge once again."

Dr. Corzine approached Jason Turner and shook his hand. "You can't beat this kind of advertising. If any of your former friends need some changes, send them my way."

Turner looked confused. "I don't have contact with those kind of people anymore."

Corzine smiled. "That's OK. I have a feeling they're going to have contact with me." He noticed Soares' glare and his smile vanished. He nodded and walked away.

As Corzine left the courthouse, a reporter asked him if verdict was a financial windfall for Corzine and the field of personality adjustment. He looked at the camera and said, "Social justice is my sole reward."

ABOUT THE AUTHOR

Richard Zwicker is an English teacher living in Vermont, USA, with his wife and beagle. His short stories have a appeared in "Hybrid Fiction," "Heroic Fantasy Quarterly," "Penumbra," and other semi-pro markets. Two collections of his short stories, "Walden Planet" and "The Reopened Cask," are available at select online retailers.

The Cobbler's Daughter

Dawn Vogel

WHEN CHETANA'S FATHER died, her uncles would not allow her to see the body. Their insistence made no sense. This was not the first time a member of the family had died. Chetana was only a toddler when her grandmother died, and yet she had helped to wash the body. Her brother had died two years previous, and she had accompanied his body to the funeral pyre, as was traditional.

Uncle Lochan said, "It is time for you to take on more responsibility in the workshop. We have many orders to fill this week, and if we all go to the funeral, how will they get done?" He handed her a stack of shoe leathers, designs already punched through the thin paper affixed to the leather.

Chetana sat down and began to sew. When the rest of the family left for the funeral, she watched them from the window of the shop, her pile of work left unfinished. She longed to follow them, but instead shed her tears for the loss of her father in his workshop, curled up on the bench where he shaped the shoes.

On Uncle Lochan's return, he was furious. "You have done nothing?" He shook his head. "You will never fill your father's *mojari*." As if to make his point, he took Chetana's father's shoes and perched them on the doorframe, a silent reminder.

Three months later, they received word that the young princess had outgrown her shoes, and the queen called upon all the cobblers in the kingdom to make her daughter a new pair.

"Might I make the princess's new *mojari*?" Chetana asked her uncle. Her mind was already awhirl with leather dyed midnight blue and thousands of tiny gems surrounding an embroidered crescent moon.

Uncle Lochan laughed. "No, but if you are very good, I'll let you take them to the palace to present them to the princess."

The day for the journey to the palace arrived, and Uncle Lochan said nothing. He had completed the *mojari* for the young princess. Chetana thought they were the ugliest pair of shoes she had ever seen, even worse than her own, which were developing holes where her feet stretched them out.

"Am I to take those shoes to the princess?" she asked.

Her uncle regarded her for a long while. "No, I do not think you shall. Your attitude is poor, and once you see the splendors of the palace, I fear you would not be content here with your family. I will go myself."

Chetana watched him go. Tears threatened to spill from her eyes, but she held them back and turned them into a fiery ball of anger in her chest. As soon as Uncle Lochan was out of sight, Chetana climbed atop her father's workbench, sitting just beside the door, and pulled his shoes down from the doorframe. They were much larger than her own shoes, but they would at least give her feet room to breathe. She didn't care if her uncle saw her wearing them. She slipped her feet into the soft worn leather.

In an instant, she was content. Though she could only shuffle about in the large shoes, they still made her believe she was taller and stronger and able to stand up to her uncle.

"Now listen here ..." she began. Her hand flew to her throat. The voice that had come out of her had sounded nothing like her own.

Chetana shuffled to the full length mirror in the workshop and gasped. She recognized her own eyes, and her clothing, but her face was different. Her chin had gone from pointy and narrow to a wide square shape. *The shape of Father's jaw.* But it was not that she had taken on her father's appearance. Instead, she looked like a boy.

She grimaced and lifted her *kameez* so she could peek inside of her *shalwar*. It was not just that she looked like a boy, she discovered. Somehow, she had become a boy.

Chetana kicked her father's shoes off, still standing before the mirror. Immediately, her appearance changed back to her own.

Her head swam. It was the shoes, there was no doubt about that. But did that mean her father had only masqueraded as a man? Surely his brothers would know if he had been born a girl, but they had never said a word of the sort. And then Chetana realized why her uncles had not allowed her to see her dead father.

The gemstones on the curled toes of the *mojari* gleamed in the lights of the shop. Chetana was drawn to them, so much more comfortable than her own shoes. How her life would be different if she were not the cobbler's daughter, but his son. She wondered if that was why Uncle Lochan had made such a point about putting the shoes up and out of reach.

Chetana picked up her father's *mojari* and put them back on the door frame. Then she began digging through the piles of leather in the workshop for a similar shade.

BY THE TIME a year had passed, Chetana had learned much about the business of cobbling. Her uncle still had her work only on the decorative elements of the *mojari* he sold, but she had been working on making a pair of shoes in secret. They looked nearly identical to her father's *mojari*—she had even taken the time to wear them in the rain and dust to make sure they were worn out in the right places. Her feet were growing, and now were almost the same size as her father's feet had been. With just a bit of straw in the toes, she could wear the new shoes comfortably.

Chetana's feet were not the only growing feet. Again word came from the palace that the princess had outgrown her shoes. And again, Chetana asked Uncle Lochan if she might make the princess a pair of *mojari*. This year, her idea was inspired by a trip the family had taken to the seashore—the shoes would be simple natural colored leather, like the sand, but their adornment would be the gorgeous blues and greens of the sea. She had even brought back a handful of small shells she could use to decorate the shoes, having drilled delicate holes into each one with a blunted sewing needle.

"You are not a cobbler, Chetana," Uncle Lochan said. "You are a cobbler's daughter. I will allow you to choose what design you sew on the princess's shoes, but I will make them. And if you are well behaved, perhaps you can come along with me to deliver the shoes to the palace."

Chetana agreed, and planned to use the design she had in mind. But the *mojari* her uncle made were a dark and muddy green, and looked atrocious with the designs and colors she had chosen. She rubbed the outside of the shoes with sand, trying to change the color to be more like the sea, but the sand only served to make the *mojari* dirty. She chose an elaborate design to cover up as much of the dirty green as she could, and stayed up late into the night, neglecting work on her own shoes so she could finish the princess's shoes instead.

When they were complete, Uncle Lochan took half an hour examining the shoes. His fat fingers probed Chetana's tiny stitches, trying to unravel them. But try as he might, he could not. Finally, he nodded. "Very well. You have behaved admirably, and I have no desire to make the journey to the palace this year. You may take these to present to the princess."

Chetana smiled and thanked her uncle. But making the journey on her own would be dangerous—a young woman should not travel the roads of the kingdom without an escort. She looked at her father's *mojari*, still perched on the door frame, where they remained except for late at night, when she needed to make sure she had rendered a part of their design correctly.

She did not go to sleep that night, as she had additions to the pair of shoes she had made as a replacement for her father's shoes. When the night was darkest, she slipped through the workshop with her handcrafted shoes. Uncle Lochan snored in his chair near the hearth, an empty jug of *sura* on its side nearby.

Chetana was not yet tall enough to reach the top of the door frame without assistance. Uncle Lochan's feet rested on the step-stool she normally used. Her only option was to move her father's workbench, now put away on the other side of the workshop.

The bench was too heavy for her to lift alone. When it needed to be moved during the course of the workday, she and Uncle Lochan moved it together. She could drag it across the floor if he were not around, but she knew the noise it made would wake even those sleeping deeper in the house.

She spied a wooden box that held shoe leathers. If she turned it on end, it would be almost as tall as the workbench, and she could stand on tiptoe to reach the *mojari* above the door. She emptied the box of its contents and placed it beneath the shoes.

Chetana tested the strength of the box with one foot at first, and then added her full weight to the box. It creaked ominously, but held her. Uncle Lochan's snores continued. She released a slow breath before stretching toward the shoes. Their supple leather lay just out of reach of her fingertips. She stretched again, with more force than the previous attempt. The box teetered beneath her, and she lost her grip on her handmade shoes. She grabbed the door frame with one hand just as the box clattered to the workshop floor.

Uncle Lochan snorted and stirred. Chetana's could drop to the floor and hope she landed quietly on the toppled box, or continue to hang from the door frame. She chose the latter, watching her uncle over her shoulder, eyes wide with fear.

Chetana's arm burned with the strain of holding herself up.

It seemed like an eternity before her uncle turned his head away from the doorway and resumed his snoring. Chetana grabbed her father's shoes with her free hand and let go of the door frame, spreading her legs wide so she landed straddling the box she had used as a stepstool.

She sighed as she landed soundlessly. Setting her father's shoes to the side, she reset the box and prepared to put her replacement shoes atop the door frame.

WEARING HER FATHER'S *mojari*, the long walk from home to the palace seemed less arduous. She had left before the sun came up, slipping out of the house before Uncle Lochan noticed her shoes or her sudden transformation into a boy. She had borrowed her father's best suit of clothing, as her own hardly fit her when she wore the magical *mojari*. Chetana looked, for all the world, like a young man on a very important errand.

As she walked, she couldn't help but marvel at how her father had lived his entire life in disguise. Had no one noticed he always wore his shoes, even indoors? Suddenly, Chetana felt faint. Surely it would not be permissible for her to wear her shoes into the palace.

She nearly turned back then and there. The only thing that kept her moving toward the palace was the certainty that Uncle Lochan would be furious with her if she did not deliver the shoes he had made to the princess.

Her first sight of the palace took Chetana's mind off of the embarrassment that surely awaited her when she arrived. The gleaming white walls shone in the noonday sun, larger and more beautiful than any building in the town where she was born. Above the low outer wall, trees and tall flowering bushes splashed a riot of color in stark contrast to the clean white lines of the palace.

Chetana took a deep breath as she approached the guards at the gate to the palace. "I come with shoes for the princess," she murmured.

One of the guards nodded. "She is receiving cobblers in the Western Garden."

Chetana's heart leapt. In the garden, no one would insist upon her taking her shoes off. Her secret would remain safe. She thanked the guard and nearly ran to the garden on the western side of the palace.

The Western Garden was abuzz with activity. Dozens of cobblers, some of whom had brought retinues, waited in a long line that snaked amongst the ornamental architecture and paths between a variety of flowers unlike anything Chetana had ever seen.

A young man with a scroll and quill approached her and looked her over. Chetana held the shoes forward, and the young man snorted. "Who made these shoes?"

"Ah, uh ..." Chetana stammered. Her father had never named his shop. It was the only one in their town, so there had been no need. She used the first thing she could think of. "The Household of Sashi."

The young man's eyes widened. "Sashi? We thought he had died."

"He did. His brother, and, uh, myself, have carried on his work."

"Hmm, brother and son, very well then." He leaned close to Chetana's ear and whispered as he gestured to the other cobblers nearby. "You're going to have to work harder if you want the princess to choose your shoes."

Chetana took a moment to look at what the other shoemakers had brought, and her heart sank. Uncle Lochan had made shoes fit for someone who lived in their town, not a princess. Around her were shoes with delicately cut leather, made to resemble a butterfly perched on the back of a pair of gold embroidered *mojari*. Another pair had iridescent peacock feathers layered atop one another to give the shoes they adorned wings.

She shook her head. Even her own idea would have looked shabby in comparison. As she began to turn away from the throng, settled on returning home, the young man tapped her on the shoulder.

"What's your name?" he hissed.

"Uh, Chetan," Chetana mumbled. She grimaced as soon as it had escaped her lips. Though there were boys called Chetan, it wasn't very good as an alternate name. Anyone from her town who heard about it would know right away that she was simply Chetana in disguise.

But the young man wasn't from her town. And as the princess and her mother approached Chetana, the young man called out, "May I present to you Chetan, of the Household of Sashi."

The assembled cobblers murmured and craned their necks to try to get a glimpse of Chetan. But Chetana barely noticed. Her gaze was fixed on the princess.

Chetana had always been long of limb and face. The princess had a perfectly round face, and the plump body of a girl who had never worked. But she carried herself in such a way that she was radiant. The yellow silk of her *sari* complimented her soft brown skin and jet black hair that twined across her shoulder in an elaborate braid.

The princess's gaze settled on the shoes Chetana held awkwardly in front of her. She pursed her lips, and then looked up into Chetana's eyes. And then the princess smiled.

If the princess had been radiant before, now she outshone the sun itself. It took all of Chetana's willpower to not fall to her knees, weeping at the beauty of the princess.

Only the princess's soft voice brought Chetana's mind back to reality. "Thank you, but I believe they are too large." The princess arched one delicate foot toward Chetana. "Perhaps next year."

Perhaps next year. Those three words echoed in Chetana's mind for the entire journey back home. Already she was concocting a plan. She had made one pair of shoes while her uncle slept. Another pair, even *mojari* truly fit for a princess, was within the reach of her talents. *Next year*, she thought.

I N THE YEARS that followed, Chetana worked tirelessly through the day, helping Uncle Lochan run the shoe shop. And then she worked on through the night to make a pair of *mojari* for the princess. Each year, the queen announced the princess had outgrown her shoes, and each year, Chetana donned her father's *mojari* to take the shoes she had made to the princess. Uncle Lochan always sent a pair of shoes with her as well, but those she tucked into the bottom of her bag.

Each year, the princess favored Chetan with a smile, but she never selected the shoes Chetana had made.

In the year the princess and Chetana were both to have their seventeenth birthday, rumors came to the village that the princess was in search of not only shoes, but also a suitor. They said she would choose her future husband from among the cobblers who brought *mojari* to the palace.

Uncle Lochan scoffed. "Why would the princess marry a common cobbler?" But Chetana watched him select the leather for the princess's shoes even more carefully this year. And when he brought them to Chetana to embroider, he watched over her like a hawk, making sure every stitch was perfect.

Chetana took months to decide what shoes she would make for the princess that year. She also thought for all that time about what might happen if the princess chose the shoes she made. Surely, if that happened, Chetana would be asked to come inside the palace, and would have to take off her shoes. And then the truth of her gender would be revealed.

She considered not making a pair of shoes to enter into the competition. She could take Uncle Lochan's shoes to the palace, and if the princess chose them, then Chetana could direct the girl to her uncle. But the thought of the beautiful princess marrying to her uncle, who had already buried two wives, seemed abhorrent. Perhaps she should make the shoes, even if she could not marry the princess.

The thought of marrying the princess caused a sudden warm

stirring in Chetana's belly. At first, she did not know what to make of it. But then she noticed the feeling came whenever a young woman who looked like the princess walked past, or came into the shop. Though it was not the same as when she thought about the princess herself, she began to realize that her feelings were adoration for the princess's beauty. She wondered if that might be something like love.

Chetana settled on a simple design for the princess's shoes, yellow leather the color of the dress that had so flattered the princess's skin, with a pattern of interlocking hearts in a simple embroidery pattern. Though they did not have the flash that many of the *mojari* made for the princess had, they were elegant and lovely. *Just like her*, Chetana thought.

Getting the embroidery just right was difficult. Chetana stayed up many long nights, working on the shoes and thinking of the princess.

One morning, she was awakened with a rough shake of her shoulder. Uncle Lochan glared at her from beneath dark eyebrows.

"What are those shoes for?" he asked.

Chetana had fallen asleep in the workshop, on her father's bench. The princess's *mojari* were in front of her, in plain sight. She tried to snatch them up, but her uncle grabbed her arms and repeated his question.

"I made them for the princess," she cried.

"For the princess? Why? She is searching for a suitor."

Chetana looked up at her uncle. His gaze flickered toward the shoes Chetana had put atop the doorframe, in place of her father's actual *mojari*. Then he looked back at her, and the two of them stared at one another for a long time.

Finally, Uncle Lochan spoke. "You are not a cobbler. You are only a cobbler's daughter. No princess will wear shoes you have made, let alone want to marry you. I will journey to the palace this year. You will stay here." He picked up the shoes Chetana had slaved over and threw them into the smoldering hearth.

Chetana wailed and rushed to the fireplace. The smell of singed leather reached her nostrils. She thrust her hands into the embers, barely feeling their heat. The beautiful yellow shoes were now gray with soot, blackened in places where the embers had already scorched them. "Why, uncle? Why must you be so cruel?"

"The world is cruel, Chetana. Get used to it."

As SOON AS Uncle Lochan left the next morning, Chetana emerged from her bedroom. She had made the best of the damage instead of sleeping. Where the shoes had been scorched, she had cut out the leather, shaping the holes into hearts that matched those embroidered. Then she added more heart-shaped holes to make the *mojari* look like they had been fashioned that way originally. All that remained was to clean the last traces of soot from the leather, and to get to the palace by nightfall, without Uncle Lochan seeing her there.

Chetana paused in front of the mirror, her father's *mojari* on her feet. She looked every bit a young man, except her hair was far too long to be fashionable for a young man. She stepped out of the shoes and ran her hands through her long, straight hair. It had not been cut since her father had died.

Tears rolled down her face as she sharpened her scissors. It took a long time to saw through the first handful of hair. The dark brown strands spilled across the workshop floor, but Chetana did not bother to sweep them up. She would not be returning from the palace. She would offer her services to the princess, and if the princess did not want a royal cobbler, then Chetana would continue onward and find a village in need of someone to make them shoes.

It was nearing noonday when Chetana began her journey to the palace. She hurried as fast as she could, clutching the princess's *mojari* to her chest. The clouds were tinged pink and orange by the time she reached the palace.

The same young man with quill and scroll who had introduced

Chetan to the assembled cobblers and palace residents the first time Chetana had come to the palace was on duty. He seemed to recognize Chetan but only frowned.

"Am I too late?" Chetan asked.

"No, but there is already a representative of the Household of Sashi who has presented his shoes to the princess."

"Can I not present mine as well?"

The scribe frowned. "In the past, the princess has seen only one pair of *mojari* from each shop. Wait here, please."

Chetana's fingers worried over the largest of the heart-shaped holes in the shoes while the scribe was away. Lost in contemplation, she hardly noticed when someone sat down beside her on the bench.

"Are those for me?" a soft voice said.

Chetana looked up and found herself face to face with the princess. None of the princess's retinue was anywhere to be seen. Trying to hide her shock, Chetana said, "Yes, of course, but the scribe ... my uncle ..."

The princess tilted her head to the side, a small frown creasing her brow. "May I try them on?"

Chetana nodded, pushing the shoes across the bench toward the princess.

The princess smiled and removed her old *mojari*. She slipped her delicate feet into the pair Chetana had made. A satisfied smile replaced her frown. The princess's gaze met Chetana's.

"I would know your name."

"I am ..." Chetana began. Then she shook her head. She could not lie to the princess. She rose from the bench and stepped out of her father's *mojari*. "I am but a cobbler's daughter. I am Chetana, daughter of Sashi."

The princess gasped. She looked at Chetana's face, then at the shoes, and then back at Chetana's face again. "You're ... Sashi ... oh dear," she stammered.

"No, no," Chetana said. I'm not Sashi. Sashi was my father.

Or perhaps my mother. The shoes ... there's magic in those shoes. I'm sorry if I deceived you. I just wanted to make shoes you would like."

The princess smiled as Chetana spoke, and finally quieted the cobbler's daughter with a single finger placed on her lips. "You didn't deceive me. I knew all along. The shoes you make are far more delicate and beautiful than anything made by men." She paused, a blush creeping over her features. "I would like for you to make my shoes for me."

"But what about a suitor?" Chetana asked. "Won't you still need one of those?"

"I don't particularly want one. Not yet, anyway." The princess smiled shyly. "Perhaps someday, when we have gotten to know each other, you could be my suitor. Though I suppose I would have to pass a law to allow you to wear your shoes indoors."

ABOUT THE AUTHOR

Dawn Vogel's academic background is in history, so it's not surprising that much of her fiction is set in earlier times. By day, she edits reports for historians and archaeologists. In her alleged spare time, she runs a craft business, co-runs a small press, and tries to find time for writing. Her steampunk adventure series, Brass and Glass, is available from Def-Con One Publishing. She is a member of Broad Universe, SFWA, and Codex Writers. She lives in Seattle with her husband, author Jeremy Zimmerman, and their herd of cats. Visit her at http://historythatnev-erwas.com.

Julia Dream

David Taub

L EANDER STOOD OUTSIDE the entrance to the strange bar, one eye on his watch, one eye on the passersby walking down Pearl Street. He'd been living in Boulder for over four years now and couldn't believe he'd never seen this place before, even if it was the very definition of a nondescript hole-in-the-wall.

One minute.

He was supposed to meet his friends at the Downer, but he couldn't face them tonight. He was just too tired of everything.

Five seconds. 56...57...58...59...midnight. Happy birthday to me, he thought and walked into the bar.

It was smoky and dark, and even if there were people everywhere, it didn't feel crowded. The jukebox was playing Sultans of Swing and a few people were even dancing, or at least swaying rhythmically.

"Give me a shot of whatever," Leander said, slapping down two twenties and his license on the countertop. "Then keep them coming until the money runs out or I give up and leave. You can keep whatever's left."

The bartender eyed his license suspiciously, looking back and forth between it and Leander and even checking the clock. "What year is it?" he finally asked.

"1992", Leander replied, returning the bartender's suspicious stare.

The bartender shrugged and gave him back his license. "I lose track sometimes," he said, then took the money and poured a shot of tequila.

"Shouldn't you be celebrating with your friends?" the bartender asked while cutting a slice of lime to put next to the shot glass.

Leander laughed. "My friends? Sure, let's celebrate with my friends." He raised the glass. "This one's for Sarah, my first girlfriend. She fell off a cliff in Hawaii and died when she was 14." He shot back the liquid, quickly biting into the lime just as the burning sensation engulfed his throat and mouth.

Another shot appeared just as he slammed down the first empty glass. Whisky this time. "And this one," he said, raising the new drink, "is for Kyle. My best friend for two years until schizophrenia ate his mind." He shot back the whisky, slamming down the glass a bit harder this time. "Have you ever watched someone's mind and personality disassemble before your eyes?"

The bartender shook his head while pouring a new shot of vodka. "Can't say that I have."

A twisted smile spread across Leander's lips. "How about this one?" He picked up the vodka shot, waving it around as he talked. "How about one for my friend John who masturbated to death last year. No. Fucking. Joke." He shot back the liquid, which burned a lot less now than the others had. "It's even got a fucking name. Autoerotic asphyxiation. Go figure."

"You know, I think I might have just the thing for you." The bartender unlocked a heavy metal door beneath the bar and pulled out a weird looking bottle, something out of a fantasy movie, with a bright green liquid sloshing around inside.

"Absinthe?" Leander asked, his curiosity piqued.

The bartender shook his head, pouring a shot. "You won't have heard of this, but I promise you'll enjoy it."

Leander shrugged and shot back the liquid, tired of listening to his own whining. Expecting more fire, he was surprised to feel a cool and smooth liquid slide down his throat. Soothing. "It tastes like ... like ..." He licked his lips, trying to get a handle on what he was experiencing. "It tastes like a full moon on a clear summer night."

"Why the hell did I say that?" he mumbled and stood up from the bar before he realized what he was doing. Suddenly very clear-headed, he wanted nothing more than to go home and sleep.

E VERYTHING FROZE, A surrealistic mishmash of distorted people and places. It was Leander's first lucid dream, the first time he had ever become aware in the middle of a dream.

"Are you a ghost?"

Leander spun around. "Who said that?" he demanded. He was supposed to have control in a lucid dream. He shouldn't be hearing strange voices.

"Are you a ghost?" A woman dissolved into focus right in front of him. Smooth, dark, ebony skin. Hair dyed bright green and woven into tight cornrows. She was stunningly beautiful.

"Are you part of my dream?" he asked. He wanted to look at the rest of her, but was captivated by her eyes. She looked so awake, a person who really saw the world around her. Who saw things as they were and not just the mirage most people lived in.

She laughed at his question. He melted, thought his heart would burst. It was such an honest laugh, uninhibited. She was who she was. And he was already in love. With a dream.

"I thought you might be part of mine," she said, keeping her eyes locked on his. "But you don't fit. So I thought maybe you were a ghost."

Leander shook his head. "I don't believe in ghosts."

That smile again. "I don't either. But my lack of belief might not stop them from being real."

It was his turn to laugh, and he could finally look away, look her over. She wore jeans and a loose fitting t-shirt, both covered

THE BEST OF MYTHIC: A SCIENCE FICTION & FANTASY MAGAZINE | VOLUME ONE

in paint, as were her hands. Her fingernails were short, an after-thought. Her hands were busy, tools to be used, not put on display for men. They were her hands, and hers alone. And they were all the more beautiful for it.

She was impossible. A fantasy figure cooked up by his depression, or some drug that bartender had put in his drink. But he didn't care. Right now, right here, real or not, he didn't want to lose her.

"What's your name?" he asked, looking her in the eyes again.

"Julia."

"No. Fucking. Way." He shook his head, snorting more than laughing.

She frowned and he thought he would die. Every emotion she felt echoed in him a thousand times stronger. He had hurt her a little bit, and her pain cut him like a knife.

"What's wrong with my name?"

"Nothing, it's perfect," Leander said, and meant it. "There's an obscure Pink Floyd song, one of my favorites. It's called Julia Dream. I'm not going to torture you with my singing, but it goes something like this: Julia dream, dreamboat queen, queen of all my dreams."

Her smile was back. "Sounds like a nice song. I'll see if I can find it on Spotify when I wake up." She paused, her smile fading slightly. "If I remember."

Leander had no idea what Spotify was—maybe it was a collection of mixed tapes or something. But his focus was much more on the last thing she had said. "Am I so forgettable?" he asked.

"Hardly." She was looking him up and down now, and he liked the expression on her face. She clearly liked what she saw. "But I never remember my dreams," she added.

"I don't think this is a normal dream," he replied and moved closer to her. Dream moved. More like floating. He just thought about being closer to her and suddenly he was. And now he could see the fading scars on the underside of her arm, just below the wrist. Parallel cuts. Obviously self-inflicted. He'd had other friends who'd cut themselves. All for different reasons. Always about pain. You don't get clarity of sight without walking through the fire.

She saw him staring at her arm and quickly pulled it away.

"Wait," he said. "You don't have to hide them from me."

"They make people uncomfortable." She looked down at her feet while she spoke, a slight tremor in her voice. "I don't like the way they look at me afterwards."

People are idiots. "It won't make me uncomfortable. I promise."

Julia looked up at him tentatively and then slowly held out her arm.

"May I?" he asked, reaching towards her hand.

She nodded and he took her wrist gently in his left hand. With his right hand he brushed his fingers lightly over her scars, the tips of his fingers barely touching her skin. The gentlest touch humanly possible. The softest caress. She closed her eyes as he moved his fingers slowly from her wrist to the inside of her elbow, skin barely touching skin the whole way. He could see she enjoyed it and that lit a fire inside him. Bending over, he brushed his lips every so lightly over her scars. Breathed on them. And then it was a soft kiss. It spiraled out of control from there.

The sex was impossibly good, as only dream sex can be. It was more than just physical. They had some kind of mystical connection in the dream, a sharing of feelings and emotions. Her pleasure was his pleasure. His pleasure was hers. It was almost unbearable how good it felt. Terrifying. Addicting. He never wanted it to end. But everything does, eventually.

He was still painfully hard when he woke, his underwear dripping from repeated orgasms during the night. Getting up, showering, getting ready. Going through the motions of life. It was tedium upon tedium.

Facing the day was a nightmare. Sitting through his university classes, pure torture. This was the real dream, last night was reali-

153

ty. All he wanted to do was go back to sleep, back to her. Somehow he knew she'd be there again.

And she was.

THE SECOND NIGHT she showed him her art. It was as amazing as he knew it would be. She poured herself into her paintings, all her pain, her joy, everything she truly saw. It was the kind of art that could change people. Help them see the world differently. It was transformative. But she was too scared to show anyone else. So she worked, and she created, and she hid it all away.

They talked about life, philosophy, religion, reality, no corner left unturned. They talked about all the big questions, the big fears. And in between, they made love. Again and again.

This went on for four nights in a row. And somehow, through it all, they never once talked about any personal details of their lives aside from her art. It was like the rest of their lives was the dream, and the only reality was what they created together. But nothing ever lasts.

Leander was afraid of going to sleep on the fifth night. He wanted more than anything to see her again. To touch her again. But he knew what he had to do. Had known it for a while now, though he tried to pretend he didn't.

"Sometimes you matter most by realizing you don't really matter," he said to himself in the mirror. Trying to believe it. He was being selfish. He wanted to be with her. But he also loved her and her happiness came first.

There was no dream sex that night. Just a long talk about her paintings. Him trying to convince her to show her work. To change the world in her own way. In the end she agreed, and that was the last time he ever saw her.

LEADER WATCHED THE second hand on the clock tick towards twelve. 58...59...noon. It was now twelve hours since he'd turned 45 and nothing had really changed. He just kept getting older. Or perhaps it was only four hours, if you count the time difference between Colorado and the café in Amsterdam he was sitting in.

There was a time when he thought happiness was possible. When he might have had the strength to leave the past behind. But three marriages and five careers later, it felt like he'd just come full circle back to nothing.

He'd spent a few years teaching English here in Amsterdam, and that had given him purpose for a while. Made him feel like he was doing something important. But overwhelming bureaucracy and a stressful home situation forced him to give that up years ago. He'd stayed in Amsterdam after his divorce, having become a citizen himself by then. Now he made a living translating between Dutch and English. It paid the bills, but that was about it.

A bottle of pills sat on the nightstand by his bed. A silent debate he had every morning and every evening. A debate he knew he was losing. It was harder and harder to find things to put in the *Why not?* column.

Leander glanced at the clock again. Jamal should be here soon, he thought, then mentally slapped himself. No, that's not her name anymore. Habits could be hard to break, and he didn't want her to think he had a problem with her transition. He felt terrible when he realized he didn't actually know her new name. Why am I just thinking of this now? I'm such an idiot!

Jamal had been one of his students when he was teaching English to teenagers. One of his favorite students, actually. He was skinny and nervous, and a bit weird, and he was bullied a lot during breaks. Leander had given him a safe zone in his classroom and they would spend the time talking about all kinds of random things. The kid was smart. And deep. He cared about bigger issues than most of the other teenagers who were focused on clothing, social media and sex. Leander had always hoped things had gone well for him later in life.

They were friends on Facebook, and so Leander saw small

glimpses now and then. He knew that Jamal had come out as a woman at some point—which must have been extra difficult considering how religious his parents were. She had moved to another city and changed her name, hiding her identity for safety reasons—which was probably why he didn't know it! He suddenly felt a little bit better. But only a little bit.

In a bout of self-pity, Leander had recently posted an old picture of himself on Facebook. It was from his early 20's, kicking around a hacky sack in a park. His former student had commented on the picture almost immediately, using her old Jamal account, "Is that really you?!?!" That stung. Twenty years will take its toll on anyone, no matter how hard you try and fight it. That six pack was long gone, as was that smooth skin and full, curly hair. He knew that. He just didn't like having it thrown back in his face. It was hard enough to accept as it was.

He tried to play it off with a joke. "Yeah, hard to believe, ain't it?"

She said she was going to be in Amsterdam and suggested meeting for coffee. And so here he was, waiting for her to show up. Hoping he'd recognize her. She was 24 now, and he had trouble recognizing most of his former students at that age. A gender change was not going to make it easier. He really didn't want to hurt her feelings.

Ten minutes later, he figured out her name.

It hit him like a shockwave. He spilled his coffee. Lost his breath. His world turned upside down. Reality turned inside out.

Julia had just walked into the café and waved at him.

S HE WAS SITTING across from him, talking excitedly about something, but he couldn't hear what she was saying. The thunder in his ears was too loud. His heart was racing so fast he thought it might explode.

Green cornrows, smooth ebony skin, just as young and beautiful as she was twenty years ago in his dreams. It was more impossible now than it was back then.

"Leander! Are you listening to me?"

"What?" he mumbled, still trying to find a footing back to reality. Everything was wrong. Impossible.

"I know who you are!" she was almost yelling at him now. "I recognized you from your picture. From when you were my age. On Facebook."

He shook his head. "What do you mean you recognized me? You weren't even born then."

The sudden doubt on her face cut him to the quick. "You don't remember...the dreams?" Her voice was only a whisper now, her lower lip trembling slightly as she spoke.

He knew she was wondering if she'd just made a terrible mistake. If it had all been in her head. And for a moment, he thought it might be best to let her think that it had. The truth would only make it worse. More heartbreak. It was unbearable. The literal girl of his dreams turns out to be real, but she's twenty years younger than him. A former student! He was old. Ashamed of the way he looked, of what he'd become. She was young and beautiful, just starting her life. It was insane. It was unfair. Un. Fucking. Fair.

In the end, he couldn't lie to her. Not to her. "I remember you," he said, his eyes watering. "I don't understand how, but I remember you."

Her smile lit up the room like a supernova. "My paintings are being shown in a major gallery. I'm the youngest artist to ever get a showing! It's all thanks to you!"

Leander wiped his eyes and took a deep breath, pushing down his feelings. A skill honed over the years. "I'm really happy for you, Julia. But that was him, not me. It was a lifetime ago."

A noise by the entrance caused Julia to glance over her shoulder, a shadow momentarily darkening her face. She relaxed when she saw it was just another customer.

Leander realized that she'd been subtly glancing out the window the whole time she'd been sitting there. "Is everything okay?" he asked, concern for her momentarily pushing aside all other feelings.

She shrugged. "I've been in the city a few days now. It's dangerous for me. I might be recognized."

"That's...," he started to say, but she cut him off.

"My life. My choice. This, right now, is about us. Forget everything else. Okay?"

He nodded, "Okay."

"Good. Now take my hand," she said, putting her hand on the table, palm up, her scars on full display, but with no shame this time. The same scars he had caressed and kissed so many years ago.

"I can't."

Julia frowned, her hand starting to close. "Is it because you think of me as a man?"

"God no!" Leander shook his head vehemently. "You're too young."

"I'm an adult," she said, opening her hand back up. "I have been for years. I've even lived together with a man for over a year. That's over now, but it was serious while it lasted. We almost got married. I am an adult. Take my hand."

He couldn't do it. "You were my student."

"And you were wonderful to me back then, as a teacher. You helped me more than you know. But I am not that small boy anymore. That was a very long time ago. Take my hand."

Could he do it? Was it possible? No, she deserved so much more than he could ever offer. He had his chance, it wasn't her fault he'd fucked it up. It was her turn now. He knew she would do better.

And yet, there she was, right in front him. Real. Waiting for him to take her hand. The way she looked at him made him feel so young. So alive. Like he still had value. Like he mattered.

Maybe. Just for a little while. Just until he felt strong again. Maybe he deserved a little happiness. Just a little.

"Jamal!" The angry scream snapped him out of his thoughts. Then everyone else started screaming as a large man with a knife starting running towards their table.

He saw the terror and recognition in Julia's eyes even before she turned around.

And then everything happened so fast.

The table overturned. Cups and plates crashed onto the floor.

Julia screamed.

Leander was jumping towards her. Shielding her.

Pain!

More pain!

More screaming.

The angry man was swearing, being held down by customers and staff.

Leander lay on the floor, unable to move. He felt cold. Tired. It was hard to focus. He knew he was dying.

Julia's face appeared in front of his, tears streaming down her cheeks. "Why?" she asked. "You saved me as a teacher, you saved me as a lover, and now you saved me again. Why didn't you let me save you this time?"

Leander smiled, and, with the little strength he had left, reached up and gently brushed a tear from her cheek. "But don't you see? You did save me. You gave me everything today. Everything."

About the Author

David Taub lives in Sweden where he works as a university lecturer and rock climbs as much as possible. His first horror novel, Comes the Dark, hit the shelves in March 2006, and his short stories have appeared in Cosmos, Andromeda Spaceways Magazine, Farthing, Neo-opsis, Dark Recesses Press, Nocturnal Ooze, Coyote Wild, Beyond Centauri, POW!erful Tales, Mythic Magazine, Mitrania (Swedish), and 9 Magazine (Greek).

The Mummy from R'lyeh

John Michael Greer

EIGHT MONTHS OF the year, Kingsport huddles between the high gray crags of Kingsport Head and the cold waters of the Atlantic. Mist comes flowing in from the sea most mornings, drifting up the narrow streets past houses that were already old when the Revolutionary War began. Later in the day, as the mist dissolves, heavy gray clouds roll in from the sea to march implacably overhead, flinging down rain or snow according to the season. In the half-light, the old families of Kingsport celebrate their archaic mysteries, and the Terrible Old Man leaves his silent cottage on Water Street to buy groceries with centuries-old Spanish doubloons.

Come May, though, the sun straggles through the clouds more days than otherwise, lights go on in the hotels on Harbor Street, and the proprietors of tourist traps on the waterfront give uneasy glances toward the Terrible Old Man's cottage and stock their shops for the summer. The Friday before Memorial Day, the roads into Kingsport fill with tourists, the carts selling shaved ice and corn dogs roll onto Harbor Street's sidewalks, and the season begins.

A week into the season, as afternoon spread golden over the old town, a brown station wagon picked its way up Green Lane and turned left into the driveway of a brick mansion of Georgian date. The moment the car rolled to a stop, two girls came pelting out the door to welcome it. The back doors of the car popped open an instant later, and a girl and a boy sprang out to meet them. Thereafter, adults joined them: from the car, a broad-shouldered man with sandy hair and a short beard, and a woman with brown curly hair and a long skirt that didn't quite move as though it concealed human legs; from the house, a stocky man in an old-fashioned black suit, and then a short plain woman with a mop of unruly mouse-colored hair.

"Hi, Laura," said the woman from the house, shaking hands. "Hi, Owen. Sennie, Barney, good to see you both again."

"Hi, Aunt Jenny," the two children chorused.

"I hope the trip down wasn't too difficult," she went on.

"Not a bit," said Owen Merrill, grinning. "I suspect you had something to do with that."

Jenny Chaudronnier, who was among other things the greatest sorceress of that age of the world, smiled and said nothing. Meanwhile Laura went to the rear door of the car and murmured something, and another got out: a woman with straight black hair drawn back hard into a braid. Despite the warmth of the day, she had a long scarf wrapped around the lower half of her face.

Jenny came over to her at once. "You must be Anne Gilman," she said. "Welcome to Kingsport. Can we offer you tea?"

"Thank you," came the muffled response. "Maybe—maybe in a while."

Jenny turned. "Michaelmas—"

"I took the liberty of ordering tea in the lilac parlor, Miss Jenny," said the man in the black suit. "Mr. Merrill, if I may see to your car and luggage?"

"Thank you," said Owen, and handed over the keys.

I T'S ONE OF those things," said Laura. They were sitting in the lilac parlor as evening deepened and the lights of Kingsport came on one by one. "Anne's family fled Innsmouth during the troubles in 1928. They went to Harrisonville, New Jersey, and pretended to be ordinary humans. Everything went well for a couple of generations, and then Anne came along. She spent her entire childhood in a room in the attic."

"That's really sad," Jenny said. "Did her family finally contact someone?"

"Not exactly." Laura sipped tea. "When we had to leave Innsmouth, my cousins Sarah and Toby Marsh moved to Harrisonville, and ended up near where Anne was living with her sister Bethany. Toby spotted a sign of recognition in the window—thank Father Dagon they kept up the habit—and so they met Anne. A year later she came to stay with us in Dunwich, to study for the priesthood. She'd literally never met another person who didn't look human, and she's still very shy about her appearance. It took a lot of work to convince her to come with us for the summer."

"I'm glad she did," said Jenny. "By Labor Day she'll have met plenty of people who look a lot less human than she does."

"That ought to help," said Owen, and finished his tea. Laura glanced at him and then at his cup. When he nodded, a slender tentacle snaked out from under her skirt. The tip coiled three times around the handle of the teapot and lifted it. Owen held out his cup for the refill.

"I imagine that helped too," said Jenny, smiling.

"Very much so," said Laura. "The first time Anne saw my tentacles she quite literally burst into tears, she was so relieved, and—" She glanced up. "She'll be here in a moment."

Jenny nodded, and instantly changed the subject to the doings of a mutual friend at Miskatonic University. Owen, who was used to the uncanny abilities of both the women in the room, sipped his tea and waited. After a minute or so, tentative footsteps sounded in the hall outside, and then Anne's voice: "I hope I'm not interrupting anything."

"Not at all," said Jenny at once. "Please come have a seat. Would you like some tea?"

"Please," said Anne, and came into the parlor.

She'd taken off the scarf that had shielded her face on the drive down from Dunwich. Though the upper half or so of her face looked fully human, the lower half flowed down into a dozen delicate tentacles that framed her mouth and descended to the level of her breasts. There was, Owen thought, nothing in the least ugly or unnatural about them; it was just that most human beings weren't used to such things.

Anne settled on a chair, took a cup from Jenny with a murmured word of thanks, then broke into a sudden luminous smile as one of Laura's tentacles came out again and poured tea. A moment passed as tea splashed, and then Anne raised the cup, let one of her mouth-tentacles wrap around the handle, and folded her hands in her lap while the tentacle carried the cup to her lips. Owen, who knew how much courage doing that in public had cost her, smiled and sipped tea in his own less elegant fashion.

TWO MORNINGS LATER, while the children ran whooping on the lawn outside, Owen came downstairs to find Jenny reading the Sunday edition of the Arkham *Advertiser*. "You'll want to read this," she said. "You know the Cabot Museum in Boston, right?"

"The place with the mummy collection?"

"That's the one. They just picked up a really remarkable sarcophagus from Ponape. Miskatonic's archeology department has some people excavating the ruins there, which is the only reason this got into the *Advertiser*."

Owen laughed, recalling the parochial habits of Arkham's daily newspaper. "So what's remarkable about the sarcophagus?"

"Take a look," said Jenny, and handed him a section of the newspaper.

Owen glanced at the black and white photo on the open page—a dark oblong shape with strange bas-reliefs and ornate inscriptions on it—then did a double-take. "The writing looks like hieratic Naacal," he said. "You said it came from Ponape?"

"Exactly." She considered him. "You know something about it."

"Maybe. Laura needs to see this."

Jenny regarded him a moment longer, and nodded.

Later that morning the photo of the sarcophagus sat on a table in the brown parlor as four pairs of eyes pondered it: Owen's, Jenny's, Laura's, and Anne's.

"It looks a lot like the description in von Junzt," said Jenny.

"Or certain other descriptions," Laura replied. Owen glanced at her; she met his gaze, nodded fractionally.

"Do you think it could be—" said Anne, and then stopped in confusion.

Laura gave her a reassuring smile, then said, "I wonder if there's any way to get a closer look at it—especially the inscriptions."

"There might be," said Jenny. "I gather the Esoteric Order of Dagon knows something about sarcophagi like this one."

Laura nodded. "If it's genuine, there are certain things we're supposed to do."

"I bet Miriam can get me an introduction," said Jenny.

"I bet she can," Owen agreed. Professor Miriam Akeley of Miskatonic University's History of Ideas department had been Jenny's and Owen's graduate adviser years back, and was still a close friend of both. "I'm up for a trip to Boston any time you like."

"I'll see what I can arrange," Jenny said, nodding.

TWO WEEKS LATER the Sargent bus left them at Boston's South Station, and Owen flagged down a taxi out front. The cab wove through traffic and narrow streets, heading for Beacon Hill, and the cabby kept up a lively if one-sided discussion about the Patriots' prospects that fall, until the cab finally pulled up in front of a nineteenth century mansion on Mt. Verrnon Street. A demure sign out front read CABOT MUSEUM OF ANTHROPOLOGY.

Inside, the receptionist was effusive. "A pleasure to meet you, Dr. Chaudronnier, and—"

"My research assistant, Mr. Merrill," said Jenny.

"Of course. I'll let Dr. Minot know that you're here."

Dr. Edward Minot turned out to be a cadaverous gentleman in his seventies, with a hooked nose reminiscent of the famous mummy of Ramses II and a mottled scalp fringed with white hair. "Ah, good morning," he said. "Pleased to meet you both. Miriam's fine? Ah, very good. If you'll come with me."

An elevator near the receptionist's desk had three buttons for the floors open to the public, and a unmarked lock beneath them. Minot extracted a key from his pocket and turned it three audible clicks to the left; the door slid shut behind them and the elevator slid smoothly down. The door opened again on the lowest level of the museum basement.

"This way, please," said Minot, and led them through a maze of corridors with stark concrete walls. "Ah, here we are," he said, stopping at a locked door marked RESEARCH STAFF ONLY. "I'm sorry to say that a find like the Ponape sarcophagus attracts far too much attention from the wrong sort." He sniffed. "Cultists. So we take precautions."

Inside the door, fluorescent lights glared down on bare utilitarian concrete and steel. Laboratory gear stood around the walls, and two technicians in white lab coats busied themselves with computer screens. In the middle of the room stood a green-black shape maybe ten feet long and four feet or so in width and height, carved on every surface.

"I hope you don't mind if my assistant takes some notes," Jenny said then.

"No, no, not at all." Minot gave Owen a benign smile. "Carry on by all means."

Owen took him at his word, and while Jenny kept Minot

talking about the sarcophagus, he walked over to it and examined it. It matched the description in von Junzt exactly: the stone like greenish obsidian, the bas-reliefs of unhuman figures bearing offerings to the tentacle-faced statue of Cthulhu, the columns of script written in hieratic Naacal.

A glance at Jenny showed that she'd gotten Minot over to the computers. "It's quite perplexing," Minot was saying. "Of course the stone defies analysis—we're used to that here—but we haven't been able to get an image of the cavity or its contents."

"That's really remarkable," said Jenny.

As Minot bent over a keyboard and put more images onto the screen, Owen pulled a notepad from his pocket and started writing. He knew hieratic Naacal well enough to copy it, and Jenny kept Minot out of the way until the job was done. He said little as they extracted themselves from Dr. Minot's underground realm, took another taxi back to the South Station, and settled down to wait for the Sargent bus to return.

Once they were sitting in the station, Jenny asked, "And?"

"It's authentic," said Owen. "The gear Minot's got would see straight through it if it was a fake, but the real ones have an inner lining of *lagh* metal, which stops just about everything."

"I've heard of it," said Jenny.

"I bet. But the sarcophagus is real, and it seems to be intact—and that means I've got to figure out some way to get into it."

Jenny frowned. "Not a good idea. They've had problems with people on our side of things trying to break in for years. There are alarms, guard dogs, that sort of thing."

"I know." He shrugged. "That doesn't matter. If you're an initiate of the Esoteric Order of Dagon, one of the oaths you take requires you to help—certain beings in certain situations—and those aren't the kind of oaths you want to break."

"Certain beings." Jenny considered him. "So we're not just talking about a fancy coffin."

"No. It's what's in the coffin that matters."

167

She nodded slowly, after a moment. "I should be able to arrange something. It may take a while." She propped her chin on her hands. "It's just a matter of talking to the right people."

O NE MORNING SIX weeks later, Owen was sitting downstairs reading von Junzt's *Unaussprechlichen Kulten* under the gaze of a dozen not entirely human Chaudronnier ancestors. He had just reached the chapter on the ancient Pacific when Jenny came in. "You might want to take a nap this afternoon," she said, "and then dress for underground. We've got an appointment in Boston at midnight tonight. Oh, and bring a tennis ball."

Owen gave her a perplexed look, and she smiled and left the parlor.

That evening, toward dinner, Owen came downstairs from a long nap to find Jenny and Laura huddled together over one of the oldest tomes in the Chaudronnier collection. "Oh, hi, Owen," Jenny said as he stepped through the doorway. "I've confirmed everything with people in Boston. We can go pick up your friend tonight."

Laura turned to Jenny and said with obvious amusement, "Owen's friend? You've been introducing him to exalted company."

"I didn't know what else to call the mummy," Jenny admitted.

"We'll settle that tonight," Laura said, and turned to face Owen. "If you and Jenny can bring our guest, Anne and I'll get everything ready."

"Easily done," said Owen.

At quarter to midnight they got out of Owen's station wagon in front of a once-elegant building. White letters on a grimy canopy over the door read THUNSTONE AND SONS. Jenny led the way to the door and knocked, and the door opened to reveal a plump old man with protuberant eyes who wore an unconvincing wig. "Miss Chaudronnier!" he said with a broad smile. "And your friend? Please come in."

Inside was an entry hall lined with wallpaper that hadn't been replaced since the Reagan administration, and beyond that a large room with a pair of couches framing a round table with a pot full of artificial flowers on top. A tall young man in baggy clothing waited there. His narrow chin, tipped with a curly beard, made his face look remarkably like a goat's.

"Hi, Will," Owen said. Will Bishop came from an old Dunwich family, and was finishing up a master's degree at Miskatonic. "So you're part of this little adventure."

"Wouldn't miss it for the world," said Will. "Jenny tells me there are some locks that need picking. You know that's a hobby of mine, don't you?" He got up, turned to Jenny. "You're sure the dogs are going to be taken care of."

"Don't worry about it," Jenny said. To the old man: "Same stair as before?"

"Yes indeed," he said with another smile, and handed Jenny an old-fashioned lantern. "They'll be expecting you."

Jenny took the lantern and led the way to an unobtrusive door. The cracked and patched concrete stair beyond it soon gave way to stonework of Colonial date, and a little further down the stonework gave way to bare damp rock.

"Just who are we going to meet down here?" Owen asked then

"Ghouls," said Jenny. "What would you expect under a Boston funeral home?"

Owen gave her a startled look. "And the funeral director's okay with that?"

"Well, of course," she said. "Haven't you read *Cultes des Goules*? Undertakers have been cutting deals with ghouls for a long time now. It makes life easier for everybody."

Owen gave her an uneasy look, and she smiled back at him.

The stair ended in a low-ceilinged cavern, and there half a dozen naked figures with grayish, rubbery skin waited for them. They had vaguely canine faces and hooved feet, and the smell that surrounded them reminded Owen partly of wet earth and partly of less mentionable things. They greeted Jenny in a language of meeps and glibbers, and she responded in kind.

"Okay, good," Jenny said in English after a brief conversation with the ghouls. "They've agreed to take us to the Cabot Museum." To Owen: "They say you look tasty."

Owen gave her a wary look and said, "That's not very reassuring."

"Don't worry, it's just a traditional compliment," said Jenny "They won't take a bite out of you while you're alive."

That wasn't very reassuring either, but before Owen could think of a response, Jenny meeped something to the ghouls, who glibbered in response and shambled down one of the tunnels. Jenny followed with the lantern, and Owen and Will came afterward, ducking to keep from banging their heads on the tunnel roof. For the next hour or so they followed the ghouls through a maze of damp and malodorous underground passages, until finally their guides stopped at a vertical shaft with a well-aged iron ladder climbing one side.

"Here we go," said Jenny. "The Cabot Museum's right above us."

She glibbered her thanks to the ghouls, who meeped in reply. As they settled down to wait, Jenny started up the ladder, and Owen and Will followed.

At the top of the ladder was a cavern with a slab of poured concrete forming one side. In the middle of the slab a roughly circular opening a yard or so across had been hacked, or just possibly gnawed. A metal surface painted beige blocked the opening from the far side.

"Before we go through," Jenny said, "it's time to do something about the dog. There's just one on this floor—that's what the ghouls say."

"I somehow don't think of ghouls as museum patrons," said Owen.

"Of course not. They consider mummies a delicacy—and

they're really good at taking just a little from each one, so it won't be missed."

"About that dog," said Will.

"Not a problem." She pulled an old-fashioned perfume atomizer out of her purse, said, "Close your eyes," and squirted him with the fluid, which had a curious musky smell.

"Your turn," she said to Owen then, and squirted him with it, then applied it to herself as though she was putting on perfume. "There—that'll take care of it."

"Dog repellent?" Will asked, clearly dubious.

"No, nothing so clumsy." She put the atomizer back in her purse.

"You don't like dogs?" Owen asked Will.

"They don't like me," said Will. "They bite me whenever they think they can get away with it. It kind of runs in my dad's family."

"If one of you can push that filing cabinet out of the way," said Jenny, "we can go on."

T HE FILING CABINET slid away so easily that its underside must have been lubricated—with what, Owen didn't want to know. He crawled through the opening and stood up in darkness. When Jenny followed, the lantern showed a bare room full of filing cabinets.

"Okay, good," said Jenny then. "We're on the right floor, and only about half a dozen rooms away from the one we want. Come on." She went to the door, opened it, and headed out into the dimly lit hallway outside.

They were about halfway along it when the sound of claws rattling on concrete sounded not far away. "Jenny—" Will said in an agitated voice.

"Don't worry about it," she replied, and kept walking.

A moment later the dog, a big black and tan Rottweiler, came barreling around a corner in front of them and started toward them with bared fangs. It covered half the distance, slowed, then stopped, and a dazed expression creased its face.

"Oh, you're such a good dog," Jenny cooed at it. "Such a good dog."

The dog pondered this assertion and decided that Jenny was right. It lowered its head, whined, and wagged its little stump of a tail in apology, then trotted over to Jenny, who scratched it behind the ears and motioned with her head the way the three of them had been going. They went to the door marked RESEARCH STAFF ONLY, and the dog trotted amiably alongside them, pushing his head up under Jenny's hand as they went.

The door was locked, but Will pulled a set of slender steel tools from his pockets and made short work of it. Inside, the sarcophagus from Ponape gleamed.

"Can you keep Fido occupied for a while?" Jenny asked Owen. "It's going to take us a bit to get the sarcophagus open."

"Sure," said Owen, and started scratching the Rottweiler's ears. The dog responded by flopping down on the floor and offering its belly to be rubbed. Owen sat down beside it, and in the process discovered the tennis ball he'd tucked into a pocket of his cargo pants. After he'd finished paying due attention to the dog's belly, he got out the tennis ball and held it up, and it immediately became the Holy Grail at the center of the Rottweiler's world. Owen chose a patch of bare wall well out of the way of the Ponape sarcophagus, and threw the ball that way. It came back to him clenched in the dog's powerful jaws and well coated with drool, but a game of catch was clearly required, and Owen picked up the damp object and flung it again.

Meanwhile Jenny intoned certain arcane words to open the seals on the sarcophagus, and her careful probing of subtle details on the carvings resulted in a sudden click loud enough to startle the dog. As the ball bounced again and the dog leapt after it, the lid of the sarcophagus pivoted silently up. Jenny leaned over the opening. Even over the rattle of the dog's claws on the concrete floor, Owen could hear her breath catch.

"That's an impressive mummy," she said to Owen.

"I bet," said Owen. He paused to extract the wet and punctured tennis ball from the dog's jaws and toss it. The dog came bounding back, and Owen had to attend to the tennis ball. He glanced back once it was flying across the room with the dog in hot pursuit, to find Jenny and Will lifting a not-quite-human shape out of the sarcophagus. It was wrapped tightly in strips of a bluish-white membrane—*pthagon*, the tomes said, the inner skin of the long-vanished yakith-lizard—with incantations in hieratic Naacal down the center of each strip. Lumps here and there inside the wrappings suggested amulets of peculiar shapes.

"There we go," said Jenny then. "Your friend from Ponape can come with us."

"My friend from R'lyeh," said Owen, and then extracted the mortal remains of the tennis ball from the dog's teeth and threw it again. When he glanced back at Jenny, right about the time the ball landed on the floor with an audible splat, the sorceress was staring at him.

"Seriously?" she said. "It's actually one of the spawn of Cthulhu?"

"That's what the sarcophagus says. I compared it with the text in von Junzt."

"And—is he—"

Owen glanced up at her. "Dead, yet dreaming—at least in theory. Supposedly all Great Cthulhu's spawn can manage that trick. The oaths I mentioned require us to try to revive him."

She took that in. "Will he be okay outside the sarcophagus?"

"Yeah. The periapts and phylacteries that matter are in the wrappings."

The Rottweiler came prancing back with a torn yellow-green shape in its jaws, and Owen resumed the game. Meanwhile Jenny and Will closed the sarcophagus and picked up the mummy. "Okay," said Jenny. "Let's get out of here."

Owen hauled himself to his feet, persuaded the dog to surrender the fragments of the tennis ball, and followed the two of them into the hall, where they retraced their steps to the room with the filing cabinets.

"Sit," said Owen, as Jenny and Will hauled the mummy inside. "Sit. Good boy." He slipped through the door behind Jenny, and closed it. A moment later claws scratched on the far side of the door, and a muffled whining sound came through it.

"I hope the dog'll be okay," Owen said to Jenny as she and Will slid the mummy through the hole into the cavern. She ducked through after it, and Owen followed.

"Oh, he'll be fine." Jenny straightened up—a privilege not granted to Owen or Will, who were both more than a head taller than she was. "Fifteen minutes from now, the spray will wear off, and he won't remember a thing." Then: "I hope you didn't leave the tennis ball behind."

"I've got it," said Owen, displaying the well-chewed fragments. "I think it's just about ready for the ghouls, though."

"I suppose you could see if they want it," said Jenny. "You never know with ghouls."

"I hope they won't try to take a bite out of this mummy," said Owen.

"With the amulets he's got on him? Not a chance. Ghouls aren't stupid." She started down the ladder. Owen glanced at Will, who gave him an amused look and followed.

IN THE SMALL hours of the morning, the station wagon pulled through the Chaudronnier mansion's carriage port, and kept going up the gravel drive alongside the rambling northern wing, to stop just outside a side door. The room inside had an altar over toward one wall, incense smoldering in a burner, vessels of strange fluids on a table nearby. Lines drawn in four colors traced patterns on the wooden floor. Laura and Anne had already donned ornate robes and gold tiaras. It took only a few moments to get the mummy settled in its place at the center of an irregular heptagon surrounded with written incantations.

"Should I leave?" Jenny asked.

"You don't have to," Laura told her. "If you want to get a chair from the next room, and sit over there, that should be fine." She turned. "Owen, there's an acolyte's robe by the door—could you help out with the libations and the incense?"

It wasn't a common experience for Owen to watch Jenny sitting on the sidelines of a sorcerous operation while he took part. Still, this was the Esoteric Order of Dagon's work and no one else's. As the salt-scented incense smoke rose and the priestesses began to chant, the dim light in the room took on a liquid quality, as though filtered through waves, and half-seen shapes clustered around the room's edges, peering in through the smoke with pale unblinking eyes: the servants of Dagon, Owen knew, come to keep watch over his human and half-human children.

"The first libation," Laura said then. Owen brought her one of the bowls, and she handed it to Anne, who poured a thin stream of wine-colored liquid on the mummy from head to foot. The *pthagon* wrappings soaked up every drop, darkening and swelling as the fluid spread.

For another quarter hour or so Laura and Anne chanted, Owen fed the coals with more incense, and Jenny watched. "The second libation," Laura said then, and Owen brought her another bowl full of clear fluid. She took it and poured it in the same way as the first, a thin stream tracing the length of the mummy. Where it touched the *pthagon* wrappings they shriveled and split, until withered flesh the gray-green color of the ocean showed through a gap in them.

"The third libation," said Laura. There were two bowls full of fluid, one greenish, one the pallid hue of the moon, and Owen brought them one at a time. Laura and Anne each took one and stood on opposite sides of the mummy. Laura caught Anne's glance and nodded, and at the same moment each of them began to pour a thin stream onto the gap in the wrappings, moving slowly from head to foot. Pale vapors rose where the two fluids mingled, and beneath—

175

Though the pages of von Junzt had taught him what to expect, Owen's eyes still widened. The ocean-colored flesh visible through the split wrappings had begun to swell.

The priestesses finished pouring the libation, gave the bowls back to Owen, and took up positions at the head and foot of the mummy, resuming their chant. By the time he got the bowls on the table again and went back to tending the incense, the gap in the wrappings was widening moment by moment as the body within filled out.

The chant wound to its end, and then Laura and Anne went to the mummy's head and began peeling aside the brittle remnants of the *pthagon* wrappings, uncovering the naked form within. He—the pronoun was impossible to evade—was humanoid in shape, but hairless. Blunt claws tipped his fingers and toes, and his face, roughly humanoid on its upper half, descended from there into a thicket of tentacles that reached well down his chest. At brow, throat, chest, hips, and ankles, phylacteries of iridescent *lagh* metal were tied with cords of braided snakeskin.

Working together, the two priestesses took off the phylacteries one at a time, and then Anne got to her feet and Laura rose on her tentacles. They stood back and waited. Owen glanced at Jenny, who was staring at the scene with fingertips pressed to her mouth, and then watched the creature on the floor.

A long moment passed, and another. The priestesses waited, unmoving. The last of the incense hissed and spat on the coals. Then, almost imperceptibly at first, the unhuman chest began to rise and fall. The clawed fingers stirred, and the eyelids twitched and opened, revealing golden eyes with crescent pupils, like those of an octopus. The mouth-tentacles twitched, and a faint whisper sounded in the still room: "*Iâ.*"

"He's thirsty," Laura said to Anne in a low voice, and knelt beside the creature and said in Aklo, "*M'wlgh kn'â-gwî y'au ph'hwlau.*"

The yellow eyes turned toward her, struggled to focus. "*Agh'wlh m'nau dhû'kh?*"

"*Kh'wlth y'au ûm'shwai,*" she replied in a reassuring tone.

He closed his eyes, opened them again as Anne knelt beside him, holding out a glass of water. The first trace of an expression showed as he stared up into her tentacled face, and with an evident effort, he caught her wrist in one clawed hand. "*Akh-ke m'nwa?*" he said.

Anne glanced at Laura in confusion, and Laura said, "He wants to know who you are. I can tell him if you like."

She considered that, and then shook her head. "Anne *m'nau.*" His grip on her wrist didn't slacken, but he let her bring the water closer, and his tentacles deftly took the glass from her hand and guided it to his mouth.

THE LABOR DAY holiday came and went, and all the roads out of Kingsport filled with tourists heading back to their homes and their lives. The big hotels on Harbor Street sank into their autumnal afterlife of weekend conventions and half-price specials, the carts selling shaved ice and corn dogs headed for their winter's sleep, and the proprietors of tourist shops in the old waterfront district gave one last uneasy glance toward the Terrible Old Man's silent cottage on Water Street and closed up their premises until spring. In the Chaudronnier mansion on Green Lane, though, the residents and guests had other concerns.

"You're sure it won't be any kind of difficulty?" Laura asked, as she refilled the teacups with a deft movement of one tentacle.

"None in the least," Jenny reassured her. "They'll both be welcome here as long as they want to stay. My nieces really like Anne. As for Zh'kau—" She sipped tea. "He's going to need a safe place to stay until he knows enough to get by in today's world."

"I don't think he'll have any trouble learning English," Owen said. He was standing by the window, looking down at the rose garden below. There, two figures with tentacled faces sat on a stone bench, apparently deep in conversation. One of her hands folded around one of his.

"I imagine not," said Jenny. "And Anne's getting a first-rate knowledge of Aklo." With a sly smile: "The family library has an old manuscript of Aklo love poetry; I think it was originally from the Chateau des Faussesflammes, part of the Malinbous collection. I've considered leaving it out for them to find sometime."

Owen turned to face her. "I didn't know there was Aklo love poetry."

"Of course. Mind you, it's very graphic, and some of the metaphors are a bit unsettling to people nowadays, but it's really sweet."

"I suppose it was inevitable," said Laura then. "Waking up after all those millions of years in a place full of strange beings, and there's one face that looks familiar."

"And he wasn't the only one to respond to a familiar face, of course. I wish them well." Owen downed the last of his tea. "Time to load up the car."

About the Author

John Michael Greer is the author of more than fifty nonfiction books, a weekly blog, and sixteen novels, including the seven-volume epic fantasy with tentacles *The Weird of Hali*. He lives in Rhode Island with his wife Sara.

The Gates

Brandon Daubs

ORRIN HEARD THE voice of his wife.

We are at the gates.

He looked up to find her silhouetted against the pale ghost of Charon, rising from the dark Hydra horizon as naked as the night of their honeymoon, and he almost drove his spider down a ravine. Three of the legs knifed out over the edge and only by digging his heels into stone was he able to stop himself. When he looked back to the horizon, his wife was gone.

Of course Corrin was obligated to share all this with Doctor Sanders when he got back to the station. Sanders listened with that sad, somber Freud-face that led some of his contemporaries to call him "Siggy" behind his back. Corrin didn't care about the affectations, though. He had ceased to care the first week after the death of his wife out here, in the cold black at the edge of the solar system, where messages from Earth or from anyone were few and far between. The only other sense of human contact they got were the brief flashes of light on the console of the FTL Personnel Relay.

Corrin tried not to think of all the people going through there, blasted bunches of particles and broken-down biopaste patterns shot from Earth to somewhere else in space.

"Corrin? Corrin."

Corrin turned back to Siggy. Sanders. Whatever.

"You've been out there way too long," said Sanders.

Corrin glanced at the mirror. He took in the dark circles beneath wide eyes accustomed to dim light and his mop of brown hair gone almost black, sponging up the shadows of this place like ink. He took in his cot, and all his garbage piled onto a narrow shelf. A half-finished anthology by Algis Budrys. A manual on FTL communications. A faded pair of VR glasses from Earth, now vintage, and a photo of his wife, turned away just enough that Corrin wouldn't have to look at it every time he came through the airlock.

He looked at it now. That face. That smiling face.

"I don't care how young and spry you might think you are," Sanders went on. "This place will suck the life out of anyone. Do something easy. Cook, maybe. I'm getting pretty sick of the protein packs Wheelie puts together."

Wheelie rolled by the corridor outside and Corrin imagined he saw reproach behind the glass lens of its eye-camera before it disappeared.

"Sure, doc," Corrin muttered. "Whatever you say."

Sanders wandered off—to complete a report on Corrin's sanity, no doubt. A pinprick of light that was the glow of a distant Sun glimmered through a glass dome overhead. Much closer was the ominous thumbnail of Charon and just at the edge of his vision, Pluto, cold as a judge. Corrin pulled the helmet back on his suit, exited the airlock and rode his spider the distance between the dwelling pod and the personnel relay to perform some routine maintenance on the cooling systems. While he worked, he watched the little flashes of light inside the conduits. Not for the first time, he wondered how the Deep Corps got away with all this folding of space and time.

He wondered if they had.

"Who knew," crackled the voice of Wheelie through the speakers inside Corrin's helmet, "that the essence of a human being would be so colorless?"

Corrin wasn't paying attention. His eye caught a different kind of light from somewhere nearby—green. The relay, having been buried into Hydra's crust long before the dwelling pod had been added for maintenance personnel, had its own dark radar screen. Probably just another asteroid that would miss them by a mile or more, Corrin thought. Just another errant piece of long-blasted satellite knocked out of Earth's orbit to make way for a new piece of junk.

He turned toward the console and his hand froze above the override.

Freya, it read, above a green blip on the black. That was not any kind of asteroid.

His wife was out there, in the dark.

CORRIN NEVER HAD found the body of his wife. Only her suit, torn almost in half, hanging like a ruined flag from a snag at the edge of a ravine hidden from the station side by a high ledge. The same ravine, he thought, that he had almost wrecked his spider in. The assumption, as he and Sanders stood staring down into the black, was that she had not seen the drop and tumbled to the other side before ripping her suit wide open and slipping out of it. She was freeze-dried meat down there, somewhere in the black within the black.

"Come inside, sir," Wheelie commanded. "I have your protein pack prepared."

Corrin ignored him. He stood by his spider outside the dwelling pod and watched the tiny Sun sink below the horizon. The sliver of light left on Charon waned and disappeared, leaving only a looming void where the stars should have been. Pluto had long since sunk below the horizon. A shadow crept over the rocky landscape unlike any shadow Corrin had ever seen, even when he closed his eyes—like a spill of ink that spread until everything was covered.

Within moments the darkness was so complete Corrin could not be sure he was standing on solid rock. He couldn't be sure he even existed.

"Come inside, sir," Wheelie repeated, and Corrin climbed onto the spider to creep out into the night. He felt the scratch of the spider's legs against stone. He listened to the sound of his own breath harsh inside his helmet while the blip on the radar embedded in the back of the spider blinded him over and over again.

Freya.

"I have not alerted Doctor Sanders to your little escapade," Wheelie said. This got Corrin's attention. He reached a hand up to press the side of his helmet.

"Why not?" he asked.

"I know he would stop you," came Wheelie's reply, "and I liked Freya as much as you did. Maybe more." Corrin didn't think Wheelie was equipped with the cognitive circuitry to make this sort of determination, but he said nothing. "I saw the radar, too. I saw the one here in the pod. I disabled it, so Sanders wouldn't follow you. I'll keep him busy. I want you to find her, and if you don't, I at least want you to get some sense of...I forgot the word."

Wheelie had not forgotten the word. A machine did not often just "forget" anything. He had been programmed not to upset his human charges here at the edge of space as much as possible and it was likely he just didn't want to say the word "closure."

In the darkness, Corrin almost rode his spider over the edge of the ravine again—almost. This time only two legs stretched out over the black. He held his breath for a long while, looking down. The lights from his spider did nothing to pierce that darkness. Corrin dismounted, lodged his grappler into the stone of a nearby boulder and rappelled down into the black. Up above, the spider's lights shut off automatically. The light on Corrin's helmet came on but it only served to light a circle of stone in front of his face, about a foot in diameter.

He tried not to imagine something reaching up out of all that dark.

"Why Hydra?" he remembered his wife asking, before either of them had known how great they would be together at Virtual Sword, at difficult tech repair, at messing up the bed, at everything. She sat near the head of a long table at their last Deep Corps debriefing, wearing the stern power suit and glasses that had drawn Corrin's attention from the first day he worked there. He stood at the door in his Air Force coveralls, ready to fly whatever tin can they wanted.

At the time, Corrin had wondered the same thing. Why Hydra? The orbit was erratic. Even the gravity, which barely existed, changed with some frequency.

"Because it's there," had been the answer.

Now that Corrin understood the point of the relay, he knew both of the answers.

Hydra's orbit was the furthest away from the sun at aphelion, which made it the best place to send signals deeper into space. Maybe more importantly, if something went wrong with the relay, it was far enough away from prospects on Charon or Pluto that at least they could be salvaged. Nobody cared if Hydra was blown into gravel. Those other places, though, already had a few shallow mines sunk in. They had potential.

Corrin imagined he heard the hum off the relay launching souls from Earth deep into the stars beyond the solar system—until he realized that was not his imagination. His feet brushed solid stone and he just about jumped out of his suit. Wheelie tried to say something through the radio in his helmet but his voice only came out a garbled mess of distortion. Power, was the only word Corrin could make out. Power something. Corrin wasn't paying any attention to him, though. He felt a rush of air nudge him into the wall and turned to see what appeared to be some sort of access tunnel, marked with the Deep Corps logo.

Open.

We are at the gates.

Corrin stepped forward. The voice of his wife was not just in his memory, this time.

Corrin. Her voice was warm in his ear. Her breath was warm on his cheek.

On the other side of the open access door, Corrin froze. His light shone on metal, rods and rods of nuclear fuel both new and expended, and piles of waste glowing a phosphorescent green in the darkness. His suit would protect him from most of the radiation, he hoped, but still, to see this stuff just piled here, discarded as the relay used it up...and that wasn't the half of it. As he lifted his head, the light on his helmet shone up past rows of what looked like hyperbaric chambers—only they couldn't be. What were they for? Who would they hold?

Almost all of them oozed a viscous black tar, as dark as the Hydra night, from the outline of doors and hatches that should have been vacuum sealed.

Corrin. Honey. Corrin shook as cold fingers brushed his chest beneath his suit. *We've been waiting for you.*

We are at the gates.

Let us in.

SOMETHING IS WRONG with the relay," Corrin said, back in the safety of the dwelling pod. He ran a Geiger counter over his suit again and again while he stood in the airlock, and kept his other hand on the decon button until the counter stopped clicking. Sanders watched him from the other side of the glass wearing his Freudiest Freud-face.

"How can there be anything at all wrong with the relay?" Sanders asked, as Corrin stepped through the airlock and began to peel off his suit. "You were out there messing with it 18 hours or more yesterday."

Wheelie rolled by with his lens-eye turned away from them both.

"I don't mean that part," Corrin said, and after a moment's pause, he decided whatever needed to happen down there was bigger than a one-man job. Much bigger. "I went down the ravine," he said.

Sanders glared at him. "I told you to rest!"

"My wife appeared on the radar."

Sanders offered a significant pause.

"I didn't see anything."

"Wheelie disabled the radar after I left."

"And why would he do that?"

Corrin glanced over at Wheelie, who was busy putting some protein packs together. "He's programmed to help," he said. "He was sure you would try to stop me if you found out where I was going. He was just covering my tracks. But listen. That's not the point."

"The hell it's not!" Sanders said, but Corrin talked over him.

"The point is this relay is way bigger than we realized. It doesn't just need a little maintenance here at this part that we can see. This part is only the tip...like the antennae. The machine itself is huge. It's buried in the crust. We've got nuclear waste spilling into Hydra's core down there. We've got discharge from some sort of hyperbaric chambers..."

Corrin trailed off. He did not like the look on Sanders' face. Cold. Indifferent. Not one single shred of surprise.

"You knew all this already, didn't you," Corrin asked. Sanders shrugged.

"Let's have some tea," he said, and he spread a hand to the table jammed next to the com panel. Corrin caught sight of a message open on the screen, sent from Deep Corps headquarters on Earth. *Your replacement tech has passed the asteroid belt.* Hmm. Corrin took a seat and Sanders produced two cups of tea from a nearby cabinet, already prepared.

"Tell me what you know about faster than light travel," he said.

"Tell me if you murdered my wife," Corrin cut in. Sanders almost choked on his tea and the look he gave Corrin was not very Freud-like at all.

185

"Get bent," he said. "What kind of question is that? I loved Freya as much as everyone did. Even Wheelie loved her and he's a goddam machine. She was like a daughter to me. I ought to taze you just for suggesting that!"

Corrin did not feel at all stupid for asking. He just then noticed the stun baton, tucked into the cabinet by the empty tea cups.

"Anyway," Sanders went on, "don't act so surprised to find all that waste down there. Faster than light travel requires a bend in the sheet of our universe, to bring someone from one part to another in a single moment. To do that, you need a hunk of matter compacted just as dense as you can make it and for *that*, in addition to the matter itself, you need a ton of power. This is humanity's first attempt at something like this so yeah, it's got to be a little bulky, a little messy, a little nuclear. There's no helping that mess down there and as for why we didn't let you know about it...you're just the repairman, Corrin. Twelve years in the force and you're a repairman in space. It's unfortunate, maybe, but there you go. The Deep Corps decided you just didn't need to know about that other part down there."

Corrin glared.

"And the chambers?" he asked. "All that crud?"

Sanders shrugged. "Like I said, it's primitive technology right now. Our range is not infinite. Most likely the chambers are to reconstruct passengers for one millisecond so they can be reanalyzed and boosted the rest of the way to wherever they're going. And as for the discharge, it's just some residue on the outside of those things, from...whatever. The nuclear waste, probably. There's no way it could be from inside. Those tanks are airtight."

Corrin's eyes flicked back to the stun baton.

"Did my wife ever go through?" he asked.

"You already know that she did," Sanders growled. "She bent onto a passing ship and took a shuttle to get here. You should know it's not so much going *through* anything, as it is being caused to exist in two places at the same time, like I already said."

Corrin pretended to drink his tea.

"Three places," he said.

Sanders frowned. "What?"

"No matter how hard you fold space-time there is always a void between point A and point B," Corrin went on. "A passenger going through would also exist, for however brief of a moment, in the space between."

Sanders narrowed his eyes. "And I suppose you think this is where you might find your wife," he muttered. "In this...space between."

"I'm going to find her," Corrin whispered.

"If you're going back to the relay, the real relay, I can't let you," Sanders sighed. "I can't risk you sabotaging something down there. Try to imagine people shot out into space every which way, not even close to their destinations...hey!"

Corrin lurched toward the door. Sanders grabbed the stun baton and tackled him down to the steel of the dwelling pod floor. The baton flashed to life but Corrin kicked it out of Sanders' hand, kicked until the sole of his boot crunched into a few of Sanders' fingers and thumped into the side of his face. Sanders cried out as old glasses skittered across the floor and Corrin finally pulled himself free.

"I'm sorry to have to tell you this," Sanders "Siggy" Caldwell spouted through the blood in his teeth, "but you are clearly insane! And don't think I've kept that out of my reports to headquarters! You've got nowhere to go!"

Corrin almost made it to the door before Wheelie appeared and stopped him with a cold metal claw snapped around his neck.

"Traitor!" Corrin managed to choke. Wheelie shrugged.

"I'm sorry," he said. "Protocols do not allow me to sympathize with the insane."

"I am not insane!" Corrin screamed.

You're not insane, he heard his wife whisper, warm in his ear. *Come find us.*

He felt her kiss soft against his cheek as Sanders zapped him in the back with the stun baton. A moment before he hit the ground, he glanced toward the photo by his cot.

Smeared with black.

Corrin's sleep was not at all peaceful. He dreamed of the space between moments. He dreamed of Virtual Sword and the endless, hideous monsters he had faced with his wife thinking that was *fun,* thinking that was a *good time.* He dreamed of her opening one button at a time at the neck of her suit and all their meetings in the supply closet at Deep Corps headquarters on Earth, and all their meetings at her timeshare in Switzerland once things had gotten serious. He dreamed of protein packs, one eaten, one left untouched and the third…the third was more rotten than Corrin had ever seen any piece of food in his life.

By the time he finally awoke, Sanders spoke with somebody new near the airlock. The dwelling pod was small enough that Corrin heard every word they said.

"Yes, we've read the reports," said the new arrival. He was still in his suit. Corrin could see part of a ship parked outside through the pod window. "You're right. It's probably nothing…but 'probably' isn't good enough. There was a pretty strange power surge about the same time Corrin was down there. Even your robot noticed it. Now, we can't be having surges of any kind while we're shooting *whole people* out beyond the solar system. We don't need for there to be any…complications. Now, don't look at me like that, doctor. I'm not discounting your reports. I'm just trying to say, maybe we ought to go down there and take a look."

Sanders shrugged. "Waste your time if you want," he said. "Whatever it was, it was just an anomaly. You'll have a lot worse if you don't get Corrin out of here. He's fixated hard on the relay. Who knows what he'll try to do?"

The newcomer grunted.

"We brought your replacement," he said. "Don't worry. We'll get Corrin back home."

Sanders muttered to himself while he pulled on his enviro-suit, grabbed his box of tools and slipped out through the airlock. "Watch him a second," he said, "somebody's got to do the maintenance around here," before the seal slid shut behind him.

A green light on the radar began to blink again and Corrin looked over to read the name.

Freya. Freya.

He grabbed the old VR glasses off his headboard and put them on. Once he flipped the switch, they cycled through a few photos of Switzerland. There was his wife, half-buried in a snowbank with her skis sticking up. There she was in front of the fire. Here was a photo of her developing the transporter. Another photo flickered past—a dark silhouette, serene against the dead light of Charon.

Corrin wondered what that space would be like, between the folds of the universe.

"What pictures you got on that thing?"

Corrin flipped up the glasses to see the newcomer standing by him. *Danner,* read the name tag on his suit. He had a face full of pretend interest, like he were speaking to a child.

"Only the best," Corrin replied. "You want to see?"

He pulled the VR glasses the rest of the way off and handed them over. Danner slipped them on—and he got a good view of Corrin's wife in her lingerie, before Corrin leapt out of bed and slugged him in the gut as hard as he could. Danner did not even put up a fight as Corrin threw him back against the communications console. His head slammed somewhere between "send" and "receive" and the VR Glasses bounced off as he slid down into a sitting position. Moments later, Corrin had stripped Danner's suit, put it on himself, and shoved his own head into the helmet. He paused only to fire off a brief message from the communications console before he ran out through the airlock.

Sanders saw him at once. He lit up the radio.

"Corrin, stop, God dammit! I know that's you!"

189

Wheelie was there, too, holding the tools. His message was more on the nose.

"Halt! Cease! Desist!"

Corrin did nothing of the sort. He jumped on the spider, which had seen more use in the previous week than it had in years before that, and skittered off toward the ravine. The spider moved barely as fast as a bicycle but Corrin still had plenty of time to dismount at the edge of the ravine, lodge his grappler into the stone and begin the descent. Only a moment passed before he felt the ominous pull of gravity grab at his back and begin to drag him down faster, and faster. He realized Sanders must have cut his rope only a moment before he hit the ground with a *crunch* and the hiss of escaping air.

He screamed. He hoped everyone could hear that over the radio. He screamed and it took everything he had to roll over and clutch the tear in his suit over his broken ribs to keep himself from suffocating, as he crawled through the access door and into the heart of the relay.

"What are you trying to do, anyway?" Sanders roared over the com. "Do you think you'll find your wife in there? Corrin! Corrin, don't do anything to that relay!"

Corrin raised his head and the light of his helmet shone off the tar oozing from the containment chambers. Each time a flash through the conduits announced the departure of another soul from Earth, more of it seeped out. Flash after flash went by and the puddle of black mixed into the waste from the nuclear rods all over the floor moved toward him.

You came back. The puddle pooled into the shadow of a familiar shape. *Corrin. Please. We are at the gates. Help us…*

The puddle froze at the sound of a clang from the cavern beyond the access door, and Corrin turned to see Wheelie struggle upright from what must have been a very long fall. His eye lens had cracked. His suspension was bent. Sparks shot out of his chassis but he still rolled doggedly forward, claws outstretched—until he stopped short, and swiveled his lens around, and around, taking in the hyperbaric chambers and all the waste.

"Help me," Corrin gasped, through the radio. He gestured toward the relay, to the dark ooze all around them. "Help me with this."

"I can see that you are not insane," said Wheelie. "But…"

"You must protect the humans here on Hydra," Corrin said. "I understand that. But you have a much larger responsibility, Wheelie, to protect the humans…everywhere. Can you imagine what's in there? Can you imagine what would happen if they got out?"

Wheelie swiveled his working lens this way and that. He settled it for a moment on the puddle that looked a lot like Freya. Then he moved to pull as many rods of fuel toward himself as he possibly could, until he collapsed into the corner under their weight. His chassis caught fire. His wheel melted to the stone and his claw arms fell limp by his sides.

"Permission to rest, sir," he groaned through the radio.

Corrin grimaced as the light in Wheelie's camera lens went out. He wondered if ever there was a machine that had done more for humanity than Wheelie just had.

He forced himself upright. He could hear more whispers now, not just his wife—and after a long moment of working at the console, he got the containment chambers open. Black discharge poured out like pus from an open wound, so thick on the ground it washed over Corrin's ankles. Tendrils wound up his legs before they broke away and merged together into the hips, the chest and arms of his wife. She did not reflect the light from the fire or his helmet lamp. Every square inch of her leeched color from everything around it.

"Leave the relay alone, Corrin!" Sanders screamed through the radio. "Please!"

Behind Corrin's wife, others began to take shape. Soldiers. Scientists. Colonists. Everyone who had ever come through the Hydra Relay on their way to somewhere else. There would be countless more—and imprint for every person who had ever appeared, however briefly, in the void between two points in the universe.

"Sweetheart," the Freya-thing breathed. She pressed her lips to his helmet, and left a smear of black across the glass. "Thank you."

Corrin's eyes drifted to the pale shape behind the command console, a pale shape that he had missed on his first visit to this place. She wore only thermal lining and a scrap of suit. Her hair hung about her like a golden spiderweb. Her face had frozen solid but there was no mistaking the round cheeks, the eyebrows just a little too thick, the lips that had always tasted a little like cinnamon. Corrin's breath caught in his throat. Whatever this thing was clinging to him, smearing his visor, squirming and trying to get *inside,* it wasn't his wife.

And there it was.

Closure.

"Now!" he barked, through the pain of his broken ribs, and Wheelie's chassis popped open to reveal a fusion core smoldering in there. Its glow lit the rods of fuel piled around it.

M OMENTS BEFORE THE "incident," as it came to be known, Deep Corps received a very simple message from the Hydra Relay from repair technician Corrin.

Stop.

They didn't stop. They couldn't. Their holdings were in danger "out past the rocks" and they needed more soldiers to keep their ships safe, more scientists to keep a competitive edge over rival companies and more civilians to fill all the space they could find. Besides, that email came from Corrin, a lunatic on his way to forced retirement. They kept sending people even after the reports of "some disturbance" near Pluto, even after a scan by a passing probe showed only four moons, not five, as it wove through a previously unmapped cloud of gravel. They kept sending people even after they began to appear near their deep space destinations in pieces, in empty space or not at all.

The order finally came from near the relay itself.

"For the love of God," Sanders blared over every radio back in the Deep Corps HQ, every radio within range of his transmission, "don't send any more people! This is Doctor Sanders of Deep Corps in the USS Cerberus, on my way past Charon. We only just barely got out alive. Hydra is gone. The relay is gone."

The gates had closed.

ABOUT THE AUTHOR

Brandon Daubs is a science fiction and fantasy writer whose stories have appeared in Grimdark Magazine, Dark Fire, 4 Star Stories, Three Crows, Mythic, Who Knocks? and the anthologies All Hail Our Robot Conquerors and Knee Deep in Grit. His short story "A Vague Inclination to Please" was a finalist for WSFA's Small Press Award in 2018. He lives near San Francisco with a dog and three kids, a wife who has been very supportive of his work, and a cat who has not. He is a proud member of both the SFWA and the HWA..

The Ice Breaker

Hall Jameson

HE LODGEPOLE PINES creaked in acknowledgment as Amanda passed beneath them; the sound reminded her of her grandfather's rocker as he sat on the front porch watching the lake, rocking, *ker-crick, ker-crick*.

The only other sounds were the crunch of her snowshoes accompanied by the whisper of the sled's runners as she made her way toward the ice. She enjoyed the two-mile trek to the lake, towing a light sled loaded with her fishing gear, particularly after a fresh fall of snow.

She caught a glimpse of the frozen lake through the orderly trunks. Swirls of turquoise and pearl marked the ice. The steep shoreline jutted over the lakes edge, met below by fingers of driftwood skeletons, softened by a froth of snow.

According to local lore, a monster (described as an enormous, eel-like creature by witnesses) inhabited these waters, a legend similar to that of any small town near a formidable stretch of freshwater. At four hundred feet deep and thirty miles long, Flathead Lake could certainly conceal such a creature. Yet, she had lived near the lake her entire life and had never witnessed anything supernatural. She craved such an encounter, but believed such a creature found you, not the other way around.

When Amanda was a girl, her mother taught her how to fish for Mackinaw trout. She dropped a silver jig with a kernel of fresh corn impaled on the hook one hundred feet below the surface, as the Macs avoided light. Strands of tinsel were tied to the top of the jig in order to create shimmering tendrils in the water. The working of the rod consisted of a figure-eight motion of the tip, followed by an upward jerk of no more than six inches. She called her mother's fishing technique the *Mac Method*, and, if the weight of her sled as she hauled each day's catch home was any indication, the *Mac Method* was foolproof. However, her mother's method was a source of contention when she described it one night at the Dewlap Pub. The old men at the bar chuffed and shook their heads at her.

Tinsel? Eye rolls all around.

A pretty gal like you should be married, not hunting and fishing. Joe here's available, aren't ya Joe? A hearty chorus of laughs.

Aren't you afraid, out there on the ice at all hours? There are grizzlies and wolves all around here, not to mention, a crazed mountain man or two. Though their tone was light, condescension soaked their bleary, beer-eyed, group expression.

"Actually, I prefer women to men," she had said. "And I'm an excellent shot."

The jibing ceased and the subject matter switched to hockey.

Less than a week later, as she was passing by Mike Samuel's hut, he emerged toting a string of three enormous Macs. He nodded to her, the color rising in his cheeks. *Must be the cold air,* she thought as she walked away, then she spotted something on the ice.

A single strand of tinsel.

THE AIR NIPPED amanda's cheeks as she pulled down the neoprene mask covering her mouth and flicked off the crystals that had formed from her breath. The trees offered protection from the bitter wind, but once she reached the open ice, the gusts assaulted her. She adjusted her mask and tightened her hood. The weather report said the wind chill could reach forty below in open areas, but the layers she wore shielded her from the worst of it. She preferred the cold to the stifling temperatures of summer, the crisp air made her feel alive.

She was alone on the lake today. No smoke drifted from the stovepipes of the nearby huts, the weather too cold even for those with shelters.

She inspected her fishing holes and discovered a thick layer of ice had formed since she had last been there. As she cranked the auger, reopening the holes, she wondered what it felt like to freeze. She had heard stories about people who had fallen through the ice and lived to tell about it. They claimed it felt like you were on fire.

She huddled close to a ledge that hung over the ice, a favorite spot of hers because the water was still deep, yet she was sheltered from the wind. She took a step, reaching for the thermos of coffee on her sled, but she slipped and fell on her ass, both legs kicking up in front of her. She started to rise, but hesitated when she noticed something suspended in the thick wall of ice beneath the ledge: an irregular form, frozen in place. She crawled closer to study it, but it was too dark beneath the ledge to make out any details. She brushed at the ice with her gloved hand.

What is that?

She retrieved the hatchet from her sled and started to chip away at the ice. A voice spoke up in her head.

Just leave it.

She ignored the voice and hacked at the ice until she had freed a chunk the size of a small boulder, the object in its center. She rolled it out into the sunlight to inspect it.

The ice surrounding the object was cloudy and patterned, making it difficult to identify any of the object's, or rather, *the creature's*, details, because surely this had once been a living thing. Was that the slip of a tail? The ridge of a spine? Multiple slender extremities? A head with a protruding jaw and brow?

It's probably a muskrat or young beaver, maybe a mink, she told herself. *Something that died just as the December freeze hit.*

Yet, the coloring of the creature was not brown, but a startling array of jewel tones that sparkled as she turned the chunk. Was it some kind of bird; an unfortunate parrot released into the wild to fend for itself? As she inspected what details she could make out, that did not seem to fit either. The head was the wrong size and shape for a bird, and the tail more...reptilian.

What is this thing?

She thought about chipping away more of the ice, but worried that without the proper tools the chunk would fracture and damage the creature, so she hauled it onto her sled and strapped it down, leaving the auger and the rest of her fishing supplies behind on the shore. It had started to snow, so she tied a red rag around a branch to mark the spot where she had left her gear.

Despite her layers, she shuddered as a chill wracked her body, but she warmed as she lugged the sled back up the hillside toward her cabin. The snow was falling heavily by the time she reached the steps of her front porch.

Mackinaw, pheasant, and venison filled both chest freezers in her garage, so she emptied the freezer compartment of her kitchen refrigerator. She threw bags of frozen peas and French fries into the sink, and placed the ice cube trays on the counter where the twelve compartments melted into tepid rectangular pools. Her cat, Toad, lapped a puddle that had formed on the kitchen floor.

The chunk filled the entire freezer compartment. She stared at it for a moment, before she let the door swing shut.

She lay in bed that night thinking about the thing in her freezer. Why had she brought it home? What was she going to do with it? And, most importantly:

What the heck was it?

THE NEXT MORNING, she removed the chunk from the freezer and set it on a towel on the kitchen floor. She dug out a chisel and hammer, and went to work, chipping away like a sculptor working on a marble block, shaping it into a more manageable size, honing it down until it was the size of a watermelon.

Okay. Now what?

Her first thought was what any reasonable person would do...

A reasonable person wouldn't have brought it home in the first place!

...thaw it out. Put it on a plate in her refrigerator like a piece of meat for her dinner—say, a venison steak or a rainbow trout from last summer's haul. Once thawed, she could identify it—a logical course of action.

She held it up to the overhead light until her arms trembled, squinting, tilting her head from side-to-side. Part of her wanted to keep it a secret, tucked away in the freezer to take out on special occasions so she could enjoy those exquisite, sparkling colors. She felt at peace when she looked at it, as if everything was going to be okay. She realized she had not felt that way in a long time.

She thought about packing it up and bringing it to the lab in Seattle where her brother, Brian, worked. When they were young, he loved this type of thing, but they had grown apart over the years. He left home for the city after High School graduation and had returned only once, when their mother was dying.

She thought of her last visit to Seattle, two months after their mother's death. She had been in the city for a fruit growers' conference and decided to surprise Brian. He had met her in the corridor outside his office, unsmiling, saying her name in chipped, careful syllables.

Amanda. What are you doing here?

He frowned at her weathered Carhartt pants, hiking boots, flannel shirt, and hunting jacket, then glanced up and down the hall to see if anyone was watching him converse with this ragged specimen of a woman.

Her brother was a snob. When had that happened?

She glared back, taking note of his snowy lab coat, skinny black jeans, and black, plastic-framed glasses. Okay, he was a nerd and a snob, but he was also a little bit cool. She resisted the urge to grab his head and mess up his perfectly moussed hair.

She imagined him examining the chunk of ice, his frown deepening, looking at her with a furrowed brow and placing a hand over his chin, professor style, while he contemplated how to tell her to go away.

No. Her brother and his perfect hair were not an option.

She leaned in toward the ice and frowned. Something had changed. The creature seemed to be in a different position than she remembered. Impossible! She placed it on the kitchen table and rolled it, studying the creature from every angle.

Of course, it's in the same position!

The lower extremities, if that was what they were, seemed closer to the body, like it was crouching, preparing to spring. A clear ripple in the chunk revealed a dark spot the size of an olive she had not noticed before. An eye? She jumped, the legs of her chair scraping the floor, as a drop of water cascaded down the surface of the ice. She took a breath, her heart pounding. For a moment, it had appeared to come from the corner of the eye.

You should just toss this thing in a snowbank and forget about it. Get it out of here!

Nodding, she rose and grabbed the chunk, but instead of going outside, she shoved it back inside the freezer and shut the door. She would figure out what to do with it later.

S HE WOKE WITH a start. Had there been a sound? A thud? Toad jumped onto the bed next to her head and she squawked. He responded with a croak, and she laughed.

"You scared me, kiddy," she said.

Drifting off to sleep last night, she had made a decision—she was going to thaw out the creature and examine it. If it were a beaver or other recognizable creature, she would dispose of it. If it was something else, then she would...

What would she do?

You'll figure that out when the time comes, her mother's reasonable voice said. She closed her eyes; she missed her so much. She thought of her brother in his pristine lab, surrounded by microscopes and test tubes, slides and beakers, itching to make a discovery; the reason he had left home. She was the opposite, longing to be discovered by something; the reason she had stayed behind.

She crawled from her warm bed. "Coffee, before I do anything," she said to the elk head mounted over the fireplace as she shuffled toward the kitchen. A cigarette dangled from his mouth, something her friend Julia found hilarious, but she found disrespectful, yet she had not bothered to remove it.

She moaned in sleepy surprise as liquid coolness soaked her socks when she stepped into the kitchen. She clicked on the light and saw puddles scattered across the floor.

Suddenly, she was wide-awake.

The freezer door was open.

She looked inside. The compartment was empty, except for shards of shattered ice. The creature—*her* creature—was gone!

A water trail led from a large puddle in front of the refrigerator across the kitchen floor and into the living room. The carpet was damp in patches all the way to the fireplace, where the glass doors were open a crack. She pushed open the doors and peered inside, but saw nothing odd amongst the charred remains of last night's fire. She tilted her head and listened, but heard no sound in the chimney. A knot formed in her stomach.

"Come back," Amanda whispered into the mouth of the fireplace. Then she shuddered and sank back onto the couch, her optimism melting away like the remnants of ice in her kitchen.

THE FEBRUARY THAW arrived with the same abruptness as the December freeze—a bully in its own right. As a result, the ice began to speak, moaning as it shifted and split; singing in joyous celebration about its new form; and gurgling as if digesting a satisfying meal. The sounds, amplified by the juicy air, made Amanda feel restless and blue.

Since her discovery of the thing in the ice and its consequent disappearance, she had become obsessed with seeking an explanation, even one considered beyond reason.

Last night there had been swatches of colored lights in the sky—an aurora borealis, according to the weather service. She questioned that. She had seen many an aurora in the northern skies, but last night's display had been due west, over the mountains. The lights hovered low in the sky, as if waiting for something. Her skeptical side argued with her whimsical side. It was doubtful that the lights had anything to do with her creature, yet the similar colors and sudden appearance seemed a strange coincidence.

The mysterious lights reminded her of other curious events in Montana, such as the recent cattle mutilations in the eastern part of the state—her friend, Jacob, was obsessed with such things. Fish Wildlife & Parks reported the deaths as casualties of December's frigid temperatures, which had plummeted to sixty-below on the coldest nights. Townies complained that the region's wolf pack had become more aggressive, preying on domestic animals due to the dwindling elk population. Jacob believed neither one.

Looking for a bit of an adventure, she had gone with him in December on what he called *a little extraterrestrial investigation*. Jacob's "investigations" usually turned out to be nothing more than a burn mark on a boulder from a vagrant's campfire, or a mysterious pattern in a farmer's hayfield, which later turned out to be the work of bored teenagers.

In this case, he wanted to see the mutilated body of a cow discovered on his cousin's ranch. She was the sensible friend, brought along to offer a bit of scientific reasoning, but when she saw the body, headless, torso sliced in precise ribbons, the internal organs removed, she had no logical explanation, other than to say that she believed the mutilation was not the work of wolves, vandals, or the result of inclement weather.

Jacob had placed the cow's head, found about twenty yards away, in a small cooler he retrieved from the trunk. When she asked him what he was going to do with the head, he said he was going to take it home and put it in the freezer.

But I'm not Jacob. It's not the same thing...

She ventured out onto the ice, trying not to think about aliens, wolves, or decapitated cows, deciding it was best to forget about the creature, rather than try to explain it.

At thirty-eight degrees above zero, the air was balmy, but the ice around her fishing holes was still solid. The middle of the lake, on the other hand, was treacherous, in a constant state of flux, shifting and cracking. On her trek down to the shore, she had seen the network of cracks and sheets of overlapping ice, as the thaw pushed them together and drove them apart.

There was no need to reopen her fishing holes; the mild temperatures had kept them liquid. As she prepared a line, a disturbance in one of the holes—a subtle rippling of the water's surface—caught her attention. She leaned over the hole, her reflection faceless on the water's dark surface.

She shouted when unfamiliar features appeared on the blank palette of her reflection: a pronounced brow, a jutting chin, sunken, glittering eyes—they locked onto hers. Colors swirled on the water's surface—familiar colors—engulfing the reflection. She fell backward, slamming the back of her head on the ice, blackness covering her like a quilt.

A THUNDEROUS CRACK jolted Amanda back to consciousness. She sat up, blinking, her thoughts muddy and jumbled. She was next to one of her fishing holes, gear scattered around her. She rubbed the back of her head with her hand and groaned, her voice echoed a second later by the lamenting ice.

Based on the sun's position behind the ridge and the cold bite of the air, it was late afternoon; she had been unconscious for hours.

She rose to her feet and shuffled back toward shore, focusing on her sled in the fading light. She remembered the reflection of the creature, and argued with herself as to whether or not it had been her imagination. It had been there for a second, then she had stumbled back and ... fainted?

Actually, it felt like you were pushed. Remember? That thing wanted you off the ice.

Come on! Enough of this crap! Your imagination's working overtime because you've been surfing the web too much, reading about Bigfoot and crop circles, and been going on "extraterrestrial investigations" with your crazy friends who bring home cow heads in their cooler. The thing trapped in the ice had been...nothing. The temperature in your freezer got too low because you left the door open a crack, and the chunk defrosted and dripped all over the place. Then Toad tracked it into the living room—he's one of those weird cats that likes water. The thing inside the chunk was just discolored ice, like when certain wavelengths are frozen and form that beautiful turquoise color. Mom taught you that. Remember? There is a scientific explanation for everything!

She clenched her fists and shook her head as she walked, so intent on self-flagellation that she did not see the jagged fissure running across a section of the ice that she had crossed a hundred times before.

She slipped through the split, plunging into the freezing water below. Her lungs contracted, the breath ripped from her chest. The weight of her clothes and boots dragged her down into the darkness. As she descended, she looked up toward the ceiling of ice—the network of cracks so obvious from her current vantage point—they surrounded the holes she had bored into the ice. She tried to kick, but that seemed to accelerate her descent.

She wondered how long it would take to reach the bottom. She looked down, but could see nothing but blackness. Once she reached the bottom, would her body eventually float upward and freeze? Would someone discover her there, frozen in a wall of ice, and decide to chip her out? Would they recognize her in the block, or would exquisite color cloak her features? Would they thaw her out immediately, or wait a day or two?

Her body burned. Her lungs ached.

So this is what it feels like to freeze. It does burn. How strange.

A creature materialized in front of her, and her oxygen-deprived brain announced that her mother had sent a Mackinaw trout to save her.

Then she realized it was not a trout.

She thrashed in the water, terrified, bright flecks dancing before her eyes. She flailed for the surface, but the creature moved with her until it was inches from her face. Swirling tentacles of radiant color encircled her head, wrapping around her neck and body. The creature opened its mouth and all she could see were rows of jagged yellow teeth. She, in turn, opened her mouth to scream, but had no breath left to do so. The burning sensation in her body had ceased, her extremities now numb and limp. She closed her eyes and longed for the void of unconsciousness, trying not to think about those sharp teeth tearing into her.

I'm sorry I took you away from the lake! The voice in her head screamed. *I'm so sorry!*

She opened her eyes and found herself surrounded by a viscous cloud, her body cradled by the ribbons of colored light, the warmth of the creature against her back. A rubbery coating covered her bare skin, insulating her from the frigid water, her clothes, dissolved. Her muscles warmed and she could feel her limbs, her hands and feet tingled.

And, she could breathe!

Her body rose toward the surface, the presence guiding her to an opening, the colored lights radiant against the ceiling of ice.

She pulled herself through the opening onto the frozen surface where she lay a moment, staring at her curled fingers, covered by the gummy purple substance. As she watched, a piece the size of a dime chipped off the back of her hand, and she felt a bite of cold air. She realized she must move; that her curious suit of purple goo was temporary.

She turned back toward the opening as the creature slipped back beneath the ice. It did not look back; it did not acknowledge her in any way. Perhaps it wanted to get deep beneath the surface before the ice caught it once again. To the west, over the mountains, the night sky trembled in a vivid palette of emerald, ruby, and gold.

She managed to get to her feet, but with every movement, more of the insulation fell away and the greedy air gnawed at her bare skin. As she made her way up the hillside in the darkness, she heard the familiar creak of the lodgepole pines, old friends urging her on.

Two hours later, she crawled up the steps to her cabin as the last of the coating fell away. Her body quaked as she started a fire in the wood stove. She dropped to all fours in front of the stove, basking in the luxurious heat, the thin layer of ice that had replaced the insulation on her skin, melting away.

From her spot on the floor, she could hear the ice complaining, its groans cutting into the night as it shifted and contracted; disappointed it had not captured anything before it returned to a frozen state.

ABOUT THE AUTHOR

Hall Jameson is an American writer and artist who lives in the Pacific Northwest with an assortment of furry and feathered creatures. Her writing has appeared in *Compelling Science Fiction, Nature Futures*, and *Drabblecast*. When she's not writing stories or taking photographs, Hall spends her time on the water, in the woods, or wrangling cats.

Playing the Hand You're Dealt

M.A. Akins

EVEN THE END of the world won't make me miss our annual poker game. It's a tradition that's been going on for thirty-five years now. Normally we get together around seven, which at this time of year, is just after dark. Today we're meeting at noon. It doesn't feel right. There's something about gambling in natural light that seems, well, unnatural. But, as I said, even the end of the world... I'm just grateful the timing worked out.

Roger, Charlie, Bill, Daryl, and I have been playing poker ever since we survived an ambush in the second Iraq war. We were the only ones. Charlie took a couple rounds, one in the shoulder, the other in his right thigh, just missing the artery. We played poker on Charlie's cot while he was in the medic's tent waiting for medevac to the hospital. That's where we played the first game, and we've been playing on that day ever since. With Daryl dying of pancreatic cancer a little less than a year ago, around the time my wife Sandy was diagnosed with brain cancer, this is the first time any of us has been absent. I wanted to be with him the day he died, but at least the other guys made it, so he didn't die alone. Sure, his wife and daughter were there too, but he needed us just the same. I called him to say goodbye, but it felt like I was cheating. Sandy understood, even told me to go, but I knew she needed me more.

207

I pull up to the wood cabin and park behind a red Porsche Cayenne. I wonder who the hell owns that? I see Bill's rusted Ford pickup and Roger's ancient Chevy, not looking any different than the day he first bought it, so it must be Charlie's. My son Matt steps out of the car before I turn the engine off. We didn't speak at all during the two-hour drive. We hadn't spoken in the last five months, so he surprised me by saying yes when I asked him to join us to stand in for Daryl.

"Look who decided to show up," Charlie says as we walk in the door. He walks up to Matt, putting his thin hand on Matt's shoulder. "I'm sure as hell sorry about your mom, Matt. That's tough. We appreciate your sittin' in fer Daryl. Wouldn't be the same with just the four of us."

Charlie's parents moved to Boston from Ireland when he was a child, and he never fully lost the accent. Charlie's dad wanted him to work for him after we came back from the Gulf and take over the family business. He went to work for Big Y supermarkets instead, loading trucks at a distribution center, never even taking a promotion to shift supervisor so he wouldn't have to be responsible for anyone but himself. He's worked there ever since.

"So, this is the mysterious cabin dad's been coming to all these years," Matt says. He looks up at the vaulted ceiling, then the loft, around to the kitchen area with a small, white two-door fridge and sink with an old radio sitting on the edge. Classical music or something like that plays. A black and white Felix the Cat clock is mounted above the sink. A single log beam stretches from one side of the room to the other, with a solitary five-bulb lamp hanging from it over the round table in the middle of the room. "Don't you guys eat? Where's the stove?"

"Not really," Roger says, opening the fridge door and revealing two loaves of bread, cold cuts, cheese, mustard, and ketchup on the top shelf while bottles of Sam Adams Boston Lager line the remaining two. Pointing to the iron wood burning stove over in the corner, he adds, "If we want something hot, which we almost never do, but if we did, we have this old gal. It's great for pancakes, bacon, and eggs in the morning. Of course, we didn't bring anything for breakfast this time."

Bill hands Matt and me a cold Sam Adams and nods, taking a sip of his own. Bill, a lobster man from Massachusetts, has always been a quiet person, at least as long as I've known him. I figured that was the reason his wife left him after only being married a few years. It might have also been he chose to spend more time with his crew on the boat. He never remarried.

I ask who brought the Porsche, and Bill and Roger turn to Charlie, who tells us his neighbor gave it to him. It seems Charlie and he got to talking this morning about the poker game, our history, Daryl, and all that when the guy takes out the keys and tosses them to him. He tells Charlie not to gamble it away. Charlie tells the guy it's not that kind of game, no heavy hitters, but the man just turns around and walks back into his house, sipping his coffee.

"We've been neighbors for I don't know how long," Charlie says. "and this is the first time he gives a shit about my day. Even gave me a damn fine cup o' Joe. Anyway, he just got that SUV too. Still has that new car smell."

"It's the luck of the Irish," Roger says.

Roger's a big man with a nervous demeanor. He used the GI Bill after returning home to get a degree in computer engineering and started his own network security company after that. He's the richest one of us, but you would never know it the way he dresses. If there was a time he wore an expensive watch, a tailor-made suit, or anything that didn't look like it came off the rack at a JC Penney's, I couldn't tell you.

"Even out in the sticks where I live, there was quite a bit of chaos at the beginning," I say and then nod towards Matt. "But this morning it was quiet when I picked up my son. I suppose people are with family or at church today."

Matt stares down at his beer.

After I buried my wife, I didn't have time to mourn her properly. As soon as I could, I stockpiled canned goods, water, and toilet paper, bought a few hundred rounds of ammunition, and filled up extra gas cans. I made sure I had enough for two and then some. If all hell was going to break loose, I would make damn sure my part of the world was secure. I wanted Matt with me, so I called him over and over again. He never picked up the phone. I drove to his place twice a week, but he never came to the door. Fortunately, my visions of apocalyptic doom never came to pass. Still, I worried about how well Matt would do under the circumstances.

"Well, boys, the family's all here and this is our church. Time fer communion," Charlie says, grabbing five tumbler glasses and a bottle of Makers Mark out of the pantry.

"For Pete's sake, Charlie, you'd think you could be a little less, you know, sacrilegious today," Roger says.

After Charlie fills each glass half way, he says, "There ain't no God. I've been a Catholic all my life, and at no time, did the priest—"

Bill clears his throat. "Gentlemen, we have a tradition. Now knock off the silly squabbling." As I said, Bill's a quiet man, a quiet man with a deep, commanding voice people listen to. He raises his glass, and we follow suit. "To Daryl and fallen comrades." My throat burns as the bourbon rushes down.

I never liked talking about religion. Sandy grew up with it, regularly going to church, praying before the meal, the whole bit, and while my family proclaimed to be among the faithful when asked, the only time you heard the Lord's name in our house was when we took it in vain. They say there are no atheists in foxholes and I always thought that meant the idea of getting killed put the fear of God in you. I guess I don't feel any different today than I did then.

The music stops.

My friend in Perth, Australia tells me the asteroid will enter the atmosphere in a short while.

The music starts again. It sounds a little like elevator music.

After some more small talk, Bill refills the bourbon glasses and we migrate to the table with a deck of cards and an old radio. Each of us puts ten dollars' worth of nickels and dimes into piles in front of us. I take the deck of cards from the center, shuffle, and deal.

"Christ! Ya think they could play somethin' a little more upbeat today," Charlie says

After a half hour with everyone except Roger winning a hand, the music stops.

Impact! In the next—

I turn the radio off as the cabin trembles, and the bourbon in my glass ripples out to the sides. Matt throws me an angry look, his What-the-hell look. I'm used to it. I pick up my cards, toss in a couple nickels and look at Bill, who tosses in three nickels. Bill won a few thousand in Vegas a few years ago playing poker. As I look at him, I can see how. His expression is as blank as the face on a statue, but with a half-burnt stogie sticking out of a mouth surrounded by a bushy, brown and gray beard.

Matt turns the radio back on, but only music plays now, some jazz piece from the 50's. He turns the dial only to find static. I look at my watch and then to Roger, who's toying with the nickels and dimes on the table in front of him. He runs his hand through his thin grey hair. It's obvious he's got a bad hand and can't decide whether to fold or not. Roger couldn't bluff his way out of anything. Charlie taps his finger on the table with the rhythm of slow faucet leak. Tap. Tap. Tap.

"Fer Chrissake Roger, we don't have all day. Would ya just throw a couple of coins on the pile and be done with it?" Charlie says. "You've got a shit hand. Ye know it. We know it."

Roger throws his cards down.

"I would like a chance to win for once. If this is going to be our last game, I want to win."

"Win? Nobody wins here except Bill. We'll all be down before the game is over. The best ye can hope fer is to walk outta here with a little dignity, which, at this point, my friend, you are sorely lacking."

"I think I can do it this time. I'm only down a little."

As far as I know, Roger succeeded in everything he did, never losing at anything except poker. He graduated both high school and college with a 4.0 GPA, star quarterback for the university, started a successful business, dated beautiful women, but never married. You name it; he succeeded at it. When we were ambushed, he took cover about fifty meters away from me behind a rock outcropping, popping off a round now and then toward an enemy none of us could see. He wanted to win then too, but knew the odds favored the other side. Still, he got careless at one point, firing without cover and charging forward, and if Daryl hadn't ordered him to return to his position, he may not have survived that day. I don't know how he didn't get killed. I'd call that a success.

Charlie looks to Bill for support. Without looking away from his cards, Bill takes his cigar out of his mouth, taps ash into the ashtray, then puts the stogie back in his mouth. Charlie takes a deep breath and resumes tapping his finger on the table. Tap. Tap. Tap.

Matt is fidgeting with his cards, folding them together, unfolding and folding. He keeps turning to the radio. I put my hand on his wrist and smile, but he doesn't notice. He's focused and unfocused at the same time. I'd seen that look in his mom's eyes all too often.

When the news broke six months ago, I didn't tell my wife. I turned off the television and radio and told her we needed to just spend some quiet time together. Because of the pain meds, she slept most of the time anyway. She was at rest now, finally calm after weeks of worrying about us, about how we would take care of ourselves without her. If she had found out, she'd have fussed about what we needed to do, as if there was anything you could do. I couldn't let her do that to herself with such little time left. Matt disagreed with me. He thought the news would be more of a comfort to her. Because of her faith, she would have believed we would soon be together again. We fought, and only after I let him know he wouldn't be allowed to see her again until the funeral if he tried to tell her anything did he agree to keep silent. She only lived another three days. We spent those few lucid moments she had reliving the good times and talking about our plans for a future that would never be.

The music stops. The airwaves remain silent.

Australia, Indonesia and New Zeal—

I turn the radio off again before Matt's reach can stop me. He flicks the knob, and music plays, the stuff my grandma and grandpa listened to from the '50s and '60s. I'm not sure. This time I get the words along with the look.

"What the hell, Dad?"

"We have a game to play, and it's your turn now that Roger has finally tossed in his hard-earned coins." I say.

Charlie chuckles. Bill stares at his hand. Roger wipes his forehead with a paper towel. After glancing at his cards, Matt folds, throwing his cards onto the coin pile.

I lay down my cards, two jacks, two queens, and a ten. Charlie and Roger toss theirs into the pile, face down. Bill, he looks at me, the corners of his mouth widening, showing me teeth clamped down on a cigar. I can't take my eyes off of that smile. He never smiles like that. One by one he puts the cards on the table, five of hearts, five of clubs, five of diamonds, nine of clubs and nine of spades. Full house. He wraps his arms around the coins as if he just won a million dollars and draws them into his other winnings.

We play another few rounds with Bill winning three more hands, Charlie and Matt one each and me taking two. As I'm dealing another, the music stops and the radio goes silent. Matt leans over the box, blocking me from reaching the dial. I shrug my shoulders.

All broadcasts from China have stopped. Antarctic stations are now silent. In approximately 45 minutes—

Charlie turns the radio off this time and keeps his hand on the dial while Matt glowers at him. After a two-minute stare down,

Charlie gives Matt a big goofy grin and turns the dial again. Simon and Garfunkel's "The Sound of Silence" is playing now. I love the song, but question the person's mentality for choosing the songs to play today.

"Don't you want to know what's going on out there? Don't you want—"

"No, Matt, we don't," I tell him. "We're playing poker. What's going on out there doesn't change what's going on in here."

"Once again making the decision for everyone?"

"I'm cool with it," says Charlie.

"Yeah, me too," says Roger.

Bill goes to the ice cooler, bringing back another round of beer for everyone. As Matt opens his mouth to say something, Bill pops the cap off of a bottle and puts the bottle in front of his face. Matt takes it from him and doesn't say anything. When Roger says he's hungry and now might be a good time for the sandwiches, we all agree, shifting the coins and cards aside to make room for the food.

"You don't know how hard it was to get this stuff," Charlie says, spreading mustard over a slice of bread. "I don't know why I didn't think about it earlier. Took me a good two weeks of scrounging around the stores to round these up. Who brought the bread anyway? I haven't seen any in the stores for at least a month."

"I bought a few loaves and froze them and saved a couple for today," Roger says. He takes a bite of his ham and cheese. "I wargamed a few scenarios, factoring in a number of possibilities, and came to the conclusion most food products would run dry a couple of weeks before today."

For the life of me, I don't know how Roger can be so methodical and still be so terrible at cards.

After we finish the sandwiches, I deal another round. While everyone is studying their hand, the music on the radio ends.

Hawaii and Berlin have ceased broadcasting.

A mellow upbeat song begins playing. The name escapes me,

but I remember dancing with my wife to it on our fifth anniversary when Matt was only eighteen months old. It was the first time she left him with a babysitter, her own mother. What if something happens to Mom? she would ask. She's very healthy and not at all old, I would tell her. What if he won't stop crying? she'd say a little later. They'll be all right. I'd say.

I watch Matt fidget with his cards after everyone else tossed in their nickels. I touch his shoulder to remind him to place his bet, and he adds a nickel to the pile. After replacement cards are drawn, we toss more coins in the pile. Matt folds again. Bill wins again.

"Ya know, Matty," Charlie says. "Don't take this wrong. You're doin' us a big favor playing for Daryl, but I gotta tell ya, Daryl you ain't. Your Dad ever tell you about him?"

Confusion rolls over Matt's face.

Roger shuffles the deck. I have to admit. I'm not sure where Charlie's heading with this or if Matt is going to lose his temper. Knowing how to read Matt was a skill I never mastered.

After his Mom took her last breath, after we cried by her bed-side, after I called the hospital, he just stared at me, his face red. He turned away from me. I called him back, but the door slammed shut. At the funeral, we stood side by side next to her coffin as people gave us their condolences. We thanked them together and carried her casket to the hearse together. The whole time he never said a word to me. I never imagined he could be so angry over such a simple request.

"He never talks about the war," Matt says.

"Let me tell you. Unlike yourself, Daryl could not keep his mouth shut for more than two minutes. Ain't that right, guys?" Charlie says, taking a peek at the cards Roger handed him. Roger and Bill nod their heads. "He always had some story to tell. I never knew a guy who could have so much to relate after only one year. One year he goes to China, the next Africa. Just to take pictures of wild animals. He shoulda been here after they made that announcement. Talk about animals. Anyway, up to the day he died, he had somethin' to say. But he wasn't always like that. No, sir. He was a quiet one in the army. At least until the day of the ambush. He got us out of that firefight with the Iraqis, directin' fire and keepin' us movin'. I knew in my heart of hearts we were all goin' to die, but here we are."

I remember the vehicles rolling up to the edge of the village, and before I know what's happening, I watched the Bradley in front of us disappear in a cloud of dust; and then, our Humvee being pelted by gunfire as if we were in a hailstorm, we stopped and I saw the disabled vehicle, its tracks blown off, the back ramp lowering, the first man out shot in the face, then Charlie running out and falling to the ground. I screamed as my driver died when he jumped from the Humvee, and I wanted to shoot back, but there was no room, and Bill pushed me out, rounds whizzing by me, getting closer and closer, as I hugged anything that offered even the smallest bit of protection. I saw the bodies of the rest of our patrol sprawled in the dirt, as bullets splashed into the soft earth around them, a burning Humvee, its ammunition cooking off, sending more projectiles in all directions. Bill vanished off to the side firing as he ran, leaving me alone, and then Daryl's voice came out of nowhere instructing us to lay down cover fire as he sprinted into that hell to get a radio from our other Hummer. I knew he was calling for evacuation or assistance, but those thirty minutes waiting for the choppers were the longest and loneliest ones of my life. I thought Charlie was dead, and could only see Roger, who looked as scared I did.

Everyone places their bets as Charlie continues.

"I was laid up in the medic tent with a couple well-placed bullet holes in me when in walks Daryl and these three. They're all carryin' somethin'; your dad and Roger had some chairs, Bill a deck of cards, and Daryl a bottle of bourbon. I can see them walkin' in like it was yesterday. But somethin''s different. Daryl's talkin'. I mean a lot. We can't get a word in edgewise."

Matt plays his hand and loses. He doesn't look angry anymore. Bill shuffles and deals.

"Fer the love of God, Bill, can't you cut me a little slack?" Charlie says after looking at the cards. "Anyway, where was I? So every year, Daryl and us get together to play poker and shoot the shit. Daryl still talks a ton and updates us on every little thing that happened durin' the year. Our last get together, he tells us he's dyin' and probably won't be makin' it to the next night. Cancer. I went to see him in the hospital just before he passed. While I was there, I had to ask him what made him change that day, the day we nearly died. You know what he told me? He tells me that if he would've died that day, we wouldn't have known him from Adam. He couldn't live with that. So, from that point on, he told us everythin' about his life."

"What's that got to do with me?" Matt asks. "What's that got to do with today, the radio, or anything else going on in the world? I don't know why—"

The song on the radio stops in the middle, and Matt whips his head in my direction. I raise my hands up as if surrendering.

San Francisco and London are silent now. This is my final announcement. I hope you've enjoyed the selections we chose for you. This station will go off the air after one final song.

The now all too familiar lyrics of REM's "It's the End of the World" come pouring into the cabin. Every television and radio station has played it ad infinitum since word of the asteroid broke. Matt puts his fist to his mouth as if to force back a sob, but he chuckles instead. Then he laughs. He laughs hard. Bill smiles then also breaks into hysterical laughter, dragging the rest of us along. We can't hear the song anymore over our own noise. I force myself to stop and breathe. The song finishes. A minute or two of silence and then static lets us know the announcer powered down the station.

Bill keeps the cards and deals each of us five cards.

"It's time to wrap this game up," he says putting a fresh cigar in his mouth and lighting it. He tosses two dimes into the middle of the table. We each in turn add two dimes to the pile, and then without hesitation, Bill replaces three cards.

Roger smiles and asks for only one card. When he sees Charlie looking at him, he looks down at his hand. Charlie asks for two, Matt three, and I take three.

Bill bets five dimes.

Roger ups the ante to six.

Charlie adds six. Matt adds six, and I add six.

Bill tosses in another five and a nickel while Roger again raises the stakes by a nickel.

The betting goes around the table twice more with Bill and Roger in heavy competition and the rest of us just playing along, matching Roger's bet. When Bill's turn comes around once more, a low vibration as if a generator has been turned on flows into the table.

Bill takes his cigar out and places it in the ashtray.

"It's time to stop pussy footin' around," he says, shoving all of his coins to the middle.

Roger's eyes open wide, but he pushes the rest of his coins in without a pause. After I add the last of my money, Bill puts his cards on the table. He doesn't even have a pair. Roger is giddy with excitement as he lays each card down one at a time. Ace of diamonds. King of spades. Queen of spades. Jack of hearts. Ten of hearts. The rest of us toss down our hands as Roger scoops in his winnings.

Matt stands up, stretches, and goes outside. I follow him as Charlie congratulates Roger and Bill smokes his cigar with a wide grin.

"Son," I say as I step out onto the porch. "Are you ok?"

"What kind of a question is that? Of course, I'm not all right." His face softens a little, and he looks up. The light dims as the sun fades behind dust filling the sky. "I still don't understand why you wouldn't let me tell Mom."

"I know you think you knew her," I say, "but you didn't. Not really. What could she have done? Nothing. That's what. Wasn't it nice to feel like we didn't have a care in the world while we were together?"

"No. She might have died a lot happier. You don't have the right to make all the decisions, yet you did."

"I don't think anyone dies happy. She was in a lot of pain, but died peacefully. We can't control everything, only a very small portion and sometimes not even then. We play the hand we're dealt."

A thin dark line grows in the distance, as a gentle warm breeze washes over us. Overhead, fireballs blaze across the sky like shooting stars.

"But you've always tried to control everything, Dad. There are too many things you can't control, and what you do control is very small."

"I've only done what I felt was best for you and your mom."

"Have you ever considered you might have been wrong on some of those decisions?"

"Sure. Who doesn't question the calls they make now and again?"

"It doesn't matter anymore. I didn't come here to rehash this or stand in for Daryl or play poker. I came to be with you because Mom would have wanted me to. Because I wanted to."

I put my arm around his shoulder as the other three file out of the cabin, joining us on the porch. The wind and heat rise, and I feel sweat run down my left side and bead on my forehead. Pine trees swat the air. As I realize how much my Son is more like my wife than I ever thought, certainly more than me, I feel a tap on my shoulder.

"The boys and I were thinkin' it might be a good time to see what that Porsche can do," Charlie shouts over the roar.

The ground shakes and rumbles, but we can still stand.

Matt yells, "Where would we go?"

Bill yells back, "Who the hell knows? Beats waiting around to die, don't ya think?"

Matt and I look at each other and shrug our shoulders. I open the door to let Matt climb in before me, but he shakes his head and gestures for me to get in first. We climb into the SUV and spin out of the driveway toward the highway.

ABOUT THE AUTHOR

M. A. Akins holds an MFA in Creative Writing from Lesley University and lives in Stuttgart, Germany, where he is a writer of Science Fiction and Fantasy when he can convince his cats to stay off of his lap or keyboard. After a long period of brainstorming, map making, and world building, he is hard at work writing the first of a five-book, young adult fantasy series. His short fiction has been published in MYTHIC and Wild Musette.

Three Minutes Back in Time

JR Gershen-Siegel

THE FAIR WAS a disappointment. Rosemary couldn't really blame her date for that. James Warren was a serious guy, and it was getting to be a serious relationship. For him to take her to something so frivolous as a fair in the DC suburbs was a rare treat indeed. It wasn't his fault that it was a bit run-down and small, a bit too old-fashioned for 1943.

His spectacles gave him a serious look, even more serious than he was. But they were also a necessity. And they had made him a 4-F. Rosemary Parker knew that a lot of her friends at the munitions plant were jealous. And she didn't even think she was that pretty, yet there she was, with a man who was going to become an actuary once he finished his exams. And he even said he would be all right with it if she went to school to become a teacher and work after—he hoped—they wed. Rosemary still wasn't sure if her answer was yes. She didn't know if his permission to work would suddenly be withdrawn if they had a child.

With her mother gone and her brother as well; it had just been Rosemary and her father, Reverend Elisha Parker. Until James came along, straight out of Concord, Massachusetts, to seek his fortune in the nation's capital and, in his spare time, join the church. A romance hadn't been on his mind, and it hadn't been on Rosemary's, either. Other young ladies at the National Baptist Memorial Church had thrown themselves at James, as he attentively listened to the choir or read aloud to the congregation.

Maybe it was her soprano voice, or maybe it was her hair, straightened carefully and flipped slightly, like one of her favorites, Lena Horne, or sometimes held back or even with a flower by her ear, like Billie Holiday. Times were tight enough that Rosemary didn't dress in the latest styles. Her hat for church was modest, as was her suit. The dresses she wore, and the occasional skirts with sweater sets, were all a bit old, so they had a bit more decoration than was currently the style. She had taken in some of her mother's old things or saved her money from her work for a blouse here, a hair ribbon there. But she was never a fashion plate.

Maybe those were the things that had attracted James first, for Rosemary had looked serious, too. Except that, inside, she wasn't. So she had convinced him to forego their usual date – watching the planes take off and land at National Airport – and instead go to a fair just outside nearby Arlington. This was even though it meant a streetcar ride and then a bus ride. James grumbled a little at that.

And now he was grumbling more, that their day was not going well at all. At least the fair wasn't segregated, like so many other places were. Its grounds were open to all, including James and Rosemary. And once they had determined the fair had little to offer, they had sat down on a bench and talked. He had wanted to discuss W.E.B. Du Bois and the recent allied raid on Rome. But Rosemary had wanted to talk about the upcoming premiere of *Stormy Weather* with Lena Horne and Fats Waller. He didn't even want to discuss the recent All-Star game.

She finally got up, tired of too many somber moments. "Rosie, where are you off to?"

"I, I just need some time to myself." She started walking away.

James dashed over. "This place isn't familiar. It's not safe for a girl like you to be walking alone." He shrugged and gestured a little at the fair. "You know, circus people."

"James! Please, these people are making a living and abiding by the law. Don't begrudge them that."

"It's, it's not helping anyone."

She leveled her gaze at him. "And you honestly think actuaries help anyone? And I mean people, not insurance companies." She started walking again.

"I, I, wait, wait, please." She stopped and let him catch up. He said, "Rosie, I'm sorry. It's just so, so frivolous. There's a war going on and our people are finally getting some recognition and are advancing. There's the good and the bad but all these people are focusing on is how to have a good time."

"And why is that such a bad thing? James – and you're not even Jim, like most men would be – James, you are missing the point. People going to a fair or the movies or to the ballpark are well aware that there's a war going on. They want to escape it, if only for a little while."

"And the advancement of our people? Do they want to escape that as well?"

"I don't know. But honestly, James, were you ever a child?"

"I don't know what you mean. Of course I was a child."

"I don't think so. You may have been shorter and immature, but it seems to me as if you've been a studious near-actuary your entire life. Were you born wearing spectacles and carrying a book?"

"Don't be absurd. It, it doesn't become you."

"James, we have our whole lives to be sober and serious. We have, the good lord willing, decades to be the pillars of the community, fine and dependable and upright citizens and all that that entails. Can you, just once, set that aside for an afternoon and, and be the child I'm not so sure you ever truly were?"

"This is hardly the place."

She spotted a different ride she hadn't noticed before. "This is

223

exactly the place." She strode toward it and he hurried to keep up with her. She reached the attendant first. "Excuse me," she said to the attendant, "I see your ride is free. But I'm puzzled as to its name—*Three Minutes Back in Time*—whatever does it mean?"

James arrived a moment later. The ride suspiciously looked a lot like a tunnel of love. "Rosie, I think this would be improper."

"Wait, we haven't heard this man's explanation as to what this ride is all about. Sir?"

The attendant took a toothpick from his mouth. "It's exactly what it says. You can go back in time to any day, but only for three minutes."

"What?" asked James. "That's impossible."

"It's very possible. Young lady, what do you think?"

"I don't rightly know. Here," she said after a moment, "if you can take me to a particular time and place, then I'll know you're not pulling our legs."

"And when would those be?"

"Rosie, you can't be serious."

"April the eleventh, 1940. At about four in the afternoon, please."

"And the location, Miss?"

"Meridian Hill Park, near the Joan of Arc memorial, sir."

"I can do that. That'll be fifteen cents, or a quarter for the both of you."

Rosemary turned to James. "Well? I can pay my own way but if you want to come along, you'd best speak up now."

"I suppose I should." He fished into his pocket. "Here's two bits."

"Now you folks get into the boat and I'll start everything up." He pulled levers and manually turned gear wheels and then plotted the location using a straightedge and a map. "Ready when you are. And you'd best set your watch, young man." James checked his wristwatch briefly.

They settled into the small boat. "Ready," Rosemary said.

It was perhaps a coworker of the attendant's pulling them along, because for some reason the boat went forward even though there was no motor and no one was paddling. The tunnel was dark and quiet and then there was music. James strained to identify it. "Tommy Dorsey?"

"No, it's Make Believe Island and I believe the band is Mitchell Ayers. I've forgotten who the girl singer is."

"That's all right. Well, I suppose such older music is a bit like a moment back in time. Not bad for two bits. But why that day in particular? What's so special about it?"

"It's, it's the day Freddie was shot and killed."

"Oh my goodness. Rosie, I knew you had lost your mother, of course. And I had seen pictures of your brother. I had always assumed he had died in the service of the armed forces, or something. But this is before we were at war. What happened?"

"It was a gang fight, James."

The scene changed in an instant, and they were out of the boat and standing in the sunshine right by a statue of a woman in medieval armor on horseback, Joan of Arc. Rosemary was stunned and then rushed over to a man sitting on a nearby park bench reading the newspaper. "Pardon me, sir, but may I see the headline, please."

"By all means," he said, handing her the paper. The front page article in that morning's *Baltimore Sun* said: *Norway to Fight to End—Berlin Dubious of Quick Victory.* The date was April the eleventh, 1940.

"Oh, my!"

"Is something wrong, Miss?"

"I, I, I'm sorry." She turned to find James and he was right behind her. "Did you see it?"

"Yes, I did, Rosie. Sir, is this some sort of a trick? Are you an actor?"

"No, young man. Now if you'll excuse me." He adjusted his hat and left, leaving his newspaper behind.

225

Rosemary picked it up, randomly turning to page 23. "There's classified advertisements and everything. I do believe it is the correct newspaper."

"Anyone could have saved theirs, though. This doesn't make any sense. Rosie, we are not in 1940. That's impossible," he repeated.

"I beg to differ. Look at her outfit."

It was a woman in a smart suit and heels. Her jacket had pockets and her heels were maybe three inches high. Her hat had a wide brim. "And?"

"And those are prewar clothes, James. Her complete outfit is from before rationing."

"I still say this is a trick. This, it can't be right. It can't possibly be true."

There was the sound of shouting suddenly. It was insults going back and forth. They both turned toward the sources of the noise, to see young men of several races in their shirtsleeves. Their slacks were the looser kind worn with zoot suits. "Freddie!" Rosemary yelled. "Freddie!"

One young man turned and rushed over. "Sis, what are you doing here? It's not safe for you." He had a baseball bat in his hands. "And, and you, you cut your hair? New clothes?"

"I'm not so sure I can explain. Freddie, you're in peril."

"It's as I said," he pointed out. "I did just warn you that it's not safe here. And who might you be, sir?"

"I'm James Warren, Rosie's fiancé." Rosemary gave him a look so James hastily added, "Well, that is to say, I have asked but I don't have a response as of yet."

"I see," Freddie said. "Sis, really, you need to go back home. It ain't right for you to watch this." He turned the bat over in his hands.

"Baseball, Freddie, baseball," Rosemary said, "I know you have season tickets for the next few years. I know your seat number and everything. It's 89R."

Freddie scowled a bit. "Nobody's supposed to know about that. You been looking through my sock drawer?"

"Freddie, I know where your seat is because I've sat in it, many times." Her voice quavered and James quickly handed her his handkerchief.

"I would never miss a lotta games."

"Freddie," she whispered, rubbing the handkerchief against her face to sop up a tear or two, "this is your last day on earth."

Freddie glanced from one face to another. "Is this for real, Mr. Warren?"

"Yes, it is. We come from 1943. I didn't believe it before. But I do now." He glanced down at his watch. "It's been two minutes and, and forty-one seconds."

"There's no time. Freddie, just know that we love you and, and you can change this."

"Freddie," James said, "leave this place so her heart isn't broken. Please."

Freddie's image started to dissolve as time was up. The last thing Rosemary heard in 1940 was the report of a gun.

And then they were back in the boat, and the music was playing, but this time it was Jimmy Dorsey's orchestra and Kitty Kallen singing, They're Either Too Young or Too Old, a lament about all the good men having been drafted. It was a hit in 1943. Just as Kallen sang, "He tries to serenade me, but his voice is changing now," the boat left the tunnel and emerged in the July sunshine.

Shaken, Rosemary let James help her out of the little boat. She was still clutching his handkerchief. He led her to a bench as a few pigeons jogged out of the way. "Are you all right, Rosie?"

"No," she said, lower jaw trembling, "I'm not. James, what do you think just happened?"

"It feels as if we really were there. And if we were, then Freddie learned how much you cared. And how much you still do."

"But that gunshot. Is it the bullet that killed him? Did we meet Freddie only to barely miss his end?"

"Maybe God spared us from Freddie's end. I know you see me as a stick in the mud. And I am. I know that about myself. But I can see your point of view, too. I know it doesn't always look like I do. But you're right. I have time enough to be a drab, gray, dull man, surrounded by numbers and bank notes and the like. So I will need you, Rosie, to pull me back from that, and bring me back to the light. But I want to do something for you in return."

"What is it?"

"I swear to you, I will be your rock. I'll never be flashy. But I will always be there. And I vow to you that I will never ignore what you say. I will never dismiss your ambitions or your dreams and claim they're worthless. My own father did that to my mother. I promise I will never, ever do that to you."

"If we were to wed, what would happen after we started a family?"

"I can't predict the future," he smiled just a touch. "All I can do is understand the past, I suppose."

She glanced back to look at the ride again, but it was gone. There was nothing there at all. "Where's the ride?"

James looked back, too. He then looked back at her, slack-jawed. "What happened?"

"Maybe it was God giving us a lesson, too, and a bit of a nudge. It wasn't just God sparing me—us—from witnessing Freddie's death."

"Whose death?" asked a voice just behind Rosemary.

She turned to see a man a year older than her in a corporal's uniform, holding two dripping ice cream cones. "Freddie? What is going on?"

"They were out of chocolate sprinkles so I got you walnuts. I hope that's okay." He handed her a chocolate cone which had been rolled in crushed walnuts. "And Jimmy, I got you your usual plain vanilla." He handed the other cone to a speechless James. "What's the matter? You two look like you've just been to a funeral, or something."

Weeping, she hugged him, and James took her cone from her so she could hug Freddie all the more tightly. "Freddie, oh Freddie."

"This was a great surprise," Freddie said. "Jimmy sure knows how to set 'em up. All I had to do was get leave and a plane ticket and let him know when I was in town."

Laughing and crying at the same time, Rosemary broke the hug and turned to look at James, who she caught eating some of her ice cream. He gave her a guilty look and then winked at her and smiled. "Freddie," she said, "I'm so glad you're here. You're the first person I wanted to tell."

"Tell me what?"

"I wanted to tell you that this is the man I am going to marry."

About the Author

JR Gershen-Siegel is a Lambda Literary Award nominee, who also won the 2013 Riverdale Avenue Books NaNoWriMo award. In addition to Mythic Magazine, she has been published by Riverdale Avenue Books, Jay Henge Publishing, Hydra Productions, and Writers Colony Press. Her work has also appeared in Theme of Absence, Empyreome, and Asymmetry Fiction.

Her current project is a trilogy of works about drug-induced time manipulation, called Time Addicts. She lives in a Victorian house Boston with her husband and twice as many computers as people.

A Level of Choice

D. A. D'Amico

Aishwarya Patel liked me in a way that was clearly against the law. I knew, but said nothing as we rode the narrow tube up into the cap with the others from our graduating class.

Holographic images of our starship home floated like thought bubbles above our heads, silvery potato shapes meant to represent our tiny made world as it traveled between the stars. I'd never given it much thought before. *Starwind* was my home. The ship was all I'd ever known, and that wouldn't change in my lifetime.

"*Star time*, Ndamona." Rashawn Ortiz smiled at me from his place near the crowded front of the slender elevator. His eyes were all pupil, glittering black saucers against the thin planes of his face. He was completely leveled out, a poster boy for medicated normal. "You excited?"

I tried to smile, but the heat from Aishwarya's thigh pressing against me from beneath where our layered formal skirts overlapped made it hard for me to breathe. The scent of her perfume shifted, becoming flowery, sweet, like the candy I'd just eaten. I glanced away.

"Are *you* excited, Aishwarya?" My voice trembled. My face hot as I became all too aware of the double meaning behind my

231

words. She looked at me, lips slightly parted. I blushed. I hadn't meant it the way it sounded.

The tube slowed. A wave of dizziness rippled through me that had nothing to do with the change in momentum, and I trembled. I tried to stand. The compartment felt too crowded, people jammed together in a tight mass like fleshy puzzle pieces, hot with mingled and sometimes stinking breath. I could feel my level slipping away.

Unfamiliar anxiety gripped me. I panted. The air in the tube seemed to vanish, and my vision blurred.

Aishwarya realized my dilemma. She slipped a hand around my neck, her icy fingers easing my head toward her lap. "Put your head down. Close your eyes and breathe."

My left arm flopped awkwardly, grazing Malala who sat suffocatingly close on the slender padded bench. She grinned, pupils huge, the soft lines of her plump face flexing liquidly as she leaned back to stare dreamily out the curved glass window.

"It's a once in five lifetimes event," she murmured as if speaking to herself.

I leaned forward to get some air, but the withdrawal symptoms got worse. "I'm fine."

"Where's your tool?"

I fumbled with the silver chain around my throat, choking back the bitter taste of embarrassment as Aishwarya pulled the lipstick-sized micro-grid injector from between my breasts and dialed up a leveling dose.

"Better?" She caressed the spot on my neck where she'd drugged me, her fingers soft and gentle.

I exhaled. The sense of suffocating faded, leaving me with a hollow feeling as I sat up and tried to smile. It'd been a long time since I'd experienced withdrawal. I'd overreacted, but nobody in the tube seemed to have noticed. Or cared.

"I think my tolerance is building again."

"It happens." She put her hand on my knee, but I felt nothing.

THE TUBE STOPPED just below the cap. People squeezed by in a hurry to see the stars. Some hesitated to level out, injectors in hand, before entering the grand viewing chamber. Three girls I didn't recognize held hands up ahead. They swung their arms to soft instrumental music emitted from thin guide strips in the floor, their gazes dreamy and far away. I envied their unworried innocence.

A image of the ship floated high above. Its pocked surface appeared elongated, its engine cones shining from a bulge in its lumpy oval tip. I had no idea where in the giant rock my home was located.

"Do you need a dose before we go in?" Rashawn tapped a pen-shaped injector to his wrist with three quick jabs; for anxiety, aggression, and a phobia he was too embarrassed to describe.

I checked my own injector. It seemed to be malfunctioning, random warnings scrolling across its sleek polished surface. It clearly needed to be serviced.

The tool monitored my socially adjustable traits, correcting mood, and guarding against breaches in morality set down by the starship's founders in the first years. Most of my levels had been determined in-vitro, some corrected before I'd even been implanted in my mother's womb. Others were latent. I showed a tendency toward bipolar disorder, and had a dose for that. There was also a possibility I'd become a trouble maker. My genetic makeup favored high intelligence but low drive, a strong factor in the rebellious, and my level for that one required two shots a day.

"Okay, we're going in. Please keep together, and level as needed." Niki, our guide, patted the ruffling on her seafoam-colored skirt, her small eyes glistening pebbles of hematite against her dark skin as she bent to press an injector to the back of her knee. Her blank but playful little smile never faltered.

I glanced at Aishwarya. She was taller than me, but slender, and stood out among the ocean of students waiting to enter the viewing platform. There'd always been something different about Aishwarya. It's what drew me to her.

"I'm having trouble with my tool." There wasn't a hint of concern in my voice. I'd been leveled for anxiety, so the weight of my problem wouldn't hit me for a while. "I should get it fixed before I do anything else."

"There's got to be an Omni-Med up here. They're everywhere." Bucket lamps set into the smooth stone ceiling illuminated the warmth of Aishwarya's round face, and I studied her eyes. Her pupils were reactive. They dilated naturally, no sign of mood-altering medication. I found that odd. We'd been friends for nearly a year, but I still had no idea what her levels were.

I stepped out of line. "I'll catch up. Don't wait for me."

"You'll miss the stars?" Rashawn smiled blankly beside Aishwarya as if it didn't really matter.

"It's okay." I'd miss standing under the crystal dome in the starship's bow, but I didn't want to end up in a hospital.

"It's a once in five lifetimes event, half a millennium in the making." Niki the guide's voice spoke from up ahead as if she were part of the conversation.

Turnaround was a special time in *Starwind's* history. Almost five centuries had passed since our ancestors had left a place called Earth for a new home. The ship had reached the half-way point. The crew had silenced the engines to reorient for deceleration, and the stars had become visible for the first time.

I was supposed to be awed by this, but my medication concerned me more.

"There'll be hell to pay if I let myself slip." I swung my injector on its chain, thinking about the trouble I'd be in if my parents found out. I was on the list for my own suite, but it wouldn't happen for a year. Until then, I was still at home, still under someone else's rules.

I pressed my injector to my wrist. A tremor tickled up my body, but the cold sensation of a dose didn't flow through me as I'd expected. An unfamiliar feeling of panic washed over me instead. I worried about bottoming out. I worried I'd change.

"I'm coming too." Aishwarya grabbed my hand and pulled me away from the crowd, leading me in a different direction.

THE CORRIDORS IN the cap seemed primitive compared to the public warrens that'd been scooped out deep within the protective mass of the ship. The walls here were little more than rough cut stone valleys. The alcoves seemed uninteresting. Nothing flashy, bright, or exciting lined the walls, and there were almost no service terminals available. Traveling at relativistic speeds made it important to have a thick plug of shielding set in the direction of travel. Still, they could've done something to liven it up.

We were further from the city than we'd ever been, close enough to the emptiness of space to see the curvature of the hull reflected in the shape of the walls. Aishwarya had been quiet for the most part since we'd left the group. She seemed content to walk beside me, holding my hand, lost in her own thoughts.

"I think I see one." I spied a wide metallic tray set in a recess at the end of an intersecting hallway. The bright red cross glowing beside it flickered, but was unmistakable.

"It doesn't look good."

"It'll have to do." I sped up, jittery, my skin cold and clammy. Goosebumps made me drop Aishwarya's hand to wrap my arms around my sleeveless bodice. If I'd only known, I'd have brought a small jacket. But it wasn't really the temperature. It was my receding level.

"Do you want me to do it?" She reached for my injector.

I pulled back. "No, I've got it."

The Omni-Med came up to my chest, its dull brass-colored finish protruding only inches from the alcove where it rested. Its icons barely glowed, and the white plastic inlay on its handles appeared chipped and melted.

"This thing looks like it needs fixing more than my injector." I laughed, uncertainty making me hesitate. I debated waiting, but the fear of withdrawal won out.

"Then don't use it." Aishwarya's eyes seemed sunken in the harsh uneven light coming from the Omni-Med. "We can go back down to the warrens. There's a terminal not too far from the tube there."

"I'm coming off. Now. I can feel it." My fingers shook as I dumped my injector onto the plate and tapped the repair glyph. I *needed* my level.

Nothing happened. I struck the glyph again. Hard. So hard my teeth chattered and my wrist hurt. I felt on edge, as if something were crawling under my skin. I hit the machine a few more times, frantic. Finally, it took, and my injector vanished behind a mesh service screen.

"It'll be okay." Aishwarya put an arm around my shoulders. I leaned into her warmth, strange sensations clouding my thoughts.

As a child, I'd felt separate. I'd felt alone. It was almost as if I were a different kind of creature from the people around me, a changeling in human form. Confusion had caused me to question my body, and my soul. I'd pleaded for answers, but in response got only an injector tool shaped like a tiny pink unicorn, and a blank feeling of numbness to blot out my true self.

Those feelings returned as the drugs thinned in my blood. The chemical mask I'd worn my entire life slipped aside, and I cried for the girl I'd never gotten the chance to become. I cried for my lost innocence.

"I know. I know." Aishwarya brushed a tear from my cheek. She leaned in and kissed me, our lips barely touching. Her breath smelled of licorice, and I turned away, sadness sinking into despair as I buried my face against her shoulder and continued to cry.

THE SMELL OF burning plastic pulled me away. Sizzling noises hissed from the Omni-Med like angry snakes. The machine crackled, its colorful holographic icons blending and then fading out altogether. I grabbed the handle. The tray burned my hands, and I screamed.

"I need my tool back!" My fingers stung, white-flecked patches of red throbbing painfully where the handle had seared my hands. Losing my injector was worse than the pain.

"Let it go." Aishwarya pushed me aside.

The glyph winked out. A shrill alarm tore the air, and frigid blasts shook the Omni-Med as fire retardant erupted from the ceiling. I coughed, tasting something bitter and dry. Then a line of brilliant red beacons illuminated the ceiling.

"I broke it!" I screamed over the clamor, eyes wide as I stared from the Omni-Med to Aishwarya. My heart felt like it would burst. "Now they'll find out. They'll know I'm not medicated, and they'll take me away!"

There were consequences for missing treatment, and not just with the law. If I came off my doses, I'd risk creating an immune response that'd leave me at the mercy of my own body. If I came down, I might never get back up.

"Let's get out of here." Aishwarya grabbed me with surprising strength and dragged me down the hallway as the Omni-Med shrieked behind us.

I F YOU'RE REALLY worried, I won't say anything." Aishwarya held my hand as we walked through the soft grass.

It was early evening, and the long filaments overhead had just begun to dim. The park was crowded. Children played ball in the clay courts beside the high barrier wall, older couples strolled through the finely manicured dwarf trees, and teenagers loitered in groups against irregularly-shaped statues in the garden plot. I searched faces as we passed, relieved when I didn't recognize anyone. Nobody paid attention to us, although I imagined a thousand glances as we reached the pavement and entered the busy heart of the city.

"Worried about what, the Omni-Med?" My voiced sounded husky and raw. I still felt sick.

"About everything." She slowed. "I know you're feeling confused. I feel it too, but...."

"You think it's because I'm off my level, don't you?" Withdrawal still clouded my thoughts, making me jumpy and irritable. I had no injector. I had no dose, and I didn't know how to get more.

The trip back down from the cap seemed like a strange dream.

We'd run until I could hardly breathe and until the siren's wail was lost in the turning corridors, and then we'd squeezed into an already crowded tube, dropping all the way back to the warrens with Aishwarya's hand in mine, our faces pressed close, the sweet taste of her breath against my neck.

"No. The drugs only keep you from realizing. They did that to me too, for a long time."

"Realizing what?" I was too confused to think straight.

"What you've given up, what you've been denied all your life. You're not who your level makes you, Ndamona." She turned down the residential corridor leading to my home, and I followed.

I stopped, my hands trembling, and stared into her bright unclouded eyes. "Oh my god... you're not on *anything* right now, are you?"

She put her hand over my mouth and pushed me against the wall. Surprise held me there, the compressed rock cold against my skin, the acrid odor of new paint strong and pungent.

"Please, Ndamona." She moved her hand, letting her fingers trail down my cheek. "Please don't ruin this for me."

I let my legs buckle, and I slid down the wall until I sat in a heap against the floor. I wrapped my arms around my chest, protecting my still injured hands. I could barely believe it, but it explained so much.

"When?" I whispered.

"Not long." She knelt beside me, her canary-yellow dress stretched tight against her thighs. She bit her lip, the gesture of a little girl caught at being naughty. "My injector clogged, like yours, and I lost my level."

I was stunned. I'd seen Aishwarya every day. We went to school together, hung out together. We were like sisters, but I never even suspected she'd dropped her medication.

"Don't you feel out of control?" I shivered and started to cry. I was exhausted, emotionally drained. The comfort of having all my flaws held in check was gone, and there was nothing to keep me from going insane.

She held out her hands. I took them, too weak to resist. "For the first time in my life, I'm the person I was born to be and not someone else's ideal."

"I don't want to be someone else," I said.

"The world isn't what you think it is, Ndamona. You've only seen it from the inside of an injector tool, but your level hides a more real and unpleasant truth. Free yourself to become what you were born to be."

I tried not to think about what I'd lost when I'd been leveled, the little girl I'd abandoned to become the young woman I was today. Pain and humiliation kept me from searching down that path. I tried to think of a future, of a world where responsibility wasn't injectable, but fear made my thoughts spin out of control.

Who would I become in that world, I thought? But I said nothing as Aishwarya dried my eyes and brought me home.

Y OUR EYES ARE all red." My mother looked me over. Her frown dragged her thin lips comically over her chin, as if she were merely pantomiming real concern. She leaned against the video wall. Cartoonish images arced out and around her like coronal ejections as I hurried by. Her gaze followed, eyes like obsidian flecks in the dark rock-like angles of her face. "How's your level?"

"I'm fine." I stammered as I pushed past her towards my room. My hands throbbed, and I had a headache.

I'd promised to keep Aishwarya's secret even though I knew it was wrong. I shouldn't have. She was in danger without treatment. I was in danger as well, but my lack of medicated control was already causing me to make bad decisions.

"You're. Home. Early."

My father glanced at me from the big futon in the corner of the communal room, his colorful agbada tunic gathered over his wide frame like a tent. He spoke as if each of his words needed time to reach me before the next could follow.

I stopped. "Are you okay?"

He moved with the fluidity of cold molasses, shifting in his chair like an exhausted sloth. "How. Were. The. Stars?"

I glanced at my mother. She'd turned to face the video wall, her body glowing a deep emerald color, enshrouded amid images of an Earthly rainforest as she hid among the trees.

"Mom...."

"Yes, dear?" She turned, face half hidden behind a creeping vine that made it look as if she'd been split in two.

"I think...." I'd planned on confessing. They should know I was off my medication. I needed more, and I needed it soon, but their strange actions had me convinced it might already to too late. "What would happen if someone fell off their level?"

"Bad. Things." My father stood. It was like the ponderous rise of some enormous undersea creature.

"Why?" My mother asked.

"Just curious. It came up in conversation today."

"It's. Illegal." My father took his first step towards us. I could see suspicion eroding his features like the slow wearing away of a mountain. "And. Horribly. Immoral."

"Just because something's illegal doesn't necessarily mean it's wrong." My cheeks grew hot. I thought of Aishwarya, and her cool composure even without her level. I'd never even known she was drug free.

"It. Does." My father took a second step.

"The original colonists had specific goals in mind when they set off for the stars. The drugs saved us all, and it's not our place to question why." My mother seemed to sink deeper into the project-ed rainforest, almost invisible now behind the dense foliage.

"Maybe it'd be better if people had a choice?"

"Who would want that, Ndamona?"

"I don't know." I squeezed my fists together, grinding my teeth at the pain. "I just wondered... there might be more than what the founders wanted. Maybe without the levels holding people in...."

"That's. Crazy. Talk."

"But what if it were somebody you loved?"

"Then it would be even more important they get help." My mother's voice echoed from somewhere within the forest, lost now only feet from where I stood. I wished she'd shut down the projection, or at least step away from the wall and the seething images that hid her from me.

"Do. You. Know. Somebody?" My father didn't quite make another step forward.

Is this what people were really like? Is this how I'd been, I thought?

"Aishwarya?" My blood froze when my mother said her name, emerging from her forest to stare at me with beady black eyes. "Is your friend in trouble?"

"No!" I shouted it, my voice shrill. They were too suspicious, even with their weird behavior and odd movements. "Aishwarya's fine. There's nothing wrong with her. Leave her—leave *me* alone!"

I ran from the suite. My mother's gaze followed as her body slowly sank back into the rainforest. My father never even had time to react.

I THOUGHT YOU were coming back. You said you would, but you never did." Rashawn looked dazed. I'd bumped into him as I stumbled into the street. He reached for me, pawing clumsily at my blouse. I didn't remember telling him where I'd be.

People lurched like cheap movie zombies across the sidewalks, moving in small groups through the intersecting spaces where neighborhoods met. Not a single one seemed normal.

"I needed medicine." I hugged myself, feeling strangely shy.

Bizarre splashes of conversation hit me like rain. I turned, distracted. An older couple stood back to back. They argued as if they were staring into each other's eyes, their facial expressions identical, their words in sync.

241

"You didn't come back."

"I know," I said.

I'd known Rashawn since we were children, since before his level. In my memories, I see only the man, the un-medicated boy he'd once been as lost as my own childhood. It'd been assumed we'd eventually marry, raise a family, and live our lives together, but I wasn't sure who'd done the assuming and why I'd never bothered to correct them. We were just friends. I could be friends with a man without needing more.

"You said you would." His petulant tone caused me to hesitate. I stared into his eyes, but saw only my reflection in their dull glossy surfaces.

"Are you okay?" I'd asked that question far too often lately. At first, I'd wondered if it were my lack of level making normal people seem strange, but now I suspected something far more dreadful. The whole world *had* gone crazy, and I'd just begun to notice.

Aishwarya had been right.

"I thought you were coming back. You said you would, but you never did." He repeated himself, stuck in a loop.

The drugs not only changed how we interacted with the world. They changed how we *perceived* it. People who'd seemed perfectly ordinary had become caricatures in the absence of medicated normal. My parents, my friends—even the way I saw myself. It'd all been a lie. I could see behind the illusion for the first time, and it frightened me.

I stepped onto the grass, my low heel twisting, and stumbled drunkenly, teetering for a moment before falling into an ornamental bush. I screamed. Flower petals the same dark blush of my cheeks scattered everywhere, and Rashawn just watched as if I hadn't even moved.

T HE SIGNAL WOKE me from a nightmare. I'd curled up in the unfinished shell of the suite being built for me. Strips of plastic sheeting covered the bare rock walls, cutaway in spots where workmen had chiseled alcoves for appliances and conduits for electrical devices. A small yard had been carved behind the living area, and lights heavy in ultraviolet were already warming the freshly manufactured soil.

"Your. Friend." My father's voice sounded like thick syrup oozing from the tiny button phone behind my right ear.

"She's in the hospital, dear." My mother interrupted in a more rapid tone. "She was off her level, but she's okay now. They fixed her."

I sat up so quickly my head spun. "Aishwarya? They can't fix her! She wasn't broken!"

"No, of course not, but they fixed her just the same."

THEY'D TAKEN AISHWARYA to one of the new clinics, built ten levels up from the warrens to accommodate children who wouldn't be born for another two years. Overflow cases from established towns were taken there. It's where they put people they wanted to hide.

I had so much to say. I wanted to tell her she'd been right, I understood that now. Thoughts weren't illegal. Desires should never be immoral. We *were* so much more than our levels let us be. I wanted to tell her I loved her. We could figure it out and make it work—even if we had to change the world to do it. It was a once in five lifetimes chance. It was *our* chance.

"Aishwarya?"

She looked small and fragile in her paper gown, her back to me as she stood by the small bed. Her hair had been pinned into a sloppy bun. It sagged to one side of her drooping shoulders making her seem about to fall over.

"I came as soon as I heard." My heart fluttered. My knees felt suddenly weak as I rushed forward and she turned.

Her face was as smooth as a porcelain doll, eyes wide and unblinking, pupils huge like black buttons sewn over an empty expression. My breath caught. My hands flew to my lips to stifle a sob.

"She's still adjusting." A pale woman in a peach-colored lab coat stood in the doorway behind me. Her words seemed to ooze carefully from her lips, as if each were a precious gift with which she was reluctant to part. "It might take a while before the medications settle in."

"You leveled her?"

"Of course. She was absolutely *drug free*. Unbelievable. It was amazing she could function at all."

Aishwarya still hadn't spoken. Her gaze followed me, but I wasn't sure if she heard my voice.

"Are you okay?" The doctor squinted, studying me. "You're... crying, I think. Perhaps you should check your level."

"I'm fine!" I snapped.

"Medication isn't something to fool around with. Your friend—"

"I said I didn't need your help! Neither did she!"

I turned back to Aishwarya. She'd wrapped her arms around her chest, hugging herself. Goosebumps tickled her exposed skin.

"She's cold." I glanced behind me, but the doctor had gone.

I took Aishwarya's right hand, pressing it to my cheek. She smelled like roses, a perfume her mother had given her on her last birthday only two months before. It seemed like a lifetime ago.

"I'm so sorry..." I whispered into her palm.

She'd seemed different even then, affectionate, almost criminal in the way she'd looked at me. I should've realized she wasn't medicated. I should have noticed, but I'd been on my level and oblivious to the rest of the world.

I glanced into the blank expanse of her eyes. She moaned, her voice the soft mewing of a frightened kitten. "You tried to free me from the haze of chemical censorship, but I fought you. I didn't understand then, but I do now. I'm sorry it took so long."

She pulled away from my hand, her body rocking, the porcelain serenity of her face cracking into an expression of anguish. A single tear spilled down her cheek.

"Step away, please." The doctor had returned. Two female

orderlies in pale blue scrubs stood beside her, swaying as if in a heavy breeze. They both wore wide smiles, but I got the impression nothing friendly rested behind those perky expressions.

"I was just...." I had so much more to say to Aishwarya, but the doctor stepped quickly between us, facing me. Her smile never wavered. Her gaze seemed to sink into me, the pupil of her left eye much larger than her right, making it look as if she were winking, as if we shared some dirty little secret.

"Please, I'd like more time with her." My throat felt dry. I shivered, suddenly realizing I was still in my party dress from the night before. I wasn't sure how they saw me while on their level, but I felt a mess.

The two orderlies stepped in behind me. Aishwarya stumbled, flopping awkwardly against the nearest woman. The huskier woman grabbed her. I lunged to intercept, but the second orderly wrapped her arms around me.

"Get off!" I kicked out. Even in her drugged state, Aishwarya had been more aware than me, because I never saw the doctor move. She snuck up behind me. A sharp stab tickled my throat, and an icy calm flooded into my blood as I lost consciousness.

A RE YOU EXCITED to see the stars, Ndamona?" Aishwarya sat beside me in the tube, a wide smile on her face, her cheeks flush. I could see my own grin reflected in the black disks of her enlarged pupils. Laughter erupted around us. Everyone seemed perfectly on their level, happy and medically adjusted, and I smiled a bit wider.

It'd been two weeks since my breakdown, and only two days since my release from observation. Both Aishwarya and I had been re-medicated. Our levels had been adjusted, our ethical and moral proclivities tuned to align with what the original colonists had intended. We'd been balanced in every way, two friends sharing a once in five lifetimes opportunity.

"I'm glad we're getting a second chance." She giggled at the double meaning.

"Me too." I squeezed her hand. Her fingers felt warm, a comforting weight in my lap.

It turned out the drugs didn't work so well a second time. They'd never been intended to cease. Going cold broke the cycle. Reintroducing new medication only made me aware of the intended effect. I wasn't a slave to it. I was free.

I remembered everything as if it were a dream, but I no longer felt the tension or anguish of needing to choose between the girl I was born to be or the woman my level made me. The tingling in my fingers, my shortness of breath when I looked into Aishwarya's eyes, and the way she blushed when she glanced at me told me I could be both.

I might not know what the future held for us, but I knew Aishwarya liked me in a way that was clearly illegal, and it made me happy.

ABOUT THE AUTHOR

D. A. D'Amico is a crazy mix of clumsy mad scientist and failed evil wizard, leading to spectacular displays of truly unremarkable brilliance. Occasionally, the stars align, and a coherent storyline is born. He's had more than eighty works published in venues such as Daily Science Fiction, Shock Totem, and his personal favorite, MYTHIC. He's a winner of L. Ron Hubbard's prestigious Writers of the Future award, as well as the 2017 Write Well award. Collections of his work, links to anthologies and magazines he's been in, can be found on select online retailers. His website is http://www.dadamico.com. Facebook authordadamico, and on painfully rare occasions, twitter @dadamico, instagram authordadamico, and tiktok.com/@authordadamico

Broken

Courtney R. Lee

HEALER!"

The cry rang through the square, wrenching my attention from the poxy old man and his vice grip on my arm. Everywhere I looked townspeople stood gaping at me: some with fingers pointed, others covering their mouths in shock, many more with chests clutched and jaws gaping. Even the other schoolchildren, who walked beside me just moments ago, now stood among the throng, surprise and disgust plain on their faces.

"Get her!" shouted Eli—a scruffy, dark haired boy I'd thought was my friend.

The crowd erupted to life, rushing me. I tore my wrist from the old man's grasp—ignoring his litany of 'praise gods' and 'thank yous'—and sped for the woods.

I didn't look back to see who followed or if they sent for the sisters. I just ran. Fast. Faster than I should have over the knotted roots and tangled undergrowth that conspired to send me sprawling. Trees and brush blurred past in a spectacle of reds, greens, and yellows. Their branches raked gashes across my skin and snagged at my hair and skirt as if, they too, intended to capture me. My chest burned and my legs screamed, but the fear that bit at my heels would not let me slack.

The woods opened into a brightly lit clearing. Momentarily blinded, I raised a hand to shield my eyes. There, resting in the shadow of Grandfather Mountain, stood our simple log-and-mud cabin. Smoke billowed from the chimney.

She was home.

I flew across the dusty field, skirting an overturned plow, and charged around the hen house, their frenzied clucks following me as I crashed through the door.

"Mama?" I called.

Startled, my mother, her fair skin and pale locks a mirror of my own, spun round dropping the bowl she'd been holding. A flood of peas rushed across the floor.

"Oh my God." Mama ran to me, peas forgotten, and grabbed my wrist, lifting and rotating my arm to inspect the mass of pockmarks that ran its length. She tipped my head by the chin and followed the trail of scars up my neck and jawbone. Then she lifted my shirt to find yet more pockmarks covering my belly. "Oh, Beth. What did you do?"

"It wasn't my fault," I cried. "The old man came out of no-where. He grabbed me, I don't know why, and it just happened. I couldn't stop it. I tried not to scream, but it hurt so bad. I'm so sorry."

Her eyes widened. "Who saw?"

"Everyone. The whole square. They tried to grab me so I ran. They're coming for us. We have to get out of here."

"Come on." She hurried to the bed, and from underneath pulled out two large sacks, already stuffed with supplies. She tossed one to me. "Go watch. I'll get the food."

I slung the heavy bag over a shoulder and bolted to the window, pulling back the drapes just enough to peek outside. "Nothing, yet. What are we gonna do?"

"We'll hole up in the woods for a few days, then head south to Charlotte." She shoved dried fruit and grain into a satchel. "From there... I don't know." She heaved the bag over her shoulder then, one-handed, grabbed the flintlock rifle, fire bag, and horn. "Let's go."

We opened the door to find a cavalcade of riders pouring down the little road to our farm. The cavalry rode in procession with a flag bearer at the fore, his banner beating violently against the wind. It was the new separatist flag, the 'Grand Union' my teacher called it, red and white stripes with the union jack stamped onto the top left corner.

The men were more likely farmers than soldiers but were still an intimidating sight in their tricorn hats and dark blue jackets. Their horses' hooves pounded the powder-dry clay, raising such dust the riders appeared to float on red clouds.

It was like a great grizzly giant took hold of my chest and squeezed. I could not breathe, could not think. I could only watch, frozen in fear, as the riders descended upon me.

Mama rammed me from behind, so I almost toppled over, "Run," she shouted, and my legs finally came back to life.

We raced for the cover of the woods, but the horsemen were too fast. They came at us from all sides, cutting us off from the field and forest and forcing us back against the side of the house. That's when the entire front line, perhaps fifteen men, dropped from their mounts and drew muskets.

Mama stepped in front of me, and wiry arms trembling, raised the flintlock. The rifle was so massive she had to tuck the butt under an arm just to keep it upright.

I lay my hand on her shoulder. "Please, Mama. It's no use. They'll just kill you."

She glanced sideways at me and shook her head. "I don't care," she said, tears spilling down her cheek to wet the powder.

"I do. Mama. Please." I wrapped my hand around hers and guided the barrel downward. She didn't fight it, and with a shuddering sigh let the gun slip from her grip and into the dirt.

"I'm sorry. I'm so sorry," she sobbed unable to meet my eyes.

I wrapped my arms around her chest, and we leaned into each other sobbing.

"Elsbeth Wythe?" A woman's voice rang out from the armed throng.

I pulled away from Mama, her whimpering protests like tiny knives to the heart, and mustered what little bravery I possessed to reply, "Yes, Sister. I'm here." My voice was much steadier than I would have expected.

The soldiers parted ranks, and an old nun plodded forward on horseback. She rode astride, her ivory habit heaped about her thighs, revealing knee high stockings and an indecent amount of translucent skin. Her head was coifed from temple to throat, so only her craggy face and sagging jowls were visible, and a black veil cascaded down her back to brush the horse's haunches.

She dropped from the saddle, landing easily—this was not a frail woman—then looked us up and down as though she were assessing hung beef. The sister finished her appraisal, and seeming to find it wanting, glared at me disapprovingly. "Sister Miriam. That is how you'll address me, girl. Do you understand?"

"Yes, Sister Miriam."

She harrumphed, "Good." She glanced at Mama then back at me. "You're quite a slippery one, Elsbeth. How old are you?"

"Fifteen."

"Fifteen. Goodness." Her arms swung out dramatically. "I've never found one so old. How ever did you fool us for so long?"

She wanted names. People who helped hide me. People she could punish. I lowered my eyes and stood silently.

The Sister crossed her arms over her chest. I could feel her watery blue eyes boring into the top of my head.

"Well, girl? Answer me."

My hands were shaking. My stomach rolled, the morning's meal threatening a reappearance. Still, I said nothing.

"Rufus." She called, her tone high pitched and musical. A giant, with a face like a brick, rode forward. "Cudgel her mother."

He dismounted and pulled a massive club from the horse's harness.

"Wait." I jumped in front of Mama and flung my arms out protectively. "Please. Don't. I lied. I pretended to get sick and get hurt, and Mama knew nothing about it. Please don't hurt her."

The old woman sneered and raised her hand to halt the giant's advance. "Of course, dear," she said too sweetly, then turned toward the troop of men at her back, and with a voice like a thunderclap, commanded them to "Mount up." The men immediately set about climbing back into their saddles and forming lines. All but a few that surrounded me and the one that still hovered over Mama, fingering his club's well-worn handle, dark stains littered the tip. Sister Miriam glanced round to him then tipped her head toward Mama and said, "Arrest her."

"Mama." I lunged for my mother only to be grabbed about the wrists by two soldiers. "Please. I don't want to go. Please. Mama!" I dropped all my little bit of weight to the ground yanked my arms, kicked my legs and resisted with every ounce of my strength, but the men were too strong. They dragged me across the earth, rocks, and twigs tearing at my back and thighs.

Mama screamed too. She screamed and cried and fought, but there wasn't anything either of us could do. The men bound my wrists so tight I could feel the blood pool in my fingertips and slung me over the back of a horse.

The horseman circled to leave. The beast's hip jabbed my stomach with one step then my clavicle with another, and I strained my neck to watch the remaining men attempt to bind Mama's wrists. She struggled against them, pulling free for a moment before they toppled her to the ground. A guard slammed the butt of his rifle into the side of her head, and she slumped over unconscious.

"No," I wailed. I dredged the power from within myself and drove it in ribbons from my fingers. The ribbons took to the wind, twisting and swirling across the yard, fighting through the current and ever-increasing distance to reach Mama. When at last they touched down, the ribbons caught onto her like hooks to a fish. I ripped the injury from her body and drew it into myself. It landed

251

like a hammer to my fingertips, the bones breaking then knitting in tandem as the crushing blow traveled up my arms and shoulders. I howled in pain but all sound was lost to the wind and pounding hooves. The injury settled into my cheek and temple where the bone cracked and splintered sending shockwaves through my skull and spine. Warm blood oozed across my face and dripped onto the horse's flank and for a bare moment, I feared the pain would never end. Then my vision flashed white and red as the broken bits of bone lifted back into place and fused. Everything went black.

A SHARP SLAP across my cheek startled me awake. I opened my eyes to find Sister Miriam standing over me. In her hand was a long wooden rod. "Get up, girl."

I sat up slowly, more to annoy her, than out of sluggishness.

The wood thwacked against my cheek again. Hot pain flared across my face.

"Ow." I rubbed the spot where she'd struck me even though the pain was already gone. One good thing about being a healer. Nothing hurts for very long.

"Then move faster next time. Now stand up."

I did, but not too fast because she could go to hell for all I cared.

Whack. That time a sharp jolt against my shoulder.

"Stop it."

She didn't. Instead, she stuck me in the ribs, then again on my shoulder, and again across my face. I ducked my chin and raised my arms over my head, screaming. Finally, I caught hold of the rod mid-swing and ripped it from her grasp. "Stop," I spat.

The sister shoved me into the cot and twisted the rod back out of my hand. "Oh, you're a fiery one. Good. I like a challenge."

"I won't do it. I won't do anything for *you*," I said knowing the lie of my own words.

Her eyes drew into slits. "You are a selfish, selfish child. You think only of yourself, not of the countless lives that have been lost at your hands."

"I've never—"

"You have through your inaction," she broke in. "For every life a healer saves there are countless more left to die simply because we don't have the numbers we need to meet the demand. Instead of using the gift our Lord so righteously bestowed upon you, you would horde it and allow these men, these heroes who fight for *you*, to suffer and die."

"That's not fair. I never asked for any of this and I don't care about your stupid war. I just want to go home."

Sister Miriam's eyes lit with rage. She grasped me two-handed by the neck and squeezed so hard my head started to pound and I thought my eyes would pop from their sockets. I couldn't breathe. I raked at her hands, panic-stricken.

"How dare you! These men are fighting to protect us: our land, our rights, our freedom and you would stand here and call those efforts 'stupid'?"

She shoved me and I careened over the bed cracking my back and skull against the hard, stone floor. When I opened my eyes, the old woman was standing over me again, brandishing her switch.

"This isn't freedom?" I said, bracing for the next strike.

She paused then lowered her arm. "Maybe not. But we don't have time for sappy sentiment girl. This is war." Her face screwed up strangely and I couldn't tell if she was about to scream or cry. "If you'd seen what I've seen, you'd understand." She shook her head as if to clear the image from her mind. "You are one person, girl. I'm fighting for a nation." She snapped out of her reverie and smacked my leg. "Now get up and follow me."

The sister took me down a long windowless hallway, candlelight flickering along the walls as we passed. To say I wasn't frightened would be a lie. I was terrified, but I clasped my hands to stop them from trembling and did my best to keep my face blank. I wouldn't give her the satisfaction of seeing my fear. We entered a massive room, broken up by rows upon rows of homespun pallets filled with ill, dead and dying men. They were only silhouettes against the light from the hearth that lined the far wall, but I could hear them. They pleaded for death and relief; they moaned and sobbed and writhed and coughed. The air hummed with their pain and hung heavy with the stench of blood, shit, and death.

My stomach heaved and I fell to my knees. I closed my eyes and breathed through my mouth to lessen the nausea, but then, oh God, I could taste it—like rotten flesh. I closed my mouth again, but the sickness had grown unstoppable and I retched all over Sister Miriam's feet.

She cursed and flung off her shoes, then grabbed me by the collar of my shirt and jerked me to my feet. "Don't like it, huh? Well, remember it's your fault." She shoved me down the central aisle and came to a stop in front of a dark-haired, dark-skinned man lying on the floor. His shirt had been removed and his side bandaged, but blood continued to swell out of the wound and pool into the recess of his belly. He was sweaty and feverish and spoke nonsense about harvesting wheat and heavy rains. Sister Miriam pushed me onto the floor beside the man, "Heal him."

"What?" I said disbelieving. "No, I can't. It's too much. You can't ask me to..." I crossed my arms, defiant. "You can't make me do it."

"Can't I?" Her brows raised. "Guards." She snapped her fingers and two young men strode from their position against the wall to stand behind the sister. They didn't look like guards. They were pimply faced boys, barely older than me, wearing simple brown cotton vests and britches. The pistols slung from their belts were real enough though.

My whole body shook and yet, ever the stubborn one, I said, "What are you going to do? Shoot me. I'll just heal again."

She laughed—a full, guttural guffaw that was more frightening than the boys and their guns. "You stupid girl. Do you really think I would be so ignorant of your abilities?" She leaned in so her face was mere inches from mine. "Let me make this clear.

You have a choice. Either you heal him now or I'll have these men hold you down and make you do it."

"You can't make me heal someone."

"Really? So, you meant to heal that old man in the middle of the town square then? How altruistic of you. And to think, I simply thought you couldn't control your power when you touched the ill. Oh well." she shrugged her shoulders. "Perhaps we should try anyway? Just to see what happens. Boys—"

"Wait." I thrust my hands out to halt the approaching soldiers, then thought better of it and sat on them. "Please, don't make me do this. The pain—"

"A few moments of pain in exchange for a life. *A life*." She gestured to the dying man. "You will not sway me in this, girl. Now do it."

"Please," I begged. The tears ran rivulets down my face.

"Guards—"

I curled up into a ball, but the soldiers were too strong. They wrestled my arms from my chest and began dragging me toward the wounded man.

"No." I kicked my legs narrowly missing the sister's shins. "Let me go. I'll do it. Stop. Please." The men released me and I collapsed to the floor. When I looked up, my eyes met the sister's. She nodded. My vision swam and I half felt, half crawled the rest of the way to sit next to the dying man. I reached toward him, my hand trembling, and touched a fingertip to his chest. The power was immediately yanked out of me. It surged through the soldier's body, curled around his crushed ribs and eviscerated organs then dragged the injury from his body and into mine. The pain slammed into me. It shredded skin and tissue as it ran up my arm like a tidal wave, my body knitting itself together again as it passed. The shredding wave ran across my shoulder and chest then settled in my midsection where it sliced into my stomach and intestines in a cruel facsimile of the man's injury. I gripped the wound with my free hand but could not stem the flow of blood.

My skin grew hot with fever and a rush of dizziness washed over me. He was killing me.

Fiery pain gripped my stomach and I felt the organs, tissue, then skin meld together. The fever cooled, the dizziness abated, and I slumped to the floor, my hand finally free. I lifted my shirt and traced my fingers over the long, angry scar running across my belly.

God help me.

The man sat up on his pallet, seemingly refreshed after his ordeal. He drew me into an embrace. "Thank you," he said, tears spilling down my neck. "Thank you for saving my life."

I hated him.

You are the hands of God. Your sacrifice is His sacrifice, your pain is His pain, and He will bear it alongside you. Do you feel Him? Do you feel His love, children? His love is infinite. It encompasses all of us: you, me, our United States, and yes, even that tyrant who would take away all we hold dear. God has laid his blessing upon us and we cannot fail." Sister Miriam spouted her rhetoric to the assemblage, as she had every morning for the past month, raising her arms to the ceiling as though she could call down the heavens.

A ragtag collection of crippled, deformed and mutilated people surrounded me, their bodies bearing the scars of countless healings. Yet they clapped and cheered, their faces rapturous. I wondered, not for the first time, which ones truly believed her words and which only played along, the way I did.

Standing just a few feet in front of me was a little red-haired girl named Ann. She was probably younger than me and might have been pretty, but for the scars crisscrossing her face and body. She cried at night. I heard her. But there she stood shouting with the rest of them.

On my right, stood Jonah. He was older, maybe twenty. Jonah lost his arm and half his teeth healing others. He clapped his lone hand against a thigh and shouted, 'Praise God' and 'Amen' like the rest, but his eyes looked glazed over like he was somewhere else in his head.

And then there was Eliza who had lost a leg, and Tomas, his whole face looked like it has been shredded then reformed, and the little girl, Sissy, who never spoke and was missing half her hand. Could they truly believe all of this or were they just pretending?

Sister Miriam finished her sermon, and we filed out of the room to make our morning rounds.

When we reached the infirmary, it was abuzz with activity. Guards and attendants raced around the room frantically collecting water and bandages while healers rushed forward to treat the new influx of injured troops. To the naive, it might have appeared as though they were eager to provide aid, but I knew better. They were racing to claim the least painful, least debilitating injuries. I held back and waited, perched against the back wall. Sometimes they didn't need every healer. Sometimes they forgot about me.

"Sister Miriam!" A voice shouted across the chamber.

"What happened?" Sister Miriam sprinted through the doorway toward a crowded area in the back corner of the infirmary. She melded into the horde of activity, then reemerged to scream my name. "Elsbeth! Elsbeth, come here now!"

"Dammit," I muttered under my breath. I walked across the room as slowly as possible, I stepped carefully over broken bodies and even pretended to trip a few times, but the distance was short and I could only stall for so long.

When I finally reached the sister, she shoved me to the floor next to a dead man. His face was crushed from cheek to jaw, his mouth gaped open in a sort of grotesque yawn, and his leg was severed at the knee and swathed in blood-soaked bandages.

Then he coughed. *Dead men cough?*

"No," I gasped, realization dawning. I tried to flee, but Sister Miriam and her guards fell in behind me, stalling my escape.

"This is the major general, girl! You must heal him. Now." She pressed me toward the wasted man.

I wedged a boot against the General's hip and held fast. "I can't. I'll lose my leg. I might die. Please, stop. I can't."

"It doesn't matter." Her voice strained through gritted teeth, "He dies, and we lose this war. Now do it." She rammed my hand into his chest and the power betrayed me. It spread across the general's ruined body and drew the injury into my own. I wailed as the pain ran like lightning through my arm, carving through my chest, my stomach, and my leg. There it bored into the flesh like a hot poker, slowly severing skin, tissue, then bone. The pain continued up my chest, into my face and jaw where the bones cracked and splintered then caved in turning my shrieks to gargles. Specks of light filled my vision while darkness crept into the periphery.

My body screamed for release from the pain. I tried to push it back into the general, but the flow was too powerful. I pushed again, this time out of myself, driving it through my fingertips. *Get out! Get out!* I reached for the nearest warm figure and pushed. The flow surged from within me, at once both pain and relief, and rushed into my neighbor's awaiting body.

She howled with such force my ears ached. I sent that to her too. My half-severed leg pulled together. The skin fused and healed. The broken bits of my face reformed. The pain abated. I was alive.

And Sister Miriam writhed on the floor next to me.

For a moment, I could only stare at the old woman, the magnitude of what just happened settling slowly in my mind. *Is this my true gift? Not a healer, but a weapon?*

"Take it back," she screeched, hands grappling for her severed leg. As I watched, the injury traveled up her body crushing bone and tearing skin along the way, just as it had done to me every time I performed a healing. But Sister Miriam's bones did not reset; her skin did not knit together. She wasn't a healer.

The side of the sister's face crumpled in upon itself as if it had been hit with an invisible mallet, her pleas wasted on a jaw too broken to form words. She clawed the floor, bloody nails biting wood, and dragged herself toward me swinging at my leg. I scrambled backward to avoid her touch, but still, she persisted.

No!" I KICKED and stomped her fingers with my shoe. "Go away. Just go away and die."

She moaned and scraped and sobbed, and I watched, keeping just out of reach as the blood and tissue poured from her broken body to pool upon the floor like red soup. Finally, she fell silent, her face a frozen scream, her eyes accusing, even in death.

I wiped bloody hands on my apron, peeled it off and discarded it next to the dead woman. By the time I mustered enough strength to stand, a mob of onlookers surrounded me on all sides, so I was forced to push my way through. My legs were so weak, I feared they would collapse beneath me, but somehow, I managed to take one step then another, my strength returning as I waded through the crowd. Only one soldier guarded the door, but I could feel the others approaching from behind, their anxiety a dissonant cord in the silence. The guard was just a boy, with brown hair and a big nose. His ragged clothes were about two sizes too big and his musket so large, I wondered how he held it aloft.

"Halt." He jabbed the air with the gun. His knees trembled.

"Please. Just let me pass."

"No." He jabbed again. "Surrender or I'll shoot."

I raised my arms as if to surrender, but instead sent tendrils of my power into the room, seeking an injury that was painful but not mortal. The boy fidgeted more and more with each passing moment. He inched toward me, but I ignored him, flipping through the wounded soldiers like the pages of a book until I found what I needed—a man with a minor burn on his palm.

I drew the burn into myself, then twisting my other hand toward the guard-boy, blasted it at him.

The gun clanged to the floor.

The guard screamed and clutched his burned hand in disbelief.

He backed away slowly, as if I were a rabid animal. I spun round anticipating an attack from behind, but no one advanced. The entirety of the infirmary simply gazed at me, their faces bearing terror, confusion, disbelief, and for a few of my fellow healers, hope. No one moved to stop me, not even the major general sitting on his mat. He knew better. They all did.

A tiny figure stepped from the crowd. She crossed the room, unafraid, and came to stand in front of me.

"Can I come with you?" Sissy asked.

I nodded and took her mangled hand in mine. She smiled.

Jonah approached me next, then Ann and Eliza and Thomas and countless others I didn't know or couldn't name. One by one they came to stand with me while the sisters, the guards and their wounded soldiers watched impotently, stymied by their own cowardice.

I turned my back on them, flushed with a kind of strength I had never before experienced. Sissy's hand in mine and an army of healers at my side, I opened the door and stepped into the sunlight.

ABOUT THE AUTHOR

Courtney R. Lee lives in Chapel Hill, North Carolina with her husband, two children, two dogs, a cat, and a leopard gecko. As quiet space in her home is at a premium, much of Courtney's writing is done in an overly caffeinated state at the local Starbucks. She is a member of SCBWI and her work has appeared in Stupefying Stories and Mythic Magazine. To learn more, visit her website at https://courtneyrleewrites.com/ or find her on twitter @Courtney_RLee.

The Alien Among Us

James Rumpel

YEAR 1 DAY 1

THE CAPSULE HAD bounced and rolled through the thick under-brush of the jungle, leaving a fifty-foot-wide scorched trail in its wake. Despite the recent clamorous intrusion into the calm, everything was now silent. No birds took flight or called out in fear. There were no animals scurrying to presumed safety. The jungle appeared lifeless, except for the site of the crash.

There, three identically clad men stood over a fourth. As the prone man opened his eyes, he gasped deeply, sucking oxygen into his near-empty lungs. His comrades spoke to him, simultaneously.

"Don't try to get up to fast, you've been in stasis for over twenty years."

"What do you remember?"

"What is your name?"

After a few minutes, the astronaut managed to sit up. He was unsteady as he leaned back against a piece of mangled equipment, but he was ready to reply to the bombardment of questions.

"I am Mission Specialist John Howard of Interplanetary Search Mission Alpha." While he answered the inquiry, he glanced down at the emblem and name tag on his left chest, as if for verification.

"Do you know who I am?" asked a mountainous man with

MISSION SPECIALIST GAVIN WHITE embroidered above the mission patch of his uniform.

A confused look appeared on John's face. "No, I don't recognize you at all. How can that be, if we were on the same mission…" He stopped, his expression composed of concentration and bewilderment. "I can remember everything about the mission, except whenever I try to picture or recall any of my crewmates, I come up blank. I can recall conversations but I can't picture the other person."

"It is worse than that," added the man with MISSION SPECIALIST DUANE MCDONALD on his name tag. "If you are like us, you can't even remember their voices or idiosyncrasies in speech patterns. It is totally impossible to identify who was with us on the mission."

"Well, that should be obvious. We're the only ones here. It has to be us."

"It is not that easy," replied the fourth astronaut, Mission Specialist Eduardo Esposa. "Think about it. We were only a three-man crew. We checked the wreckage, there were only three suspended animation compartments on the ship."

"Not only that," continued White, "Someone or something pulled us all out of the compartments and laid us here, outside of the ship."

"We've gained consciousness, one by one, out here," explained McDonald.

John held his hand up, needing time to analyze the new and extremely troubling information. "Are you telling me, that one of us didn't come with the capsule? One of us is not from our mission?"

"It could be more than one. For all I know, I am the only true human among us," declared McDonald.

"But I remember it being a three-person mission. And there were three opened stasis compartments," pointed out White. "I think we should operate on the assumption that there is only one alien."

"Technically, we are the aliens," explained Esposa. "Whoever the imposter is, they were here when we arrived."

"That's impossible." John gathered his strength and rose to his feet. "There has to be some way to determine who wasn't with us on the ship. Wouldn't it be the one who was awake when everyone else regained consciousness?"

Esposa shook his head. "I'm thinking this being would be smart enough to pretend to be unconscious in order to carry out its ruse."

"Of course, you say that. You were awake when I came to."

"Let's remain calm," instructed Howard. "I think Esposa has a legitimate point. There must be some other way to identify the imposter."

"We could ask questions that only people from Earth would know the answers to," suggested John.

"Yeah, like we are all going to know what team won the World Series in nineteen forty-two," scoffed McDonald.

"Not like that…"

"Remember, John, the being we are dealing with has the ability to block very specific parts of our memories. I'm guessing it would be able to extract enough info to answer a few trivia questions."

"You're right, White…"

"Call me Gavin. Maybe we should go around and introduce ourselves. It might even give a clue as to who is the imposter." Each member of the crew proceeded to tell a small bit about themselves: their hometowns, when they joined the Interplanetary Search Mission, and other minor details. McDonald joked about being a Pisces and enjoying long walks on the beach. Not surprisingly, none of them claimed to be from a mysterious planet or mentioned wanting to enslave the entire human race.

"That was a waste of time," concluded McDonald.

"Whoever the alien is, they could have killed us instantly if that was their goal. We are stranded in the middle of a jungle and who knows what else is out there or what it's going to be like once darkness hits. Why don't we just, all, work on scavenging the capsule, checking inventory, and setting up some sort of shelter for the night."

With varying degrees of enthusiasm, the crew agreed with Gavin's suggestion. They each set about the tasks before them, though all kept a wary eye on each of their compatriots.

YEAR 1 DAY 2

A DAY AND a half of constant labor produced positive results. The four marooned astronauts found enough food for five or six weeks. A prefabricated shelter was constructed. In two days, the crew did not encounter any forms of higher animal life. Aside from a few grubs and insects, the planet seemed to be devoid of any lifeforms. Water could be found abundantly in the morning dew and persistent short rain showers. Tests of the water proved it to be entirely safe for human consumption.

The jungle around them was extremely dense. Any exploration away from the crash site was extremely difficult and time-consuming, with the exception of the burnt and flattened path the capsule had left in its wake as it crashed onto the planet.

Most importantly, the beacon the crew was sent to set up on the planet's surface was fully operational. This beacon, along with the multitude of others, similar to it, which the vessel's computer theoretically placed along the route to this planet would allow any subsequent ships to locate the crew. The computer, however, had not survived the crash. Any interplanetary communication, beyond the beacon, had been rendered impossible. The failure of the computer had also destroyed any recordings which would have indicated the identity of the true astronauts.

As the quartet sat around a makeshift dinner table, they finally addressed major issues.

"I question whether we should activate the beacon," said White.

"Why?" asked Esposa.

"Do we really want to bring more people here. Remember, one of us is an alien. The plan might be to lure more humans here so they can infiltrate our population or take our vessels."

"First of all, we have to quit applying human tendencies to the alien. We have absolutely no idea how its mind operates or what it wants." Howard stood as he spoke. "Secondly, if that was what the alien wanted to do, why even wake us up. It could have activated the beacon on its own after reading our minds."

McDonald spat out some reconstituted vegetable mix and spoke, glumly. "No ship is coming from Earth. We all knew this was a suicide mission from the start."

Esposa chastised his crewmate. "That's not true. It is entirely possible that Earth has developed faster than light travel in the twenty years that we were en route. They could be here in a week after the beacon is established."

"Or, all of Earth could be dead and gone. We have no idea what happened in that time."

"Well if they haven't gotten faster than light travel, we are going to be stuck here for at least twenty years. Had the capsule not crashed we could have set the beacon and started our return trip."

"You're stating the obvious, Gavin," declared Howard. "Something else that is obvious, is that if we are going to have to wait twenty years for rescue, we have to develop better housing and find a way to grow food. I don't think there are any animals in this area. We have to explore."

"We also will need to find edible plants and start growing crops," added Esposa. "The path of the capsule is already cleared to some extent. We could start gardens there."

"We are not a flippin' colony. If we were sent to colonize this hell hole, they would have sent women with us." McDonald stood quickly, sending his canvas folding chair flying as he did so. "No one is coming. We aren't going to survive for long. And on top of everything else, there is some stupid alien spying on us. Face reality; we are dead men." He reached back as if to reset his fallen chair, but suddenly stopped, gave the chair a scoff and waved in its direction. He stormed out of the shelter, slamming the door as he did so.

YEAR 1 DAY 5

O N THE FIFTH day, after countless hours of debate, the crew activated the beacon. Minor progress had been made investigating the planet. There were many plants that, to the best of their knowledge, the crew found safe to eat. They even found some of the vegetation to be tasty. Construction of a more permanent shelter had begun and they had surveyed a few square miles of the immediate vicinity.

McDonald, who had begrudgingly returned that second night and agreed to do his share, was the first to speak after the beacon was initiated. "Okay, now that we've done that. I have an announcement." He drew a small device from the pocket of his uniform. "This is an explosive. I rigged it from some of the material off of the ship, but trust me, it will be deadly. So, unless the alien wants to die along with the rest of us, you better come forth right now."

"Hold on, Duane," White stepped forward, his hands raised. "You don't want to do that."

"Oh, yes I do. If by some miracle the beacon actually leads more people here, they are not going to be violated, like we were, by some unnatural being. I'd rather we all die than allow that foul creature to exist."

"It hasn't done anything to any of us," proclaimed Esposa.

"Not one time has any of the individuals in this group acted against us," added Howard. "There is no evidence that it is anything other than benevolent."

"Then why doesn't it just show itself. If it doesn't mean any harm, then just tell us."

"Put down the device, Duane. Killing all of us isn't the answer."

"I don't have to kill any of us if the creature simply shows itself."

"Maybe it's not a creature. Maybe there's something else entirely at work here," suggested Howard.

"Yeah," continued Esposa. "Maybe there were always four of us and our memories got changed during the crash...I don't know...but there has to be hundreds of possible explanations for what's going on."

"Let's just wait and see. We can figure it out without having to resort to this." White, carefully, moved a step closer to the red-headed, weapon brandishing astronaut. We have time. God knows, we have time. We can wait. Keep watching. If there is an alien, maybe it will slip up or decide to come forward."

"Whatever it is, it has played with our minds. It needs to be killed."

Howard and Esposa stood silently as White continued to try and negotiate with McDonald. "And if that is what it comes to, then we will do so. But, for now, we need everyone so that we have the best chance for survival. Please, give me the explosive. We will keep it. If we need it, we will use it."

"I'll keep it. I'm going to watch each of you. Don't give me a reason to use it."

"Sure. We trust you."

"I want my own shelter. I'm not sleeping in the same building as the alien. I'll work with all of you, but I will not let any of you near me when I am not awake, understand."

"Of course. That is an excellent idea. Now put down the explosive.

Looking dejected, yet, at the same time, relieved, McDonald turned the explosive in his hand, deactivated it, and replaced it in his clothing.

The four men stood silently for a prolonged period of time.

"Okay, let's make lunch," said Howard.

YEAR 1 DAY 38

JOHN HOWARD SWUNG the improvised hoe towards the soil with all of his might. The blade barely sunk into the grass covered ground, but when he pulled the handle back towards himself a large chunk of sod broke loose. He had been working at clearing the soil in this area for three days and had managed to create a decent sized area of weed free, exposed soil.

He stopped to catch his breath and take a quick sip from his water bottle. As he raised the hoe above his head, preparing for another mighty swing, he heard rustling from the edge of the jungle. He froze with the hoe above his head, his eyes searching the dense underbrush for the source of the sound.

The thick vegetation parted and a woman stepped into the clearing. John recognized her instantly, it was his late wife, Jenna. He let the hoe fall from his hands to the ground behind him. He stood, unable and unwilling to move, as she walked in his direction.

When she was about ten feet away, she stopped. "Hello, John."

"You're not Jenna."

"That is true. But don't you wish to see and talk to her."

"I can't. She's dead. She died three years before the mission began."

"You miss her. At least, look at her and remember her."

"I don't need to see her, to remember her," declared John. But he stared at her, intently.

"I have no intention of ever hurting any of you. I want you to survive. I want you to be happy."

"Seeing Jenna is not making me happy. It is making me quite sad."

"I understand, but you are lonely. I thought seeing her would help."

"I loved her so much. I still do. It's been so long that it is starting to become more difficult to see her, to truly see her beauty, in my dreams. I guess being able to see her now will rekindle many memories. For that I thank you."

"You are welcome. I only wish the best for all of you."

With that, Jenna turned and ran, briskly, back towards the jungle. Howard started to follow, maybe hoping to grab and capture the creature, but he stopped. Instead, he turned and sprinted in the direction of the camp.

H OWARD WAS EXHAUSTED. He struggled to catch his breath, as he reached the remains of the capsule and the shelters in which the astronauts now resided. He quickly located Gavin White working on the ship's computer, trying to bring it back to life.

"Gavin, where are the others?"

"I'm not certain. Eduardo was gathering fruit to the south, earlier. I think, McDonald was exploring, trying to add on to his map."

"Go find McDonald, right now. I will go look for Esposa. Bring him right back here as soon as you can."

"What's this about?"

"I'll tell you soon enough. Find McDonald, quickly."

I N LESS THAN twenty minutes the four castaways were gathered together in their camp.

"What's this all about, John?" asked Esposa.

John took a deep breath and exhaled slowly. "About half an hour ago, I saw my wife. She...the alien, in her form, approached me while I was working on the garden. It said that it meant no harm and wanted us to be happy. Were any of you together at that time."

"I was out by the deep ravine, trying to find a way across," answered McDonald. "I was there the entire afternoon."

Esposa held up a bag of bright orange fruit. "I was collecting fauxmangos. You found me up in a tree."

"So, none of you know any of the other's whereabouts?" Howard's eyes moved from person to person, focusing intently on each of them.

"I was here, working on the computer all morning," said White. "I do have something to tell you, though. I know I should have told you earlier, but I wanted to wait to see if it happened again. Two nights ago, I was visited by my partner, from when I was in college. He looked the same as he did then. I knew it was the alien, but it felt so good to talk to Michael. It was late at night and everyone was asleep in their cabins. I had gone for a walk, to think. He met me near the garden. I raced back here after we finished talking, but all of your cabins were locked."

"Well, I haven't been visited by anyone. The alien probably knows I would drop it on site," interjected McDonald.

"I haven't, either," said Esposa.

"But that doesn't mean either of them is the alien," explained White. "We could just as easily be making up our stories."

"I know." Howard nodded. "If one of you actually is that alien, I just want to say that I believe that you do not mean us any harm."

"Well, I don't." This time, it was McDonald who looked from person to person. His look could only be described as a glare.

YEAR 2 DAY 1

THE ASTRONAUTS COMMEMORATED the anniversary of their arrival on the planet with what could barely be called a celebration. They ate vegetables and fruit from their expansive garden. They looked at the progress they had achieved. They now had six sturdy permanent buildings in their camp. The supply shed was nearly filled and they had created a freshwater reservoir. The beacon had been kept operational the entire time. The quartet was surviving.

"I still wish we could get the computer up and running. It would be nice to be able to send out some form of communication beyond the beacon," announced John.

The beacon was designed to send its location a great distance. It is not made to send messages. We could change the transmission to a two- or three-word message, but then it might not be able to relay our location."

"We know, Gavin," asserted John. "I was just wishing out loud."

Eduardo changed the subject. "You know, it has been over a

month since any of us have even mentioned the alien. I hardly even think about the fact that one of us might not be human. The last time I thought about the alien was when my mother came to talk to me last month."

"I still think the alien still is a threat," McDonald responded. "If anyone ever does come for us, we will have to do something. But, for now, I agree, we have to just go on living, day to day.

"Well, to each of you, I say thank you. We've survived because we have worked together, worked through our differences." Here, John looked directly at Duane. "I don't know how this is going to end, but we keep going."

All four compatriots raised their glasses of fermented fruit, nodding agreement.

YEAR 5 DAY 113

THREE ASTRONAUTS STOOD over the grave. The marker, constructed from metal pulled from their ship, had an embroidered nametag fastened to it: MISSION SPECIALIST DUANE MCDONALD.

After a short traditional ceremony, Gavin White raised his head. "You know, he was a stubborn son-of-a-gun but he always had our backs. He always had the best interest of us and mankind at heart."

"I agree," said Esposa. "And the last couple of years he was actually enjoyable to be with."

"He really wanted to map this planet. I think he was always looking for some sign of civilization, some sign that there was life somewhere on this planet." John pointed to a mountain peak, barely visible through the vegetation. "I think we need to officially name the mountain after him. Not just because it is where he fell and lost his life, but because it signifies who he was."

"I totally agree." Eduardo picked up a worn paper map from a collection of McDonald's belongings. "I am going to continue to survey the planet. I promise to continue his work."

"I think we all will," added Gavin.

YEAR 12 DAY 76

G AVIN WHITE LAY, nearly motionless, in his bed. The minuscule movement of his chest with each shallow breath was the only visible sign that he was still alive. His body, weakened by the ever-spreading cancer was on the verge of giving up the fight, surrendering to the inevitable end.

The door to the cabin opened and a handsome, young man entered the room. "Gavin, it's me, Michael."

Gavin opened his weary eyes and fought the pain in order to turn and gaze upon the image of his long-lost friend. A soft, unintelligible mumble emerged from his lips.

Michael took Gavin's hand in his own. Gavin had once been a strong and powerful man, now his hand, like the rest of his body, was shriveled and weak. "You don't need to say anything, Gavin. I am here with you. I will stay with you until the end."

YEAR 12 DAY 77

T WO GRAVES OCCUPIED the makeshift cemetery on the outskirts of the camp. The more recent of the resting places, like the first, was adorned by a marker which featured the nametag from a uniform, the uniform in which Gavin was buried.

The two remaining astronauts no longer wore their uniforms. Years earlier, John had mastered the art of creating fabric, using an improvised loom. They wore pale brown clothing fashioned from the thread-like roots of a jungle plant.

"He was a good man," eulogized John. "He didn't deserve the physical suffering he had to endure at the end. He will be greatly missed."

"What do we do now?" asked Eduardo.

"We continue living. There is nothing else to do."

YEAR 23 DAY 199

J OHN CLOSED HIS eyes, letting the heat of the afternoon sun soak into his aged skin. He had asked Eduardo to bring him out into the clearing one last time. The open area had shrunk a great deal during the last few years; there was no one capable of maintaining it as it should have been. A shadow moved across his face, drawing his attention. He opened his eyes to see Eduardo standing above him.

John's friend took a seat next to him. Eduardo's hair, once thick and coal black, was now almost pure white. Wrinkles filled his face, giving the impression of a mosaic pasted together by a child. John spoke, "You are looking old, my friend."

"I dare say, not as old as you." Eduardo smiled. "Is there anything I can do for you?"

"You can finally answer my question. I'm not going to live long enough to ask again. Are you the alien?"

In answer, Eduardo's body and clothing began to change. Slowly it morphed, transforming to a completely different appearance. Soon the image of Jenna, John's beloved wife, sat before him. She wore blue jeans and a purple blouse. John remembered that purple had always been her favorite color.

Jenna took John's hand in hers and smiled.

John smiled back, looking into the eyes of a love he had lost so many years earlier. "Why? Why masquerade as one of us?"

The alien, still in the form of Jenna, replied. "I had been alone on this planet for thousands of years. I had endured loneliness that no one could ever imagine. I wanted to experience companionship, brotherhood. Had I revealed myself to you, you would have accepted me, but you would have always thought of me as something different, something alien. I wanted to, truly, be one of you and be part of something I have not been part of for an incredibly long time."

"But, why introduce the suspicion. You could have, simply, taken the place of one of us."

"I will never take the life of a sentient creature. I know what it is like to experience the loss of someone, everyone. I refuse to inflict that on any being."

John shook his head, ever so slightly. "I think we might have accepted you had you been honest with us."

"You very well may have, but I made my decision and I am happy with the outcome. For the last twenty years, I have not been lonely."

"You will be alone again, very soon, I fear."

"I wish it wasn't true, but I know. I will have new memories of friendships to fill some of the emptiness."

The two did not speak to each other again. They sat in silence, an old man and his beautiful wife. The sun set and darkness fell across the shrunken clearing.

YEAR ? DAY ?

Scarcely detectable in the thick underbrush lies the skeleton of a space ship. In a far corner of a section of jungle, which was once a clearing, are three shallow graves. A short distance from the graves, a beacon still sends a faint signal out into the heavens.

Next to that beacon sits a shapeless, translucent being. Rarely does the creature move. It is waiting, always waiting.

About the Author

In 2018, after 35 years as a high school math teacher and coach (tennis and wrestling), **James Rumpel** retired. Since that time he has greatly enjoyed spending time with his wonderful wife, camping, and training for half-marathons. In addition, he has had the chance to fulfill a lifelong dream by using some of his free time to try his hand at writing short stories. He has been lucky enough to see nearly one-hundred of his works appear on the internet or in print, though, to be honest, he finds his greatest joy in simply being able to turn some of the odd ideas circling his brain into stories.

The Unkillable Man

Topher Froehlich

THE MIRACLE BABY was his first name. Delivered stillborn, he was carried halfway to the hospital morgue upon a cold metal platter, when his stubby fingers, fresh with stickiness, began to wiggle as his stopped heart resumed its beat. The nurse bearing him away nearly dropped him to the floor when he opened his eyes.

Few of his career's following acts would match the emotion of that first resurrection, though many would inspire far greater awe. His mother wept on and off for months, for every reason: gratitude, sudden paralyzing confusion, wonder for the fragility and miraculous nature of life, and a terror she kept secret, the unspeakable fear that maybe her little miracle was in fact a tiny devil.

The medical staff spent a week being puzzled, before letting go, only bringing up the story on occasion, when in need of an anecdote to entertain a patient or pass a few minutes in idle co-worker gossip. Swiftly, the sense of reality being turned inside out dissipated among them. The story was demoted from unbelievable miracle to as-yet explained curiosity, then finally to an easy-to-digest lesson. *We only thought he had died*, they consoled themselves. *We must be more careful in the future.*

The second time he skirted death's shadow created a bigger

fanfare. Now a roughhousing lover of horsing around, The Miracle Baby had grown into a young boy who was always in motion. Regardless of his aptitude he played every sport. Free time was given to hiking, bicycling, camping, canoeing. His leftover energy he channeled into (the sloppiest) tap-dance.

On the occasion of his second victory over the Grim Reaper, the boy was scampering in the woods among a pack of friends. At play pretending to be merry men, wielding sticks to have sword fights, the children became carried away. In their fervor they imagined themselves a mob of villainy, surrounding a lone hero and chased their friend, the former Miracle Baby, up a boulder, where, in an imitation of a feat of derring-do, he leapt to seize a tree branch and instead fell fourteen feet and snapped his neck.

A few frantic jabs, from foot and stick alike, proved to all the children their friend was not joking. Hysteria took them - panic erupted, sobbing commenced and scolding responded unkindly to tears. "Shut up, shut up," the most afraid hissed. Fleeing the scene, the dispersed and traumatized little ones all told their tales at home. But when a congregation of disturbed parents and solemn policemen returned to the rock it was to find a boy midway through the process of snapping his own neck back into place.

The old story received a resurgence. Before he knew it, the Miracle Baby was the Luckiest Boy Alive, a modern day miniature Harry Houdini. Defier of death! The town's own local celebrity. Everywhere he went there were free favors (he never paid for pizza or ice cream again) and back thumps, folks who wanted to pump his hand and ask over and over again what it was like. Had he seen a light? Heard the voice of Him?

In different conditions, the ingredients were ripe for a storm of either great fear or mistaken profundity. Another town might have lost their sense and insisted here was a Messiah. In Stonebrook, people were too casually cynical to take religion too seriously, and too confident in their economic stability to see anything as much of a threat. Besides, the Luckiest Boy Alive was too goofy to stoke such fevered sentiments. His buck teeth, flat flaxen hair, and most especially his voice, nasally and ever on the verge of laughing, made one want to hand the kid an ice cream and ruffle his head, not fall to the floor in supplication. The town adopted him as their collective kid brother, the neighborhood rascal.

Like many a boy before him, in the bountiful throes of youth, the Luckiest Boy Alive had an innate sense that he was invincible. Having twice bested death, never one day allowed to forget it by his community, that sureness of his own invulnerability swelled and swelled and swelled.

The experiments soon commenced.

The Luckiest Boy Alive tested his luck. Rather than dip his toe in the lake, as they say, he went ahead and cannonballed into the depths of his potential.

The first, second and even seventh time he jumped out of his mother's car, as it hurtled down the highway, it shocked the poor woman and caused her months of insomnia, multiple cases of strep throat from screaming herself hoarse and drove her to such emotional and mental anguish, she seriously considered never letting her son leave the house again.

By the time the town had voted to put up a sign warning other drivers of the boy's predilection toward leaping from cars, his mother had adjusted her attitude to that of, "as long as he's safe." She did not wish to be the one to hold him back from expressing himself, as her father had done to her, driving a wedge between dad and daughter by forbidding her to continue "wasting time with watercolors."

"He doesn't do drugs, gets good grades, shows me respect and so... what can I really complain about? It makes him happy."

Everywhere he went, a pal recording video followed. Documenting it all for the Luckiest Boy Alive to upload to his Youtube channel, "Illneverdie". Friends would shoot fireworks right at his chest. He would take weights to pool parties and hang out, breath held, for thirty minutes or more. He let speedboats drag him, one foot tied to a rope. He tried to crowd source funds for purchasing a cannon, as he thought it would be great fun to get shot out of it.

In private, he went further. Conducted attempts on himself that were less spectacle, nastier. He burned his fingertips with matches, then an iron, then left his hands on the stove. He suffocated himself with plastic bags. One time he even put his hand in the garbage disposal. Though it felt like his hand had been shredded and devoured, he pulled it whole and unblemished from the sink. Despite the fact that he was fine, even he felt terrified and never put his hand in there again.

His stunts were not universally beloved. One Halloween, he dressed as a witch and let his friends set him on fire. The day after the video went up, the Luckiest Boy Alive found himself sitting with the authority figure he most respected in life: his gymnastics instructor.

"You're almost a young adult now, so I'm not going to mince words here. What you're doing is acting like a jackass. Turning yourself into a sideshow. Like one of those morons who shoot porta-potties into the sky. This right here," and as the Coach flicked a finger on the paused witch-burning video, the Luckiest Boy Alive was sure he was about to be lectured on *'how very dangerous'* this all was, as if he didn't *know already*.

"This," the Coach said, "well you tell me. What does this say?"

"Huh?"

"When people watch this video, what do you think they're thinking?"

"I don't know. That it's cool?"

"Did it never occur to you that maybe you could be doing something more constructive than lighting yourself on fire cause it's 'cool'?"

"You mean like... you want me to foil bank robberies?"

"What? No. Nothing of the sort. Just think about the example you set. Think about what this video says about you. Right now it says, *I will hurt myself for attention. I don't care about my body.* Is that what you want people to think of you?"

Whatever, the Luckiest Boy Alive thought to himself and though the Coach couldn't read minds, the message could not have been plainer.

The Luckiest Boy Alive did not think about this meeting for more than a year. Irene Crayple forced him to remember it. At eight years of age, she had attempted to recreate his car-jumping stunt, hurling herself out of her family's minivan at seven a.m. on a Saturday, on her way to soccer practice.

The Luckiest Boy Alive took down all his videos and did not perform for the next twenty years.

I N A MONTH's time he would be known nationwide as the Unkillable Man. The dawn of his return was unassuming, as dawn on day's of incredible things tends to be.

The city park where he was to arrive was blessed with summer sunshine and a packed weekend crowd. By midmorning, the great green getaway was humming with its visitors' contentment.

The Unkillable Man entered anonymously. Attired in plain jeans, a wrinkled gray tee, and running shoes, he cut a forgettable and bland figure. His hair was nondescript, his face utterly ordinary, his lanky frame unremarkable. No one paid him any attention as he stepped onto the stage of the empty outdoor amphitheater, where occasionally concerts or Shakespeare were performed. Why should they? No announcement ushered him to their attention. Not even the barest explanation was offered for his presence.

No attention was paid him until the first gunshot rang out. The sound alone sent people running, screaming. Those closest were transfixed. Unaccustomed to the crack of gunfire, they searched for the source of noise, perhaps hoping for a more mundane answer to their confusion, and what they saw was forever burned into their memories.

The Unkillable Man stood, handgun held to his temple, the

stage stained with his blood. Three more times he shot himself in the head. Each blast the only sound in the world. His head and shoulder ran with crimson. His whole body shuddered ceaselessly with spasms. For a moment that lasted less time and felt longer than the shooting, he stared out at them with what many thought was a mix of accusation and imploration. His quivering face was about to explode in either tirade or tears.

Silent, he dropped his emptied weapon to the ground and strode toward his audience. Pinned by horror and, an amazement they would never dare to admit feeling, they watched him open-mouthed and rooted to their seats. As he passed through the crowd, some were tempted to reach out and touch him, to be sure he was real. They followed him with their eyes as far as they were capable, but by the time the police had come to the scene no one was sure where the man had gone.

After three days of relentless pursuit, the authorities uncovered him and took him to jail. His tenure there was short lived. Following a highly publicized and heavily scrutinized court case, the Unkillable Man's indefatigable and ever-inventive legal team had this public display of violence ruled as performance art.

The Unkillable Man was free to continue with his work, the only consequence to his equally derided and praised attempted execution being the stipulation that going forward, he must always announce his shows in advance and acquire the necessary permits and various bits of insurance required of any life-risking showman.

By all accounts, the Unkillable Man was greatly displeased by this as he felt it was paramount to his mission to operate without warning. "It dilutes the message," he confided to his closest friends. What message, they wanted to know and received hand-waving answers in lieu of.

The second performance, years removed from the first, was anticipated with a level of hype the world's various mass media conglomerates could never dare to dream up. An audience of a million persons attempted to descend upon the grounds where the Unkillable Man planned his next appearance (a place most commonly used for music festivals). Admission was free, only inciting the public interest more. Police patrolled attendance ruthlessly, turning away more than a third of the potential spectators.

Without a TV screen to amplify the spectacle, only the closest could see what was happening. The Unkillable Man had waited, in silence, for hours, while the crowd enveloped him in an endless circle. Screaming for his name, his autograph, his blessing, his attention, none of which he gave, eyes shut until show time at six p.m.

Promptly he rose and drew back his coat to reveal he wore a bomb strapped to his chest. The crowd screamed not like civilians in the presence of a weapon, but fans in the ecstatic hysteria of a much-worshipped musician tuning their instrument.

With his customary lack of fanfare or showmanship, the Unkillable Man unceremoniously clicked the detonator and exploded. Bits of blood and bone whacked the closest viewers in the face, and the people threw up their arms and cheered as if they had been sprayed with confetti.

Slowly the dust cloud dispersed and there stood the Unkillable Man. The crowd swore he was at once whole and unblemished, and at the same time limbless, his skin charred and blackened. The effect lasted perhaps a minute, a tortuous sixty-second span in which the shocked and silenced onlookers wondered whether this was an optical illusion even as they knew their eyes were not lying. But if he could be both murdered and alive, then what did anything they had ever seen before this moment matter at all, for suddenly every natural law was violated, invalidated, shattered and destroyed.

Then the Unkillable Man grasped the rope lowered for him from a helicopter and rose up and away from the people. Now they saw he was unhurt, they were sure of it, and thus their worries were, for the moment at least, banished and they whooped and cheered and screamed in relief.

"The cheers disturbed him," one close friend of the Unkillable Man's confided, anonymously, to an outlet circulating a photo of the much talked about entertainer, drifting over a sea of enthusiastic fans, his face carved with repugnance. "I don't think it's what he expected. Or what he wanted."

Millions were now asking: who was the Unkillable Man? How did he survive bullets and explosions? The twenty-four hour news cycle fed these and other questions to the hungry populace without break. Speculation was both predictable and rampant, from the easily-discarded theories that he was an alien to the more palatable, popular theory that he was the greatest magician who ever lived, a man who had single-handedly revitalized not only a long-dead art but an entire nation's sense of wonder for the unexplainable. The armchair psychologists also came out in full force, every other think piece on the web weighing in on whether this mad man was driven by a death wish or an adrenaline addiction. Some writers were so bold as to claim the Unkillable Man was a symptom of his generation's nihilism and narcissism.

All these topics possessed the public imagination but were of no concern to the man himself. "They do not yet understand," he thought to himself whenever he encountered such reactions. "I have to be clearer."

The stage was set for the Unkillable Man's renaissance. All his greatest and most memorable demonstrations were to take place over the next decade, in which he remained a figure of fascination, each performance attended by hundreds of thousands of spectators.

For five uninterrupted hours, he swung from a hangman's noose, choking and sputtering while his admirers looked on, alternately cheering him to withstand his predicament and vomiting in disgust. Of course, there were also those who took selfies, with the strangling man as their backdrop.

He tied himself to a concrete block and spent ten hours drowning in the depths of a Great Lake, his tortuous underwater experience live streamed to an estimated audience of twelve million.

Three days the Unkillable Man stood naked in Antarctica. He spent four weeks in Death Valley, blistered, burnt, dying of thirst, watched by onlookers in air-conditioned buses. For two years, he starved himself, sitting in cafes and restaurants, not permitting himself even a glass of water. This was known as "The Global Hunger Tour", in which the Unkillable Man traveled to 93 countries to starve.

Claims of his selling out became lobbed with regularity after the Unkillable Man opened up a charity in his own name and charged admission to all shows to finance his non-profit. Donations to the Unkillable Man were directly funded to organizations devoted to suicide prevention, gun control advocacy, pro-choice movements, world hunger associations and relief funds for communities adversely affected by disasters or disease. Much of America's right wing derided the Unkillable Man for his actions. They saw these donations as politicizing the hitherto purity of the Unkillable Man's public pain. "Stick to shooting yourself," became a common complaint. "I don't watch your shows to listen to your politics."

Without a parachute, the Unkillable Man skydived. He stood on a highway and was run over by 9 sixteen-wheelers, repeatedly. He subjected himself to spearings, stabbings, guillotines, water boarding, being drawn and quartered, and the electric chair.

When he came under criticism for only suffering show-offy deaths, the Unkillable Man deliberately overdosed on a pharmacy's variety of drugs, willingly injected himself with diseases ranging from typhoid fever to malaria, and routinely ingested carbon monoxide.

His grip on the zeitgeist became firmer than any President's. Although his friends described him as good-natured and quick to laugh, the masses judged him to be the most serious, severe and humorless man who had ever lived. The longer he continued with his work, the louder his critics became. His shtick was getting old, they said. Repetitive and banal. What frustrated them most, what frustrated even his devoted fans, was the lack of explanation or clear purpose. Just why was the Unkillable Man bothering to do any of this? Mere attention? To propagate his own brand of masculinity? To eventually launch a political campaign many feared would be a colossal success?

His frustrations equaled theirs. The Unkillable Man could not believe that still his points were not getting across, not to anyone. After more than a decade.

In all his years in the limelight he had turned down seven-figure offers to star in movies, ludicrous book contracts and ungodly amounts of money in brand deals. At the same time he had refused all self-promotion, eschewing giving interviews in any form.

Thus when it was announced he was going to be the featured guest on an investigative reporting show, the public was more shocked than it would have been had he announced he was going to swallow a live grenade or a king cobra or both.

44 million people watched the interview live.

For years he had been their mime of anguish. To hear him speak caused a majority of viewers a cognitive dissonance. They had imagined he sounded resonant, rich, godlike. Instead his voice seemed like it would be how an anthropomorphic squirrel spoke, quick and congested.

Asked why he had agreed to an interview at last, after years of silence, the Unkillable Man said:

"I always hoped the work spoke for itself. People have always wanted me to explain myself and I would say, my art does all the talking. It says exactly what I want it to. But more and more as the years have gone on, I don't know if that's true. I hear people saying, oh he's glamorized suicide. Or, he's contributed to desensitizing us to violence. My favorite is when I hear that everything I do is no different than, say, a Youtube clip of someone getting hit in the balls. As if I want people laughing!

"You'd know it's not supposed to be funny if you paid any attention at all to what I'm going through. Everyone gets so caught up talking about the part where I survive, they forget about when I'm suffering. Sure, I eventually get cut down from the noose, but when I'm up there, I feel every second of it. Just like anyone would. With the rope around my neck, I am actually gasping for air. You know, I lose all brain function. In that moment I don't remember I'll be all right. In that moment, I am *dying*. Every gunshot, every stabbing, let me tell you, anyone who says your body gets used to it, is full of shit. When I am drowning I am drowning for real. On the Hunger Tour, I was in agony. Agony. Every single moment of every single day. I'm not exaggerating. I felt it all. You know? The only people who understand that, are people who have lived through starvation. I didn't ever hear them laughing. During the tour, when I sat with other people undergoing the same torture, who were starving, only for them it wasn't voluntary? Complete acceptance. I was welcome, as one of them. There was no judgment, there was no, 'oh why does he do this?'"

"I am still not sure I understand why you are doing these things. You want people to see you in pain, but why?" said the interviewer

"It's not about my pain," said the Unkillable Man. "I am showing people death. I am showing them what death really is. There is so little attention given to those who are dying. And even less caring about what they're going through, what they're really feeling. Too few of us want to comfort anyone dying, or even think about them, unless we're forced. We want the dying and the dead kept out of sight, out of mind. We reduce them to the abstract. Whether it's victims of genocide or cancer, in our minds, they're off someplace that isn't here and doesn't matter. We choose not to see or dwell on them. It isn't real to us. I'm trying to put death in front of everyone. To show you how real it is.

"What incredible irony, that people would accuse me of not taking this seriously, because I take dying more seriously than anyone. That's what my art is about."

If there were any supporters of this outlook, their viewpoint was the minority and it was drowned in the immeasurable backlash the Unkillable Man faced for his words. His sin was twofold, each unforgiveable to his longtime audience. One, he had dared

285

call himself an artist, seeking to elevate his position when, nearly everyone agreed, what he did required no talent whatsoever. Just sheer genetic luck. Second, he had the audacity, *the nerve*, to lecture them! And what a paltry, sentimental, meaningless lecture it had been to cap off the insult. All those years, all that human suffering, all for a credo with the depth of a Hallmark Card.

Seemingly overnight, those who had been proud to witness the Unkillable Man's mettle became embarrassed. Their hero was no indestructible wise man. He was a pretentious, moralizing fuddie duddie. With the mystery dispelled by a pitiful excuse for a reveal, the Unkillable Man's preachiness was exposed. Many wished he had been an adrenaline junkie after all. If, critics argued, this had been his intention all along he had done an abominable job expressing it. Worse, they were nearly unanimous in deciding, the Unkillable Man was woefully unaware of the inherent contradiction in his act, a paradox with no way around it.

"We aren't saying the Unkillable Man hasn't felt pain," one wrote, summing up her peers' thoughts best. "We're saying surely even he is aware that, for all his anguish, he is never actually at risk of dying. He can't die. How can he claim to be showing us death? He's literally just wallowing in his own misery."

The few shows the Unkillable Man performed over the next couple of months were poorly attended, widely mocked, relentlessly parodied. Even the former Miracle Baby himself wasn't putting his heart into it. The death knell to his mission was in a critical observation that the Unkillable Man, after years of failing to succeed in his message, knew personally to be true: you cannot make people take death seriously, when you turn it into a spectacle.

Obscurity was coming for the Unkillable Man. He knew it and knowing it, retired without announcement. He was remembered as a passing fad, an embarrassing relic of youth, as if everyone had woken up together to his mediocrity and blushed to recall what so short a time ago had seemed magnificent and somehow, though it was difficult to remember why, important.

Eighteen years later he died choking on a tuna fish sandwich in the privacy of his home, attended only by his golden retriever. The obituaries were late to correctly identify him as the Unkillable Man, and what little stir his belated end finally caused was mostly confined to shrugs of indifference and remarks in the vein of, "So he died then. He was a phony after all."

ABOUT THE AUTHOR

Topher Froehlich currently exists somewhere in Queens, New York. When he isn't writing, he amuses himself by doing silly voices, including uncanny impressions of, among others, Gollum, Elmo and Patrick Warburton. He's been known to make short films and might do it again someday. This Muppet of a man has written for Brooklyn Magazine and his fiction will appear in a forthcoming issue of Abyss and Apex. Look out for him online @topherfroehlich.

The Frost Mother

Caitlin E. Jones

All hail Good Velka, Mother of Frost.

THE WORDS WERE still cut into the panels of ice when Sasha finally made it around the mountainous slope, wet slush of melted snow under her boots. She knew they would be there, as famous as the landmark was. The red of the words had long turned rust-colored, but the inscriber still clutched his sliced palm, blood streaking red forever along his exposed hands and pearly rosary. He had frozen where he knelt, encased beneath a gleaming shell of ice, a half-lidded gaze that eternally spoke of peace. Acceptance.

Sasha clutched her walking poles in tight fists, breathing puffs of steam through her head cover. The snow had ceased for a moment, but the temperatures around the range clung below freezing. Frost stuck to her fur-lined coat, ice picked its way at the seams of her seal boots. Every patch of exposed skin burned with the heat of an unseen sun.

To pay respects was to die, so Sasha moved forward with a nod. She needed to accept the grisly scene anyway: Saintly Nielson was only the first marker, a warning to travelers that now entered the Graveyard of The Frost Mother.

Sasha pressed forward in short steps and careful breathing; the magic shielding her was wearing thin with each step she made into the Frost Mother's land. The mountains crowded now around her where they had- all of her life, been so distant. Their jagged, frost-topped peaks towered around her, their forceful masses filling patches of sky with rock and snow. The pine forests and sparse ground below were no longer visible, with fog banks so dense that Sasha thought she'd wandered too far up and into the clouds. Only ice remained.

Her lungs burned for more air, but cried out when she took a breath. The enchantress had warned her of this, the pervasive cold that strangled from the moment you ascended the summit. It was worse than Sasha imagined, a kind of cold that reached for your brain. She let her mind wander- however troubling, back to the Gardens of Eternal Summer, hoping Vesna's gifts were enough to guide her forward, passed the bloodless bloodshed of Mount Bantok. It was her earliest memory, after all.

Y*OU WISH TO go where, my flower?" Enchantress Vesna asked, the innocence in her voice burying with an edge. She was a tall, pale woman, her beauty a rapturous, overwhelming thing that combated the mountains themselves. She looked almost ugly now though. Vesna must have not liked being outwitted, but then, Sasha had never really wanted to stay in the gardens forever. Vesna had to have known that her spell would not keep to someone so proud, so restless.*

"I must go to the Hinterlands! Up the summit and to the castle." Sasha exclaimed, tears rolling down her cheeks, a rose in her hands. The one she had stolen from the enchantress' hair in a flurry of memory and fear. "Please, I cannot stay in these gardens forever. Kai will be lost."

"Kai?" The enchantress tipped her head.

Who was Kai? Sasha paused, for the flowers in the garden had known, whispering their truths into her ear after the rose had broken the spell. She wasn't a flower, or an enchantress. She had come here with a mission in mind. Kai was her mission, her guiding light, her everything.

"The Hinterlands are eternal winter, endless death," Vesna contin-

ued softly. "They are my sister's keep and anything that crosses into her land is hers to claim. Your Kai is dead."

"That's not true, your flowers have spoken it," Sasha said, pointing to the garden's occupants. The flowers stretched forward in approval. "The lilies do not mourn for him, the hyacinth bells do not ring for his funeral. I have time, I must return to the road."

"Then I consign you to death, my flower. I cannot allow it," Vesna said, turning away in tearful remorse. "I will not let Velka claim another."

"But if I can defeat The Frost Mother?" The name slid from Sasha's lips before she remembered why she knew it.

Vesna wheeled forward with inhumanness, her eyes black, her skin full of cracks like glass, her hair undone. She hovered up to Sasha, her voice coming through in a hiss. "We do not speak that name in these most sacred gardens."

Sasha shied away, keeping an eye on the gate. "I can... defeat Queen Velka, I know how. I know how the shard affected her."

Vesna fell back, dark magic fading from her eyes and face. "You... believe the shards can be removed?"

Sasha nodded, edging away again.

Vesna laughed musically. "And, do you know what it takes to remove them?"

Sasha still didn't know. She could not get a straight answer from Vesna before the enchantress gifted her with a Spell of Warming and sent her on her way.

Sasha had traveled many miles since her journey had re-started, and her memories of Kai became clearer with each day.

Kai, a boy from her village, east of the Hinterlands. where the mountain range encircling the valley like sets of snowy teeth. Kai was her best friend. This had been the same for seventeen years, and promised to be the same forevermore after that.

Every year, The Good Kindred of Season would come and go through the mountains. Spring, summer, autumn, and winter. That was the Frost Mother's duty, to greet the winter. She had always been a kind, benevolent sorceress, managing the weather from her isolated home in the mountains.

Then something had changed a year ago, in 1816. The story that passed through the pub doors and around the worship alters was that Vesna had tried to cross the mountains to bring the springtime, but Velka no longer wanted to retreat into her home. Why should she? Why must winter be the most hated season, and spring the most loved?

Whatever occurred between the two powerful enchantresses in that mountain range, it sent Vesna into an eternal garden, walled away from the world. Summer and autumn, not heard from, and so Velka remained, and winter crept onward and onward until the months seemed to not matter.

The clutch of winter made people tired of all the snow at first.

Then scared, because crops were freezing in the ground.

Then angry, as villages ran low on stored foods and lower on what livestock they could spare to slaughter.

Village leaders from across the land were sent to reason with Velka, but none returned. The village men then grouped in thousands, whoever was strongest, most able enough to make the climb through Bantok's summit. Each village sent their groups to plead and beg and threaten the Frost Mother- if they had to, to allow the season's change. Months passed, and few ever returned. Most did not want to go back.

Sasha's village grew particularly despondent and troubled, a morass befalling anyone it could touch.

It was worse for Kai—always so cheerful, always so kind. A depression claimed him in the Year Without a Summer, and he so turned reckless and violent and withdrawn, only smiling at the falling snowflakes, or during visits from the Frost Mother, making her rounds through the village on her horse-led carriage. Offering a journey into the mountains for anyone who would take it. No one did, fearful of what ill omen she might bring next.

Except one day, when his joy so consumed him, Kai took the

Frost Mother's hand. She kissed his fingers to numb him of cold, and then his forehead, to forget about Sasha, and home, and all the nice things that winter had taken from them. He bundled himself into the Frost Mother's carriage, and was gone. Sasha wasn't sure when she expected to see him again.

Sasha had not expected to see her village elder again either, but she spotted his frozen body on a shelf of ice that bordered the Frost Mother's pond. His pose suggested he'd been scolding whoever killed him. Sasha held her breath, making a slow trek to the pond of shining ice. Bodies littered the top like a statuary. Men and women from all over the mountain range, some eras and eras old by the make of their clothes. No blood, nothing broken, though the clutch of endless winter had left more than a few open to the elements. The shine of exposed bone through flesh, left by ugly gashes in skin where corvids and carrion birds had staked their claim.

Below the ice, more bodies appeared beneath Sasha's feet, their clothes floating, suspended in the eternal swim from which they never surfaced. Most wore the same blissful grin. Dying for the sake of the Frost Mother was an honorable cause, after all.

Sasha shivered at the pond's edge, fighting the urge to retch onto her snowshoes. This wasn't a battlefield of corpses. This was a grim, defiant trophy case.

I'm coming, Kai. Stay alive, I am coming. Sasha bundled her scarves up and tightened her shoes, preparing to cross the ice in full force. She kept her unanswered question in the back of her mind, and all who could not answer it…

A*RE YOU SURE this is the way, little crow?"* Sasha asked. *The paths were growing snow-patched and rough as she followed the bird.*

The bird cried from the tree branch, fluttering down until it had landed on her shoulder. "Saw Kai this way. Saw Kai."

Sasha sighed, stroking the animal's beak before it flew off again. The strange bird had been her only company since she had fled from Vesna's

293

clutches. She regretted not taking lessons in crows' speak from her grand-
mother before her passing; it might be so useful now. But crows were ev-
er-present and ever-watchful, so Sasha trusted that the bird could not lie to
her enough to lead her in the wrong direction. She hopped onto the crum-
bling remains of roadside wall, arms out as if to give her winged friend
company. They were closer to the Hinterlands; the nearest mountain was
a wall that followed them up the roadside, veins of limestone cutting into
its cold, gray rock. Lush, freezing water wept from the cliffface in springs,
creating streams of life in the remarkable stillness. Clutches of wild flow-
ers bloomed wherever the water touched, small but present. Even the Frost
Mother could not remove all of springtime.

Another question bloomed in her mind then. "Mr. Crow?"

The bird cawed from the sky.

"What does it cost to fix the shard that has infected the Frost Mother?"

The crow cackled into the air, flying into a sharp circle over Sasha's
head. "Always a Frost Mother. Always a Frost Mother."

"I don't understand," Sasha said.

"Find Kai! Let's find Kai." The bird was off again, flying into the
treeline and leading Sasha further away from the eternal gardens.

KAI..." SASHA BREATHED his name to keep focus. Her steps
were so small that they scarcely counted for walking. The ice
looked at though it was frozen to the bottom of the lake, but each
time her snowshoe landed, the ice crackled beneath, threatening
the same fate as so many villagers before her. She could see the
entrance to the mountain's peak from where she stood, and from
there, the way into the Frost Mother's palace. One step, another,
eyes forward.

Ice gave under her feet and gasped, looking down at the cracks.
The ice had split between her feet, and the body of a pale-faced
woman stared up at her through the gap. Her fingers were shriveled to nothing, her eyes were sunken, sallow cheeks so thin that
they gave way to bone. Sasha was trapped by her dead stare, by the
gleam of the golden chain that still hung around her neck.

The woman's fingers suddenly twitched. Her dead gaze turned upwards.

"You can stop here, if you like," she said, words muffled through bubbles in the water. "We all do. Your friend might join you soon... it doesn't hurt."

Sasha couldn't look away, but shook her head. Her hands drifted to the ice ax at her hip.

Skeletal hands shot through the gap, fingers latching an iron grip on Sasha's ankle. She screamed, but fought the urge to swing her weapon, kicking back at the dead creature instead.

"Hail to the Frost Mother... hail to the Frost Mother... Strike me down, please." the corpse chanted, crawling closer and closer out the ice. She was rotting the more she came into the sun, her flesh melting away like snowfall. Her eyes and nose were gone, her teeth were jagged and horrid as the mountain face.

Sasha grabbed the woman's bony wrist and kicked the corpse in the torso. Most of the body sank back into the ice, but her arm remained latched onto her ankle until Sasha threw it down into the water.

Closing her eyes, Sasha fell to her knees on the pond and choked on a sob.

"They aren't real... You weren't real. Natalia said that." she whispered, touching her lips. Peeking through her fingers, she could already see truth: the gap in the ice was gone, and the corpse woman had returned to her final resting place, peacefully floating once more.

T*HERE'S NOTHING REAL on Mount Bantok. That is how it claims so many," Natalia told Sasha in warning. They laid side by side- though not of Sasha's own volition, given the knife that Natalia held. The young woman's arm was banded over Sasha like a venomous snake.*

Her journey had taken another detour: she'd been captured by a band of highwaymen just a day from the mountain base, and if not for Natalia's defense, Sasha's journey might have ended at this detour. A daughter of the king thief, Natalia was a rough, unladylike figure that had taken Sasha as part of her "collection," which somehow seemed to include more questionable things than a human.

Nevertheless, the young thief had a good heart, and seemed more interested in making sure Sasha was prepared to fight the Frost Mother than turning her into a servant. Their current position in bed was mostly ruse, should her proud father look into Natalia's room.

"We have sent men- good men, up to mountains," Natalia said, her gaze pulling on Sasha's. Her eyes and hair were the same ebony color, and her accent deeply soaked with the Eastern Hinterlands. "She tricks you if she does not freeze you. Her magic is too cruel. I have seen a few of ours return, mad from corpses rising- demons and ghosts in the ice. The Frost Mother kills the weak, recruits the strong, and we are left to suffer. This is what happened to your Kai, I do not doubt."

Sasha's heart sunk. "So she will test me to the point of death when I cross the summit? She has already claimed Kai. Perhaps… Vesna was right."

Sasha's doubt was met with a knife blade at her cheek.

"I did not say this," Natalia grimaced, retracting her weapon. "I said you must be ready for unimaginable horror, if you so wish to save this Kai. Save us all. Your heart, it seems good. Your regrets, few. You have no weakness that she can take. I must hope anyway: there is no place for respectable thievery when whole villages starve under dangerous winter."

Natalia's smirk made Sasha laugh.

Natalia sighed, rolling over on the mattress' side. "Tomorrow, I will give you climbing tools, food- better clothes. Something to defend yourself from the cold when foolish magic wears off. You can borrow Ba—" She gestured to her reindeer that slept on the floor. "And make the rest of the journey into the mountainside, though I do not think he will cross the summit with you."

"I'll see that he returns, thank you," Sasha whispered.

Natalia's gaze bore into her still, scrutinizing and brilliant. Sasha met it for a moment too long, that same question bubbling into her throat.

"Natalia... when you defeat the Frost Mother, what does it cost?"

The thief sighed, a shred of doubt passing into her confident expression. "I will ask you again then, you are... quite certain you do not want to stay here? Send someone else to save Kai? I would always keep you well-dressed and fed and you could come on raids. Rise up as the second strongest woman in our band- I am first, of course. But it is a good life, even when it is harsh."

Sasha shook her head, Vesna's pleading eyes in her thoughts. "I must do this. It is all I have left."

Natalia furrowed her brow. She nodded to herself, as if confirming something and leaned in closer, a loose grip on the knife. The way her mouth brushed Sasha's was so slight that they both froze. Natalia held her ground as she whispered truth against Sasha's lips.

"Winter is a kind of freedom, because it takes the things we did not realize we had."

THE PALACE OF the Frost Mother was less grand than Sasha had imagined, and far more befitting of the Frost Mother's nature. Carved out of the summit's icy sides, it jutted out as if it had always been a part of the mountain, jagged and lifeless and covered in snow. The temperatures were so relentless that Sasha was beyond the cold, her body numbed and warming itself instead. She doubted that was a good sign.

The air was still so thin and slowed her down more than she wanted. She pressed forward, step after bold step until she had crossed the threshold of the palace and slipped into its stone walls. No decor, no portraits- only ice.

"Kai!" she called, trying to undo her snowshoes and run at the same time. Her voice echoed back tenfold.

"Come in..." The voice that called was feminine and harsh. A briskness carried it through the air that reminded Sasha of the first bout of northern chill in autumn.

Slowing her breathing, Sasha followed the voice's call with instinct. She knew nothing of this palace, and yet, without a second thought she wound her way through the icy corridors and found herself in the Frost Mother's throne room.

Velka's beauty was much like her sister's: Sasha could not stare at her without feeling overcome. Her face was a sharp point, her eyes consumed in the deepest blue. She wore a gown of fine black silk and coat of stark white fur, the heads at the end confirming its make was of Arctic fox. Velka stood in front of her throne, full of crystalline ice, two carved polar bears emerging from the face of her chair's arms.

Kai stood at her side, as dark-haired and tall as ever. His presence almost sent Sasha to her knees: his face was blue with cold, his eyes were beginning to sink, his body a mirror of the corpse woman from the lake.

"Oh, Kai." Sasha breathed. "Kai, I've come back for you! We have to go home."

Kai's eyes turned on Sasha, harsh and unreadable. "Who... are you now?"

"It's me," Sasha pleaded. "It's Sasha, remember?" But for all she could remember before Vesna's spell, she could not place who she was to Kai either. Her attention veered to the Frost Mother. "I beg of you, Good Velka. You must end the eternal winter and allow Kai to go home."

The Frost Mother made no movement nor opened her mouth, but her voice echoed through the halls. "Your companion can leave when he wishes, if he wishes. But to end the winter will be impossible."

"Nothing is impossible. The other seasons must happen, or the Hinterlands will die. Is that what you want? That is not the Good Velka we have come to know." Sasha said.

The Frost Mother paused, a small, cold smile on her lips.

"Then you know why I have changed, girl," her voice offered. "So few realize what has happened, save my siblings. Was it Vesna that told you?"

In truth, Sasha couldn't remember, but still words tumbled

from her mouth. "I have... known what corrupted you. You broke the Mirror of Reason when you decided that winter wasn't enough. The shards entered your eye and have made you cold to humanity."

"Correct," The Frost Mother said, denying nothing.

"But winter must end sometimes."

"Perhaps..." The Frost Mother tilted her head in a sharp question. "Who is to say that I will be the one to stop it though, while I am Frost Mother? There is no winter without me."

Sasha's retort faded into nothing. She shivered and fell to one knee, weakness clung onto her body.

"Dear Sasha... you are dying." The Frost Mother's voice offered no compassion though. "Let go of this folly. It will be fruitless, and you will be so much happier if you simply join your Kai..."

In the fog of winter chill and the numbing warmth, Sasha's mind was still caught by a single, solitary idea: the memory she'd clung to, the knowledge of what had corrupted Velka. Not a story she had been given by Natalia, not the highwaymen, or the royals, and fisher-women, and the enchantress she had met in her travels.

She shuddered a breath and let her mind dig deeper, somewhere past the foggy memories of Vesna's spell. To her village, her parents, or grandmother. No one had told her. She had simply known the fate of Velka, and knew that in this choice, she would be made to watch an old god die.

This idea took hold around the memory of a murky mountain pass, and a chatty crow that led her into the Hinterlands.

Sasha huffed, her breath fogging the air. "There... must always be a Frost Mother."

The Frost Mother tilted her head to the other side, a waning smile on her face like a setting moon.

"What... Sasha?" It was Kai that spoke, a sudden clarity and shock to his voice. More himself in the way he spoke her name. "Where is this? Where have I been?"

Sasha willed herself to stand and ignored him, pulling the ice ax from her belt. "There will always be a Frost Mother."

The Frost Mother finally smiled in earnest, though her eyes remained cold.

"Hail to the new Frost Mother…" The words finally left her mouth, and Velka opened her arms wide, more herself than she had seemed in many winters. "Oh, now. Now I must hasten away to warmer countries…"

Sasha charged Velka, her voice a primal, unnatural howl against the palace walls. The ax was swung, and Velka smiled in summer heat as she welcomed the sharp, violent end of the pick ax.

NATALIA HAD MADE it all the way to the river's bend before she finally relaxed, and it was warranted. Ba was growing tired in the increasing heat. He had done well though, and she needed him to make it passed the Hinterlands, even if she planned to release him when she left. Planting boots in the high grasses, Natalia led her reindeer to the riverside and allowed him to drink.

Spring was quietly returning, sending the snow retreating back into the mountains and returning the earth to green, vibrant life. Natalia welcomed the change, taking it for nature's sign that she had made the right choice in leaving her father's band of thieves. The work and travel of it all had begun to bore her, so she had freed all of her birds and servants before burning the rest of her exotic collection. With nly her clothes and a few books keep her company in her travels, she was headed north of the Hinterlands, though if that did not suit her, she would keep going. Natalia intended to see the whole world until she found a place that was wholly hers.

She stroked Ba's bristled coat and stared up at the mountains for a moment, their imposing, beautiful forms crowning the valley in stone and ice. Her mind drifted back to the village girl again, months gone since they had parted ways and Sasha had ventured up to defeat the Frost Mother.

Natalia squinted up, the mountains growing clouded and the

wind changed. A flash of lightning echoed from the thunderheads, and Natalia turned to Ba to repack and move.

She froze in place then, matching the river's flow as it covered in frost. Ba made an uncomfortable noise and trotted back as a carriage rolled parallel, across the river, through the grass as if the trail was nothing.

The carriage was led by two snow-white horses, so pale they appeared to be transparent. A young man, dark-haired and tall, coached the animals on as they passed the unseen road. Behind the rustling curtains of the carriage, a young woman leaned out of the window, pale and lithe and still enough of herself that Natalia knew her face. Her eyes were a foreign place though, consumed by the deepest, coldest blue.

The carriage rolled to a stop at the river's edge until Natalia and the young occupant could see each other. Ice crinkled in the grass where the wheels rested.

Natalia made a frivolous attempt at a bow. "Hail to the new Frost Mother."

The young woman opened the carriage doors and stepped out. Her face was etched with a sullen coolness, as though she embodied the whisper of the first northern wind. She was still Sasha though, somewhere deep inside the layers of ageless magic.

"I remember you," she said to Natalia. "You have grown away from what you were once."

"So have you, I see," Natalia said, her smile weary. "I thank you for the spring."

The young Frost Mother curtsied in response, and offered her hand. "It is by your hand I am crowned such responsibility. I remember your offer... Will you not join us on our journey to the furthest mountains? I have often thought of you."

Natalia bit her lip, a hand still on Ba. "Not yet. But someday soon, I think."

The Frost Mother nodded, her dark braid curtaining behind her in a sudden grasp of wind. "I will come for you then."

301

Natalia felt something warm in her chest. "Safe travels then, Frost Mother. Winter lingers in the mountains."

"Yes, how cold it is... how large and empty it all looks." Sasha gathered her skirts and returned to the carriage, rapping on the roof with her knuckle. "Onward then, Kai."

Natalia sighed, hugging Ba's neck as the newly crowned Frost Mother had vanished into the valley's glow and onward into colder mountains. The promise of spring followed her path, wild flowers peeking out of the frosted wheel tracks and reaching to the sun, welcoming the new season.

ABOUT THE AUTHOR

Caitlin E. Jones is an author, editor, and a lover of all things Victorian and fantastic. Raised in South Louisiana, where the myths roam wild, she has since worked in Berlin and Sydney, and made a living out of collecting adventures. She is currently in pursuit of a BA in Literary Studies with a minor in History. Her debut novel, Chimehour, was published in 2018.

Blood in the River,
Tears on the Sand

Timothy Mudie

I STOOD HIP deep in the River, just past where the reeds ended, my bare feet sinking into the silt, my testicles shriveling from the cold. At my side stood my father, hand on my shoulder to steady me before the priest.

"Don't be frightened, Yuny," my father whispered, eyes straight ahead. But I wasn't frightened. I had prepared for this.

I did not flinch when the priest raised the knife. Bright sunlight glinted off its polished blade, a blade that had cut many boys before me, and would cut many more after. With his left hand, he gripped me by the chin and squeezed, and I pushed out my tongue. Deftly, he sliced off the tip, but only the tip because the River needed me to speak, and to make its wishes understood. He traced shallow circles around my eye sockets, but did not cut my eyes because the River needed me to see. He sliced my palms, but did not take a finger because the River needed my hands. Blood spilled from my open mouth, ran down my face in rivulets, seeped from my palms. It dripped into the water and swirled away into the River's current.

Eight years old, and I was bonded to the River for life. Like my father and his father and his father before him. My blood flowed into the River, and its water flowed into me.

THREE DAYS LATER I woke in the dead of night, everything black under a cloudy sky, the air heavy with promised rain. I had spent the day working our farm. Picking early melons, feeding the goats and chickens, pulling weeds amidst the grain stalks, trying not to wince when rough fibers pricked my scabby palms. The River rewarded my father's service with fecund soil and bountiful crops, overflowing its banks each summer, covering the fields all the way up to our cottage, always stopping just before it got too close. Each spring, when the harvest came, our flax and figs and radishes grew tall and fat. Busy days this time of year, I would collapse into bed straight after dinner and sleep soundly until sunrise. But when the River called to me, I woke instantly, fatigue banished from my body.

The River spoke to me in bubbles and the rattle of pebbles rolling over each other, the snap of a crocodile's jaws. I understood perfectly. I dressed in the darkness and slipped out of our cottage into the night.

Following the tug of the River's command, I walked for nearly a mile until I reached the outskirts of town. Along the way other boys joined me, no one speaking or looking at each other, all of us pulled along by the magic in our veins. Before long there were dozens of us and we formed our own stream, the hushed clop of our footsteps on the dusty streets joining the River's voice in our ears.

I knew where we were heading before we arrived. The Temple of the Moon. Still under construction, it already stretched so high I could see it from our cottage on a clear day. It was to be the tallest building in the town, a display of the Moon's power. Scaffolding wound up its walls, just a different shade of black in the moonless night. We surrounded it.

Moving in sync, like a line of marionettes, we lifted our arms. Our mouths opened, and we exhaled. All the air in my lungs roared out, until I felt emptied, but it kept coming, all of us breathing a susurrus that swirled and eddied around the half-built walls of the temple. Humidity pressed on me. My arms quivered as I held them up, palms skyward.

A tremendous peal of thunder cracked open the clouds, and rain began to pour down, confined to the area just above the temple. Great sheets of water fell, hitting the ground hard, churning the dirt to mud and spraying droplets outward, drenching me from head to toe. Out of the corner of my eye, I saw onlookers hanging from nearby windows, watching from the shadows of alleyways. No one tried to stop us. If the Moon had problems with our actions, they seemed to think, let the Moon's acolytes put a stop to us.

Minutes passed as the deluge continued, until the ground below the temple was so saturated that it was more water than dirt. The sandstone walls sank into the muck. As soon as the stability was gone, the walls simply collapsed, wide bricks falling out of place and crashing down. None of us stepped back as they landed, sometimes mere inches from our toes. Not ten paces from me, one of the bricks from the top of the wall dropped directly onto one of the other boys, stoving in his head with a crunch so loud I heard it over the rumble of the rain. Terror jolted through me, but I stood in place, arms up, hissing air past my teeth, until the rain finally ceased.

By the time it stopped, what was planned as the greatest temple the world had known was reduced to a haphazard pile of cracked and pitted stones.

We all turned and walked silently away. Boys peeled off from the group in ones and twos along the way, and by the time I reached my family's cottage I was alone.

I SLEPT THROUGH the rooster's crow the next morning, not waking until I heard a sharp rap on my bedroom door the instant before it creaked open. My father stood silhouetted against the morning sun. I sat up slowly, rubbing crusty sleep from my eyes. I'd crawled into bed seemingly minutes before dawn.

"I'm sorry, Father," I said, rushing to dress, the scarring tip of my tongue muddying my words. "I'm awake now."

I expected to see annoyance, reprimand, but if any emotion showed on his face, I would have to name it sorrow. "You were called last night?" he said.

I nodded. Had he felt the pull as well? A residual jerk from his time as a River acolyte? Once the River was in your blood, it never left. But perhaps he had simply looked toward the town and noticed the absence of the temple.

"It went... well?" he said, and again I nodded, more hesitantly this time, remembering the panic, the crack as the boy's skull shattered.

I heard a hiss of steam from outside my room, my mother putting out the morning's cooking fire. She'd left waking me to my father, was going about her own day. She never spoke to me about the River.

My father tilted his head toward the bed. "Sleep an hour more," he said. "You'll need your rest."

Gratefully, I collapsed back into bed half-dressed. I began to doze before he even shut the door.

"Be safe," he said as he did. Then he added, "It will all be worth it," but he had turned away so I couldn't be sure whether he was speaking to me then at all.

T HE GREATEST MOMENTS were when the River set us to run. No goals, no ambitions, simply loosing us boys to cavort amongst the town, the magic of the River coursing through our bodies. When this happened, I felt as though I could explode, as though the River's power inside me would wash away my skin and leave me a being of pure energy. I never stopped laughing.

Packs of acolytes would run through the streets, kicking up clouds of dust in our wake. Bakers gifted us pastries fresh from the oven, and shopkeepers handed out dried figs and honeyed walnuts. Smiles would be plastered to their faces, but they handed off their offerings warily, using the tips of their fingers as if we were dogs that might nip them in our frenzy.

Sometimes we passed other groups of riotous boys, these filled with the heat of the Sun, the glow of the Moon, the dry crackle of the Desert. We crashed into each other like flocks of birds caught in a tempest. Jostling and scratching and shouting, but never any real harm, not in those joyful times. The River and the Sun and the Moon and the Desert and the rest all had their magic, all needed to work together. It was only dangerous when things fell out of balance.

A DOZEN OF us surrounded the man, cutting off any chance of escape. Like the others, I babbled at him, nonsense words gurgling from my throat, spittle flecking off my shortened tongue. I took a step closer.

"Please," he begged, hands actually clasped before him. "You don't need to do this. I will leave and never return. I'll never tell anyone what I've done."

I knew he was not talking to us, but to the River. I knew that the River would not be moved by his appeals.

The man knew it too. He hung his head. Light from a high-up window glinted off his bald brown pate. He glanced around the room. Strange devices of glass and iron hung from pegs and sat arranged on shelves. I had never seen anything like them. "Not here then. Somewhere else, I beg you."

Across from me, a boy croaked like a bullfrog and leapt onto the man's back. He reared his head back, opened his mouth to bare his teeth, and lunged at the stumbling man's neck. The man threw himself backwards toward the floor, panicked, not actually trying to fight back, falling onto the boy and buying himself a moment's reprieve. The River boiled inside me as I moved forward with the others, closing in, my vision tunneling until all I saw was the man on the ground in front of me. Further, until the only thing I saw were his eyes, wide and white and terrified, like a horse that's broken its leg and knows its end is coming. That was the moment I realized what the River wanted me to do, and something inside me lurched to a stop. In the six years since I'd bonded to the River, I'd done much I never would have otherwise. I'd smashed temples, washed away idols on waves that raced to the sea, gorged myself on still-living water buffalo bloated with silt and wrack. I had seen people die. I had painted myself in blood. I had seen fear in people's eyes, but never like this. I'd never felt it was really me they were afraid of, and that made me fear myself.

While the other boys tightened the circle, I froze. Inside every part of me, the River strained like a dog against its lead. I held fast, refusing to attack the man. It wasn't necessary; the other boys had him on his back, his arms and legs flailing in a fruitless attempt to ward them off. But the River compelled me. I watched as my feet lifted and stepped toward the condemned man. As my hands curled into claws. As my jaws opened to bite. As I launched myself into the fray.

There was so much blood it blurred my vision. My teeth found a finger and I bit down without knowing whose it was. A screech rewarded me, but it could just have easily been from one of the other boys. My fists fell and rose again and again. Every hit added more moisture to the man's body until it soaked him through and filled his lungs. He gurgled as he died, choking on blood and river-water. I wondered if all the boys were as certain as I that they had landed the fatal blow. I wept the entire time, but the River controlled me. After smashing the equipment that lined the walls, the other boys left me crying, the River carrying them out, leaving me behind to think about what I did, to learn that it could not be disobeyed.

Alone, lying on my stomach, sobbing hot tears into a sticky puddle of blood, I don't know how long I mourned. At some point, a hand touched my shoulder, and I spun around, scared and ashamed.

The girl was about my age and the dead man was her doctor and from her hiding place in the wall she had seen everything. Her name was Matia.

Y OU ARE GUILTY nonetheless," she said. Matia traded me a clean wet rag for the pink one in my hand, and I resumed wiping blood from my face and hands. "No one forced you to bond to the River."

"My father—" I said, but she cut me off.

"You could have run. Did you even attempt to refuse?"

I didn't answer. Of course I hadn't. I never even thought to. Bonding to the River was simply something the men in my family did. And I had wanted to be a man.

"You run through town, harassing people simply trying to go about their days. You break things, brawl in the streets. You take offerings for the River that people cannot afford to part with. All of this is fine, but when the River wants you do something you disagree with, then you whine and cry. Then, suddenly, you are not responsible." Venom in her voice, fire in her eyes. I shrank before her like a water lily after the receding floodwaters abandon it on the sand.

"But what am I to do?" I asked.

"What are—? What am *I* to do?" Matia spread her arms and spun in a circle. "Doctor Baufra was going to get me away from here. Your people will find me eventually. Your people or some other's."

"But why?" I asked. "Your doctor. Why did we kill him?" As I asked the question, I realized it was the first time I had. The River never told us why it made us act, we simply moved in its currents. And Matia was right; I had never wondered.

While I cleaned myself, Matia had washed the doctor's face as best she could. She'd folded his mangled hands over his breast. She'd closed his eyes. She shed not a single tear.

"Because he cured me," she said quietly. "Doctor Baufra did something that the River could not do. Death was growing inside me, and he stopped it."

"Surely the River could have cured you. If not the River, then the Sun, the Grain, something."

"There are limits even to magic," she said. "But the so-called gods can't have people knowing that."

I stifled a gasp at her blasphemy. I tried as well to hide my admiration. What most awed me wasn't just her strength, but that she drew it from no magic, no god, solely from her own deep well.

"What can we do?" I asked.

For a long time, Matia didn't answer. I worried that she had written me off, that she would cast me aside like an empty prawn shell. But finally, she spoke. "You will help me," she said. "You'll help me, and I'll help you, and together we'll get away from here."

I shook my head. "The River will drag me back."

"Then we'll go where the River can't reach."

MOSTLY, MATIA KEPT me in the dark. The more I knew of our plan, the more involved I was, then the more we were at risk. At any moment, the River might have taken control, seen through my eyes, realized what we meant to do. I kept to myself, waiting anxiously while Matia made arrangements and procured our equipment, skulking around town with a hood low over her face, buying what she could, stealing what she couldn't.

But she could not buy or steal a camel, and that was where I came in. I tried not to think of it as stealing. That I persuaded the merchant to give up one of his camels. After all, I didn't really have the force of the River behind me, and that the merchant couldn't know that made no difference. I still felt a twinge of guilt when he threw saddlebags and two waterskins into the bargain.

In less than two days, we were ready. All our possessions were packed in the saddlebags. The saddle itself was prepared so that it needed only be strapped onto our camel and we could be on our way. In the bags was food and clothing, a tent, all the coins that Matia could scrounge from Doctor Baufra's cottage. Matia had also packed pieces of the doctor's equipment, though it had been mostly destroyed by myself and the other boys. I didn't know if she took it for a particular use or sentimentality. Finally, there was a wide coil of stout rope. We would leave late at night, and hope that the Moon did not see us.

"If the River knows what I'm doing, if it senses me trying to flee, it will stop me," I told Matia. I paused, forcing myself to say the next words, terrified of what her response might be. "You will have to go on without me."

"I should," she said. "But I won't. I keep my promises."

I failed to hide my elation. "I'll do whatever I can, I swear. But the River—"

"Stop it, Yuny," Matia said. "You are not the River."

I nodded, but she was wrong. Of course I was the River, and it was me. When I had bonded to it, that was for life. Part of me feared that if I did manage to get far enough away that I was outside its control I would simply drop dead.

But I did not say any of this to Matia. I nodded, and said, "No matter what my mind wants, my body won't be my own. I will fight you. I'll try to turn us back."

She grinned. "What do you think the rope is for?"

M Y BONES RATTLED with each step the camel took, and it was not even walking quickly. I dreaded how it would feel if the beast broke into a trot. The ropes looped around my body, my wrists tied to my ankles, everything bound tight to the camel's back just behind the saddle where Matia rode. She turned around to make sure I was okay, and I smiled tightly.

The Moon peered down through scattered clouds like a great all-seeing eye. I wished we could stick to the shadows as we made our way through the streets, but it was impossible. At least it was the middle of the dry season so there was no rain and the River sat low beneath its banks. Even the slightest diminishment of its power could be all the edge we needed.

There was no one else in the streets. "The way is clear, I think."

311

"Now you've done it," Matia said without looking back. I humored myself that I heard a smile in her voice.

Perhaps I doomed us after all, because just moments after Matia's answer, I felt a twinge in my limbs that did not come from the uncomfortable rope. I gnashed my teeth and wriggled like a worm on a fishhook. Over the buzzing in my head I heard scratches and shuffling of feet and a sound like drops of water hitting a still pool.

"Your friends are here," Matia said, leaning forward and spurring the camel to a livelier pace.

I heard them before I saw them, and felt them as well. The other River acolytes, pouring from side streets all around us. One jumped from the roof of a short building as we passed, but he misjudged the timing and landed on the dirt in front of us, barely rolling out of the way of the camel's hooves.

I thrashed my body, trying to loosen the ropes. I wrenched my head forward to try and gnaw through them. "Let me go!" I shouted. Matia jabbed her heels into the camel's haunches, and it rushed forward.

Twisting my neck, I saw the boys falling behind despite their unnatural speed, their inhuman perseverance. In my heart, I wished to be free, for the River to let me go, but my mutilated tongue spewed anger and encouragement to them. But the distance between us grew, and I started to believe we might really get away. Then the horses joined them, a half dozen with riders jouncing and whooping on their backs.

They gained on us. My eyes remained fixed on the galloping animals as they drew closer. Our camel ran as fast as it could, but soon, I knew, our pursuers would be close enough for the boys to jump, tackling us all to the hard dry ground. The nearest horse drew up almost alongside us. The boy riding it, who couldn't be more than ten, stuck a knife between his teeth and tensed himself to leap. Against my will, I urged him on.

The instant before the boy attacked, something in my peripheral vision flashed orange and black. Colors I'd seen over the years and learned to fear, that all River acolytes feared. All acolytes of any god. Save the Sun.

My head turned and watched as the Sun acolytes' trained hunting dogs swarmed us all, one chomping hard on the leg of that nearest horse, which went down, throwing its rider against the nearest sandstone wall. They wove between the camel's legs, and it stumbled, but miraculously held its footing and barreled onward. Shouts and battle cries of the Sun, the Moon, the Grass, the Viper, of seemingly every god there was, filled the air. All the gods of the world had come for us. I wondered if Matia wished then that we had killed her when we'd slain the doctor. Surely that would be preferable to whatever fate these gods and their magic had in store for us. The River let me close my eyes.

The sounds of combat rose around us. And fell. I opened my eyes, and saw a maelstrom of acolytes, horses, dogs, coiling snakes. They punched and kicked, ripped and tore, bit and scratched. None of them could pull themselves from their frenzy long enough to pursue us. I caught the eye of an acolyte I recognized, and he tried to run from the fray and chase us, but a hand caught his ankle and pulled him down. He turned to fight off his attacker. The River, it seemed, had other things to deal with. All the gods coming together, swirling their magic into one small space, was overwhelming. I still writhed and tried to loosen the ropes, but with every second the acolytes grew smaller. Soon the whole town grew smaller too.

All night we raced across the desert, and all night I raged against Matia but she never responded. Worn out by sunrise, I tumbled into sleep. When I woke, I was still strapped to the camel's back, but I didn't try to escape. My body was my own.

To BE SAFE, Matia kept me tied to the camel, feeding me and holding a waterskin to my lips when necessary, for another night and day. When she released me, my limbs throbbed so hotly I half-feared they would burst into flames. Pins and needles danced across my body as blood resumed its normal flow.

Matia and I sat under the shade of a canvas tarp, napping much of the day, waiting for the cooler night to resume our travels.

"You have a destination in mind," I said. "You claimed you didn't."

She shrugged. "I have an idea."

"Where?"

"Somewhere far away. Where the River will never find us."

"Thank you," I said softly. I knew she still blamed me, that she always would. And she should. She owed me nothing, and still she took me with her. I hardly understood how it was possible, but I wanted to. Desperately.

For a second, she let her palm rest on the back of my hand, gave it a squeeze so miniscule it could have easily been an involuntary twitch. But she said, "You're welcome."

The sun sank beneath the sand, and we resumed our flight.

"I saw fear in your eyes at the oasis today," Matia said, seated across from me at our table, dipping a piece of bread into vegetable stew.

"I didn't think you noticed," I said.

She smiled. "Oh, Yuny. How many years now? Of course I noticed. You never could hide your emotions."

"Not even a bit?" I asked.

She snorted. "You fell in love the moment you saw me. It was so obvious, you may as well have written it in the sky."

"For you I would," I said, smiling. But the smile faded quickly. We tried not to talk about those times. I tried to forget them. And most days I could. The oasis where we gathered our drinking water was no River, was barely more than a large palm tree-ringed puddle. When we first arrived at this place where we built our home, I admitted that I did feel tempted by the water.

It sang to me of power. Those first years, Matia journeyed to draw all our water, but time passed and the song grew quieter until it was nothing more than a whisper then nothing more than a memory. Though I dreamed it would happen, I never once woke in the night to find my feet had carried me back to the River.

Matia pushed away her bowl. "So what were you scared of?"

I shook my head and tried to laugh off my fear, but one look in Matia's eyes and I knew that wouldn't work. I answered truthfully. "I felt something. That tug I used to feel when the River took hold. Not as strong, but it was there. And the water, it was like something was rising up, coming for me."

Matia stood and crossed the room to where she kept Doctor Baufra's implements. Her implements now. She'd added to them over the years, become a healer in her own right. People came to her when they were sick or needed a broken bone expertly set. The people here didn't seek to cure themselves with magic. If anyone here knew of the River it was only as a story.

"I wonder if it's been looking for you all this time," she said, but it sounded more as if she were musing to herself than really speaking to me. "The one that got away, that stole a piece of its power." She turned back to look at me, placed her hands atop her ever-rounding belly, atop our child. "This is true desert here," she said fiercely. "We're stronger than the River. If it wants you, let it come."

I had no response for her, my brilliant powerful wife. All I knew was that when I had bonded with the River it was for life, and I was still alive.

A WET HACKING COUGH woke us an instant before a knock on our door. Matia and I both vaulted from our bed. It wasn't completely unusual for someone to come to us in the middle of the night—medical ailments can strike at any time, after all—but something about the cough seemed to me both familiar and wrong. In her moonlit eyes, I could see Matia felt it as well. All our years here I had anticipated that one day the River would return, that it would send an acolyte to fetch me, though I knew it couldn't control someone this far from its power. Whoever it sent would work of their own accord.

We crept toward the door. Along the way, Matia grabbed a long curved blade from her medical shelves. At the door we stopped, holding our breath. If it were truly someone coming for help, I had to think they would shout their need. Instead, the person outside knocked again. Matia stepped back, blade held ready. In one swift motion I threw the door open, prepared for a torrent of water to burst in and wash our lives away.

A hunched person stood in the doorway, a darker outline against the night. As my eyes adjusted, I gasped. Because, though the years had withered him, I recognized my father.

"I..." he said. "I didn't believe... Can I come in?"

"Absolutely not," Matia snapped.

"Matia, please," I said. "This is my father."

"I know who he is," she said. "And he needs to turn around and return whence he came."

My father loosed a string of phlegmy coughs. "I only want to talk," he said. "Please." He looked from me to Matia and back, and though I hesitated when his eyes lingered on Matia's curved belly, I let him in anyway.

He sat at our table while I poured him a cup of water. Matia stood back, arms crossed, eyes slit. I gave him the water and sat in the seat across from him.

He sipped it and looked at me. "It tastes different here."

Matia shot me a look. I'd said the same thing when we first arrived.

No one spoke for a while. Finally, I needed to break the tension. "Is it mother? Has she—?"

"Your mother is fine," he said, shaking his head. "The town, the River... Things are hard back home."

I could tell from the way Matia leaned forward that she wanted to speak, but she held back, and my father went on.

"The magic isn't so strong as it was. The crops don't grow like they used to. No one bonds with the gods anymore. They're fading away."

"Good," said Matia. But she waved off any response and turned away.

My father leaned forward and spoke urgently. "You need to come back with me, Yuny. The River will forgive you. You still hold its power within you, and while you're gone it will never be whole. It needs you. I need you."

Tingles of energy spread through my body, as if my father had brought part of the River here with him. He'd been bonded for life as well, so I suppose he had. And now the River let him leave town so he could come fetch me back to its currents.

"You knew what the River would make me do," I said. "How could you do that to your son?" My eyes watered, a few tears dripping out and pooling in the scars on my cheeks. I hadn't known I wanted to ask him that.

"It's what we do," he said. "It's worth it. Please, Yuny." He fell to his knees, actually twined his fingers in supplication. He cried now as well.

I didn't stand. My legs felt weak. Watery. "No. I will not come back. If that dooms the River, so be it. The town will survive without its gods. There is enough magic in the world."

Though he begged, I would not waver. Finally, he angrily spat, "So be it. You have abandoned us all," and left. Sagging against the doorframe, drained of emotion, I watched until he disappeared in the pre-dawn gray.

Matia's hand touched my shoulder. "Come back to bed," she said softly. "We can wait a bit to begin the day." I nodded and followed her.

We laid side by side until well after the hot sun began to

beat down. My hand rested above her bellybutton, feeling my child kick and kick, its little legs churning like it was swimming up from the depths of some great water, fighting to reach the surface.

ABOUT THE AUTHOR

Timothy Mudie is a writer of speculative fiction and an editor of many genres. In addition to *MYTHIC*, his stories have appeared in *Lightspeed*, *Beneath Ceaseless Skies*, *Deep Magic*, and various other magazines, anthologies, and podcasts. When he was a kid, he wanted to be a paleontologist until he read *Jurassic Park* and realized that just writing about dinosaurs would be a lot easier. (He's not sure how true that turned out to be.) Timothy lives outside of Boston with his wife and son.

The Dryad's Muse

Tom Jolly

D RYADS DIDN'T HAVE cell phones.
Dr. Matt Hamilton looked at the clipboard for his scheduled patient, and not for the first time, wondered how some
of the supernatural creatures that visited Redstone Clinic made ap-
pointments ahead of time.

"Thanks, Medjine."

The zombie receptionist nodded. "You are welcome, Dr. Hamilton. The patient is waiting for you in exam room two."

Hamilton never expected his career to involve curing monsters.
It was pure chance that brought a werewolf to the clinic's door, and
Hamilton's nature led him to sew up the bullet wound in its leg. It
was never really a choice for him.

After that, all the supernatural creatures within the city seemed
to have decided that he was the guy to go to; the one who would
ask no questions and keep his mouth shut. So his patient list was a
supernatural sampler of monsters and curiosities. Every day, a new
flavor.

The dryad was his first patient of the day, though it was already
2PM; the clinic opened late and stayed open through the early evening hours to accommodate nocturnal patients. He wrote down the
time on his clipboard. A dryad! He knew a bit about them, but had

319

never had one as a patient. Something new to deal with. He entered the exam room, not knowing what to expect.

The girl in the exam room was carrying a small potted red oak tree. She was strangely beautiful despite her green skin and hair made of strands of grass and tufts of leaves, moving as though a gentle breeze blew through the room. "Hello, Carielle" he said, "I'm Dr. Hamilton."

She saw him staring at the small tree and she held it up for him to see. "It's my home," she told him.

Hamilton wondered for a moment how she got here in the middle of a big city without arousing any comment or suspicion, but by now, he understood that everyone in the community had a few tricks up their sleeves to help blend in. He looked at his clipboard. "Carielle, I can't say I'm very familiar with dryads. Can you tell me a little about yourself?"

"I wanted to be an Earth Mother," she said, "but do you know how hard it is to find a nice earth elemental in the middle of a city?"

He shook his head. "No, I can't say that I do. So why not move out into the country?"

Carielle sighed. "You can't get a good espresso in the country."

Hamilton smiled. "Eternal love or good coffee. Always a tough choice."

She frowned. "Are you mocking me, mortal? Because I can..." she stopped and looked down at the little potted oak tree, and sighed. The branches twitched. "I can do very little."

Hamilton had to keep reminding himself that his patients weren't human, and some would just as soon tear his arm off as talk to him. "I'm sorry if I offended, Carielle," Hamilton said. "I was just making a little joke. Tell me what brings you to the clinic today."

She pulled her sleeve back and Hamilton winced. Her left hand was missing, sickly yellow veins trailing away from the stump up her arm. "My first home was over one hundred years old, on Willow Street. There was an old house there, and they tore it down to put in condos, and my tree was in the front yard. I knew they were coming soon to cut it down, but the oak had a sapling, and I had to move my belongings to this tiny home. I had to give away a lot of things."

Hamilton really wanted to ask her what things you could store in a three-foot tall oak sapling, or for that matter, a full-sized oak tree, but he resisted.

"When I transferred myself to the young oak, I found that it was sick. I took the sickness from it so it would thrive. It is part of being a dryad, keeping your home healthy. And the sickness should have died then, since they prefer the oak to the essence of our own bodies. But it came over to me, as though part of both worlds, the living and the magical."

Magical! Hamilton hated that word. He'd spent the last year trying to classify various creatures by their substances: what they were made of. If he could measure it and quantify it, he could start dealing with their illnesses in a more traditional fashion. In some ways, he felt like a doctor from the 1800's, trying to define bacterial diseases before they even knew that such things existed, excising the specter of "possession by spirits" that was so popular in those days. Not that that didn't actually happen on occasion, he'd discovered.

The dryad was part of a class of creatures who didn't require human belief, and could dematerialize when they needed to, or appear as solid when necessary. Their "cells," if you could call them that, could convert to a gaseous form that could merge with their host-tree. In most cases, when a group of creatures had similar abilities, such as the shapechanging were-creatures, they shared similar cell structures and were genetically close to one another on the evolutionary ladder. Though the dryad would be disgusted to know it, she was closely related to Bigfoot, sort of a giant, ugly, stinky dryad that could adopt an entire forest. He found it interesting that dryads could mate with earth elementals, putting them in the same cellular class. He itched to go write in his notebooks.

"Generally," Hamilton said, "diseases can't travel between species unless the species are very close. In your case, I suspect the disease you have is a mutation of a common oak disease. This is particularly bad for your community, because you can potentially act as a host for the disease and can spread it to other dryads if you have any social contact with them."

He took the stump of her arm in his hand and examined it. It was as light as balsa. The yellow veins tinged toward brown as they approached her stump. He sat back on his stool, picked his iPad up off the desk, and did a quick search on oak diseases. "The most common diseases in oaks are funguses. If we can identify the fungus, then we can find a systemic fungicide that should be able to treat it. The local nursery or arboretum can probably identify it if they have a sample."

"I have a sample you could give them," she said. She reached into a pouch made of woven grass and pulled out a shriveled brown object. He leaned over to stare at it. It was her missing hand.

"Hmm. I had something more like a leaf in mind. That might not go over well at a plant nursery." He picked up his iPad again. "Look, do you remember what the oak looked like when you took it over? Was it sick then?"

She nodded. "It looked so sad. Like a Charlie Brown Christmas tree."

"Charlie Brown? Your previous tree must have been near someone's TV set, I'm guessing." On his iPad, he brought up a website showing pictures of various oak afflictions, then flipped it around so she could see it. She gasped and put her hand over her mouth, pushing the screen away. "Oh! What a horrible machine!"

"I need you to identify the damage you saw on your little oak before you cured it. We might be able to figure out the fungicide needed to kill the infection."

She reluctantly took another look at the iPad. He scrolled down the page while she looked on in horror. Finally she said, "There! It looked like that!" Then she turned her head away. "The humans that created that are terrible people."

"This is here so others like me can find cures for these diseases. These are not bad people. They share these images to save trees."

She sniffed and wiped a tear away, mollified.

"It looked like oak wilt. Pretty common. The fungicide brand they mention here is called Alamo. If you can transfer the disease back to the oak, before you use the fungicide, it'll be safer for you. I don't know what it'll do to your existing body."

"That would be impossible. Would you give your child a disease to make yourself feel better?"

He drummed his fingers impatiently on the top of the iPad. "Okay, I see your point. But I'd like you to be here when we apply the stuff. If there's an adverse reaction, maybe we can control it."

She looked uncomfortable. "It's alright. But I have no place to stay. And there is no sun in here."

"There's rooftop access from a stairway in back. You can relax up there in the sun while we see if we can get some of the fungicide. I'll come up and get you, and we can run some tests." He stuck his head out the door of the exam room. "Agatha?" The Oracle was standing just outside the door, as if waiting for something. "Ah. Of course. Could you please guide Carielle to the rooftop stairwell? Once you're done with that, please pick up a bottle of this," he showed her a picture of the fungicide on the iPad. "Take some money out of petty cash for it. I'll be seeing my next patient while you're gone."

"He's in Room 1. Very moody fellow!" said Agatha.

Hamilton picked the clipboard up from Medjine's desk as he walked by the receptionist. He knocked and entered the exam room. The man inside was tall and thin, all angles and lines. A compass and a ruler stuck out of his pocket. He was pale and sickly, his clothing expensive but at the same time worn and shabby. "Hello, Doctor," he said. His voice was as rough as sandpaper.

"Hello Mr. Steel. I see you signed in as an architect's muse. You say you're feeling depressed? Weak and lethargic?"

"I try to whisper words of wisdom, design inspiration and aspiration, into the minds of youthful architects and builders! The beauty and simplicity of huge swathes of cement, the purity and geometric construction of perfect surfaces, smooth beyond comparison! But do they listen? No. They want confusion and chaos, nothing matches. Organic forms, they cry! They have ceased to listen to me." He hung his head. "I am dying."

Hamilton considered the creature. Muses fell into the category of very, very small gods. They existed because people believed they existed or wanted them to exist. They seemed to consist of a sort of matter that was related to thoughts just as light was associated with matter. But this implied that thoughts actually had some sort of reality like photons, and could be converted into the thought-matter that gods and spirits were made of. Like the association between light and matter, he assumed it took quite a lot of thought to coalesce into an entity like this. But there was no $E=mc^2$ in what everyone else called the supernatural realm. At least, not yet.

"You were larger before this, I take it?"

"Oh, huge! Very popular in Russia. My head could barely fit through a doorway, so large was I. But even there the interest has faded."

Hamilton scratched his head. "I don't understand. If you are *the* muse for architectural design, and architects are ignoring you, how is it that they have any great ideas?"

Steel shrugged. "Some dullards use old ideas and copy them, or perhaps something completely unrelated to architecture inspires them. Sometimes evil muses in other arenas of creativity cross over the line, afflicting the minds of willing slaves with their witless ideas! Like the muse to birds, teaching architects how to make beautiful nests in China! See how that turned out?"

"So your sickness appears to be something that a doctor like me can't cure. I can't change the thoughts that will keep you from wasting away. I can't tell you how to do your job, but I'm guessing that a muse has to follow the basic leads of his...subjects...and expand on the creative directions they already wish to pursue. For example, a writer's muse wouldn't try to influence a fantasy writer to write a medical thriller, would she?" Hamilton asked.

"But the very fundamental nature of architecture is mathematics," the muse replied. "The purity of a flat plane, a perfect cube, the exactly executed circle, these are the firmaments upon which I am built! How can I defy my very nature as a muse of mathematics to... to...educate these simpletons!"

Hamilton chuckled.

"What do you find so amusing, doctor?"

"You just called yourself a 'muse of mathematics'. Perhaps you aren't dying. Maybe you're just changing professions."

His eyes darted around the office, anxiously, his hands trembling. "But I *like* buildings! Math and buildings belong together! They will fall down if I am not there to guide the architect's befuddled thoughts."

"So I suppose it'd be important to find out what other influences are affecting their creative processes and add your little spark of brilliance."

"Not just a 'little spark', but yes, perhaps."

Hamilton sat down on the stool and thought for a moment. "Recently," he said, "a lot of new architects have been moving toward greener designs. Things that incorporate gardens, trees, and lots of plants. Terraced areas, hanging gardens, green walls, that sort of thing."

"But plants are so chaotic! Messy and unaligned."

Hamilton's thoughts drifted back to the dryad. Plants. Chaotic plants. But they weren't, really. "Are you familiar with fractals at all?"

"Yes. No. Not so much."

"It turns out that plant growth obeys certain mathematical rules. There's a bit of chaos in there; I suppose humans are naturally attracted to that at some level. But basically, plants obey the same fundamental mathematics that your buildings contain."

"I...think I see."

Hamilton tapped slowly on the clipboard, thinking. Could the muse use a muse? "I'd like you to meet someone. She might be able to help you expand your creative horizons."

"They are already as vast as the seas," Steel said. He looked down at the floor, and sighed. "But I will try almost anything at this point."

T HE TWO OF them stepped out onto the roof. The area around the clinic was hilly, and the tops of dozens of other buildings were visible nearby, trees towering over many of them. In one corner of the roof, gathering the Sun's rays, was a small potted oak tree. As they watched, a misty cloud coalesced around the small oak tree and materialized into a solid form.

"Hello, Carielle," said Hamilton.

"Hello, Doctor. Have you retrieved the medicine so soon?"

"No, not yet." He paused and turned to Steel. "I'd like you to meet Steel. He's a muse of architecture."

Her face turned red. "A minion of death! Covering life with barren cement abortions!"

Steel just stared at her. "She's very pretty."

Hamilton almost laughed, but refrained. "The muse needs your help. He needs to learn how to adapt his musings to include plants."

She tilted her chin up in the air and turned her side to them, managing to look insulted and smug all at the same time. "Why would I ever help such an atrocious beast as this thing?"

Steel saw the stump of her hand. "You're hurt!" He stepped toward her.

"Stop!" she cried, holding out the other hand.

His chest thumped into her extended hand. He looked down at it and backed away, a wan look on his face. "It has been thus since the Hanging Gardens," he said, head hanging down.

Hamilton was stunned into silence for a moment, remembering that muses were essentially immortal. "...of Babylon?" he asked.

A look of consternation crossed the muse's face. "Yes, I think it was called that. The terraced gardens. The vines overgrew the sides, hanging down from terrace to terrace. The twisted trunks of jasmine and grape vines climbed the walls like trunks of stone. It could have lasted forever." He put his hand on his forehead, tears welling up in his eyes. "But a visiting prince and his mistress came to the gardens, and she ate of the fruits and nuts hanging from the trees and bushes and vines. What she was allergic to, no one knows, but she died that very night. The gardens were burned to the ground the next day, and the architect, my friend and student, was tied hand and foot and given to the prince's dogs to eat. I have never suggested such a design to my students since then."

"The Hanging Gardens? You were the muse for *The Gardens*?" Carielle shouted.

"I was. I vowed never again to cause the death of a student."

Hamilton watched Carielle shake. He couldn't tell if it was from rage or something else entirely. He'd never seen such a confusion of expressions on a face before, flickering across her countenance like a lightning storm. Was she going to kill him or hug him?

"I will help you!" she finally screamed at him. "We will see gardens that will make humans weep with joy when they set their eyes upon them! The trunks of mighty oaks will be the pillars of towering temples of life!"

Steel peered at her askance and started to say, "There would be certain structural considerations using trees..." but she ran to him and clutched him in a powerful embrace, weeping in joy.

He patted her arm and looked dubiously at Hamilton. Then the muse smiled and nodded. And grew a little taller.

Of course, the muse wasn't exactly a substitute for an earth elemental. Hamilton wondered how an ephemeral creature made of thought-particles was going to relate to a gaseous phase-changing creature like Carielle, but had a feeling it would work out. Somehow.

He also thought about mentioning the fact that humans understood a lot more about allergies and poisons than they used to, and were much less inclined to feed peons to the dogs these days. But now was not the time.

327

He retreated to the stairs. They could take care of themselves.

Carielle visited Hamilton a year later to thank him for his help. Her hand had grown back by then, and she was literally glowing with verdant health.

"The giant structure downtown, that's your doing?"

"That is Steel's doing. The thousands of trees and vines on each terraced level are mine." She smiled an Earth Mother's smile. "The glass terrarium capping the top was a combined effort."

"It looks like someone imported a Mayan pyramid into the middle of Los Angeles."

Carielle nodded, long grass and leaves rippling atop her head like wind in a forest. "A thousand homes and offices, and four thousand trees. I am the Earth Mother of that urban forest. It has set an example. Other dryads in the city have begun...securing...human architects."

"You mean seducing?"

She shrugged. "The architects involved have not been unhappy, I think."

Hamilton laughed and shook his head. She smiled shyly at him, and he couldn't decide whether to pity or envy the architects.

ABOUT THE AUTHOR

Tom Jolly is a retired astronautical/electrical engineer who now spends his time writing SF and fantasy. His stories have appeared in Analog SF, Daily SF, Compelling SF, MYTHIC, and a number of anthologies. His latest book, "An Unusual Practice," about a doctor whose patients tend toward the supernatural, is currently available on Amazon. To find more of his stories, visit www.silcom.com/~tomjolly/tomjolly2.htm.

The Demon Piper of Holy Hill

Sean Patrick Hazlett

G OD MIGHT FORGIVE Chuck McDonough for letting a leaky faucet go this long, but his wife, Linda, had higher standards. Throwing on his bathrobe and stepping into his slippers, he girded himself—retrieving a wrench required an icy excursion.

He entered the garage from a door in his den. The wind rattled the garage windows; its chill seeped through the cracks with a bite burrowing so deep, Chuck could feel it in the hollows of his bones. It was that old New England warning: when the wind whistles, a storm is nigh.

When he crossed the threshold, something rustled in the darkness. Chuck shivered. He flipped on the light. Trudging past cardboard box columns, old computer peripherals, and broken appliances, he noticed nothing out of the ordinary. So he grabbed a wrench from his workstation, then headed back toward the den.

He stepped onto something soft. He lifted his foot and looked down.

Rat droppings.

He cursed, then wiped his slipper on the concrete. He returned to his workstation and gathered some rattraps he'd kept there for emergencies.

For the next thirty minutes, Chuck set the traps. When he finished, he went to the kitchen to tighten the faucet.

Linda was cooking eggs while watching the morning news. Chuck hugged her from behind.

"Where've you been?" she said.

He shrugged. "Seems we have a bit of a pest problem."

"What? Like termites?"

"Rats, I think. I'll know for sure later today when I check the traps."

Linda's eyes widened. She put her hands on her hips, elbows flaring outward in her classic my-husband-is-an-idiot stance.

"Shouldn't we call a pro?" she asked. "Rats get in the walls. They could chew the wires and burn down the house. Not to mention we have a small child."

He nodded. "Yeah, yeah. I know. And technically, they're in the garage, not the house. Let's see what turns up this afternoon, then we can decide whether to call someone in."

She rolled her eyes and threw her hands in the air. "Fine. Do it your way, Chuck."

Deep down he knew Linda was right; she usually was about these things. But he refused to admit he might be wrong.

A female newscaster's voice filled the lull in their conversation. "The recent break-in at the American Red Cross Blood Center in Leominster has local officials scrambling for donations this holiday season. So please call the number below to make an appointment." She faced the weatherman. "Well, Bob, any updates on the big storm?"

The camera panned to a man who wore a smile like he was auditioning for a late night infomercial. He gestured toward a map where lime blobs shimmered toward the town of Harvard. "It looks like the good folks of central Massachusetts will be celebrating a white Christmas. And by all indications, this one'll be the blizzard of the century. So make sure you stock up on supplies."

Linda tapped Chuck on the shoulder. "You going to the dump today?"

He smiled. "Guess I am now."

"Good. Make sure you also stock up for the storm."

A piercing shriek echoed from the second floor.

Chuck and Linda raced upstairs to Missy's room, where they found their four-year-old cowering in a corner.

Lifting Missy from the floor, Chuck hugged her with fierce intensity. She trembled in an unsettling manner. "What's wrong, Missy? Tell Daddy what happened."

Hyperventilating, she struggled to speak.

Linda grabbed Missy's chin and tilted it toward her. "Tell Mommy what's wrong, dear."

Missy's breathing had gotten more regular. She opened her little hazel eyes, regarded Chuck, then shifted them to Linda. "I saw a tiny gray man."

Chuck tensed up. The rat infestation was worse than he'd thought. "He still there?" He stood up, balling his fists.

Linda shot Chuck an annoyed expression, then faced Missy. "How big was this little man?"

"I don't know, Mommy, 'bout as big as your hand?"

"You sure it wasn't a rat?" Chuck added.

Missy shook her head emphatically. "No, Daddy. It was definitely a man—a gray man."

WILFRED TULLY ACKNOWLEDGED Chuck's arrival at the Harvard Transfer Station with a sullen nod.

"How's it going, Wilfred?" Chuck said, flashing a polite smile.

Wilfred grunted and continued dumping his plastic bottles into a hunter green bin.

Chuck tried to fill the silence. "How's Joanie doing?"

Wilfred shook his head. "That gal will be the death of me. But she's getting better. Been hiking a lot since rehab. Guess that's something."

According to the town gossip, Wilfred's daughter had been doing a lot more than hiking. One of the more salacious rumors

Linda had relayed from her book club was that some of the older teens—including Joanie—had been holding orgies on conservation land. Small towns being what they were, the local police had investigated the allegation—though they'd never managed to catch the teens in the act.

Chuck bit his tongue, managing a "well, that's good to hear she's getting back on the horse. Speaking of horses, did you ever find your mare—what's her name—Duchess?"

Wilfred wiped away a tear. "Yeah. We found her."

"What happened?"

Wilfred rubbed his eyes. "They found Duchess's rotting carcass up in Shaker Village. Inside the Stone Barn ruins."

Chuck put his hand on Wilfred's shoulder. "Jesus, man. I'm sorry."

"That ain't the worst of it neither. Vet said somebody had shoved a pumpkin inside her womb. Some twisted bastard kept her alive like that for weeks. It was only recently that she died."

"How'd they keep a horse up at the Stone Barn ruins without people noticing?"

"Your guess is as good as mine. I figure they kept her somewhere else then moved her to the barn just before she died."

"What kind of a sick animal would do something like that?"

Wilfred held up his forefinger. "Wait. I ain't done. When the vets performed their necropsy—fancy word for a horse autopsy—they found a placenta inside her."

"Duchess was pregnant?"

"When the lab tests came back, the vet told me they found semen inside her—human semen."

Chuck wanted to vomit. "Sweet Jesus."

Wilfred spat. "Well, with all them pentagrams and occult symbols carved into the ground and chalked on the old stone walls, I'd say we got ourselves a bunch of Satanists."

"Is Chief Denmark on the case?"

"He is, but he's 'bout as far from a clue as the sun is from Saturn."

At a complete loss for words, Chuck just nodded. The two men passed the next half-hour in silence as they sorted and disposed of their garbage.

WHEN CHUCK RETURNED home, Linda nearly tackled him with her hug. "I'm so glad you're home."

He stepped back. "What happened?"

"We can't find Mr. Whiskers."

"What about his GPS collar?"

"It was in the den—torn off," Linda said in choppy breaths. "The dog's also pretty shaken up."

He rushed to the den to find his dog quivering on the couch and covered in his own filth. Chuck patted his knees. "Come here, Duffy."

Duffy whined and quaked, refusing to budge.

"C'mon, boy." Chuck whistled.

Convinced no amount of encouragement would get Duffy to move, Chuck grabbed his dog by the collar and dragged him across the carpet and into the kitchen. Duffy squealed in protest.

"Can you clean Duffy up?" Chuck said to Linda. "I'm gonna check the traps, then look for Mr. Whiskers."

Normally Linda would have chided him for the request, but instead she just nodded. Now Chuck was certain she was terrified.

Chuck stepped into the garage. A sharp pain stabbed his foot. "Son of a bitch!"

He removed the trap from his shoe and leaned against the wall while he waited for the throbbing to subside. Once the initial shock had passed, Chuck began to wonder. He'd never set a trap there. Yet there it was, right where someone would step on it.

He flipped the light on, then limped carefully through the garage, checking his traps. The rest remained right where he'd left them. And every single one had been sprung. But that wasn't the oddest thing; nothing had taken the bait.

Chuck scratched his head. What kind of rat would spring a

trap but ignore the bait? Coming up with nothing, he reset the traps. Then he returned to the kitchen to find Linda comforting a bawling Missy.

He kneeled and stroked his daughter's hair. "What's wrong, honey?"

"She's worried about Mr. Whiskers," Linda answered.

With nothing to say, Chuck just shrugged.

Linda shook her head. "Catch any rats? From all that commotion, I'd say you did."

"Nah, I just stepped on a trap."

Linda raised an eyebrow.

"Okay, fine. I surrender. I'll call an exterminator first thing in the morning."

"Good." Linda ran her fingers through her hair. "I don't think the cat's in the house. Can you post some flyers?"

"You mind if I do that tomorrow? It's getting cold out."

"Exactly," she said with confidence. "If we're cold, he's cold."

Defeated, Chuck shambled to the closet, put on his coat, and left. For the next hour, he canvassed all Harvard's public spaces from the Transfer Station to the Town Common.

He wasn't the only one.

Photos of missing dogs, cats, and the occasional rabbit papered every flat, public surface in town in a collage of sorrow. Like a broken man just going through the motions, Chuck added his cat to the grim menagerie.

His last stop was Harvard's General Store. There, a teenage boy clad in black snickered as Chuck posted his last sign. He wanted to throttle the kid, but a scowl was all he could muster.

CHUCK COULDN'T SLEEP. The vents had been jiggling all night. He cursed himself for not calling the exterminator the instant he'd discovered the rat droppings.

As he dozed off, a piercing shriek catapulted him from his

bed. Before he could think, he was barreling down the hall toward Missy's room.

"Daddy!" she howled. "The monster men were coming to take me away!"

Moments later, Linda arrived, bleary-eyed. Missy wailed. Linda struggled to calm her.

Chuck grabbed his daughter's arm. "What's this?"

Linda squinted. "Oh my God! Do you see what I see?"

"Are those...bite marks?"

"Jesus Christ, Chuck. Why didn't you call the exterminator? If you'd only listened to me...Now I have to take Missy to the hospital. God knows what diseases those rats were carrying."

Linda's words stabbed Chuck's heart. He had to do something. Anything.

"I'm calling Pete Hollowell," Chuck said.

Linda checked her watch. "It's three in the morning."

"I don't care. Pete will understand. Go ahead and take Missy to the ER." It suddenly occurred to Chuck that the dog wasn't around. "Where's Duffy?"

He sprang to his feet and searched throughout the house. "Duffy? Here, boy. Duffy, where are you?"

Chuck clenched his teeth, trying to decide which crisis to tackle first. Once he calmed himself down, he dialed Pete Hollowell.

After three attempts, a woman finally answered. "Who the hell is this and why are you calling at this hour?"

"This is Chuck McDonough. I have a serious rat problem."

Mrs. Hollowell took a deep breath. "I'm sorry, Chuck. Folks have been calling at all hours. Pete's been working 'round the clock. I haven't seen or heard from him in two days. When he checks in, I'll let him know you called. To be honest, I'm real worried. Pete has never gone dark like this."

"I understand," Chuck said. "I'll try again tomorrow."

Something wasn't right. Against his better judgment, Chuck called 911.

To his chagrin, he got a pre-recorded message directing him to "press one" only in the event of a life-threatening emergency. He hesitated to go that far. Instead, he threw on his coat and drove to the police station.

T O AVOID THE mob surrounding the police station, Chuck parked about half a mile down the road at the end of a long line of cars. A light dusting of snow from earlier that evening had covered the roadside in slush. He trudged through it toward a crowd of nearly a hundred screaming townsfolk.

When Chuck reached the crowd's edge, old Jim Cooney, the town rabble-rouser, motioned for Chuck to join him.

"What the heck's going on?" Chuck said.

Cooney shook his head. "People won't admit they're seeing the gray men in their homes. I didn't believe it neither till I seen one of them eating a rat in my garage."

Chief Ed Denmark walked out of the station carrying a megaphone. "Please disburse. We'll be holding a public hearing in the Town Hall this evening to discuss our effort to contain the infestation."

Cooney jutted his chin toward nine figures hovering just outside the edge of the crowd. "Wouldn't be surprised if those Satan-worshipping mongrels had something to do with this mess."

While Chuck put no stock in such superstitions, he did find the teens creepy. Then, when he saw Wilfred's daughter, Joanie, among them, he felt guilty for thinking that way.

The crowd dispersed as if slowly awakening from a dream. Chuck was making his way back to his Jeep when a woman sprinted past him yelling, "My boy! They've got Noam! Snatched him right outta his bed."

He stopped dead in his tracks. The poor woman made him sad and intensified his sense of urgency for his own family's welfare. He got in his Jeep, determined to send his family out of town. Instead of driving home, he headed to Worcester, intending to book a hotel room. On the way, he called Linda. "How's Missy doing?"

"Fine, considering..."

"She get any shots?"

"No. Just antibiotics. The doctor told us to monitor the wounds and call him if the swelling doesn't go down over the next several hours."

"Good." Chuck took a deep breath. "I want you and Missy to meet me at the Holiday Inn Express in Worcester. We'll stay there for a few days until I get this rat problem sorted out."

"Okay," she said. "There's one other thing."

"Go on."

"The doctor said he'd never seen bite marks like these."

"He have any idea what had attacked our daughter?"

There was a long pause. "No."

Chuck sighed. "All right. Take good care of Missy. I'll see you in Worcester."

A FTER CHECKING INTO the hotel and catching a few hours of sleep, Chuck drove to Ayer. He wanted to stop by to see his mother at the Nashoba Park Assisted Living Center just to make sure she was okay. It was always a struggle seeing her; it broke his heart. Sometimes she was sharp as a tack; other times she'd barely recognize him. And as she got older, the bad times were beginning to crowd out the good ones.

"Who's there?" his mother said.

"It's me, Chuck."

"But you're a full grown man. Chuck's barely thirteen."

Chuck groaned. This was gonna be a rough visit.

He set a chair against his mom's bed. He grabbed her hand with both of his and kissed it. "How ya doing, Ma?"

A flash of recognition lit up her face. "Oh, Chuck! So good to see ya. Why don't ya come see your Ma more often? Sometimes I feel like ya stuck me in a corner and forgot about me."

He smiled. "How could I ever forget you, Ma?"

"That's my boy. How's life treating ya? How's that girl you're seeing? What's her name again?"

"Linda, Ma. Her name's Linda. We're married with a daughter. You remember Missy, don't you?"

Her face reddened, but like a good Irish woman, she played it off brilliantly. "Oh, sure. I remember Missy. How's the family?"

"To be honest, Ma, not great. Things are crazy in town. We got rats in the house, and all our pets are missing. Heck, most of the town has a rat problem."

Her jaw tightened. Her eyes seemed to sharpen as if her mind had become suddenly lucid. "I heard this story before. Did the stranger come yet?"

"The what?"

"The stranger. This isn't the first time it's come, and it sure as hell won't be the last. And it'll keep coming long after we're all rotting in the ground."

"You're not making any sense, Ma."

She glared at him. "Back when the Shakers were here, a mob beat them at the Whipping Stones for their beliefs. Your grandma was always saying that that mob didn't come out of nowhere. A stranger had appeared on Holy Hill where the Shakers worshipped. That stranger had riled up the townsfolk to torment the Shakers."

"The stranger?"

"It is drawn to places of terrible sorrow. It feeds off the pain of good folk. It comes here to sire its offspring. Your grandma once told me about the disturbing ritual. The stranger collects the seed of its henchmen and seals it in a rotting gourd inside a horse's womb. The stranger's followers then force-feed the mare a diet of human blood. Forty days later, the abominations are born."

His mother's story sounded insane. Yet she was more coherent now than she'd been in weeks. "What are you saying, Ma?"

Then, just as quickly as her eyes had brightened, they lost their luster, reverting to a dull and unfocused mess. "Who are you?"

Chuck lowered his head in frustration. He gave his mother a kiss, then left for Worcester to check on his family.

T HAT EVENING, CHUCK returned to Harvard. It was snowing so heavily, it was almost impossible to see. When he finally arrived at the Town Hall, it was standing room only. Chief Denmark was already in the middle of his presentation.

He was holding a shoebox.

"We've all heard the reports," Denmark said. "Hell, I've seen 'em myself, the devil men crawling in my walls. But it wasn't until I shot one that I believed they were real."

Denmark paused, then opened the shoebox lid and reached in.

He held the thing up to the crowd as if to give the townsfolk sufficient time to fully comprehend the horror. There was a collective gasp, then an eerie pall of silence as the townsfolk gawked at the specimen.

Roughly six inches tall, the creature was covered in coarse gray fur. It had red eyes, sharp canines, and three horny nobs curling from its forehead.

"As some of you are well aware," Denmark continued, "these things are carnivorous. They started with our pets. Now, they're coming for our children."

"We know all that," Wilfred interrupted. "The real question is what you're gonna do about it."

Denmark glowered at Wilfred while he lowered the small corpse back into the box. "I'll get to that. Right now, we don't know what these things are, but we do know we can kill 'em like any other pest. Only difference is they're smarter."

Denmark motioned toward his deputy, Bill Farnsworth. Farnsworth brought over an easel and planted a white cardboard poster with a map of Harvard on it.

Denmark slapped the map with an extendable pointer. "Over the next twenty-four hours, each family is gonna pack up what it can and evacuate the town."

More gasps.

Denmark held up his left hand, signaling silence. "Then, the Harvard police with soldiers and Marines from Fort Devens will cordon off the town until more help arrives."

"Until more help arrives?" an exasperated voice said from the audience.

Denmark raised his voice. "We don't know exactly what we're up against here. Once we eliminate the threat, you can return to your homes."

The chief's decree sent the crowd into an uproar. Denmark tried to shout over the commotion, but the furious voices drowned him out.

Three sharp raps resonated through the room. The crowd grew suddenly quiet. Nine teens in dark cloaks fanned out from the entrance, forming a line perpendicular to it. A hooded figure shrouded in a coal black burnoose and carrying an ivory-white staff emerged from behind them. The stranger strode down the aisle, then stopped halfway between the entrance and Denmark's podium.

Chuck's eyes focused on the staff. It had tiny holes in it at equal intervals—like a pipe or flute.

"Identify yourself," Denmark said, his voice wavering.

The figure raised the pipe, drawing it to the darkness within its hood. Then it played the most beautiful melody Chuck had ever heard.

A maelstrom of images, sights, smells, and sounds inundated Chuck's mind. All around him, Chuck could sense others were receiving the same broadcast. The visitor offered a bargain—an end to the infestation in exchange for nine human lives.

It lowered its pipe and waited.

Denmark's eyes went wide as saucers. He shook his head as if recovering from a dizzy spell. "Your bargain makes no sense. With enough people, we can wipe out the vermin on our own. And you still haven't told us who you are."

The stranger stood like a statue of obsidian for what seemed like ages. Then it raised the bone pipe and played another song—a song so dark it filled Chuck with dread and woe. His heart ached. His stomach fluttered with a murderous guilt. The dirge signaled an end to normalcy and the dawn of despair.

A great gray and greasy flood of verminous men slithered out of the vents and from the shadows. Soon, thousands of them swarmed menacingly on the perimeter of the crowd.

Denmark held out his hands. "Wait! Stop!" He took a deep breath. "Please. Leave. Give us an hour. To deliberate. When you return, we'll have your answer."

The stranger gave a slight bow in assent. It raised the pipe to its hidden lips and played again. Chuck's heart beat with thunderous force in awe of the majesty of the piper's tune. The filthy, gray masses retreated into the shadows almost as quickly as they'd appeared.

The stranger turned and marched out of the hall, his nine teenage thralls in tow.

There was a brief silence—like the eye of a storm. Then, pandemonium.

"We should just abandon the town like Chief Denmark ordered," Mrs. Garber said.

"No one's getting nowhere any time soon," replied Wilfred. "There's a storm raging."

Deputy Farnsworth shouted, "Everyone keep quiet! We're going forward with the evacuation. Storm or no storm. You've seen those things."

"I seen them kids up by the old Stone Barn!" Jim Cooney yelled. "I say we follow 'em there and burn that piper with 'em. I'd betcha dollars to donuts that thing brought the gray men with it."

Many murmured in agreement.

"Enough!" Denmark bellowed. "We're gonna hold a vote. The options are: one, abandon the town; two, surrender names to the piper; and three, chase the stranger to the barn and burn it."

"Wait," Chuck interrupted. "Aren't we gonna have a debate? Surrendering nine people is insane. We can't just decide who lives or who dies."

"What do you propose?" said Denmark.

"Let's stick to the original plan. Who better than the government to flush these things out?"

"You dumb motherfucker!" Cooney shouted. "When the Army comes, they'll turn the town into Fallujah. And when the dust settles, there won't be any houses to come back to."

Many folks grunted in approval.

"And you propose what? Chasing some devil piper into its lair, which you think is the old Shaker barn because you once saw teenagers there?" Chuck retorted. "That's nuts. As for the other option, if we're despicable enough to sacrifice nine innocent lives, then what? How would we choose them?"

Cooney grinned. "Well, that's easy, ain't it? We volunteer some folks who ain't innocent. Seeing as those teens got something to do with this mess, I say we send them."

"How dare you, you son-of-a-bitch!" Wilfred yelled. "My daughter just kicked heroin. She's only beginning to get back on her feet. Just because she started running with the wrong crowd, don't mean she deserves to die."

"How do you know that thing's gonna kill her?" Cooney countered.

Chuck edged in. "Well, if we're gonna explore this ridiculous line of reasoning, what makes you think the piper would accept his own followers as an offering?"

"All right. Enough!" Denmark shouted. "We've had our debate. Now it's time to vote."

Denmark repeated the options and asked for a show of hands. Farnsworth duly counted each vote, scribbling on a notepad. When he finished tabulating the final tally, Wilfred fell on his knees, and screamed.

WE'VE DECIDED," DENMARK said, a tinge of guilt betraying the firmness of his voice.

The stranger waited.

Denmark continued, "You're free to take the nine young men and women who've accompanied you here."

Broad grins creased the faces of the piper's acolytes. From their reactions, Chuck would have sworn they'd been expecting this. The piper lowered its hooded head in assent, turned, then raised its pipe and began to play.

The gray men again emerged from the woodwork and shadows. The stranger marched toward the exit. Entranced, they streamed out of the Town Hall, flowing like rotten gravy. The townspeople followed in their wake. There wasn't a soul in the building that didn't want to watch the vermin leave.

The townsfolk followed the piper and its verminous entourage into blistering winds and blinding snow. Faint rivers of dull gray sludge converged on the stranger as it piped its mesmerizing music. Rather than smothering the eerie preternatural song, the winter wind seemed to amplify it.

The townspeople trailed the piper from Harvard Common all the way to the beach of Bare Hill Pond. The piper continued to play while hordes of pest men swarmed onto the ice like maggots on a festering blister. And like a festering blister, the thin layer of ice broke like rotten skin. The gray men drowned by the thousands.

The stranger and his nine minions faded away into the churning blizzard.

The townspeople returned to Town Hall, fumbling through near whiteout conditions. And there they slept, waiting for the storm to pass.

WILFRED SCREAMED.

Groggy, Chuck checked his watch. It was only three a.m. He'd been asleep for fewer than three hours. He tapped Wilfred on the shoulder. "What's wrong?"

Wilfred had his iPhone in hand. He showed Chuck a live video feed of men approaching some ruins. They carried bottles and rags. A girl's voice pleaded, "Please, don't do it. We are prepared to die to protect the Master."

"If you stay, you'll burn too," said a voice that sounded like Jim Cooney's.

Chuck jumped to his feet. "Chief Denmark, we need to get to the Shaker barn ASAP. Cooney's raised a mob."

Denmark hesitated the way people do once they've made a decision to look the other way.

Chuck tapped his watch. "C'mon, Ed. We're losing time. You really want their deaths on your hands?"

"But...I thought they were..." Denmark couldn't finish his sentence.

"Already dead?" Chuck supplied.

The chief's face reddened. He averted Chuck's glare, then nodded.

Denmark led a group of men and women outside. The snow had stopped falling, but the blizzard had piled massive snowdrifts along the roadside. And with the current crisis, no one had bothered to plow the roads.

Wilfred's keys shook in his hands. "If any of ya wanna come with me, I got a pickup with a snowplow."

Chuck and Denmark nodded.

Denmark turned toward Farnsworth. "Grab some folks and take the police truck. Meet us at the old Shaker barn."

"You mind driving, Chuck?" said Wilfred. "I wanna stay in touch with Joanie. Make sure she's all right."

Chuck grabbed Wilfred's keys. Everyone climbed into the Dodge Ram. White-knuckling it all the way down Route 111, Chuck turned on South Shaker Road.

Men were yelling on the video.

"Hurry," said Wilfred, shuddering.

Chuck slammed his foot on the accelerator. The men arrived at their destination several minutes later.

Screams.

The three men raced toward the ruins. A crowd was closing in on the structure. Cooney lit a rag sprouting from a bottle and lobbed it at ten figures huddled in the ruins.

Denmark pulled out his service weapon and aimed it at the mob. "Stop!"

More rags were lit. A salvo of Molotov cocktails engulfed the ruins in a firestorm.

Gut-wrenching screams filled the air. The smell of meat wafted on the chill wind. All but one hooded figure stumbled from the ruins. The victims flailed in agony until they collapsed and their bodies smoldered in the snow.

Wilfred fell to his knees and wept.

Reaching the crowd, Denmark commanded, "Hands up! You're all under arrest."

The mob complied. Cooney tried to bargain with Denmark, "C'mon, Ed. You know they was all dead anyways."

"Keep. Your. Fucking. Hands. Up," Denmark warned.

More trucks arrived on the scene. Cops and concerned citizens converged on the site.

Farnsworth recoiled when he saw the charred corpses in the snow. "What the hell happened?"

Denmark pointed at the mob. "Handcuff them."

As the cops herded the suspects to the police station, Chuck and Denmark stayed behind. The fire still raged in the ruins. Yet amidst the flames, a solitary figure stood watch.

Its cloak had disintegrated into ash, but it still carried the pipe of bone. Much like the vermin it has exterminated, it had three horns curving downward from its brow—a harlequin without a hat. Its face was pure white, and its black eyes stared at the two men with a sinister intelligence.

Though he couldn't explain why, Chuck was certain the piper

could have prevented the murders with its music.

But it didn't. It had let this happen.

Denmark grabbed Chuck's arm. "C'mon, we gotta go."

He followed Denmark, leaving the stranger to wallow in the cinders.

S HORTLY AFTER THE thaw, Chuck had returned to the ruins. There, he found no trace of the dark visitor. When he'd told Denmark the tale, the chief had advised him to let sleeping dogs lie and never to mention the incident to another soul again.

A week after the mob had burned the piper's acolytes, Chuck felt safe enough for Linda and Missy to return home.

The town had dedicated a single day for grieving. Townsfolk attended the funerals of Pete Hollowell, the nine dead teens, and eight other children who had gone missing during the infestation. A single day to acknowledge the truth of that awful incident before burying its foul memory forever.

Chuck mourned their suffering. He couldn't imagine the depths of such sorrow, the tragedy of parents burying their own children. Their loss made his reunion with Missy all the more bittersweet. He hugged her with all the love he had and kissed her goodnight. For tomorrow would be the first day of the rest of his life. And for that, he was grateful.

O NE YEAR LATER, the town gathered at the Stone Barn ruins to remember the souls they'd lost on that horrible day. Standing on the snow-covered hill, Chuck was thankful he and his family had survived what had been the darkest episode of his life.

Since that black day, he'd often wondered what had become of the piper. But like all nightmares, the thought faded away, buried by the banality of everyday life.

That evening, Chuck drifted off to sleep lulled by the most enchanting music he'd ever heard.

Linda shook Chuck awake.

"What is it, honey?"

Linda paced frantically, her face ashen. "Missy's gone!" she said through a burst of tears.

Chuck leapt out of bed, grabbed his robe and slippers. He raced down the steps and stormed out his front door.

Footprints.

A path of small footprints led from the front lawn to the street. Chuck glanced over his shoulder and shouted, "Linda, call the police. I've found Missy's trail."

Chuck jogged down the street following Missy's tracks. For once, he thought, the snow would work in his favor.

He traced Missy's footsteps all the way down to the Town Common. There, he lost Missy's path to a swirl of other child-sized footprints that converged on Bare Hill Pond.

"No. Oh, God, no."

Chuck sprinted toward the pond. His breath steamed in the frigid air. In the distance, a mist obscured whatever secrets lay hidden there. He ran harder, desperate to reach the water's edge.

When he did, he collapsed and wailed.

As far as he could see, small bodies bobbed like buoys among chunks of ice in the murky waters. And among them, floated the remains of his beloved Missy.

ABOUT THE AUTHOR

Sean Patrick Hazlett is an Army veteran, speculative fiction writer and editor, and finance executive in the San Francisco Bay area. Over forty of his short stories have appeared in publications such as *The Year's Best Military and Adventure SF*, *Year's Best Hardcore Horror*, *Terraform*, *Galaxy's Edge*, *Writers of the Future*, *Grimdark Magazine*, *Vastarien*, and *Abyss & Apex*, among others. He is also the editor of the *Weird World War III* anthology.

About the Editor

SHAUN KILGORE is the author of various works of fantasy, science fiction, and a number of nonfiction works. He has also published numerous short stories and collections. His books appear in both print and ebook editions. Shaun is the publisher and editor of *MYTHIC: A Science Fiction & Fantasy Magazine*. He lives in eastern Illinois. If you want to learn more about my other books and publications, please visit my website at www.shaunkilgore.com.

Made in the USA
Middletown, DE
29 April 2021